SCORN OF THE BETROTHED

A DARK ENEMIES TO LOVERS ROMANCE

CAVALIERI BILLIONAIRE LEGACY
BOOK FIVE

ZOE BLAKE

Poison Ink

Blake, Zoe
Scorn of the Betrothed

Cover Design by The Pretty Little Design Co.

SONGS FEATURED

Chopin's Prelude No. 4 in E Minor
Frédéric Chopin

Cello Suite No. 1 in D Major by Bach
Johann Sebastian Bach

Someone to Watch Over Me
George Gershwin

Don't Cry
Guns N' Roses

Con Te Partirò
(Time to Say Goodbye)
Francesco Sartori (music) and
Lucio Quarantotto (lyrics)

Vivo Per Lei
Andrea Bocelli and Gianpietro Felisatti

Io Che Non Vivo
(You Don't Have to Say You Love Me)
Pino Donaggio (music) and
Vito Pallavicini (lyrics)

Dance Me to the End of Love
Leonard Cohen

Tu Vou fa L'Americano
Renato Carosone

Sinfonia Concertante
Wolfgang Amadeus Mozart

Adagio for Strings
Samuel Barber

At Last
Etta James

CONTENTS

INTRODUCTION

Enter the world of the Cavalieri Billionaire Legacy, where love is as treacherous as the secrets they guard.

Each man in this notorious Italian dynasty is bound by duty, honor, and dark desires woven into their very bloodline. The Cavalieri men know what they want—and nothing will keep them from claiming it.

In *Scandals of the Father*, a powerful man's hidden obsession with a young woman threatens to unravel as the dark rumors of his past close in.

In *Sins of the Son*, vengeance and desire pull Cesare back to a shattered past—and to a woman who will never forgive him.

Secrets of the Brother plunges Enzo into a twisted web of family secrets and forbidden love, as he struggles to protect the woman he yearns for most—his late wife's sister.

In *Seduction of the Patriarch*, revenge pushes a Cavalieri man to the edge as he uses seduction as a weapon against the very woman he swore to protect.

And in the electrifying *Scorn of the Betrothed*, a forced marriage meant to prevent a mafia war becomes a battlefield of passions, with Matteo struggling to control his fiancée—a woman as fierce and defiant as him

When enemies turn to lovers, the line between love and hate is dangerously thin.

CHAPTER 1

ANTONELLA

 alermo, Sicily
February

"BAD GIRL, swaying your hips like this in front of other men—when you're supposed to be mine."

A powerful arm had wrapped around my waist from behind and snatched me to a man's chest before he leaned down to rasp in my ear.

In shock, I craned my neck to stare into a pair of piercing dark eyes, glaring at me from behind an elaborate black leather Carnevale devil's mask covering the upper portion of the man's face.

The rest of him was dressed in unrelenting midnight black, from his heavy brocade jacket and tails to his tall riding boots.

His?

I twisted around in his grip to press my palms against his chest and push, trying to break free of his grasp.

For nothing.

The man's chest was harder than a brick wall.

While it may be common practice for drunken men to touch and grab the women in the crowd during the wanton revelry of Carnevale, this was different.

His intense gaze raised the hairs on the back of my neck. A primal reaction to being caught in a predator's sights, to be sure.

And what the hell did he mean by "when you're supposed to be mine?"

Shaking off the increasing panic which twisted my stomach, I tried to wrench away from him again as I fired back. *"Parlari, tischi-toschi. Va eccati!"*

He was clearly Italian and not a tourist, so I deliberately insulted him in Sicilian.

I wouldn't dare call him arrogant and pretentious before telling him to go jump in the sea in a language he could understand!

I wasn't that brave.

His lips twisted in a smirk. *"Christa e a zita, muoviti ddruocu, colomba mia birichina."*

Accept your fate and don't move.

I froze.

He had responded using two nonsensical, slang Sicilian phrases that only someone familiar with the language and culture would know.

He had also called me *colomba mia birichina.*

My naughty little dove.

My fingers clawed at the brocade of his costume, panic tightening my throat even as a spark of awareness seemed to warm my insides.

It could be nothing…

Dressed as the popular character Colombina from the Commedia dell'Arte in keeping with this year's Carnevale theme, his calling me little dove, the literal translation of her name, was not significant.

Except that it felt significant in a territorially possessive sort of way.

The pounding of the blood in my ears warred with the pounding drums from the live music only steps away.

Who was this man?

And why was he so fixated on bothering me, when there were countless half-dressed, fully drunk women gyrating and attempting to twerk he could choose from?

The chaos of the Palermo Carnevale ebbed and flowed all around us, a dizzying kaleidoscope of shattered crystal shards in crimson, cobalt, amethyst, and jade.

Revelers danced feverishly to the pounding beat of the tambourines from the *pizzica tarantelle* performed in the center of the *Piazza Garraffello*.

His arm tightened around my waist, pushing our hips together. "Stop fighting me, little dove. You can't win."

My feet were lifted off the ground as he swung me in an arch, moving in time with the music.

The mandolins, violins, and high-pitched, plaintive cries of the female singers lyrically calling out for lost lovers added a Dionysian, almost unhinged, energy to the night.

As he carried me off, closer and closer to the edge of the crowd, the tips of my shoes scraped along the smooth, worn cobblestones of the piazza.

I gripped his shoulders and arched my back, still trying to break free. "You're making a mistake!"

Clearly, this was some suitor of my twin sister, Antonia.

He had to be. It was the only explanation for the way he was holding me.

His hand moved down my lower back. "Are you trying to get out of your punishment?"

Sciatiri e matri!

Punishment?

Had he said punishment?

No.

He couldn't have.

Furiously I scanned my brain for another word—any other word—I could have mistaken for the word punishment over the loud music.

My mouth opened on a choked cry as he cupped my ass and growled, "This cute ass is going to feel the sting of my belt. I'm going to teach you a lesson about flaunting your body for anyone else but me."

Before I could shake off my stunned reaction and respond, we were both shoved by the crowd surrounding us. The sudden impact loosened his grasp just enough for me to finally twist free.

I ducked low to squeeze between two revelers before snaking through the dense crowd. Jostled by the throng, I pitched sideways, too afraid to glance back at my pursuer.

All around me the air reeked of sweat, cheap wine, and fried food. The fabrics of the rented Commedia dell'Arte costumes exuded a musty scent of dust, mothballs, and neglect.

There were swaggering men dressed as Pulcinella with their gnarled nose masks askew and their bulging stomachs barely contained within the thin white linen of their ruffled tunics.

A number of smarmy Pantalones in flowing black capes and pointed nose masks. And countless women dressed as sexy Pierrots with black-and-white striped thigh-highs under laced corsets complimenting their pouting, sad clown makeup. My sister being one of them, with the exception of her thigh-high leather boots.

Not wearing a mask here was a mistake.

A mask gave people anonymity, which most used as a license for lecherous behavior.

Many would argue that was the true soul and purpose of Carnevale. To have one last debauched celebration before the austerity of Lent.

My sister certainly would agree.

How we could be twins and such polar opposites was beyond me.

I hissed as the stiffened collar of someone's Harlequin costume scraped my bare shoulder.

Again cursing my choice of Colombina, with her off-the-shoulder white peasant blouse and cumbersome petticoat skirt, as a costume.

Finally, I broke free of the crowd along the other side of the piazza, which was flanked by a crumbling brick wall covered in colorful graffiti, a sad remnant of World War II bombing.

Dilapidated, broken, bombed-out buildings surrounded the entire piazza, giving it a forlorn yet strangely timeless aesthetic. No one bothered to repair them, despite their being located in Palermo's center.

Welcome to Sicily.

I crept my way along the wall, wedged between the swelling crowd and the powdery rubble of the decaying bricks, searching for my contact.

A clandestine meeting with him was the only reason I was here tonight.

Certainly not to take part in the drunken festivities like my sister. My contact had said the chaos of Carnevale would be the perfect cover. No one could overhear our conversation.

For a split second, I thought the man who grabbed me was my contact.

He had certainly been making enough unwanted advances of late, but no.

This man was too tall, too strong, too *everything* to be the desk-bound bureaucratic attorney I was meeting with.

And it was imperative that I met with him.

Time had run out.

I had fulfilled my end of our bargain. It was past time for my contact to fulfill his.

Otherwise, my father would…

A hand wrapped around my upper arm and threw me backward against the wall. A warm body pressed into my front, pinning me against the bricks.

I opened my mouth to scream but never got the chance.

The man from earlier had found me.

His mouth descended on mine, cutting off my attempt to cry for help, not that I'd be heard over the festival music.

His lips smashed mine against the sharp edges of my teeth as his tongue thrust inside.

He tasted like the sweet lemon icing from the *taralli al limone* pastries the food vendors sold along the square.

But that was the only sweet thing about him.

His kiss was brutal, possessive, and entirely too arousing.

I didn't even know this man.

There was something taboo and wrong about giving in to his embrace like this.

And yet… it was very Carnevale.

As they said, when in Rome. Or, in this case, Sicily.

My lungs burned as he stole every breath of oxygen from my body.

His hands reached up to grasp my head, strong fingers weaving into my hair, gently twisting, causing just a slight sting of pain, which added even more of a frisson of awareness to his every touch.

He broke free, but only to yank his mask off and toss it aside. "Fuck this thing."

My eyes widened as his head lowered again. "No. Stop! I don't know who you—"

His mouth claimed mine again. His tongue swirling around mine, he moved his hand to snatch at the heavy fabric of my skirt just over my hip.

Cool night air teased my upper thigh where he pulled my skirt high.

My hand covered his fist in an attempt to pry his fingers loose. I had let it go too far.

He growled against my mouth as his teeth sank into my lower lip. "Stop trying to play the virgin with me. We both know it's not true."

Ice water replaced the rising heat in my veins.

He didn't want me.

He wanted my sister, Antonia.

Of course. Who would want the shy book nerd who hid from the world by devoting herself to her cello playing when they could have a vivacious, fun-loving party girl?

Anger gave me strength. This time I succeeded in jerking my head to the side, ending our kiss.

I reared my arm back and slapped him across the face so hard my palm stung.

His eyes narrowed as he gripped my upper arms. "What the hell was that for?"

My lips thinned. "Listen, I don't know who you are, but—"

He cut me off, scowling down at me, his towering frame once more pressing me against the ancient wall. "What the fuck do you mean you don't know who I am? Have you spread your legs for so many men you don't even recognize your own fiancé?"

Sciatiri e matri!

Matteo Cavalieri had finally arrived in Palermo to claim my sister.

CHAPTER 2

MATTEO

*W*ell, this marriage was off to a shit start.

I'd spent the last month and a half arguing with my cousins, Enzo and Cesare, over my plans to marry Antonia Carlotta Fichera.

Not that I blamed them.

My intended bride's nickname was, after all, the Lucrezia of Sicily.

A virginal bride she was not, but I wasn't marrying her for love, so what did it matter?

This was a business arrangement, nothing more, nothing less.

Her father, Antonius Carlo Fichera, was a powerful *capo* in Dante Agnello's organization and would be instrumental in keeping the peace after we assassinated Salvatore Giovanni Mangana, Dante's former vice capo who had attacked my family, over a month ago.

The last thing my family needed was any more drama from the Sicilian mafia and if my taking a less than desirable bride secured their safety, then so be it.

At first, I was surprised and relieved at my father and uncle's show of support for my decision. I should have known better.

Behind the scenes, they worked with Sebastian Diamanti to find alternative solutions, causing a delay in my return to Sicily.

There weren't any.

Not short of a bloodbath taking out half of Dante's men, which would turn him from a reluctant enemy ally to a pure enemy.

So, with no more delays, I set sail for Sicily to claim my somewhat tarnished bride.

Might as well enjoy a pleasant cruise around the coast on the family's yacht before I faced the gallows.

On the upside, a woman as promiscuous as Antonia would be unlikely to object to my more *unique* demands in the bedroom.

Every cloud had a silver lining.

I was due to meet with her father tomorrow evening, so saw no reason not to enjoy myself at Palermo's famous Carnevale festivities.

Despite being assured by her father that my blushing bride was dutifully at home awaiting our reunion, I wasn't the least bit surprised to see her dancing in the middle of the raucous crowd.

I was surprised at how ... *different* ... she seemed.

True, I had only met Antonia briefly on Dante's yacht when I was helping my father and Liliana out of a rather delicate situation, but still...

After following in my father's rather clandestine footsteps, someone in my profession needed to be a quick study of character. Which wasn't gleaned just from what someone said, or their actions.

I had learned from my father to study *everything*.

Every micro expression.

Every movement.

Every detail.

And something was *off* about Antonia.

On the yacht, she displayed a brassy crassness typical of individuals with nothing meaningful to say or offer to society.

Everything about the woman had screamed "pay attention to me," from her heavy makeup to her tight dress and loud laugh.

She also had no problem hanging on the arm of one man while still trying to throw herself at me.

Something I intended to put a stop to.

While this was not a love match and I may have accepted that my bride came with a less-than-ideal reputation, that didn't mean I would accept her cuckolding me.

I refused to share my toys.

At least that was one perk of this messed-up arrangement.

Most men dreamed of getting a wife who acted like a whore in bed.

My challenge would be in restricting her to *only* my bed... which I planned to do with restraints if necessary. Her days of jumping on the nearest man were fucking over.

Tonight, as I gazed at her from afar before approaching, she was different.

She had little to no makeup on, and her blonde hair flowed freely down her back in soft waves. It seemed longer than I remembered and far more flattering than the crunchy, hair-sprayed style she wore on the yacht.

I could just imagine wrapping my fist in tonight's silky curls and pulling hard as I fucked her from behind.

Then there was her attire.

Instead of taking advantage of the permissive atmosphere of Carnevale to wear something suggestive and revealing as I would have expected her to do, she wore a voluminous ruffled skirt and simple white, off-the-shoulder peasant blouse with no jewelry or other adornment.

It would almost be considered modest, especially for this festive occasion.

I became transfixed when she danced.

Despite the fast-paced 6/8 time of the *pizzica tarantelle*, she seemed to move to a slower rhythm than the rest of the crowd.

Her hips swayed to every third beat, instead of every other one, so her movements were more seductive.

I assumed it was an artifice to entice and flirt with the males in the crowd until her head fell back and I realized her eyes were closed. She seemed lost in the music, dancing solely for her own pleasure.

To my surprise, I experienced a surge of jealous rage when I realized several men had circled around her swaying form, like wolves drawn to a penned lamb.

Now was the time to stop this behavior.

My new bride might as well know now, I expected strict obedience from her.

The fact her obedience would also come with her complete submission as she was down on her knees pleasuring me added just a slight shimmer to that somewhat thin silver lining.

The moment I laid hands on her, my confusion over her changed demeanor only increased.

Gone was the thick, cloying, rose-scented perfume I remembered. It was replaced with something fresh and clean, with hints of grass and verbena.

Then there was the way her dark eyes widened at the sight of me, a soft blush blooming on her cheeks as her full lips parted on a gasp. As though I had startled a maiden in the woods.

And when I kissed her.

Fuck.

The woman had me believing I was the first man to kiss her.

Could Antonia have been manipulated, like my father's new

wife Liliana, into playing a role at that dinner? Was she more innocent than the rumors suggested?

I had almost believed that... then she'd moaned into my kiss.

It was a soft, throaty moan.

If I were a gullible man, I'd think she wasn't even aware she was doing it.

I wasn't fooled. Quite the opposite.

I realized this was why other men were drawn to her.

One of the oldest honey traps.

The ultimate femme fatale... the virgin whore.

Most men had a hard time resisting an innocent damsel in distress.

Myself included.

I'd have to be careful around her.

She obviously enjoyed using her body and her skills to convince any man she was with into believing they were the only one.

And I had almost fallen for the wide-eyed, sexually shocked look, and the way her pulse elevated when I tightened my grasp on her waist. Thank God the others were not here to see my almost-folly.

I would have to be more on my guard around her in the future, but first I had to find her. Again.

The minx escaped my grasp when we were shoved by some drunken revelers.

Before I could grab her, she had disappeared into the crowd.

I'd just caught up with her and kissed her when she slapped me and managed to wriggle free a second time.

Snatching my mask from the ground, I secured it over my face.

Time to go bride hunting.

CHAPTER 3

ANTONELLA

*W*ith shaking fingers, I yanked on the knot securing the colorful crimson-and-gold scarf around my waist.

After shaking it out, I wrapped it over my head like a kerchief, to cover my blonde hair.

For the first time damning the Norman heritage in my ancestry.

Usually, I couldn't help but feel thankful for my blonde hair. It was one of my few distinguishing features and reminded me of the only photo I had of my mother, who also had long, blonde hair.

Or did have...

Not now.

Carefully avoiding swinging arms clutching bottles of wine, greasy plates of street food, and groping hands, I maneuvered through the crowd of masks, capes, pantaloons, feathered hats, and trailing gowns.

Vigilant to avoid any attempts to draw me into a *carola* as the chain of dancers was led along by a similarly attired Colombina character banging on her tamborine to the beat of the onstage *pizzaca* music. A stage filled with frenzied dancers and a small orchestra of strings and bass.

With the creeping darkness, Carnevale inched closer to its more pagan roots.

For the second time, my ankle rolled when my heel slipped on a smooth cobblestone.

In frustration, I sent another curse up to the thigh-high, high-heeled boots my sister convinced me to wear. Between them and the tight corset I wore under my peasant blouse to avoid bra straps so I could have bare shoulders, I was hobbling and could barely breathe.

I longed for my usual black turtleneck, slacks, and ballet flats. The standard for most female cello players since it allowed ease of movement when straddling the instrument.

In order to warn Antonia, I had to escape from Matteo Cavalieri.

As I weaved my way through the increasingly drunk crowd, I seized the opportunity of *Peppe Nappa*'s appearance.

With the entire mass of people surging toward the entrance to the piazza, the noise level swelled as the big-headed, straw-stuffed effigy came tottering into view on a makeshift parade float.

The bandleader shouted into the microphone for all to hail the arrival of the King of Carnevale. He then prepared to read off *Peppe Nappa's* last will and testament.

I refused to stop, shouldering my way through, even when someone spilled wine down the side of my skirt.

When I was sure I had lost Matteo, I risked a moment to pause and rise on my toes to search over the tops of everyone's heads.

It only brought my already short stature up to normal height, so I saw little.

An American tourist grabbed me around the waist and tried to lift me against his chest, slurring out licentiously, "I'll give you a ride on my shoulders if you'll give me a ride later."

Urgh. Gross.

Not wanting to dwell on why this man's embrace was repulsive while Matteo's had made me want to melt into his arms, I pushed the offender off me with a firm knee to his groin.

Why hadn't I thought of that with Matteo Cavalieri?

I shivered. Because the idea of angering a powerful man with that move terrified me.

He was a Cavalieri, after all.

They all had what I'd call a smoldering, violent reputation.

Unlike the regular mafia families, there was nothing overt or out in the open about their presence. Their legendary family name allowed them to hide behind an air of sophistication and civility.

Being worth billions didn't hurt either.

Pivoting in another direction, I continued to search all the slutty Pierrot clowns until I spotted Antonia.

I dodged under outstretched arms as people shouted, raised their fists, and playfully hissed.

This was all in good fun, as *Peppe Nappa's* supposed crimes were read aloud. In reality, these crimes were the hidden crimes and scandals of local officials from the past year.

In a daring display, Antonia had her legs wrapped around a large man dressed as Il Capitano.

He had her bent backward to indulge himself in licking her breasts, which threatened to spill out of her tight corset.

Approaching the pair, I tapped Antonia on the shoulder. "We need to talk."

She glared at me before snaking her arms around her companion's neck. "What?" she cried out over the din.

I shouted back. "We need to talk! It's urgent!"

17

With an exaggerated huff, she opened her legs and slid down his length. Then, grabbing the bottle of wine from his grasp, she turned and rubbed her ass against his crotch. "What *is* it, Ella? God, you can be such a freaking killjoy." She took a sloppy swig of the wine.

From the looks of it, she'd already had way too much fun.

She had wasted an hour carefully applying her sad clown makeup, only to have it smudged and smeared all over her face. Her eyes were glassy from what I hoped was only alcohol but was probably something stronger, and she swayed on her too tall high-heeled boots.

Ignoring the hurtful comment, I said, "You have to leave. Matteo is here."

She paused in raising the bottle to her lips again, frowning. "Who?"

"Matteo Cavalieri. Your fiancé."

She shrugged. "Who cares? You said you were going to take care of all that."

Fuck.

My contact.

My head swiveled as I searched the crowd again, then turned my attention back to Antonia. My contact would have to wait. First, I had to get her out of here.

"I said I was working on it. You have to leave before he finds me—you—us." *Again.*

She turned her back on me and stuck her tongue out suggestively to her partner who, judging by the bulge in his costumed pantaloons, was enjoying the attention. "You're overreacting, Ella. It's not like he knows I'm here."

Oh, he definitely does. Sort of.

I circled around the two of them and tried to get her attention again before she could once more get her legs wrapped around his waist.

I gestured with my head toward her man. "Weren't you two supposed to get married? That would solve the issue."

The man dropped Antonia on her ass. "Huh?"

Antonia shouted, "What the fuck?" up at him. Then kicked him in the shin with her high-heeled boots.

He hopped back, grabbing his shin. "Fuck you, Antonia. Why'd you have to fucking kick me?"

I helped my sister to her feet.

She brushed off her ass and fluffed her hair before scowling at me. "He wishes. Really, Ella. Manfredi is not my boyfriend. He's just the guy I fool around with while my boyfriend is... *busy.*"

This just keeps getting better and better. I assumed Manfredi would marry her and help my sister escape, since they were always together.

Focu 'ranni! What a mess.

If we both didn't live at home with our father, I would have learned this important bit of information sooner.

Unfortunately we did, which meant we were rarely alone and always assumed we were under surveillance.

Something I learned from my mother—before.

Out of the corner of my eye, I spotted Fino, my contact. "I don't have time to argue with you, Antonia. Go home now. I'll see you there as soon as I can."

Following Fino's lead, I made my way to the other side of the central fountain. "Where have you been? I've been here for over two hours, waiting."

He raised his finger and pointed to the parade float. "Wait. This is my favorite part."

With great fanfare, the bandleader declared a death sentence on the effigy. It was already listing to the side on the parade float because of the wine sprays soaking its worn clothes and straw.

The crowd cheered as the effigy was set ablaze by a masked

19

official. Everyone danced around the makeshift bonfire to the band's rendition of another *tarantelle*.

My fist twisted in the ends of the kerchief I was holding tight under my jaw. "Fino, I don't have time for this. We need to talk. Now."

This night was like herding cocaine-crazed squirrels with their tails on fire.

Finally, the tall, spindly man turned to me. Dressed in yet another Il Capitano costume, its brightly colored uniform hung on his thin shoulders the way it would on a coat rack.

Before speaking, he worked his mouth several times, resembling a cow chewing cud. "What is so important that we had to risk an unplanned meeting?"

I yelled over the crowd's cheers at *Peppe Nappa's* head burning to a husk. "You have to arrest my father now. Tonight! We're out of time."

His long fingers dug into my upper arm, pulling me close enough for his puckered lips to hiss in my ear. "Lower your voice!"

I bristled. Using the middle of Carnevale as cover for this meeting was his suggestion, not mine. "You promised if I stole those files, you would arrest my father for my mother's disappearance. I've done my part."

After years of my father telling me my mother was a whore who abandoned us, I had grown suspicious.

In secret, I provided information about my father's mafia activities to Judge Marzio Delluci in the Anti-Mafia Investigations Directorate.

The purpose was to convince him to launch an investigation into my mother's disappearance.

But when I reached out to the Judge's office, it was Fino Buratti, his associate, who responded, telling me it was too dangerous for me to communicate directly with the Judge.

"It's not that simple. There is a legal process we need to follow."

"You've been telling me that for months. I have no more time. My father is going to force my sister to marry Matteo Cavalieri if we don't stop him."

Fino worked his jaw in slow circles, his raised eyebrows giving his sallow face a ghoulish appearance. "Matteo Cavalieri? Of the Cavalieri family?"

"Yes."

"From Abruzzo. The winemaking family?"

I threw my arms up in the air, not understanding why the identity of the person my father was forcing my sister to marry held any importance. "Yes! Yes! Now, are you going to help me?"

He worked his jaw again. "Can I presume your sister will travel to Abruzzo for the upcoming nuptials?"

I crossed my arms over my chest. "Not exactly."

He stared at me.

The last thing I wanted was to give him another option to weasel out of his promise, but he was determined. "She wants me to switch places with her to stall for time while she convinces her"—my nose wrinkled as I tried to find the correct word for my sister's lover—"boyfriend, to marry her instead."

I pointed a finger at his chest. "But that is our absolute last-resort plan. I'm expecting you to arrest my father so we don't have to resort to it."

He stared off over my shoulder, his eyes shifting left and right. "The Cavalieris have operated above the law for decades. This could be our chance."

"Chance for what?"

He waved his hand in front of me. "I need to take this information to the Judge."

When he turned to go, I grabbed his sleeve. "What about my sister?"

21

Stepping far too close to me, his gaze traveled to my chest before meeting my eyes. "You'll need to travel to Abruzzo in her stead. It can't be helped. This is too good of an opportunity to pass up."

"And what about the investigation into my mother's disappearance? You promised to show me the file."

I flinched at the coldness of his spindly fingers when he touched my shoulders.

His touch was nothing like Matteo's warm, calloused hands.

"Just be patient. I will say this. If you don't continue to do as we say, then you can forget about any investigation into your mother's whereabouts."

It felt like a lead weight settled in the pit of my stomach. Just because they were the law didn't mean they operated any differently than the mafia.

Everything was a power play.

Everything was about influence.

Everything was about greasing palms and exchanging favors.

No one cared about the people who got crushed by all their schemes, mind games, and manipulations.

Like my mother.

Before I could respond, I spied Matteo over Fino's shoulder, shoving his way through the dancers, a look of cold, hard determination in his eyes.

My eyes widened.

Ducking from under Fino's clammy hands, I gathered up my heavy skirt and pivoted on my heel, disappearing into the crowd.

CHAPTER 4

MATTEO

*N*o sooner had I laid eyes on my runaway bride than a man stumbled into my path.

Shoving him aside, I raced forward but lost her again.

When I next caught sight of her, she was in the northwest corner of the piazza.

She had ditched the skirt and peasant blouse and was now displaying her every curve in a pair of thigh-high boots, a tiny skirt, and a white lace corset.

Che due palle!

The woman was already in the arms of another man.

Worse than that, she had her legs wrapped around him like a fucking bitch in heat.

Storming up to them both, I twisted my hand into the back of her hair and pulled her off him.

As she fell back into my arms with a cry, I rumbled into her ear. "What the fuck did I just tell you about other men?"

The man she was with yanked on her arm. "Get your hands off her!"

I cocked my head to the side. "Manfreak? Is that you?"

Behind his mask, his eyes widened, then narrowed. "It's Manfredo, asshole."

"I'm never going to remember that, so how about I just call you little dick and warn you not to touch what's now mine again, or I'll rip off your head and shove it up your ass so you'll know what a real asshole looks like. Deal?"

Gasping and giggling, Antonia's shoulders shook with hiccups before she lurched backward. Only my grasp on her hair kept her upright.

With unfocused eyes, she fixed her gaze on me. "Matteo Cavalieri, is that you behind that sexy mask? Come back for seconds after the yacht?" She laughed and patted Manfredo's chest. "We could do a threesome! Oh, my God! That would be so much fun!"

In yet another unsteady move, she toppled against my chest. Splaying her fingers wide, she ran her hand over my torso, then grabbed my cock through my pants. "Want to be on top? I'll let you fuck my ass."

I frowned.

The flirtatious inference, as if she didn't already know I was here. The raunchy invitation.

Was this yet another act? Perhaps to avoid my wrath?

There was no fucking way this woman could be drunk.

Less than fifteen minutes had passed since she'd been out of my sight. Even if she had been doing shots of strong *Centerba,* she wouldn't be drunk this fast.

To steady himself, Manfredo placed a beefy hand on the shoulder of the nearest person. "No one's shoving anything up my ass."

As she drew her fingertips over my lower lip, Antonia rolled her eyes. It wasn't the sensual caress I was sure she meant it to be. More like the pawing of a drunken cat. "I said *my* ass, Manny, not yours."

His lower lip jutted out, resembling a toddler who had been denied a sweet. "Why do I have to share your ass with him?"

With her arm around my neck, she swung her body backward to face Manfredo. "Because Daddy says I have to marry him, so you better get used to sharing me."

With a clenched jaw, I rubbed my hand over my eyes.

What the fuck had I signed up for?

As Manfredo clenched his fists, the skin around his neck turned a mottled red. "I'm not fucking you with him in the room." He then swung his arm wide.

Using my grip on Antonia's hair, I bent her forward while ducking myself, to avoid the hit.

After releasing her, I squared off with my fists raised. "Apparently, one black eye wasn't enough."

Manfredo grabbed a wine bottle from a nearby cart and smashed it on the edge of the cart's counter. He raised the jagged edge and jabbed it toward me. "I'm going to en ... enjoy ... stepping in your ... blood!"

I winced. "We need to work on your threats."

Evading a second jab from him, I managed to seize a round serving tray from the same cart. Ignoring the cart owner's shout of alarm, I dumped the crispy, golden-brown sticks of *scagliozzi* on the ground before holding it before me as a shield.

Manfredo stabbed the bottle into the wooden tray several times, causing a shard of glass to chip off.

As he leaned back and raised his arm for another blow, I flipped the tray in my hand until it was horizontal and slammed it against his Adam's apple.

Man's apple.

Gagging, Manfredo dropped his improvised weapon and grabbed at his throat.

Unfazed by the cheers from the surrounding crowd, I tossed some euros at the cart owner, then turned to deal with Antonia.

She was gone.

Vaffanculo.

* * *

DARKNESS WAS DESCENDING. Every minute that passed where she was alone, she was in more danger, whether or not she recognized it.

The flames from the burning effigy rose higher and burned brighter, the flickering light illuminating the group of Carnevale revelers who were growing even more uninhibited.

Their dancing had taken on a frenzied, abandoned air as their bodies swayed and jerked erratically to the music.

Revelers started grabbing anything burnable and throwing it into the flames. Angry shouts from the vendors mixed with excited catcalls from the revelers when yet another cafe chair or small table was smashed to pieces on the cobblestones and tossed onto the fire.

Some had even taken to wasting decent wine by throwing entire bottles at the bonfire. Blue flames sparked from the wine as the ethanol burned off, releasing a burst of energy when the bottle shattered. A small glass shard flew into the crowd, but they seemed unfazed.

Families with children departed while older tourists retreated to their hotels, signaling the start of the wilder phase of Carnevale, where masks and costumes allowed for explicit behavior which would otherwise be deemed unacceptable in public.

Already there were couples and even small groups in various forms of undress, writhing in each other's arms.

To shield my identity, I pulled my black leather devil's mask back over my eyes.

If I were to be photographed at this event, it could compromise my future *endeavors* for the family.

Where the fuck was she?

At last, as the band launched into a rousing rendition of "Pizzica di Torchiarolo," I spotted her near the entrance to the piazza, close to the burning effigy.

I smirked at the lyrics about marriage, a chain, and a grenade. Fitting.

In an attempt to evade me, the clever minx was back in the longer skirt and peasant blouse.

Even adding a concealing headscarf she must have nabbed from one of the many costume and mask vendor carts that surrounded the piazza.

She could give lessons in spy craft. Perhaps there was hope for her yet.

I knew at least my father would approve of the evasive tactics she was using.

Too bad for her, they wouldn't be enough.

She was good, but I was better.

I was still several paces away when a group of four men surrounded her.

She cried out as they pulled off her headscarf and pawed at her breasts, tearing her blouse.

Breaking into a run, not caring who I knocked over in my pursuit, I quickly reached her.

With a twist of my hands, I flung the first man sideways by grabbing his sweat-drenched shirt. I then kicked at another's vulnerable kneecap.

The moment he bent over in pain, I caught him with an uppercut to the jaw. He was out cold before he hit the ground. After throwing a punch and hearing the satisfying crunch of bone as my knuckles connected with the third man's nose, the fourth ran off.

My disobedient bride attempted to do the same, but I swiftly caught her around the waist before she could take two steps.

Breathing heavily from my exertions, I yanked her hips back so her ass rubbed against my already hard cock, rasping against her neck, "Not so fast, *colomba mia birichina.*"

A tremor ran over her body at the contact before she strained against my hands. "Let me go!"

My hand ran over the tight silk of her corset as I moved to cup her breasts, which were swelling over the lace edge exposed by her blouse's torn neckline. "To the victor go the spoils. I've now fought two duels for your... well, we can't say maidenly honor, now, can we?"

She clawed at my hand as I pushed my fingers inside the edge of her corset and cupped her warm flesh. "Stop! Don't touch me."

As the soft weight of her breast settled against my palm, my blood boiled.

A feral need to quell her rebellious objections rose from deep inside of my chest, even as my cock swelled to painful proportions.

Was I a sick fuck for finding this persona of hers more arousing?

The crass wanton who threw herself at me with promises of raunchy anal sex held no appeal for me.

But this...

Her feigned virginal fear.

Even with her nails digging into my flesh and protests rushing from that sweet mouth of hers, I couldn't help but notice the vulnerable way her body shivered under my hand in reaction to my touch on her skin.

That did it for me.

At this point, I didn't even care if it was all an act.

I just wanted to fuck her until she stopped running away from me.

I wanted to fuck her until she finally submitted to her fate.

I wanted to fuck her until I burned away all thoughts of any other man in her life.

She was my effigy, and I wanted her to burn for me and me alone.

Uncaring about the surrounding crowd, I moved my other hand to her waistband.

She bucked within my grasp, warning me, "I'll scream."

After slipping my hand inside her skirt, my fingertips brushed the silk of her panties. Pushing my fingers under the thin fabric, I cupped her pussy. "I'd be disappointed if you didn't."

I pressed two fingers between her cunt lips, gently sweeping my thumb over the soft curls between her thighs.

Fuck, she was already wet.

With a firm tug on her blouse, I successfully freed it from her waistband, allowing it to fall down her front until it reached the tops of her thighs, effectively concealing my actions from everyone except the most ardent observer.

After pulling her head back against my shoulder, my left hand dropped to her throat. My teeth sank into her earlobe just as I tried to push my two middle fingers inside of her.

She was too tight.

"Stop clenching against me."

She whimpered. "Please, you have to stop. This isn't right."

My fingers tightened around the slim column of her neck as I gently squeezed. A warning.

I tried to push both fingers inside of her again.

Still, her body resisted.

Not to be deterred, I pushed one finger inside. Her inner muscles clamped down around me.

A frisson of unease and confusion lingered in my mind.

Her pussy was so damn tight. Too tight for someone as promiscuous as her reputation claimed.

As a practice, I usually stayed far away from virgins. They were not ready for my particular tastes in the bedroom. Even so, it was hard not to imagine I felt the slight resistance of her maidenhead against the very tip of my finger.

Perhaps it was just wishful thinking.

It had to be.

I thrust the thought aside as I ruthlessly recalled her suggesting an anal threesome just moments earlier. She probably did some kind of Kegel yoga shit to keep her pussy tight.

The tip of my tongue teased the spot just behind her ear and lingered, savoring the salty taste of her skin.

I swirled my finger inside of her until the tight inner ring just inside her entrance opened and I was able to push a second finger in. I then thrust them both in and out, using the heel of my palm to apply pressure just above her clit.

Once again, I was treated to a low, throaty moan.

"You like that?"

She gasped when I again pressed my palm into her sensitive flesh, taunting her with the nearness of my fingers to her sensitive nub.

"Beg me to touch your clit."

Her spine stiffened, then she twisted her shoulders in a feeble attempt to break my grip. "No! I hate this."

I placed my arm across her chest, just under her collarbone. "Liar."

We were so close to the flames, the heat from the fire breathed against our skin. A devil's kiss.

Using my index finger and thumb, I pinched her nub.

She rose on her toes. "Ow! Ow!"

Keeping the painful pressure on her clit, I rasped, "Want me to stop?"

Her hand wrapped around my wrist as she tried to dislodge mine. "Yes! It hurts."

"Then be a good girl and beg me."

She breathed heavily, clawing at my wrist with both hands. "I don't know how. Please, you have to stop."

My arm tightened over her shoulders to stop her from squirming. "Open those pretty lips and tell me what a dirty girl you are, then beg me to make you come."

Her cheeks flushed so furiously I could feel the heat radiating from her skin against my jaw.

Blushing on cue.

I had to admit I was impressed.

I was sure she found it a useful skill.

Her fingernails dug into my skin, causing a pleasurable sting of pain. "Here? I can't come with all these people staring at me. Please, let go."

"I'll prove you wrong." With that I gave her pinched clit just the tiniest twist to bring a fresh wave of stimulating pain to between her thighs.

"*Sciatiri e matri!*" she cried out. "Please!"

Close enough.

As I moved my hand up to once more clasp her throat, I thrust my fingers into her tight cunt, increasing the rhythm.

In front of the bonfire, only a few paces from us, a woman stood wedged between two men in white bauta masks, black silk cloaks, and tricorn hats, appearing as a silhouette.

The man at her front tore her blouse open as she wrapped her arms around his neck and her legs around his waist.

Her body rose so she could press her bare breast into his mouth before her head fell back and she slowly sank down onto his exposed cock.

Keeping up the pace with my fingers, I bit her earlobe. "Does watching them turn you on, *colomba mia?*"

Her breathing shallowed as I rubbed my cock against her lower back in an attempt to ease the growing pressure.

A small crowd began to form around the threesome in front of us as the bauta behind the woman lifted her short skirt, exposing her ass.

He then lowered his zipper and pulled out his cock. Fisting the woman's hair, he positioned himself behind her.

The woman in my own arms stilled and held her breath as we both watched the man bend his knees and rub the head of his cock between the woman's ass cheeks.

I shifted my free hand to her waist. "We both know what is about to happen next, don't we?"

Still pistoning my fingers in and out of her body, I clasped her ass with my other hand. "He's going to thrust his cock ... deep ... inside her ass."

A low keening moan rattled from the back of her throat as her head fell back onto my shoulder.

I continued to whisper darkly in her ear. "See how her back stiffens from the feel of the head pushed against her tight hole?"

In perfect synchronization, the silhouetted threesome's movements seemed like a choreographed dance. The man in front arched his back as his hands held the writhing woman under her thighs, forcing her ass up higher. The man behind took advantage, thrusting deeper.

The woman screamed.

My bride gasped. I was fascinated and intrigued by her reaction to the spectacle.

After crassly suggesting we partake in just such a threesome earlier, she now watched this display with bated breath, as if she had never seen something so raw and erotic before.

Softly, she whispered to me, her voice high-pitched yet shallow, her breathing rapid. "Is she hurt?"

I pushed my fingers under the curve of her ass to tease the

center of her cheeks through the heavy folds of her skirt. "Yes. Right now that man's cock is piercing her in two, causing an unforgettable agony and ecstasy."

The women cried out again as both men ruthlessly double-teamed her. Pounding into her body as if they were fighting over a rag doll between them.

In that moment, my intended bride came.

I had to wrap my arm around her waist to hold her upright as her knees buckled.

She turned her head to stare up at me.

What could only be described as innocent wonder clouded her desire-hazed eyes.

It was becoming harder and harder not to fall for her wiles, not to believe the lie in her gaze.

I pulled my hand free and pushed my cream-covered fingers into her mouth. "Suck."

Her eyes widened and she tried to pull her head back.

I placed my other hand around the back of her head. "It wasn't a request. Suck my fingers."

The tip of her tongue swirled around my fingers.

Just the sight of her mouth being pried open as I forced her to clean her own cream off my skin almost had me coming right then and there.

I pulled my hand free and slammed my mouth down on hers for a brief, rough kiss, before I threw her over my shoulder and stormed through the crowd.

CHAPTER 5

ELLA

For several dizzying moments, my entire world became swirls of color, flashes of light, and the pounding of drums.

Then stars burst behind my eyelids as my stomach connected with his shoulder. It took a second to process what was happening.

"Let me go!"

No response.

I closed my fist and pounded on his back. "Stop! Let me go!"

I gasped at the sharp sting of his open palm connecting with my ass. The heavy skirt fabric did nothing to protect me.

"Settle down," he warned.

I pressed my hands against his back and tried to lift my torso while turning my head over my shoulder. "Don't tell me to settle down and don't you dare spank me again or I'll scream!"

He spanked my ass again. "If you don't behave, I'm going to flip you onto your back and do what I'm planning right here and now. Audience or not."

My mouth dropped open.

His actions in the piazza made it clear that this was no idle threat.

He freaking meant it.

And who knew who would stop to watch as well?

He had a mask on to conceal his identity during any debauchery. I did not.

Since the piazza was already descending into a Roman orgy, another man was more likely to join in than to stop Matteo if I cried out for help.

How on earth had I gotten myself into this mess?

I gritted my teeth. My sister. That was how.

All the trouble I'd ever gotten into in my life could be directly traced back to my sister.

Her entire life's philosophy seemed to consist of a careless, it-seemed-like-a-good-idea-at-the-time point of view, with no thought to the consequences.

Consequences were for other people to worry about. The people following in her wake cleaning up her mess.

I curled my fingers into his brocade jacket. "Please! You're making a mistake."

"I disagree. Apparently, my only mistake was in letting you run wild this past month. That ends tonight."

My eyes widened.

How did it end tonight?

The music from the piazza faded the further he carried me through the darkened streets of Palermo, heading to the shore. His footfalls clomped over weather-beaten wooden planks, the hollow sound echoing up from beneath it as he carried me down the dock, out over the water to where the boats were moored.

Sciatiri e matri!

Mother and Savior, he was going to kill me and dump my body in the sea!

The irony of my not thinking through the consequences of what I did next was not lost on me.

I wrenched his jacket up until the tanned skin of his back was exposed. Taking a quick breath, I opened my mouth wide and sank my teeth into his flesh, biting down with all my strength.

Matteo gave a shout and twisted away before I could draw blood.

I kicked forward and launched myself backward out of his grasp, falling onto the hard dock before I rolled onto my knees.

"What the fuck?"

Was all I heard from him before I gathered my skirts and took off.

Unfortunately, in the darkness and in my haste, I ran further out onto the planked walkway instead of back toward the shore.

His heavy-breathed pursuit dogged my steps, spurring me on. My lungs screamed, my thigh muscles burned.

"Dammit, woman! Stop right now!"

My mistake was in looking back at him over my shoulder. My only warning was his suddenly wide eyes. Swiveling my head forward, all I saw was the dock edge, and that I was about to plunge into darkness.

The soles of my boots slid on the weather-beaten surface of the last plank. My arms windmilled in a futile attempt to regain my balance and not fall into the dark, foreboding waters.

In that fraction of a second, I could practically feel it...

The bitter cold water enfolding me.

The shock of it stealing my breath as I struggled to the surface.

My skirt wrapped around my legs, tangling in the heels of my boots. My arms flailing in a fight to keep my head above water. Not having enough air to even scream for help. The frigid water stiffening my muscles, slowing every movement into a sluggish and strained effort.

Catching only a glimpse of the lights of Palermo in the distance as I sank deeper and deeper toward death.

Suddenly, a powerful arm grabbed me and yanked me away from the edge.

His black leather mask was all that much more sinister in the darkness. "What the hell were you thinking? You could have drowned," he raged.

I was thinking that you were going to kill me.

I was thinking I needed to get the hell away from you.

I was thinking how badly I wished I could just scream out my real name so you would leave me alone.

I was thinking if you found out I was Antonella and not Antonia, it could get my ungrateful sister into even more trouble or worse ...

I was thinking about the sheer insanity of my standing in the middle of the public piazza and allowing you to intimately finger me.

I was thinking about the most intense orgasm of my life from only your finger.

I was thinking if anyone found out what we'd done, my father would make me marry you instead of her.

I was thinking that you still thought I was my sister—and your intended bride.

Placing my hands over my flushed cheeks, I breathed heavily. *"I wasn't thinking."*

"You're damn right you weren't."

Before I could evade him, he reached down, scooped me into his arms, and headed back up the dock toward the anchored boats.

The feeling of being a trapped mermaid at the mercy of a ruthless demon sea captain came over me. "I can walk."

No response.

"Did you hear me? I said I could walk."

"I heard you. I just wasn't listening."

Stepping down a small side dock, he stopped along a massive twenty-five-meter Pershing 82 yacht.

A man in uniform with a gun strapped to his belt approached the railing. "Is that you, sir?"

"It is, Aldo. Push out the gangplank."

I couldn't let him carry me onto that boat. "Help! I'm being kidnapped! Call the police!"

The security guard chuckled as he released the latch on the entry gate and drew a lever. "I see you caught a live one, boss."

After a loud clang, a motorized metal gangplank slowly extended from the boat to the dock.

I squirmed in Matteo's arms.

As much as the words burned like acid in the back of my throat to even say the man's name, let alone use it as leverage, I cried out, "My father is Antonius Fichera! He will see you killed for this!"

Matteo glowered down at me. "I'm well aware of who your father is."

With his power, money, and mafia ties, even the mere mention of my father's name struck fear into the heart of any Sicilian.

I should have known an arrogant Cavalieri wouldn't give a damn. Their money and influence far eclipsed even my father's extensive reach.

The sea churned and broke against the dock pilings below the plank he carried me along. Aware that it was my only alternative for escape, I shivered at the prospect of entering the icy water. It would mean certain death.

Once we were on the boat, Matteo casually tossed out. "Tell the rest of the crew we are not to be disturbed—no matter what they hear."

My mouth dropped open as I looked over Matteo's shoulder

to see his guard's reaction to such a strange request. Aldo saluted and said, "Of course, sir."

The remote din of the Carnevale music and the clang and metallic hum of the gangplank being pulled back from over the water and into the boat accompanied us as we crossed the deck.

My only escape route was now gone.

The breach between the boat and the dock was far too wide to even contemplate jumping.

Matteo carried me through a spacious lounge filled with low sofas and ottomans, all in varying shades of gray with smooth, gray wood accents. Without saying a word, we descended deeper into the boat and along a narrow corridor.

I thought about crying out, but knew it was futile. If the security guard with the gun didn't want to challenge Matteo's authority, it was doubtful a steward or porter would. Not to save an unknown, drowned-rat female, at least.

After kicking open a pair of double doors at the end of the hallway, we entered a massive stateroom. My head swiveled from left to right, instinctively searching for a way out. Again, the room was decorated in the same soft shades of gray.

An enormous bed dominated the space.

Matteo set me on my feet and turned to close the doors, sliding the bolt lock into place.

Locked in.

On a boat.

Far away from where anyone could hear my screams.

Focu 'ranni. How the hell did I get myself into this? Oh right, my sister.

I backed up several steps and said, "You're making a terrible mistake. You need to let me go."

He crossed his arms over his chest. "Sure."

My eyebrows rose. "Really!"

He nodded. "Absolutely. I'll just let you waltz off this boat in your see-through shirt with your tits on display. No problem."

It took a second for my chilled brain to register his words.

First, the sarcastic tone.

Then the absurdity of his assurances.

Finally, the bit about my tits.

I looked down. The white lace corset was on display beneath the white linen of my blouse. The damp air and spray from the waves cresting against the dock pilings had rendered it almost translucent. I could even see the dark shadow of my areoles.

With a cry, I crossed my arms over my chest. "How dare you!"

Matteo tilted his head. "How dare I what? Look? Oh yes, I'm sure you're more accustomed to extracting some form of payment for a peek."

He pushed away from the door. "So tell me, what is the standard high-class-whore rate sheet? Cash for a peek. Jewels for a taste. Luxury car for a fuck?"

I raised my arm to slap him.

He caught it mid-air. "Slap me again and I'll slap you back. Understood?"

I gasped. "You'd slap a woman in the face? You brute!"

With his fingers firmly wrapped around my wrist, he wrenched me forward. My hands pressed against his chest as he smirked down at me. "I never said it would be across the face."

My cheeks warmed at his implication. Averting my gaze, I said through clenched teeth, "Let me off this boat."

"Fine. You can leave."

Unbidden, a surge of hope warmed my core. Then reality crystalized it into a rigid block of ice.

My gaze narrowed. "Just like that? You'll let me leave."

He brushed a damp curl of hair off my cheek. "Of course. As soon as I'm finished."

"Finished what?"

Please say talking to me. Please say talking to me. Please say talking to me.

His finger reached under my chin and tilted my head back. In this better light, the painted gold lines which highlighted the contours of his devil half mask stood out in stark relief.

The corner of his mouth lifted as his gaze wandered over my face to land on my mouth. "Finished disciplining you."

CHAPTER 6

MATTEO

The silver lining to this hot mess of an arranged marriage agreement turned molten and settled in my cock. It was odd not giving a fuck about trying to hide my more feral tastes in the bedroom.

"Take off that stupid disguise."

She blinked and stood still before me.

I stroked her lower lip with my thumb. "Don't start the bullshit shy act with me now, Antonia. Drop the skirt."

Her brow furrowed at my use of her name. Perhaps she didn't appreciate being referred to by the feminine version of her father's name. Maybe she was more of a Tia.

That was a concern for later. Now I just wanted to see her naked and tied to my bed.

She took a step back. "This isn't a disguise. And we ... can't .. not until we're married."

"Says the woman who offered me her ass in a threesome less than an hour ago."

Her mouth dropped open. "She did what!"

I cocked my head to the side. "What?"

43

She shook her head as she gathered the folds of her skirt and took another step back. "I mean, you must have misunderstood me."

"Some things a man does not misunderstand. Being offered anal is pretty damn near the top."

Her arm swept behind her to cover her ass as she pushed out her chin. "Well, this time you were mistaken."

The deep blush coloring her cheeks was an inspired touch. Resisting the temptation, I had to stop myself from falling into her sweetly poisonous virginal honey trap once again.

My chest tightened.

Fuck.

The sight of her almost going over that dock edge and possibly disappearing beneath the sea's dark depths nearly stopped my heart. The seconds it took me to reach her and pull her back in time were some of the longest of my life.

My jaw clenched as anger replaced fear.

By once more exhibiting her careless and irrational attitude, she had again put herself in peril. Whether it was playing with fire by agreeing to trick me on Dante's yacht or flirting with other men in front of her current lover or acting like a fool at Carnevale, she seemed to lurch from one poor decision to the next.

While the last thing I wanted was this marriage arrangement, it was obviously the best thing for her.

Someone had to take control of her. If not, she wouldn't make it out of her twenties.

I shrugged out of my costume jacket and shirt but left the leather devil's mask on.

Time for a little role-playing.

Her gaze traveled over my naked chest. "What do you think you're doing?"

My hands lowered to the top button of my costume's black breeches. "I'm pulling out my cock so you can suck it."

"I'm not putting *your thing* in my mouth!"

Leaving my black riding boots on, I widened my stance. "Care to make a bet?"

"You're disgusting.'

I winked. "You haven't even tasted me yet."

She lunged past me for the door.

With ease, I captured her long hair and twisted my fist into her locks, pulling her back against my chest. "Does this look familiar, baby?"

I gripped the torn edges of the neckline of her blouse and finished tearing the thin fabric down the front, then covered her breast over the lace corset with my free hand. "You couldn't take your eyes off that woman."

"That's not true."

With a swift spin, I took hold of her neck and guided her backward until she met the wall. "Liar. I could feel your pulse as you watched those men fuck her."

Just like it did then, her pulse rose, a rapid flutter against the center of my palm.

With the sleeves of her torn blouse loose around her fore-arms, she grasped my wrist and tried to pull me away.

I reached down and shoved her skirt off her hips, ignoring her cry of protest.

I then twisted the thin strap of her simple white silk panties where it arched over the soft rise of her hips.

Her attention to detail in wearing something so sweetly innocent should be admired. If nothing else, she played the inno-cent maiden act to the limit. I had to give her that.

"Did you enjoy watching her lower herself onto his cock? Could you feel the pressure between your legs and imagine what it would feel like to have your pussy stretched?"

I twisted harder.

She rose onto her toes as her panties tightened over her cunt.

With my lips a breath from hers, I said, "No. That wasn't the part that really turned you on, was it, baby?"

Her panties snapped in my hand.

I tossed the silk aside and replaced it with my hand, cupping her cunt. "It was when the second man flipped up her skirt, spread her ass cheeks ..."

She closed her eyes and tried to turn her head.

I flicked my fingers against her pussy, giving her a sharp spank. "Don't close your eyes. Look at me."

Her eyes flew open as she whimpered.

"Come on, baby. Be a good girl and tell me how it made you feel to watch that stranger's cock slowly disappear inside of that woman's ass."

"Please—"

"There will be time for begging later. Right now, I want to hear you say it. I want to hear you say it made this pretty pussy wet."

My finger pushed inside of her again. Proving my point, she was already warm and wet.

Tears filled her dark eyes, her lashes wet from her attempt to blink them away. Although her mascara was slightly smudged and her hair was a mess of damp curls, she was strikingly beautiful.

Way more beautiful than she looked a month ago on Dante's yacht.

There, she was all brittle artifice under a thick layer of makeup.

Here, her face was clean and fresh, only a black watery smear under her eyes to indicate that she had worn makeup earlier.

"Did your cute little asshole pucker when you imagined how it would feel to be violated by a big, thick cock?"

She shook her head as much as my hand around her throat would allow. Her fingernails dug into the skin of my forearm where it held her. "No. No!"

Chuckling, I leaned in and flicked the tip of my tongue against the corner of her mouth. "That's right. I almost forgot. You don't have to imagine it, do you, baby? You've let other men bend you over and fuck your ass before, haven't you, you dirty girl?"

She blinked, all of her micro expressions registering pure shock and horror at the idea. "No! Never! I would never!"

Well, fuck me. Perhaps my bride did have at least one virgin hole left.

"There's only one way to find out if you're telling the truth."

"What are you going to do?"

"Did I say you could ask questions?"

She shook her head.

I released her throat and moved to a silvery gray pine chest at the foot of the bed. I had purchased a few toys in Rome before leaving for Sicily, anticipating just this moment.

After raising the lid, I selected the riding crop with the bulbous ridged handle and turned back to her.

I slapped the leather tongue of the crop against my palm. "Get over here and kneel on the chest with your hands on the footboard."

Her gaze followed the length of the crop, but she remained in place.

"Now," I barked.

She visibly jumped before, with shaking steps, she approached my bed.

I tapped the smooth wooden top of the chest with my crop and narrowed my eyes.

With a sniff, she gingerly raised her right knee and lifted herself onto the chest. After getting settled on both knees, she bent forward and placed her hands over the edge of the low footboard.

Damn, she looked amazing in only her corset and those damn fuck-me boots.

My cock lengthened at the sight of her bare ass and her legs, how they contrasted against the black leather encasing them up to the tops of her thighs.

It was incredibly sexy how the corset pinched into her waist and exposed slivers of her lower back through the laces.

No wonder other men couldn't keep their hands off her. If this marriage was going to work, I might have to lock her in a convent and only see her for conjugal visits.

I pushed her hair over her shoulder with the leather tongue of my riding crop.

She bit her lip as she lowered her head, letting a cascade of spiral curls cover her face. The damp had made her blonde hair more of a golden brown. "Are you going to kill me?"

What an odd thing to ask.

Were her Sicilian lovers so boring they played no bedroom games?

It was possible that she had never experienced bondage before.

"Don't be silly, *colomba mia birichina*. We're just going to have a little fun, but first you need to be punished for all the running away you did tonight."

"Punished?"

The leather tongue of my crop teased the curve of her hip.

She shivered and arched her back away.

As I stepped near, I placed the riding crop across her throat. "Tell me you've been a bad girl."

When she remained silent, I pulled the riding crop toward me, allowing the rod to press against her throat.

Her head tilted up . "I've been a bad... bad girl."

"Now ask me to whip you."

"What?" She attempted to turn her head to look at me.

"Face forward," I commanded.

She complied. Her shoulders rose and fell with her rapid breath. "Please tell me you're not going to hurt me with that thing?"

"Would you rather I use my belt?"

"I'd rather you let me go."

"Not an option. Now you're wasting time and trying my patience. I gave you an order."

Her throat muscles contracted as she swallowed. "I don't know what you want me to say."

I leaned over her kneeling form and whispered into her ear. "I don't want you to *say* anything. I want you to beg me to punish you."

Her tongue flicked out to wet her lips.

My balls tightened.

Soon.

It was the one pleasure I was allowing myself for now.

The pleasure of her cute mouth.

I rubbed the end of the riding crop along her jaw. "The longer you defy me, the angrier I will get, and the harder I will shove my cock down your pretty throat after your punishment."

CHAPTER 7

ELLA

*T*his wasn't happening to *me*, it was happening to my sister.

It was my sister, half naked, bent over a strange man's bed.

Not me. Not me. Not me.

My mind couldn't escape harsh reality, no matter how many times I repeated the twisted mantra.

This was happening to me.

I was half naked, bent over Matteo Cavalieri's bed.

This wasn't my world. It was my sister's.

She was the one who delighted in toying with men.

Who had been using sex as a tool to get what she wanted since she was sixteen. She was the one who reveled in embarrassing me by recounting all the kinky things she had done in some random man's bed the night before.

Not me. Not me. Not me.

I was the quiet sister. The shy one. The one who hid behind her books and music.

The virgin one.

I tilted my head to look at him through my curtain of hair.

His sudden appearance at Carnevale had been alarming. His appearance now was terrifying.

At Carnevale he was a tall, dark, handsome man in an alluring costume who boldly kissed me.

Now, he was Matteo Cavalieri.

Towering over me with his superior height and heavily corded with muscle, bare chest exposed, he exuded power and authority. His body practically hummed with it.

Even the strange tattoo of a passionflower surrounded by what looked like pagan symbols added to the demonic mystique which was certainly helped by the black leather mask and breeches with riding boots.

Then there was the riding crop.

Sciatiri e matri, the riding crop!

I wasn't so sheltered I knew nothing about bondage sex games. I just never thought I'd be a participant. Ever. Not in my wildest, deepest, darkest fantasies had I ever imagined this scenario.

Of course, I never imagined a scenario where I would let a man finger-fuck me in the middle of the square while we watched a primal threesome silhouetted by flames.

My knuckles turned white as I grabbed the footboard harder. "I know I got … carried away … in the piazza, but you have to understand, it wasn't at all like me to do something like that."

Positioning himself behind me, he brushed his hard cock against my ass cheeks. "We both know that it was *precisely* like you."

There was a tug against my lower back from his pull on the corset laces. He continued. "You obviously have never been shown true discipline. That is about to change."

I squeezed my eyes shut as another tug on the corset laces rocked my body. I so badly wanted to scream, *My name is*

Antonella! It's my sister you want! It's my sister's actions you want to punish. My sister is your bride, not me.

I pulled my lips between my teeth to keep from crying out.

My father did not share an explanation or his reasoning for why he was ordering Antonia to marry Matteo. He shared nothing with his daughters.

I assumed it was to curb the same behavior Matteo referred to, but I could be wrong. Not understanding the true motivation, if I alerted Matteo to who I really was and ruined my father's plans, I could face far worse punishment.

Punishment like my mother faced.

The corset loosened, then floated to the top of the trunk as the heavy weight of my unsupported breasts pulled against my chest because of my bent-over position.

Shame, fear, and vulnerability washed over me as if someone had drawn a warm blanket back, exposing my naked skin to the chilled air.

Then came anger.

Anger at my father for being a cold-blooded bastard.

Anger at my sister for selfishly putting me in this position.

Anger at myself for allowing it all.

Rising on my knees, I covered my breasts with my arm as I faced him and spit out, "Fuck you and your discipline!"

With his leather mask, bare chest, breeches, and boots, he looked like a ruthless medieval executioner. His lips slowly curved into a smile. "You have no idea how badly I was hoping you'd say that."

His hand whipped out to fist my hair. Shoving me back into a kneeling position, where I stared in horror at the riding crop he held high.

Then, in a flash, he brought it down on my ass cheek.

I couldn't even cry out.

My mouth opened but there was no sound, just a pitiful sucking noise as I forced breath back into my lungs.

If I hadn't known he was holding a riding crop, I would have thought he'd tapped a live electric wire against my skin.

He whipped me three more times in rapid succession. The pain escalated with each one.

I clenched my jaw to keep from giving him the satisfaction of hearing me cry out or beg. But with each strike, it was getting harder and harder to remain quiet. My skin burned from the pain and humiliation.

My body jerked at the feel of his palm rubbing over my ass instead of the kiss of the crop again.

He moved his hand in strangely soothing circles, as if by rubbing my skin he could dissipate the pain. "It won't work."

My words came out as a distorted hiss through my clenched teeth. "What won't work?"

"You trying to defy me by keeping silent."

He pulled on my hair, wrenching my head back as he leaned over me. His lips brushed mine. "It only makes me want to punish you harder."

Releasing my hair, he raised his whip hand again. This time striking me just under the curve of my ass, on the top of my thigh. My body rocked forward. He struck again on the other thigh.

I moaned.

Instead of hating myself for breaking, I felt a rush of warmth inside my chest where the tightness I usually felt from stress and anger eased.

The leather tongue of the riding crop came down on my flesh several more times. Now the pain was a pulsing heat, the leather drawing my blood closer to the surface of my skin. I was aware of every touch, every breath, every nerve ending.

My world was shrinking to nothing more than raw, primal

sensations. My mind, usually a chaotic tumble of thoughts and worries, was … silent.

All I could focus on was my body and the strange, creeping pleasure I was feeling as the hot pain turned into a pulsing warmth.

I moaned again, this time deeper and longer.

"That's it, babygirl. Admit it. You like to feel the sting of the leather on your pretty little ass."

He struck again and white sparks erupted behind my eyelids as my inner thighs clenched.

Again, he stopped to rub my skin. "Let me hear you moan again. Tell me how much my dirty girl wants this."

My back stiffened as I bristled.

He chuckled. "Still going to be stubborn?"

Without warning, he slid the riding crop between my open knees and whipped it upward, slapping my pussy.

This time I cried out and slammed my legs closed, curling up on my side.

"Get back on your knees," he commanded.

"No! You have to stop! You're making a mistake."

He pushed his fingers between my legs, pressing his fingertips against my clit.

"You're like a cat in heat, baby. All wet and ready for me."

My mouth dropped open. Shocked to my core that the unfamiliar sensations I was feeling were from arousal. How was that possible? I was in pain. I was being humiliated. I was in a rage that he was treating me this way. Wasn't I?

Sure, the man towering over me was a muscular pillar of power and dominance, but that sort of base thing appealed to my emotional, sexy, crazy sister, not someone logical like me. Right?

I knew if I screamed, no one would come.

To further defy him would only worsen my punishment. Seeing no other choice, I grasped the footboard with a sob and pulled myself back up onto my knees, once more bent over. "I hate you for this. Is this how your marriage to my sis— is this how you plan to treat your wife?"

He went down on his haunches at my side. He pushed my hair away from my cheek as he studied my face. "This is exactly how I plan our marriage to be."

I blinked. Not expecting him to say something so freaking honest.

He rose to his full height and cupped my chin, tilting my head up. "If we are to have even the slightest chance of happiness, you need to give in to me now."

"I can't."

In a weird, twisted way, what he said had as much impact on my life as my sister's.

I may not be fucking men for validation, but I sure as hell was constantly bending over backward for it in other ways.

Always saying yes to my family's selfish demands. Never speaking up for myself. Always the one in control, the voice of reason. It started after my mother left or was forced to leave.

I walked the tense tightrope of hiding my true feelings of anger, fear, and frustration behind the calm and controlled mask of the dutiful daughter. I had no idea how to even express myself anymore.

He ran his thumb over my lower lip. "Well then, it's a good thing I'm not giving you a choice in the matter."

He tossed the riding crop onto the bed in front of me then stepped behind me. His left hand gripped my waist as he raised his right arm.

I tensed and turned my head away, bracing for the strike.

He continued to spank me with his open palm, causing a fresh wave of humiliating heat. It was definitely more embarrassing having him punishing me directly with his hand as opposed to the riding crop.

The crop was detached. And in a way too kinky.

But his hand? His hand was warm, firm, and intimate.

As he spanked me harder, his hard cock brushed against my ass, and I wished he would take it out so I could feel his skin against mine instead of the rough material of his pants.

I cried out when he switched to his left hand, freeing his right hand to press down on my lower back, raising my ass even higher, like I was asking for his punishment.

I moaned again, my head falling forward, my eyes closing. "Please, I can't take much more!"

"Then beg me to let you come."

My eyes popped open. Blood pounded in my ears and my entire existence faded into a haze of heated pain ... and something else ... something darker and more threatening. "What?"

He spanked my left cheek. "Beg me to let you come."

He really was insane if he thought I would ask for something so outrageous. "Never."

His spanking intensified. "I'm warning you."

My back arched as I tried to shift forward, but his grip would not allow it. "Ow! Ow!"

My head spun. Reality slipped away. Nothing else existed but my body's reaction to every painful touch of his hand.

"Give in and I'll show you how pleasurable it can be to lose control."

His right thumb slipped between my cheeks to press against my asshole, and a bolt of lightning shot up my spine.

I was no longer on this boat.

I was that woman by the bonfire, surrendering to those men, turning all control over to the primal, driving force of pleasure.

Then I was myself again, with Matteo's hands between my legs giving me an orgasm so intense my knees buckled.

With tears in my eyes, I finally obeyed. "Please, Matteo—'

CHAPTER 8

MATTEO

*H*er tears were not fooling me.

In the extremely limited times I had interacted with her, she had propositioned me twice.

This was all part of her virgin sex game role-playing.

Lucky for her, I was a kinky bastard who was here for it.

She truly needed to be disciplined, and I meant to continue doing so until her promiscuous, irrational behavior stopped—but that didn't mean we both couldn't also have a little fun.

She was going to be my wife, after all. I was entering this bullshit arranged marriage out of duty to safeguard my family.

That didn't mean I should damn the rest of my life to a cold marriage bed.

I picked up the riding crop and flipped it in my hand until I was holding it along the smooth bamboo rod.

Her adorable ass blushed a fiery pink after my earlier ministrations. Now I pushed the riding crop's bulbous, ridged handle between her knees. The length of my hand and half the width of my palm, the handle was crafted to be the perfect dildo.

I placed just the right amount of pressure on her lower back to keep her still, while forcing her to arch her back.

"Let's see if I can make you scream even louder than Our Lady of the Bonfire."

She let out a shocked gasp as she turned her head to look over her shoulder at me.

"Eyes front," I commanded as I raised the rod between her legs.

The moment the length of the bulbous handle pressed against her pussy, I was treated to another sharp inhale from my intended bride. By subtly applying pressure, I inserted the handle between her cunt lips.

"What are you—"

"I didn't give you permission to speak," I said, giving her right ass cheek a quick spank.

She whimpered in response but didn't object further.

In a slow, rhythmic movement, I moved the handle back and forth between her thighs, using the rounded ridges to stimulate her clit.

Adjusting her grip on the footboard, she moaned. "Oh, oh God!"

I applied more pressure as I gently increased the pace. "That's it, babygirl. Give in to me."

Her head tilted back. "Oh! Oh! Oh!"

Soft golden curls cascaded down her back to cover my hand on her lower back. I had to resist the urge to grab her hair and pull hard.

I knew if I did that, I wouldn't be able to restrain myself from whipping out my cock and thrusting deep inside of her.

Now was not the time. Not yet.

Without her even realizing it, her hips rocked back to match the thrust of the riding crop handle.

A burst of masculine arrogance warmed my chest. There was

no fucking way I was going to draw attention to her body's movements, knowing she would stop just to spite me and herself.

Besides, it would deprive me of the decadent pressure against my still straining cock as her ass brushed it.

Knowing she was close, I matched the pace of my riding crop thrusts with her elevated breathing and the rocking of her hips.

I leaned over her. "You like the friction of that riding crop handle?"

I pushed up against the handle, applying more pressure on her clit as she mewed in response.

A deep rumbling emanated from my throat at the grinding of her hips against the handle as she lost all abandon.

Her hand reached between her legs where she tried to push the tip of the handle inside of her.

I pulled back. "Not so fast. Only good girls get fucked. Disobedient girls get a rub-off and no more."

Her shoulder blades contracted, and her hips lowered when I bent over her kneeling form to place a kiss in the center of her back. As I moved my lips against her now sensitive skin, I said, 'I want you to ache for the feel of my cock entering you, filling you."

A guttural moan was her only response.

As I moved the riding crop faster, I used the tip of my tongue to trace down the center of her back, along the raised edge of her vertebrae. "With me, you will learn there is a difference between those shallow orgasms you get from mindless encounters with bumbling imbeciles, and a soul-searing one that is only possible through complete submission—but only if you behave."

The carrot and cock method of obedience.

"Please," she breathed. "I need—"

"I know what you need."

I just would not give it to her. Well, at least not the full length, not yet. She needed to learn there was pleasure in anticipation.

As I caressed her hip, I slid my hand under her body to cup and squeeze her breast. Her sensitive nipple hardened between my rolling fingers. "Next time, I'm going to take the riding crop to these pretty nipples of yours."

Her body bucked in response to my seductive threat.

I nipped at the curve of her ear. "You like that, my pain princess? You like the idea of me tying you up and swatting at your vulnerable nipples until they pulse with fiery pain and become so sensitive the slightest touch of my tongue would give you an orgasm?"

Her thighs clenched around the bamboo rod.

She was so very close. It seemed that my blushing bride enjoyed filthy talk.

"And the moment you come, I'll pound my cock into your tight pussy. Stretching it until you scream for me to fuck you harder and faster."

Her body bucked in my embrace again. A long, keening moan floated through the air before cutting off as she held her breath and stiffened, a shiver running down her spine.

When she finally let out the breath she was holding and her body sagged, I wrapped her hair around my fist and yanked her sideways on the wooden chest. With her still in a kneeling position before me, I growled, "Open your mouth, babygirl."

With lust-hazed eyes, she obeyed.

I inserted the riding crop handle coated in her own juices past her lips and over her teeth, then thrust.

Her shoulders hitched when I poked the back of her throat. She lifted her hands to grasp the rod.

"Put your hands down or I'll tie you up."

She blinked back unshed tears and lowered her arms.

"Good girl, now suck it clean. Taste your own cream."

Her cheeks hollowed as she sucked on the riding crop handle.

While I watched her, I unbuttoned the rest of the buttons on my costume breeches and pulled out my cock. Wrapping my free hand around the turgid length, I pumped my fist up and down the shaft while I eased back the pressure.

When I couldn't take it any longer, I carefully pulled the handle from her mouth and tossed it aside. My fingers dug into her cheeks as I gripped her jaw and forced her head back. "My turn."

I thrust my cock past her lips.

Her eyes widened as she tried to draw her head back.

My grasp on her hair prevented it.

As I pushed my cock deeper into her wet mouth, she kept her tongue pushed down. It was almost as if she didn't know how to suck a cock, which of course was not probable.

More likely, she was being stubborn or playing her games again.

"If you don't start using your tongue and sucking my cock like the pro I know you are, I'll take that riding crop handle and shove it up your ass until you do."

With a whimper, she placed a hesitant hand around the base of my cock and swished her tongue from side to side under the sensitive skin of the shaft.

"Circle the head," I ordered.

Her tongue moved around the bulbous head until I once more pushed deeper, gagging her.

Tears rolled down her cheeks as she gagged and sputtered around my thick shaft, trying to pull back.

"Don't you dare take my cock out of your mouth," I warned, staring down at her.

The sight of her struggling to swallow my flesh made my cock swell and lengthen.

Fuck, it was sexy as hell.

I would not last as long as I wanted after denying myself all evening.

My balls tightened as I pulled her head closer to my hips. Her lips stretched around the wide base of my shaft, her small hands pushing back against the tops of my thighs.

The vibration of her frightened scream sent an amazing jolt up my cock, straight to my balls.

I came.

With a little mercy, I pulled back slightly, allowing my come to coat her tongue instead of choking her by jetting straight to the back of her throat.

The second I pulled my still semi-hard cock free, she clutched her hand to her naked chest and bent over, coughing as she spit my come out onto the top of the chest.

While holding onto her hair, I pushed her face down close to it. "I should make you lick up every drop."

She coughed again before rasping, "Please, I'm sorry. I didn't mean to spit it out."

Whether she was a girl who hated to swallow or was telling the truth, I couldn't discern. Next time I'd ensure she swallowed the entire mouthful.

Before I could threaten her with just that, there was a commotion above us on the deck.

Worried about trouble, I pushed my cock back into my breeches as I swiped off my devil's mask and reached for my shirt and jacket. "Get dressed."

Her arms covered her breasts. "You tore my blouse."

As I swiftly stormed toward the door, I tossed instructions over my shoulder. "Grab one of my shirts from the closet. If you know what's good for you, you won't leave this room until I come and get you."

The cries of alarm and heavy thuds of boots running over the deck grew stronger as I swung the door open and raced down the narrow hall.

CHAPTER 9

MATTEO

There was chaos on the upper deck as men holding semi-automatic Beretta PMXs rushed onto my yacht.

Not expecting this level of trouble, I only had a skeleton crew with me. Despite the odds of four to one, my men had taken stronghold positions and were prepared to fight.

I raised my hand. "Hold."

A dark figure strolled down the dock and over the makeshift gangplank his men had extended onto my boat.

I leaned both hands on the railing as I watched him approach. "Didn't figure you for the pirate type."

Dante Agnello shrugged. "My girl likes the outfits."

He re-buttoned his Armani suit jacket the moment he stepped onto the deck. "Mine's bigger," he observed, looking around.

Leaning against the railing with crossed arms, I responded, "You know what they say about men and overcompensating with fast cars and big boats."

Dante laughed as he extended his hand. "How are you, my friend?"

Unfolding my arms, I reached out and shook his hand. "As well as can be expected."

"And your father and Liliana?"

"The-most-interesting-man-in-the-world and his new bride? They are happy hermits up north at his ranch in San Vito di Cadore—but you already knew that."

He shrugged again. "I keep tabs."

With a flick of my hand, I motioned to his men. "So, what's with the welcoming party?"

Dante rubbed his forehead, then let out a frustrated sigh. "The girl's father is furious. He's threatening to tear apart Palermo looking for her."

"Interesting. Too bad he didn't show this much interest in her whereabouts sooner or we wouldn't be in this mess."

There was no point in diplomacy.

If Antonius Carlo Fichera had shown even half as much interest in his daughter as he had in Liliana's godfather, Salvatore Giovanni Mangano, and his plans to try to oust Dante as the boss of their mafia syndicate, I wouldn't even be in Sicily preparing to marry her.

I placed the blame solely at her father's feet for letting her run wild and fuck inappropriate men under his command.

Clearly, the girl had been acting out for attention.

I had since learned her mother ran off when she was just a young teen. It was all so classic rebellious teenager bullshit, it would be tiresome if she wasn't now in her twenties and my forced fiancée.

After a quick glance over his shoulder to ensure his men had maintained a respectful distance, Dante turned back to me. "On this, we are in agreement. However, that does not solve my problem this evening."

With a sweep of my arm, I motioned for him to join me in the forward deck lounge. "If you agree to leave your pets on shore, I could offer you a drink."

After a ghost of a smile, Dante kept his gaze on me as he called out, "Leave us, but guard the plank."

His men filed off my yacht, leaving only two to stand guard over the temporary gangplank they used to board.

As he followed me to the lounge area, he said, "No offense, friend, but you aren't going to serve me one of your family's wines, are you? I prefer to drink red only when I dine."

After stepping behind the bar, I placed two digestivo glasses on the upper counter. Holding up a bottle of *Amaro Montenegro*, I said as I unscrewed the cap, "No offense, *friend*. I only offer those bottles to *invited* guests."

Pouring the aromatic liquor in both glasses, I pushed one toward him.

He lifted the glass. *"Cin cin."*

"Cin cin," I responded, sipping the nutmeg-and-orange-sweetened bitters.

Making our way to the railing, we both looked out over the harbor for a moment, taking in the sparkling reflection of the moon off the water, the blinking green and red harbor lights bobbing in the distance, piercing the darkness.

The crisp winter air was acrid with the fragrance of char and roasted nuts from the steady stream of thick smoke rising above the stucco buildings marking the location of *Piazza Garraffello*. Carnevale continued in full swing amidst the glowing windows and streetlights of Palermo, as it would until way past dawn.

Dante leaned on the railing. "While I'm pleased that you are keeping your promise, I confess I'm confused as to why you would want to stir up trouble with your future father-in-law."

My knuckles whitened as I gripped my glass. "The man should thank me for dragging her away from Carnevale where she could have gotten into all sorts of trouble."

Like parading around in barely more than a corset, fucking a man in public, and offering me an anal threesome, to start with.

"I was doing him a favor. Trust me."

Dante frowned. "I hadn't heard she was at Carnevale. That's not like her."

I snorted and raised my glass to take a sip. "Really? Because it sounds *exactly* like her to me."

He shook his head. "Strange. Either way, I need to return her before her father and sister find out you were the one who took her."

Despite wanting to point out that her father's sudden Catholic concern for his daughter's maidenly virtue was far too late, I bit my tongue.

As to why her sister would give a fuck, I had absolutely no idea.

I was aware Antonia had an identical twin sister named Antonella, Ella for short, but my sources said they were not particularly close. It was odd for twins, but not unusual, especially twins with such polar opposite personalities.

As far as I had learned, Ella was a shy little thing who was only interested in her studies and playing the cello. By all accounts, she was absolutely nothing like her sister, Antonia.

I couldn't even find evidence of Ella having a boyfriend.

It was crucial that I know of all the males surrounding this situation in case one decided to play knight in shining armor to Antonia's damsel in distress. Including Ella's boyfriend if she had one, since I wouldn't put it past Antonia to cross that line if it suited her purposes.

Judging by her innocent ingenue act earlier, it was a necessary precaution.

Dante continued. "Her father hasn't given his full blessing to this union yet. If he deems you a threat more than an asset, the plan is done."

"There is no need to remind me. I'm meeting him tomorrow when I play the gracious future son-in-law for Shrove Tuesday dinner after the parade."

Martedi Grasso, the last feast day before Lent, was not one of my favorites. It was traditionally full of obnoxiously rich sweets as Italians cleared out their pantries before the weeks of fasting.

He drained his glass. "Good. I will not ask questions about tonight, but from this point forward, I need you to truly act like a fucking groom and stay away from the sister."

The sister? Ella? The shy cello player?

After tossing the rest of my drink over the railing, I turned to him with a furrowed brow. "Dante, what the hell are you getting at by warning me away from her sis—"

Before I could finish, the bride in question, defying my express order to stay in the room, appeared.

My anger intensified when she stepped fully into the light.

She looked beautiful—*and thoroughly fucked*—even though we didn't get that far.

Her golden curls were tousled and teased. Her lips cherry-red and swollen. Her cheeks still had a high blush that I was certain would match the lower cheeks I had whipped with my riding crop.

It didn't help that she looked sexy as fuck wearing one of my white dress shirts tied off at the waist over her voluminous skirt. Neither did it help that I knew under that shirt was a white lace corset and that her torn panties were probably still laying on my bedroom floor.

With her head bowed and her hands twisting the fabric of her skirt, she whispered, "Good evening, Don Agnello, is Father really mad?"

Dante smiled with warm affection at her as he approached and lifted her arms to kiss the backs of her hands. "For you? I lied and said you were with me and some associates enjoying a musical concert at the church. I told him I would have you home soon."

I viewed the touching scene with growing anger.

Antonia in church? Seriously? That wasn't even remotely believable.

Was Dante also one of Antonia's lovers?

He could have fooled me the night I was on his yacht with my father and Liliana.

All of Dante's body language toward Antonia showed he found her to be an annoying troublemaker. He expressed the same sentiment during the wedding.

Right before he told me he needed to marry her off before she caused a civil war in his syndicate by sleeping with two different, powerful married men.

My bride wrapped her arms around Dante's waist and buried her head in his chest. "Thank you, Don Agnello."

What the fuck?

He tipped her chin back and winked. "You're still going to catch hell for *forgetting* to tell your father I asked you to join me for evening Mass."

Her lips thinned. "Yes, sir."

Sir?

My fingers clenched into a fist as I stepped forward. "Get your hands off her."

Even if he were one of her lovers, that ended the day he asked me to be her fucking fiancé.

Dante didn't turn to face me. Nodding, he instructed her, "Go with my men. I'll be right there."

I clenched my teeth. "She isn't going anywhere, not until I say so."

She looked between Dante and me, then quickly pivoted on her heel to race toward Dante's men and down the gangplank.

My gaze narrowed. She was going to pay for her disobedience.

Dante turned to me and threw his arms in the air. "What the fuck was that? What did I just say about only concerning your-self with your bride and not the sister?"

Really? What the fuck is with him and the damn sister?

"Antonia will soon be a Cavalieri, and that means she and her sister, Ella, will be under my protection and therefore my concern, not yours. Remember that."

I could only assume Antonia would want her twin sister, Ella, to be with her to have family near while in Abruzzo.

If what I learned about the shy sister was any indication, hopefully she would be a positive, calming influence on my bride.

"Soon, but not yet. The Fichera girls remain under my protection until then. See that you remember that."

Dante was a powerful Don in Sicily and a tentative, if reluc-tant, ally of the Cavalieri family.

It would serve no purpose to continue arguing with him. By the end of the week, I would be back in Abruzzo at the Cavalieri winery with my troublemaking bride, planning our ill-fated wedding.

I watched as Dante joined her on the dock and walked toward his car.

All the while thinking of how I would maneuver to get her alone Tuesday night before dinner, to punish her for her open defiance of me.

My cock hardened as several intriguing disciplinary options crossed my mind.

CHAPTER 10

ELLA

*T*he hard slap across my face was a surprise, but not unexpected.

My father did his best talking with his fists.

He wagged his thick sausage finger in front of my nose. "After the stunt you pulled last night, I will tolerate no more sass from you. You will be at dinner to welcome your sister's fiancé and you better be on your best behavior."

Blinking back unshed tears, I nodded. "Yes, Father."

"You and your fucking sister are useless, just like your whore mother."

I swallowed past the bile in the back of my throat but remained silent. I knew better than to object. The last time I did was when I was fifteen, and all I got for it was three cracked ribs.

"The least you both can do is entertain my guests."

The bitter taste in my mouth increased.

I knew what he meant by *entertain*.

"Yes, Father."

After he stormed off, I walked softly down the terracotta-tiled hallway which stretched through the center of our villa. It was a trick I learned from my mother when she was still with us.

Always step lightly on the balls of your feet.

Never let the heels of your shoes clack against the hardened clay.

Noise was bad.

Noise alerted my father to where we were inside the villa.

Pulling open the glass lattice-window doors, I stepped outside into the lemon grove. Losing myself among the glossy, emerald-green citrus leaves, I inhaled the sweet fragrance of the *zagara* blooms mixed with the sharp citrus scent of the lemons.

As I ran my fingertip over the pocked smoothness of a lemon clinging to a nearby branch, I realized it would be harvested soon. My mother loved the lemon harvest.

I missed her.

I wished she was here now to give me advice. Her presence would have provided comfort, even though I could never confess what happened with Matteo last night.

Matteo Cavalieri.

My sister's unwanted fiancé.

That wasn't how I saw him anymore.

Last night I tossed and turned in my bed, plagued by dreams of a towering demon in a devil's mask.

In my dream, he had a long black whip, and he used it to force me to dance among the flames of a raging fire until I burned to cinders.

I didn't need a degree in psychology to analyze that dream.

Crossing the gravel path, I opened the door to a small, enclosed gazebo nestled in the center of the lemon grove. Its white paint was chipping and the cushions on the wicker chairs and lounge inside had long since faded, but this was my happy place.

I pulled my cello out of the cupboard where I had locked it for safekeeping until I could get out here and sat down.

Pulling the instrument close, I raised my bow and slowly began to play Chopin's "Prelude No. 4 in E Minor."

It was my favorite song to play when I was feeling moody or pensive. The minor key and simple yet solemn melody made it both beautiful and heart-wrenching.

I glided my bow over the cello strings to play the five-note melody over a series of downward-spiraling block chords, the longing and ache portrayed in the music matching my own tormented feelings.

What kind of evil person dreamed of her sister's fiancé?

A sharp, tightening pain in the center of my chest formed when I faced that I was lying even to my inner self.

I didn't just *dream* about Matteo Cavalieri.

I couldn't justify what I did last night, no matter how hard I tried. And I had tried!

Twisting myself every which way, coming up with every excuse I could think of.

I did it for my sister.

It wasn't my fault.

He forced me.

But always with the same result. Liar. Liar. Liar.

The only bright spot in my cloud of doom and gloom was that my sister had snuck in before my father noticed I was missing and passed out in her bed, completely drunk.

It was doubtful she remembered anything from last night.

I simply had to ensure that she and Matteo didn't have a chance to talk privately tonight.

If things went as planned, Fino would expose my father and the wedding would be canceled, keeping the truth hidden. Easy.

I sighed. My plan sounded like the terrible plot from a

sitcom, and tonight's dinner would probably turn out as comically bad as any slapstick sketch.

I bowed a *womp womp* noise on my cello.

I set the instrument inside and returned to the villa, in search of caffeine.

My sister was in the kitchen eating a plate of *spaghetti aglio olio e pepperoncino* for breakfast or, more to the point, a late lunch. The starch, oil, garlic, and chili peppers made it one of her favorite hangover cures.

Without saying anything, I made two espressos, then reached under the cabinet behind the tins of olive oil for the bottle of *Fernet-Branca* my sister hid there.

This was her second favorite cure.

After adding a splash of the bitter amaro to her espresso, I returned the bottle to its hiding place. (Father didn't believe in letting women drink outside of a glass of wine with dinner.)

Crossing to the table, I placed it in front of her, then sat with mine.

She barely looked up as she slurped a forkful of pasta past her lips before muttering, "*Grazie.*"

"*Prego.*"

Finally, she looked at me. "Is that from Father?"

I raised my fingertips to my cheek, then nodded.

"Honestly, Ella. When will you learn to just stay out of his way?"

"Says the girl who's being forced into marriage by him?"

She shrugged. "You'll figure it out. Besides, I saw Matteo last night…"

"You did?" My stomach twisted as I braced for her response, watching her closely for any change in expression.

What would I do if she suddenly raged at me for fucking her fiancé?

I could argue the finer point that I didn't technically have sex

78

with him—I only sucked his cock after he whipped me with his riding crop and made me come with the dildo handle.

Yeah, that was way better than if I had slept with him. Sigh.

She twisted a forkful of pasta against the bowl of her spoon. "He's pretty freaking sexy. All those muscles and those callused hands. Plus, you know how much I like my men tall. I bet his cock is huge."

I raised the back of my hand to my lips after choking on a sip of espresso. When I could breathe again, I struggled to keep my voice calm and casual. "You shouldn't say such things, Toni," I advised, using my nickname for her.

Antonia rolled her eyes. "God, you're such a fucking prude, Ella. Maybe if you were willing to put a piece of wood other than that stupid cello between your legs, you'd finally attract a man."

There were countless reasons why I shouldn't fire back that I had sucked her man's cock the night before.

For starters, it would ruin everything. Not to mention that Matteo thought I was Antonia when he propositioned me.

There was every reason to believe that if he knew I was the "boring" twin, he would have stayed away even if he wasn't about to become engaged to my sister.

Spinning my empty espresso cup between my hands, I said, "So, have you changed your mind about marrying him?"

If she said yes, I'd have to tell her about last night.

If she said no, I would keep my mouth shut … Ironically, what I should have done last night.

Focu 'ranni.

She kicked back her espresso in one gulp. "I don't know. Maybe."

Dammit. What was I supposed to do with maybe?

"You honestly want to move to the middle of nowhere in Abruzzo or worse yet, up north in the Dolomites, where his father has a ranch?"

She wrinkled her nose. "Of course not. If we married, he'd have to move here, or maybe we'd live in Rome."

"That's not going to happen, Antonia. His family has a massive winery business in Abruzzo. Everyone knows the Cavalieri men physically work at the winery along with their staff."

I sent a quick apology prayer to the Holy Madonna before pressing on. "And they expect their women to do the same. I heard the wives and girlfriends even slog through the muddy fields during harvest time."

She pulled a face and let her fork clatter to her plate. "Eww. But they have money!"

I collected her plate and espresso cup on my way to the kitchen sink. We only had a few more minutes before the staff arrived to start preparing for dinner.

We used to have live-in staff, but after Mother's disappearance, Father fired them all and initially refused to allow anyone in the house. He said it was because he couldn't stand the noise.

I knew what he really couldn't stand was having any witnesses to how he treated Antonia and me.

Any witnesses to what he—

I shook the disturbing thought off as I ran her plate under the faucet. "So? Money isn't everything."

She tossed her napkin aside. "Speak for yourself. It should be illegal for a man who has billions to make his wife work. I'll just tell Matteo I refuse to work. That as his wife, it's his duty to provide for me and obey me and buy me whatever I want."

After finishing her plate, I leaned a hip against the counter. "Yup. That's exactly what it says in the Bible."

Another quick apology prayer.

"But ... I heard the Cavalieri men are cruel to their women and really, really cheap! Matteo's cousin, Cesare, didn't even buy his fiancée a diamond engagement ring."

Antonia gasped and rose from her chair to approach me. "What?"

I nodded sagely. "It's true. He gave her a simple gold necklace. And not even a new one! He repaired some old zodiac charm she already owned."

Antonia placed her hand over her heart as if she had just heard he tortured puppies or kicked the homeless. "That is disgusting."

Eavesdropping on the staff while they gossiped after learning about Antonia possibly marrying into the Cavalieri family was paying off.

I continued. "It gets worse. You know the other cousin, Enzo, the one who's marrying his dead wife's sister?"

She nodded. "Yeah, the tall, brooding one."

"That's him. I heard he refuses to stay in this gorgeous mansion he owns overlooking the piazza and instead forces his fiancée, Bianca, to live in squalor in some ramshackle cottage in the middle of a dirt field."

She clutched her stomach. "I think I'm going to be sick."

I pushed my advantage. "And that is nothing compared to Matteo's father."

Her eyes widened. "I met him on Dante's yacht. His name is Benedict, I think. Insanely hot, but super scary."

"He forced a woman half his age to marry him after only knowing her for barely a week, and he now makes her spend night and day with him on his *horse* farm. Apparently, he wants to keep her pregnant with lots of kids, so she'll have no choice but to stay with him."

"A horse farm!"

"The horse farm Matteo will inherit one day as Benedict Cavalieri's heir."

Her lips thinned as her eyes narrowed. "I'm not living on some godforsaken horse farm!"

I patted her shoulder. "You might not have to … I'm sure you heard the rumors about what happened to Barone Cavalieri's first wife." I leaned in and whispered conspiratorially, *"Murdered by him.* There were also rumors about Enzo's first wife who died mysteriously when she—"

Antonia covered her ears. "Enough. I don't want to hear any more! Father can't be serious about forcing me to marry into this horrible family of arrogant, cheapskate murderers!"

My hands gripped her shoulders. "Toni, Father doesn't care about you. He cares about three things and three things only: his reputation, his greed, and his business. You have to trust me to get you out of this."

She stamped her foot. "When?"

I backed up. "I'm working on it."

"Well, work harder! Because I refuse to marry that man!" she said before storming off.

A bad deed done for good reasons wasn't really bad, right?

I was sure that was in the Bible somewhere.

No, my inner voice answered, *but there is an ancient proverb. The road to hell is paved with good intentions.*

Speaking of hell … I had a dinner with Matteo in a few hours to survive.

CHAPTER 11

MATTEO

"*W*hat is the useless skin around a vagina called?"

I closed my eyes briefly. This would not be good.

Antonius Carlo Fichera boomed out, "The woman!" Then slapped his thigh as he leaned forward, laughing at his own joke, sounding like a braying donkey.

Wow. That was even worse than I thought it would be.

My future father-in-law was holding court among his dinner guests.

The very first thing I noticed was they were all men.

Clearly, the *capo* preferred dining with his *soldati* and not their wives or girlfriends, as was customary at a formal dinner party. It had always been my experience that if a man was required to wear a tuxedo, then there would be women present.

It reminded me of the old *tavoliddus* mafia dinners from the sixties where the *mafiosi* would feast on meat, cheese, and expensive wine given, or more precisely stolen, as a tribute from the poor villagers, before ending the night with a mock liturgy.

With the men whipping the white tablecloths around their

shoulders, pretending to be bishops and priests *blessing* the only females there, the prostitutes.

All bullshit, egotistical masculine energy.

What did I expect from a man who named his daughters Antonella Carlotta and Antonia Carlotta after himself?

The ice in my Campari and soda rattled as Antonius slapped me on the back. "Great joke, right?"

I forced a smile. "I can honestly say I have heard nothing like it in quite some time."

He slapped me again. "Don't go stealing it like you're stealing my daughter!"

Again, the donkey brayed as the rest of the room laughed along with him.

I laughed through clenched teeth, covertly checking my watch. "I won't."

Where the hell was Antonia? I wanted to speak with her before we were all seated.

It was clear, given the stilted entertainment, I would not be getting the quality alone time I had enjoyed last night, but that didn't mean I didn't have some strong words for her.

The men all turned as Antonia and her sister, Antonella, appeared in the parlor's arched doorway but did not enter, as if waiting for permission.

I knew the women were twins, but damn. If it weren't for their attire and makeup, I wouldn't be able to tell the two apart.

Antonia was wearing heavy eyeliner, large gaudy jewelry and a tight, cleavage-baring, black cocktail dress, much in the style I remembered from when I first met her on Dante's yacht.

The shy sister, Antonella, wore a more modest A-line dress in pale cream with a high collar, a strand of black pearls her only adornment.

With their golden hair, they looked like the good and evil versions of two angels.

Too bad I wasn't being asked to marry the good angel.

Antonius motioned for the women to enter. "Girls, come over here and greet our guests."

Both women moved to stand dutifully near their father.

Antonius placed a hand around Antonia's waist. "So this one is finally going to make herself useful by doing her duty and marrying."

I frowned as I focused on his hand. It wasn't quite at her waist but higher, more like on her ribcage, and close to her breasts. Odd.

The crowd cheered as Antonius motioned for me to come closer. "This is my possible future son-in-law, Matteo Cavalieri. He's from the mainland, but his money ensures I won't hold it against him."

More laughter.

Fuck, this was painful.

My gaze settled on Antonia. Her lip curled slightly as she tilted her chin up and broke my gaze by turning to the other guests. Coldly ignoring me.

Well, what did I expect? The warm and loving embrace of a fiancée?

I raised my glass in a toast. "Thank you, Signore Fichera. I'm honored to become a member of your family."

Antonius raised his palm as he exchanged an amused look with his men. "Take it easy there, Matteo. No one said you'd be part of the family … yet. We haven't talked terms. You are after all, getting the daughter of one of the most powerful *capos* this side of the island. I'm not just going to give her away."

Interesting not-so-subtle hint that he would expect a dowery.

I wondered if Dante, their *Capo dei Capi* and head of the entire syndicate, knew Antonius was referring to himself as such.

It appeared we may have cut off the head of one snake, only

ZOE BLAKE

for another to appear in its place. Perhaps Salvatore wasn't the only one in the organization with dreams of taking Dante's shaky throne.

He placed his hand on the back of Antonia's neck and pulled her in even closer before saying, "And you're not bringing much in return."

Just a legendary family legacy dating back to Italy's kingdom era, a billion-dollar fortune, and respectability for his daughter.

Antonia barked a laugh as she placed her hand on her father's chest. "Maybe you shouldn't make me marry him then."

I remembered her laugh being more soft and musical last night. Come to think of it, she'd had a horrible, brash laugh at the dinner with Dante as well. Strange.

I watched as she cast a coy glance across the room.

The subject of her attention was a married *capodecina* in Antonius's ranks named Alessio Bonucci.

This must be one of the men Dante was worried about after Salvatore's assassination. The reason I was being pressed into service to marry Antonia and get her out of Sicily before she could cause any more trouble.

Either her father was completely unaware of her extracurricular activities, or he was baiting me by having his daughter's lover at the very dinner at which our engagement was being announced.

Antonius glared at his daughter, showing his mercurial temperament. "You'll marry who I tell you to marry."

Antonia's smile faded as the other guests looked down at their drinks or turned their heads to avoid the awkward encounter. "Of course, Father."

With his grip on her neck, he gave her a shove forward. "Go and greet my guests like you were taught."

I slammed my drink down on the nearest surface and stepped forward, fists clenched.

A hand on my shoulder stopped me. I looked over to see Dante at my side.

He gave an almost imperceptible shake of his head. "Not yours yet to protect. This is his house and his daughter. Remember that."

I clenched my jaw as I inhaled through my nose.

The guests in the room surged forward to greet Dante before I could respond. Everyone but Antonius, who remained by the fireplace mantle.

Dante stretched out his arms. "Antonius, do you not greet your Don?"

The man's upper lip lifted, baring his canines for just a second before his sneer morphed into a bitter smile. "Of course, Don Agnello. Welcome to my home."

Unlike with the others who were greeted with warm slaps on the shoulder or embraces, Dante swung his arm forward when Antonius approached. After a moment's hesitation, Antonius bowed low and kissed his ring.

Nice play.

Surveying the room to garner the reactions of the other guests, I spotted Ella.

Partially hidden behind a high-backed upholstered chair, she stood silent and still. As if she hoped we would all forget she was even there. It was easy to see why she was called *the shy one.*

Antonia's laughter caught my attention again. This time she had her arms around the neck of another *soldati* as his hand crept low on her back, practically cupping her ass.

Having had enough, I stormed across the room and grabbed her forearm to dislodge her grasp. Keeping my gaze on the man, I said, "You don't mind if I chat with my fiancée, do you?"

The shorter man stepped back and bowed his head before hurrying away.

Antonia ran the tip of her finger along the inside edge of my tuxedo lapel. "That wasn't very nice of you, Matteo. I was just being friendly."

"Like you were being *friendly* with Manfredo at Carnevale?"

Her finger traced the waistband to my tuxedo slacks along my belt. "Exactly."

I gripped her wrist. "I thought I made it clear last night that I wouldn't tolerate such behavior moving forward. Perhaps you need another reminder from my riding crop."

Antonia leaned forward. "And just how will you remind me with your riding crop?" she whispered suggestively, the tip of her tongue sweeping over her heavily glossed red lips.

My gaze traveled down to her other hand but didn't see a drink in it. That would be the only explanation for her sudden, overtly flirtatious insinuation, which was a stark contrast to how she behaved on my boat, but similar to her comments at Carnevale.

Perhaps she was on some form of medication? Or shared her father's mercurial personality.

I inwardly sighed. Fantastic.

A woman cleared her throat behind me. "I heard riding crop. Are you talking about your horse ranch, Signore Cavalieri?"

I hadn't realized Ella had crept up on us.

Releasing Antonia's wrist, I responded, "Not exactly."

Ella trained her eyes on her sister, despite talking to me. "I've heard it is *so far north* that more than half the people speak German and most of the restaurants in town serve boiled beef and *Gulasch*."

Antonia covered her mouth, her shoulders jerking as if she were gagging. Her response was muffled by her palm. "That isn't true, is it?"

Curious as to Ella's motives for bringing up such an odd fact, I shrugged. "It's what the skiers who visit seem to want."

Ella kept her face slightly averted from me with a curled

wave of hair covering her cheek and jaw. "That's right! It's nega-tive two degrees Celsius there right now, and it will stay that way through April. My! Isn't that *interesting*, Antonia? Right when Palermo gets warm and is bathed in bright sunshine, Matteo's family horse ranch will still be *deep* in the middle of a dark winter."

Antonia looked over my shoulder past the both of us to give someone a sly smile and a wave before glancing at her sister. "I think it sounds positively archaic. I can't imagine why anyone would want to live in such a boring, backward part of Italy."

My thigh brushed Ella's hand when I shifted to the side to block Antonia's view of whoever she was attempting to flirt with while in my presence.

I was not expecting the shock of awareness, nor Ella's sudden gasp.

She snatched her arm around her middle as she took a step away from me.

Still not meeting my gaze.

Something teased at the back of my memory.

Refocusing on Antonia, I said, "You'll learn to appreciate its charms once you are there."

"God, you can't seriously think I'd agree to visit, let alone live there."

The corner of my mouth lifted as I raised my glass to take a sip. "Good thing I wasn't planning on asking for your approval on where we live."

The champion horse ranch I helped run with my father was a huge part of my life.

Not only was it in the Northern Italian Alps, which had some of the most grandiose and stunningly beautiful vistas in the world, it was also extremely lucrative.

Not to mention its barely guarded border with Austria and Germany allowed my father and me to slip in and out of the country without records or surveillance, which was a useful asset for our more clandestine pursuits.

Antonia flipped her long hair. "I have no intention of going through with this marr—"

"Dinner is served," interrupted a uniformed servant.

CHAPTER 12

ELLA

I wrapped my arm around Antonia's elbow and pulled her away from Matteo before he offered his arm to escort her into dinner.

Lowering my head, I hissed, "Are you trying to antagonize him?"

Antonia tried to pull free, but I tightened my grip. "I don't know what antagonize means."

I inhaled through my nose, and barely resisted the urge to roll my eyes. "It means piss him off."

She cocked her head to the side, arms raised to adjust her earring. "What do I care if he gets pissed off? I'm not marrying him."

I glanced around to ensure none of the guests, especially my father, had overheard her. "*Dio Santo,* Toni! Don't say such things so loud. Do you want to get us into trouble?"

This was partially my fault.

To keep her away from Matteo, I exaggerated the horrors of marrying him.

Now she had become stubborn and belligerent over the

whole affair. Mainly because she just assumed I would fix every-thing like I always did.

No matter how hard I tried, I could not convince her of the real danger she was in over this mess.

Antonia pulled free of my grasp and gave a dismissive flick of her hand as she made a beeline for Alessio. "You're overreacting, Ella."

Before I reached the dining room, a hand encircled my waist and pulled me close to a warm body leaning into my back.

For one startled moment, my body thought it was Matteo and responded. My nipples hardened and my breath caught in a quick gasp.

I was reacting to his touch despite the surrounding guests and my precarious situation as reason fled my mind the same way it had when his thigh grazed my hand earlier.

What the hell was wrong with me?

"Looking as beautiful as always, Antonella."

I shivered with revulsion when I realized it was Falcone, an old associate of my Father's. As in, older than my father. As in, old man who shouldn't be touching a woman younger than his own daughter.

Without turning to meet his gaze, I tried to pull away.

His grip tightened.

When I would have taken more drastic measures, I caught my father's eye.

He looked over my shoulder at Falcone, then back at me. Instead of insisting the man unhand his daughter, he raised his glass and called out, "Looks like you got yourself a handful, Falcone."

Eww.

Falcone stroked my hair while still keeping a proprietary grip on my hip. "She looks just like her mother at this age."

Bile rose in the back of my throat.

My father spit on the floor. "That whore. The only good thing about that woman was her tits. Too bad Antonella didn't inherit them."

I swallowed past the lump in my throat as I stared at the floor. Hearing my mother referred to as a whore never got easier. No matter how many times my father did so, which was often.

It also wasn't unusual to have to endure obscene comments from my father and too-familiar touches from his *soldati*.

In fact, my father often encouraged it. Forcing my sister and me to walk among his male guests as if we were possessions, allowing them to briefly touch and ogle.

My father tilted his chin up. "At least Antonia did and knows how to show them off. And why not? It's the only thing a woman is good for."

Antonia turned at the sound of her name. "What, Father?"

"Your tits."

She smoothed her hands down her waist as she pushed her chest out, displaying her cleavage. "Thank you, Father."

"Antonella, be nice to Falcone. The next marriage I arrange may be yours. It's past time you and your sister got out of my house and made yourselves useful."

I'm going to be sick.

The room spun as my eyelids fluttered.

"Falcone, is it? You don't mind if I take the privilege of a future brother-in-law and escort Ella into dinner, do you?"

Matteo wrapped his hand around my upper arm and drew me away from Falcone's grasp.

Later tonight, under my bedcovers, I'd reflect on his failure to recognize me.

Part of me was relieved, since it would have set off a cluster-fuck of problems, but on the other hand, I was a little disappointed.

Another tiny, rebellious part of me wanted him to have stormed across the room, taken me in his arms, and declared he had never been deceived for one moment.

The music playing would, of course, be Rota's "Love Theme" from *Romeo and Juliet*, as arranged by R. Hayman for the Boston Pops Orchestra. My favorite version because of the raw passion and drama of the notes, instead of the usual solemn, plaintive interpretation.

Sigh. I was a music geek, even in my fantasies.

It was silly, of course. It wasn't like I wanted to marry Matteo Cavalieri in my sister's place.

But still ... it would have been nice. In a fucked-up, make a mess of my life, betray my sister, anger my father, ruin my life sort of way.

Falcone frowned and tried to snatch my arm back. "Actually, I do—"

Matteo used his body as a barrier between me and Falcone, smoothly stepping closer to my side. "Excellent. I knew you'd understand."

He placed his palm on my lower back and led me into dinner.

Visions of last night flashed through my mind, of when he placed his hand there to hold me still so he could force the dildo handle between my legs until I came. My cheeks burned at the memory.

Tilting my head forward so my hair would fall over my cheeks, I stole a quick glance at him from under my eyelashes and said, "Thank you for the rescue, *brother*."

He winked. "No problem, *sis*."

There was no reason why our playful banter should cause a sharp, piercing ache in my chest. I touched a fingertip to the corner of my eye. No reason at all. It was endearing that his nickname for me would be *sis*. Yup, super endearing.

We circled the long, polished oak table before Matteo pulled out one of the ornate, filigree-backed chairs for me to sit. Then took the seat next to me.

No. No. No. Think nothing of this. It didn't mean he suddenly recognized me. It definitely didn't mean he'd prefer to sit next to me. It was a future brother-in-law sitting next to his future sister-in-law. Nothing more.

And not even that, if Fino came through in time.

My father groused from the head of the table. "Wrong daughter, Cavalieri. The one you're buying is over there." He gestured wildly, spilling his drink on a passing servant. "Antonia! Get away from Alessio and go sit next to your groom."

Antonia stamped her foot under the table. "Why should I have to sit next to him? Make him sit next to me!"

"Get your ass out of that chair and sit next to him."

With a glare at me, she deliberately knocked over her water glass with a swipe of her hand, saturating the tablecloth and seat cushion after rising.

Since I was the one switching seats with her because everyone else was already seated, there was no mistaking that she did it deliberately to punish me.

It would be a miracle if I survived this dinner without bursting into flames from embarrassment.

Bracing my palms against the edge of the table, I moved to push back my chair when Matteo placed his hand over mine. "Don't move."

He faced the man on his left. "A lady should not have to rise once seated, wouldn't you agree?"

After a moment, the man tossed his napkin onto his plate, rose, and made room for Antonia.

An anxious glance down the table to the end told me my father was deep in conversation with his *consigliere* and had not witnessed the exchange.

I leaned over to Matteo. "It's fine. Really. My father will be angry if he learns I allowed one of his *soldati* to sit on a wet chair."

Matteo winked at me again. "Then it is a good thing the servers are already taking care of it."

Sciatiri e matri! A wink should not be so charming and sexy and adorable all at once.

Facing forward so he couldn't read my reaction, I saw the servants had indeed already replaced the chair with one of the extra ones that usually remained in the corner of the dining room and placed several cloth napkins under the plate to cover the water damage.

Antonia slouched in the chair to his left and folded her arms with a huff.

A servant approached from behind to pour the prosecco as other staff members brought the antipasti platters. The sharp, pungent aroma of anchovies and oil rose from the platter of *pitoni a la missinisi* someone placed to my right. It battled with the crisp, clean scent of the *'nsalata ri limuni e arancia's* orange and lemon slices, their chartreuse and coral colors vivid against the crystal bowl.

Antonia spat out, "Don't give me prosecco, you idiot. I hate the bubbles."

When her arm stretched out to swipe the glass, Matteo, with lightning-quick reflexes, snatched the glass off the table before she reached it.

Without missing a beat, he leaned over to her and said softly but just loud enough for me to hear, "I'd be happy to drink yours, babygirl."

My stomach twisted.

Babygirl.

He had called me babygirl last night.

Open your mouth, babygirl.

In a breach of etiquette, I reached for my glass and drained the contents before the toast. A nearby servant rushed to refill it as I tried to ignore Matteo's questioning look. "Thirsty?"

"You could say that."

Antonia leaned forward. Her lower lip thrust out in a pout. "Stop talking to my sister. You're supposed to be paying attention to me."

Matteo laid his hand over his heart. "My apologies."

Not finished, she continued in a fit of pique. "And don't call me babygirl. I can't stand that nickname. It makes me sound like an insipid child's toy."

Matteo grinned. "You liked it well enough last night."

I choked on my sip of prosecco, the bubbles going up my nose.

Antonia frowned. "What are you talking about?"

Before Matteo could repeat himself, I reached over my shoulder and snatched a small pewter tray from a passing servant's hands. "Would you like some preserved artichoke hearts, Matteo? Our cook makes them with Sicilian oregano. It's way more intense than the oregano in Italy."

Antonia grabbed the glass of *Moscato Bianco* offered to her. "What the hell is wrong with you, Ella? You're acting weird. Put down the stupid platter and let the servants earn their keep."

I leaned back in my chair, cradling my glass of prosecco to my chest. "Yes, Antonia."

I needed to calm the fuck down.

If Antonia, the Queen of Narcissism, was noticing my behavior, it meant it was painfully obvious.

Matteo cleared his throat. "So, Antonia ... have you read any good books lately?"

She eyed him up and down. "What are you, eighty? No one reads books anymore."

To cover my sister's rude response, I answered without thinking. "I'm reading *Bread and Wine* by Ignazio Silone."

Matteo turned and stared at me for so long, I thought I may have somehow given myself away.

He cocked his head to the side as his brow furrowed. "Book two in the famous trilogy about Abruzzo?"

Uh oh.

I raised my arm, holding my glass high, signaling I wanted more prosecco. At this rate, I'd be under the table before the *secondo piatto*. "Is it set in Abruzzo? I hadn't noticed." *Liar.*

Matteo looked puzzled, for good reason. The Abruzzo region was practically a second character in the book.

To cover my gaffe, I asked, "Are you reading anything?"

The corner of his mouth lifted.

The mouth that kissed me last night.

"*On Persephone's Island* by Mary Taylor Simeti."

A book about Sicily written by a woman, no less.

I tried very hard not to be impressed.

As a man, if he were going to read a book on Sicily, I would have expected it to be one of any number written about our notorious association with *Cosa Nostra*, the mafiosi, of which my father played an integral role. Not a poetic travel journal.

He chuckled. "Admit it. You expected me to say something Neanderthalish like *The Making of The Godfather*."

I smiled against the lip of my prosecco flute. "Not true." *So true.*

When the servants cleared the antipasti platters, Matteo stopped them. "Wait!" He then pivoted his head between us. "You girls didn't get any? Did you want me to serve you something before they clear?"

Antonia waved her hand. "We're not hungry."

I nodded.

Replacing the platters were three large shallow ceramic bowls of *lasagni cu rau ri maiali e ricotta*. I had to tighten my stomach muscles to keep it from growling at the lingering scent of the cinnamon, cloves, and fennel used to prepare the pork before it was added to the *ragu*.

Unlike Antonia, I was too nervous about Matteo's arrival to eat before dinner, away from Father's criticizing gaze, like we usually did.

I licked my lips, but then quickly sucked them tightly between my teeth in case one of the guests, or worse, Father, noticed me salivating over the creamy dollop of ricotta on top of the freshly made pasta ribbons.

Without asking first, Matteo lifted my plate and scooped a large portion onto it. He then reached for Antonia's plate.

She leaned back to meet my gaze behind his back and mouthed, *what should we do?*

I shrugged and mouthed back, *no idea.*

We both reached for our freshly poured glasses of *Nero d'Avola* red wine and returned matching, tight-lipped smiles in response to Matteo setting the plates back in front of us.

With this course, Matteo joined in the discussion among the men about some new trade agreement the Italian government had entered into with a Middle Eastern country, undercutting the Sicilian orange trade.

Antonia and I each pushed our food around our plates as I listened, and Antonia pretended to.

After a suitable amount of time, I excused myself from the table and smoothly took my full plate with me. As I neared Antonia's chair, she slipped her own plate behind her back. I grabbed it on my way by.

The kitchen was a warm, frenetic scene of chaos and energy as the staff prepared for the next course. I passed through it to a small antechamber next to the pantry that served as a dish room, where I scraped the plates.

Before returning to the dinner table, I gave our cook, Maria, a kiss on the cheek and told her how well things were going.

99

For the meat course, a roasted rabbit with pomegranate, I did the same maneuver but not before my father stopped the conversation to call down the table. "Watch it, *porcellini*. You don't want to get fat like your whore of a mother before she ran off."

Piggies. My father's pet name for us at the dinner table. I dreamed of one day firing back that my mother was a slim size forty-four.

"Yes, Father," we answered in unison.

It was a relief to escape the table once more.

The last course, cheese and fruit, was already plated and ready. Outside, the kitchen staff took a break for some fresh air, grabbing a smoke together.

I scraped the plates and set them on the counter before going to the side entrance of the pantry and entering the attached greenhouse near the kitchen.

Inhaling the earthy, sweet, warm air deep into my lungs, I crossed the black-and-white tile floor to the glass lattice-window door, foggy with condensation, which led to the lemon grove.

Resisting the urge to run through the trees to my gazebo sanctuary and just lose myself in my music, I closed my eyes and slowly breathed in the crisp, citrus air.

With reluctance, I turned to head back to the dinner party from hell, only to find Matteo blocking my path.

CHAPTER 13

MATTEO

*W*ith my arms stretched across the doorway, I stared down at the intriguing Antonella, my bride's sister. Tilting my head to the side as I carefully observed her response, I said, "I'm on to you."

Her body started as she immediately lowered her head, breaking eye contact. "I don't know what you mean."

I stepped into the beautiful lemon grove.

There were at least fifty lemon trees with low hanging, glossy, green-leafed branches, enclosed within an ancient rock wall. Judging by their height, the trees were at least two generations old, if not older. It gave the atmosphere a secluded, timeless feel.

My arm stretched up to rub a smooth leaf between my thumb and forefinger. "Yes, you do."

Keeping her face averted, she tried to move past me. "I need to get back inside."

I blocked her path again. "Not until we talk."

She backed up a step and turned. "You only have a moment before my father starts to worry."

I laughed. From what I had already seen, she and Antonia could self-combust at that table and the only thing their father would notice would be the annoying cinders falling into his drink.

At the sharp turn of her head and glare, I fisted my hand and pretended to clear my throat. "I'll get to the point, then. You're playing a dangerous game."

Her slim shoulders stiffened before she ducked under a branch and moved deeper into the grove. "I'm playing no game."

It took very little effort to follow her lithe form and cream-colored dress as she weaved among the lemon tree trunks. "I see you and Antonia share the same passing interest in the truth."

She paused and turned to face me, a flush rising in her cheeks. "That is not true. I'm nothing like my sister."

The vehemence of her response gave me pause. Could I be mistaken about her motives?

My shoes crunched over the mixture of white gravel and crushed seashells that made up the narrow, winding paths through the tiny orchard.

To re-establish a connection, I said, "You're right. I misspoke. I'm well aware of your differing accomplishments. In fact, I've heard a great deal about your superior musical abilities. I'm looking forward to hearing you play."

After casting me a sour look that would have rivaled the ripening juices in the yellow fruit clinging to the surrounding branches, she continued to press deeper into the grove. "There is no need to patronize me or kiss my ass, Signore Cavalieri. It is my father you need to impress, not me. I'm not involved."

"But you disapprove."

"I have done nothing to indicate I have an opinion either way."

My lips quirked upward. I had interrogated Western European spies who were less cagey.

Observing a slight break in the trees, I took advantage of the clearing and circled around to cut her off higher up the path. "As much as I hate to disagree with a beautiful woman... we both know you are lying. Or should I say, being less than forthcoming?"

She shifted to the left.

I stepped to the right, blocking her.

She shifted back to the right.

I shifted to my left.

With a frustrated sigh, she finally looked up at me. "You're making a mistake."

My brow lowered.

"Get back on your knees," I commanded.

"No! You have to stop! You're making a mistake."

I then pushed my fingers between her legs, feeling her tight, clenching heat.

"Say that again," I ordered.

Her large, chocolate-brown eyes searched my face before she cleared her throat and said again, this time softer and lower. "You're making a mistake."

Despite her attempt to hide it, I had no doubt it was the same voice as last night.

Fuck. Wait. No.

The idea was highly improbable.

Everything I had learned about Antonia's twin sister argued against the preposterous notion that it was Antonella and not Antonia I took to my boat last night... that I *disciplined* last night before shoving my cock down her throat.

Regardless of their being twins, clearly, their close relation as sisters meant they had similar speech patterns, turns of phrase, and tone.

My original theory that she was deliberately trying to sabotage my arranged marriage because she didn't want her twin sister to move to the other side of Italy was far more plausible and realistic.

My hands wrapped around the gnarled branches on either side of her head, forcing her to back up a step and press her body along the trunk. "I don't make mistakes."

Her chin jutted out. "Spoken like a man."

I gave a firm nod. "At least a confident one."

"One person's confidence is another's arrogance."

"I take it you don't share your sister's *appreciation* for the opposite sex?"

"I have yet to find one worthy of my regard."

She might as well have stepped back in time and been Katherina saucily warning my Petruchio of her waspish sting.

I leaned forward.

The scent of her perfume caught on the evening breeze. Fresh-cut green grass, a hint of saltwater and verbena. Same as the perfume Antonia was wearing last night, and vastly different from the cloying rose, ylang-ylang, and bergamot fragrance she was wearing now.

The perfume embodied the dual personalities of both women.

Antonella, fresh and innocent, with a melancholy sweetness about her.

Antonia, flagrant sex-on-a-stick, sweaty bodies, and hedonism.

Of course, she put on quite the innocent performance last night.

Perhaps that was why Antonia wore her sister Antonella's perfume.

I had already noticed her studious attention to detail when playing the part of virginal ingenue. She found inspiration nearby. Clearly Antonia was mimicking her sister.

My gaze drifted to her mouth. It shouldn't have. It was

wrong. I definitely should show more discipline, especially toward my future little sister-in-law.

Still, Antonella had the most adorable mouth.

Pink and full, with a small Cupid's bow indentation over the top lip. She only wore what looked like a simple neutral gloss which enhanced her lips' natural blush tone.

The tightness I had felt earlier suffering through that terrible dinner returned when I thought of the thick coating of red matte lipstick on Antonia's lips. It was so heavy it formed a ridge down the center of her bottom lip and often smeared over her teeth.

Again, I thought of last night, when Antonia was mimicking her sister and wore only a sheer gloss over her lips. While it was clearly an act on her part, I wished it were real.

Wished I was at least marrying the sweetly innocent sister with the sharp wit.

Instead of the sharply experienced sister with the dull intellect.

It wasn't possible, of course. For the same reason, Antonella needed to stop her dangerous interference.

"Perhaps that will change when you are in Abruzzo."

Her eyes widened and she lowered her arms to grip the trunk of the tree behind her, as if to steady herself. "Abruzzo? Why would I be going to Abruzzo?"

"That is why you are subtly interfering with the marriage your father arranged for your sister with those poisoned darts about the Cavalieris, is it not? Because you don't want her to move so far away from you. I came out here to tell you that I would be more than happy to welcome you into our home."

She snorted. "I just bet you would. I'll remind you again. I'm nothing like my sister."

Too late, I realized how lascivious my offer sounded. "You have my word that my offer, and my intentions, are honorable."

Her arms crossed over her middle, a defensive sign of unease. "Your word means nothing to me, Signore Cavalieri."

"Matteo."

"What?"

"My name is Matteo. If I'm to be your brother, I'd prefer you use it."

"No, thank you."

I took a step closer. "You used it at dinner."

She inhaled sharply. "My mistake. It won't happen again."

I was enjoying this cat-and-mouse game with her far too much. "I'm going to have to insist that you do."

She rolled her eyes before lowering her gaze. "Fine."

"Say it."

She raised her head to me again. "Say it?"

"My name. I want to hear you say it."

This was a dangerous game, and Dante's warning thrummed in my head.

Stay away from the sister. Focus on your bride.

I now knew why he had issued such a stark warning.

The sister was enchanting, especially when confronted with the brute crassness of her twin.

Between her engaging conversation at dinner, the serene, almost sorrowful, way she carried herself, and her witty banter now, I was finding my bride's sister extremely intriguing. I couldn't resist teasing her, just a little bit.

She licked her lips, and my traitorous cock hardened.

"Matteo."

Fuck. My cock lengthened further.

It's fine.

As long as I didn't touch her, I was still at least in the realm of respectable behavior.

My thoughts, on the other hand…

She continued. "You are mistak—you're wrong. I have no

desire to follow my sister to Abruzzo. I just know what she's like and doubt she will be happy there."

"I agree."

"You agree?" She stepped forward, almost brushing my chest. "Then why not call off this ridiculous wedding proposal?"

"Not an option. There are elements at play."

"Now who is playing games?"

I reached out and cupped her chin before she had a chance to lower her head and hide her expression from me. "Listen to me, you need to stop interfering. Now."

My jaw clenched as I ruthlessly attempted to ignore the shiver that coursed over her body at both my touch and commanding tone. The Dom in me rose up. *Literally.*

Fuck, she'd be absolute perfection as a submissive. A concept that would probably send her sheltered life into a tailspin as she clutched her pearls. Still... Again, my thoughts betrayed my dubious but honorable intentions.

Ignoring the pulsing need in my cock, I focused on the matter at hand. "You need to trust that I am what's best for your sister right now. Her troublemaking is coming to a head. She needs to get out of Sicily."

Her head jerked to the side as she tried to loosen my grasp.

It didn't work.

I shifted my hand to wrap it around the side of her neck to hold her steady.

Her soft brown eyes darkened to a smoldering black. "Says you. And what? You're doing this out of the kindness of your heart? What do you get out of this? I know it's not money. You have plenty of that, or are you one of those men where more is never enough?"

More would never be enough of her.

With an internal curse, I pushed the treacherous thought away but not before tempting the devil by leaning in close to whisper in her ear, once more inhaling her sweet fragrance. "I always want more, especially if it gives me pleasure."

This time, she broke free.

Throwing her body weight backward, she pitched to the side to avoid the tree trunk before stumbling onto the gravel path.

Her hand flew to her head as she swayed, seemingly disoriented by the sudden movement, before her ankle bent inward on the loose and slippery seashells as she tried to take another step.

I caught her before she fell. "Dammit. When was the last time you ate? I know it wasn't at dinner."

She slowly shook her head. "I can't remember. It doesn't matter. I'm fine."

After swinging her up into my arms, I growled, "I'll be the judge of that."

Surveying the garden, I spotted an ornate, whitewashed gazebo tucked among the trees and headed for it.

CHAPTER 14

ELLA

I squirmed in his embrace. "Let me go!"

His intense gaze stared down at me. "It is uncanny how much you and your sister sound alike."

It would poke the bear to say something.

I knew I should keep my mouth shut.

That he hadn't recognized me yet made me bold. Too bold.

"Are you saying my sister has also screamed at you to let her go?"

I held my breath with barely concealed curiosity over his response.

He winked. "A gentleman never tells but I will say this, if she did, that's not what she was screaming later."

My cheeks burned.

Well, ask a stupid question...

My only consolation was he would probably think it was shyness at his crass talk and not humiliating memories of my wanton display on his boat last night.

"You're disgusting."

"That's not what she said."

With narrowed eyes, I fired back. "Actually, that is exactly what I said to"—I bit my lip—"what I imagined she said."

He swung me around so he could push open the gazebo door with his back, then carried me inside. After placing me on the cushioned side bench which ran around the octagon-shaped inside perimeter, he surveyed the space.

I crossed my arms over my middle and resisted the urge to dive for my cello as if I were protecting my child from harm. It was oddly threatening to have him here, inside my private sanctuary.

Having any man here really, but in particular, *him*.

Matteo Cavalieri exuded a dark energy about him. I wasn't the least bit fooled by the casual demeanor and dry wit. They were all deflections, reflections in a warped mirror. It was what he wanted people to see.

That was one perk of being a wallflower, of being the shy sister who was often ignored. I had honed my skills in observing people and their interactions from the sideline.

That was also how I learned of my father's involvement in my mother's disappearance.

People had a way of forgetting I was nearby.

With Matteo, the indications were fleeting.

The emotions played across his face like the shadows of the swiftly moving clouds above; intense and almost sinister one moment, all sunshine and laughter the next.

But it was there.

It was in the tension in his jaw when someone said something he didn't like. In the covert way he clenched his fist down at his side. The way his lips tightened as if he were biting off the words he wanted to say.

He wanted others to be lulled into a false sense of security at his casual, easygoing attitude, and in the half-interested, almost bored way he contributed to the conversation when it turned to mafia business and local politics.

After all, it was the threat you failed to anticipate that was the deadliest.

It fascinated me that the others around him didn't seem to pick up on the signs. The glaring, flapping red flags that Matteo Cavalieri was a dangerous man to cross.

He may have the others fooled, but not me.

Matteo crossed to a small cupboard above a shelf of crystal bird figurines that were my mother's, which I rescued from my father's wrath when I was a teenager. "Where do you keep it?"

I leaned to my side to pull my dress out from under my hips so I could yank it as far down as possible over my knees. "Keep what?"

"Your stash of snacks. You have to keep some snacks out here."

My fingers curled in the fabric of my skirt. *Lucky guess.* Lifting my chin, I said, "As a matter of fact, I don't keep any—"

"Here they are," he called out triumphantly after taking only two seconds to correctly theorize I hid my snacks in the old oil can tucked into the back of the cupboard.

Damn him.

He popped open the improvised lid and pulled out one of the *Nucatuli Eoliani* cookies I had squirreled away from Maria's Christmas baking. The decorative cookies filled with mandarin liqueur, almond paste, and cinnamon stuffing were my favorite.

Stepping up to me, he held out a cookie. "Eat."

My mouth watered at the thought of the rich, buttery, sweet pastry and spicy filling.

Tightening my stomach muscles so it wouldn't growl, I shook my head. "I'm really not hungry. Too full from dinner. Speaking of which, the others, especially my father, will wonder where we are. I don't want any hints of impropriety."

"You father doesn't give a damn where you are. He is with his cronies in the billiards room discussing business, and your sister snuck away with that asshole Alessio."

My back straightened. "I'm sure it's not what you think."

"And I'm equally certain it is *exactly* what I think. But your sister is my problem for later. Right now, my concern is with you." He tempted me with the cookie again. "You're lying about dinner. Now eat."

I pulled my lips through my teeth and turned my head.

He sighed. "Have it your way. But remember, I tried to be a gentleman about this." He threw the cookie back in the can and tossed it aside.

Then, before I could react, he swooped down and pulled me into his arms before lifting me high and taking my place on the cushioned seat. He then settled me on his lap.

Immediately, I tried to jump off, but his arm tightened around my lower back. His fingertips dug into my hip.

Just like last night.

Stop thinking about last night!

He retrieved the cookie and broke it in half. The scent of orange zest and cinnamon permeated the air as he placed one half between his lips and chewed. "Mmmm. I can see why you like these. The pastry is almost creamy, and the filling has just the right amount of sweetness with only a hint of dark molasses."

My stomach growled. Gasping, I tightened my arms around my middle, praying he hadn't heard it.

The corner of his mouth lifted. "Gotcha."

He held the second half of the tempting cookie close to my lips. "Now be a good girl and open your mouth."

Sciatiri e matri!

The sharp sting when he pulled on my hair and growled, "Open your mouth, babygirl."

I swallowed, keeping my lips tightly closed.

He tightened the arm around my waist, forcing my shoulder against his chest. "If you don't obey me and open your mouth, I'll have no choice but to toss you over my knee and spank you like the bad girl you are being until you do."

My mouth opened on a gasp. "You wouldn't dare!"

Except, of course, he *had* dared. Last night.

My mind was too agitated to determine if it was better or worse that he had threatened my sister with the same punishment for disobedience last night. Although, strictly speaking, he threatened me.

Except, was it still only a threat if he actually went through with it?

Was he cheating on my sister if he now knowingly was trying the same punishment on me, even though he'd already done that move last night?

Or was it just part of his arrogant, domineering, entitled Cavalieri confidence to simply assume he had a right to order any woman within his reach about?

A stabbing pain increased in my temple as my round-robin thoughts brought on a headache, which wasn't helped by my low blood sugar and stress levels.

"*Brava ragazza.*"

He pushed the sweet into my mouth.

Reflexively, my lips closed around his fingertip. The salty taste of his skin bringing back even more embarrassingly intimate memories.

I yanked my head back to remove his finger as I slowly chewed.

He watched me closely. "Now is not the time, but soon, you will explain to me why you are depriving your body of vital nutrients."

I swallowed. "I'm not your responsibility. What or how much I eat is none of your concern."

Something flashed across his eyes.

There it was! That fleeting glimmer of darkness. A sinister shadow.

He pushed his right hand into my hair, brushing the side of my neck with his wrist as his gaze never wavered from my mouth. "*Buon Dio, donna.* You shouldn't have said that."

My palms pushed against his chest as my eyes widened. "No! Wait! Don't!"

I was not strong enough to hold him back.

His mouth crashed down on mine. With a gentle yet persistent squeeze to my throat, he forced my lips open as his tongue thrust inside. He tasted like burnt sugar, butter, and red wine.

He pressed his palm between my shoulder blades, pulling me closer, his tongue ravaging my mouth.

At some point, my hands went from pushing against his chest to twisting into the lapels of his tuxedo dinner jacket.

He groaned against my mouth. "Fuck, you taste sweet. Good enough to eat."

His hand moved to the hem of my dress as he caressed the top of my thigh.

My inner thigh muscles clenched, and a surge of heat pooled low in my abdomen at just the thought of his fingers inside my pussy again.

His fingertips caressed my hip then teased the silk edge of my panties.

I moaned.

The arm against my back stiffened as his shoulders tightened right before he wrenched his head back. "*Che due palle!* Dammit."

He shifted me off his lap and furiously paced back and forth within the tight confines of the gazebo, like a panther caught in a cage. Running his hand through his hair, he cursed under his breath again before turning to me. "Please forgive me, Ella."

Falling to one knee before me, he grasped my hands in his.

For one incredulous moment, defying all common sense and reason, I thought he was going to propose marriage to me, renouncing any commitment to my selfish sister.

"That should have never happened. I don't know what came over me. There is something about you that pulled at me. A strange familiarity I can't explain."

I was right. This man was dangerously perceptive, like a poisonous snake just waiting to strike.

If I stayed here with him much longer, he would guess the truth.

I allowed my hair to cascade over my cheek as I turned my head away from him. Hiding my guilt behind a false veneer of maidenly outrage, I attempted to yank my hands out of his grasp. "I can. It's called I'm the twin sister of your fiancée."

He winced. "I know. Her not taking that commitment seriously yet is no excuse for me to behave in a similar manner. I know better. I'm deeply sorry for my transgression. You have my word it will never happen again."

His words sank in like a lead weight inside my chest.

He'd never kiss me again.

Never hold me.

Never stare into my eyes as if he were reading my soul.

It should be a good thing. So why did it hurt so badly?

"I won't ask you to keep this a secret. You have every right to—"

"My sister doesn't need to know. *No one* needs to know."

If Fino came through and arrested my father soon, this would all be just a terrible memory.

A confusing, twisted, kinky as fuck, terrible memory.

He rose as I stood.

Right as I was about to turn and walk with as much dignity as I could muster through the door, he cupped my cheek again as he towered over me. "If the situation were different. If I had a choice—"

My eyes flooded with tears. "Don't."

It was the story of my life. Always being looked upon as the poor man's version of my vivacious and fun-loving sister.

Even though I convinced myself I wouldn't want to change positions with her for the world. In fact, the very last thing I'd want would be being forced to marry Matteo Cavalieri and yet...

It still hurt to be a mistake. Again.

CHAPTER 15

MATTEO

*W*hat a fucking mess.

The lights of Palermo shifted and sparkled as I viewed them through the swirling amber liquid in my glass. Lowering my drink, I took a large sip, relishing the whiskey's burn.

My head fell back onto the lounger as I propped my bare feet up on the boat railing. After changing into a loose-fitting white linen shirt and beige slacks, I had made my way to the upper deck, needing solitude.

The water gently lapped at my boat's hull, only muted snippets of conversation heard over the still waters as families and couples walked along the promenade nearby.

Gone were the rowdy music, the flashing lights, and orgy bonfires of a few nights ago.

Like a cloak of sackcloth over a sinner, the solemnity of Lent had descended over the city.

The quiet, somber tone suited my guilty, reflective mood.

I kissed her.

Dammit, I kissed her.

My fiancée's sister. Her freaking twin sister at that.

While I didn't necessarily have the moral high ground over my promiscuous future bride, I had at least been committed to being faithful and demanding the same from her.

Technically, we were barely even engaged, and it was clear the bride objected to the union, but that was no excuse.

I rubbed my eyes. Her sister. Why did I have to kiss her sister?

The answer was dangerous. Too dangerous to even contemplate.

I wanted Ella. It was that simple, and that complicated.

The report I had on Ella emphasized her shyness. The reports were wrong.

She wasn't shy. She was oppressed. Between the crass personality of her father and the brassy one of Antonia, Ella was surrounded by brutish behavior and noise. No wonder she retreated into herself and her music.

It made a man want to swoop in and rescue her.

But this was no fucking fairy tale. She wasn't a trapped princess and I sure as fuck wasn't her knight in shining armor. This was real life, with deadly consequences.

"I need a cocktail immediately!"

I turned to see Aunt Gabriella, resplendent in head-to-toe Chanel resort attire, waltzing toward me.

Rising, I approached her. "Aunt Gabbie, what are you doing here?"

She rolled her eyes. "I really hate your father for teaching you to call me that as a child."

I smirked as I gave her a kiss on each cheek. "You know he does it out of love."

Her gold bangles rattled as she gave my arm a squeeze. "Where is the bar? I need a drink."

I crossed to the black marble-topped bar at the other end of the deck lounge and reached for the sterling silver cocktail shaker. "Not that I'm not thrilled to see you, but what the fuck are you doing here?"

After slipping her silk scarf, on point with its gold anchors floating on nautical navy blue, from around her throat, she gestured to the liquor bottles. "Vodka, dear. I never drink gin after noon. Make me a dirty martini. You know how I like it. Seriously shaken and absolutely filthy."

I hid a smile as I reached for the Belvedere bottle. We all knew how Aunt Gabbie preferred her cocktails.

It was one of the first things she taught me and my cousins the moment we were old enough to be trusted not to drop the glass liquor bottles.

As I shook the cocktail shaker, I repeated. "Aunt Gabbie? Why are you here?"

Before she could respond, Dr. Pantona came huffing up the deck stairs. He took a barstool, reaching into his linen blazer for a handkerchief and mopping his brow while he glared at Gabriella. "You could have waited for me!"

She patted his hand. "My apologies, darling. I was eager to see my nephew."

Strictly speaking, I was her nephew-in-law. Typically, the sister of an uncle's dead wife didn't have a close relationship with the extended family, but that was not the case with Aunt Gabbie.

I placed the dirty martini in front of her with a clink, then nodded at the good doctor. "What's your poison?"

It seemed playing bartender was the only way I was going to get answers.

Dr. Pantona stuffed his handkerchief in his blazer front pocket and said, "I'll take a *Tarocco Spritz*."

I leaned on the bar top. "Do I look like I have blood orange juice behind here?"

A light flick of her wrist sent Aunt Gabbie's bracelets jangling as she reached for her cocktail. "He'll take an *Amarena Spritz* instead."

Dr. Pantona frowned. "What is in that?"

She raised her martini glass to her lips and paused. "You'll like it. It's not a proper drink. It has cherries in it."

After measuring the balsamic vinegar and spiking the brandied cherries on a cocktail pick, I measured out the *Carpano Bianco* and *Punt E Mes*. I tossed them both over ice and finished with prosecco and soda water before sliding the glass in front of him.

I then refreshed my simple drink of ridiculously expensive whiskey and followed them to the lounge chairs overlooking Palermo's harbor.

Before I could sit, Alfonso appeared.

"For fuck's sake, Aunt Gabbie! How many more do you have in your entourage?"

Aunt Gabbie pressed her hand to her chest. "It's not my fault! He insisted!"

Alfonso headed straight to the bar and grabbed himself a beer. Twisting off the top, he tossed it in the trash can as he took a swig before smiling. "I did. She wasn't going anywhere near this place without me."

Aunt Gabbie rolled her eyes again. "Stuff and nonsense, Palermo is perfectly safe... now. It's not the eighties anymore." She swept her arm over the harbor. "There are pasty tourists walking all about."

I hooked my foot around the leg of the nearest lounger and pulled it closer to her before sitting on the end. "Aunt Gabbie, I need you to listen closely. Sicily is not safe for you right now."

She patted my cheek. "Darling, I'm a rich and beautiful woman. Everywhere is safe for me."

Alfonso choked on the sip of beer he had been taking when

she spoke. While I rolled my neck to ease the tension from the fast-moving migraine her incredibly naïve words were causing.

I tried again. "Our family is in a very dangerous position between two powerful factions of the Agnello syndicate. If Dante doesn't hold on to his power, there is a risk of retaliation against us for Salvatore's assassination."

She pinched the metal cocktail pick between her fingers and tapped it against the rim of her glass before pulling the plump olive off it with her teeth. "And what has that to do with me? I'm a De Luca, if you recall."

She may not share our name, but she was a Cavalieri through and through and the de facto matriarch of our unruly clan.

"Nice try."

She shrugged. "I had to come and save you from a terrible mistake."

The burn from the swallow of whiskey I took was not enough to deal with this. "The only way Dante stays in power is with Antonius's support, and we don't get that without this... favor."

"Favor? Is that what the kids are calling it nowadays?"

"Aunt Gabbie..."

"Fine. If you are determined to ruin your life, the least you can do is make sure it's a long one."

My brow wrinkled.

She tilted her head in Dr. Pantona's direction. The man was currently asleep against his lounger, his untouched drink tipping at a dangerous angle in his hand. "It's why I brought the doctor. This girl has a... reputation."

I leaned back, already uncomfortable with where this was going.

She pointed at me. "As do you, so I'm not playing favorites. You both need to get blood tests before any *marital relations*. We should also be assured the girl isn't knocked up."

Well, this just kept getting worse and worse. "Knocked up? Really?"

"Don't tell me it hasn't occurred to you that is why they are in such a hurry to shackle this girl to you and ship her across the country to Abruzzo?"

I couldn't lie. The thought had occurred to me. After all, there were ways to get a subtle message to the capos she was toying with to keep it in their pants and back off without forcing her into a marriage with me.

I looked over at Alfonso, who was resting his forearms on the railing as he admired the view.

He cast a look at me over his shoulder. "Don't look at me. I'm just the driver."

Just the driver. Sure. And Aunt Gabbie was just the unrelated aunt.

"The situation is very delicate right now. I don't think I should cause any waves by insisting on a blood test."

Her eyes narrowed. "What did you do?"

I broke eye contact as I raised my glass. "What makes you think I did anything?"

"All my experiences with your gender. Now spill."

I cast a glance over at Dr. Pantona and Alfonso.

Alfonso turned and stretched his arms. "I'm going to get *all* her luggage."

She turned. "Don't think I didn't catch the inflected tone."

He winked at her. "I'd be disappointed if you didn't."

Alfonso tapped on the doctor's shoulder to rouse him, and they both left us alone.

Aunt Gabbie quirked a brow over the rim of her martini as she finished it.

Taking her glass, I crossed back to the bar.

She followed. "Quit stalling."

Stuffing ice into the shaker, I let out a frustrated sigh before blurting out, "I kissed her sister."

Aunt Gabbie threw her head back and laughed.

My jaw clenched. "It isn't funny."

She waved her hand in front of her as if catching her breath from all her laughter. "I disagree."

"Dammit, Aunt Gabbie. I'm in a real mess here."

Covering her lips to stifle her chuckles, she nodded. "So why the sister and not the bride?"

I cleared my throat. "I kissed Antonia too."

Kissed and fucked her with the handle of a riding crop before shoving my cock down her throat. But my aunt didn't need to know the details.

She bent forward over the bar and rested her forehead on her hands, bursting into laughter again.

Her martini sloshed over the rim as I slammed it down in front of her. "I'm not telling you any more."

"Okay, I promise I'll be serious. So you kissed them both. Any chance you mistook one for the other? They are twins."

I shook my head. "Not a chance in hell. Ella is sweetly innocent and intelligent, with a surprisingly sarcastic wit. Antonia is loud and bold and over the top in every way, from her behavior to how she dresses."

"Any chance you could convince the father to give you Ella instead of Antonia?"

"This isn't a market stand in the piazza, Aunt Gabbie. I can't just switch out my purchase. Besides, as I've explained, there are reasons why it needs to be Antonia."

She lifted her martini as she winked at me. "Her whorish ways."

I rubbed my eyes as the migraine moved to my temples. "Please don't refer to my future bride as a whore." Even if she was one.

"There is no shame in it, darling. Only men have an issue with women's sexuality. Besides, if a rake can be reformed with marriage, why not a whore?"

"You're not helping. I need to tell Antonia that I kissed Ella."

"Are you insane? That is the last thing you should do."

"It's the right thing to do. I don't want a marriage built on lies."

"It's the stupid thing to do. Besides, you're marrying for all the wrong reasons as it is. One more won't hurt."

When I didn't respond, she reached over the bar and laid her hand over mine. "Are you sure that is why you want to tell her?"

"What's that supposed to mean?"

She patted my hand, her gold bangles jangling again. "I'm just saying it would be a clever way of ruining everyone's marriage plans if you pissed off the bride by kissing her sister."

Fuck.

Could that be the real reason I kissed Ella?

After all, despite our issues, I'd had an amazing connection with Antonia the night before. It hadn't escaped my notice that she seemed to be a completely different person when I got her alone, away from her father's and other men's influence.

The moment we were alone, she seemed to drop the brassy, over-sexualized attitude and was as unaffected and innocent-seeming as her sister.

Was it possible that while Ella hid inside of herself behind a wall of shyness, Antonia reacted to her surroundings by putting on a promiscuous show, like her father seemed to enjoy?

It hadn't escaped my notice how her father seemed to encourage his men to admire his two poor daughters as if they were trophies on his mantle.

That must be it.

The innocent demeanor I witnessed the other night with Antonia was not an act like I assumed.

She must be closer to her sister Ella's sweet personality in real life, when away from corrupting influences or trying to please her father.

And if that was true, then most of the rumors about her behavior must be false.

"Aunt Gabbie, you are a genius."

"Of course I am, darling. But why?"

"They are twins. *Twins!*"

"And?"

"Don't you get it? The sisters are not opposites after all. They are the same! It explains everything. Why I kissed Ella. Why I had a connection with Antonia on the boat, but not at dinner last night. Why her personality seems to keep changing. Everything."

"If you say so, dear."

The tightness in my chest eased.

This arranged marriage might be off to a shit start, but at least I finally saw a light at the end of the tunnel. Once I got Antonia out of Sicily and away from her father, her true nature would come out.

My future bride would be as sweetly innocent and charming as her sister, Ella.

CHAPTER 16

ELLA

*A*ntonia flopped down into the chair opposite me in the library. "So I let Alessio fuck me in the ass last night."

My cello bow rattled as I dropped it and it fell against the base of my cello before hitting the floor.

Bending over to pick it up, I frowned at her before checking to see there was no one in the doorway. "What the hell, Toni You shouldn't say things like that."

She let out a dramatic sigh as she pulled the gum in her mouth past her lips in a long strand before sucking it back in. "God, Ella, don't be such a whiny nerd. All the girls do anal nowadays. It's what men expect. You'd know that if you weren't such a prissy little virgin."

My cheeks warmed. For the first time since it happened, I didn't regret what I'd done with Matteo on his boat.

I had to bite my tongue from firing back at my sister with, *oh yeah? Would a prissy nerd allow herself to be whipped with a riding crop as part of a sex game?'* But I didn't.

I adjusted my bow and continued to practice my cello. I had a class next week, and I wanted to be prepared. Father thought a university education was a waste for females.

His exact words had been "you don't need to go to school to learn how to spread your legs and cook pasta."

Thankfully, I convinced him that advanced music lessons counted as a legitimate feminine pursuit and playing an instrument would be a desirable skill in a wife who would be expected to entertain her husband's guests.

It was a disgusting throwback argument, but it got me what I wanted.

After a few bars, Toni interrupted me again. "Why are you in here with *that thing* and not in the gazebo, like usual?"

Leave it to my sister to finally notice something outside of her own selfish sphere when I least wanted her to. I continued to play and kept my gaze averted. "It was cold and damp in there. It's not good for my cello."

It had nothing to do with the fact that Matteo, *her fiancé*, passionately kissed me in that same gazebo not all that many hours ago.

"What is that song you're playing? It sounds familiar. Not like that posh crap you usually play."

My bow hand paused. I hadn't even realized it. I should have been practicing "Cello Suite No. 1 in D Major" by Bach as a warmup.

Instead, I had absentmindedly been playing "Someone to Watch Over Me" while my mind drifted to thoughts of Matteo and last night.

I adjusted my grip on the fingerboard and fiddled with the position of my fingers over the strings. "Nothing. Just an exercise. Did Alessio agree to marry you, so you don't have to marry Matteo?"

There was a strange pressure in my chest at just the thought of her marrying Matteo. Before, I was against it because my father was being boorish and unfair.

Now?

I gave myself a mental shake. There was no point in dwelling on how my reasons may have changed. The point was, our endgame remained the same.

She laughed as she adjusted the chain on the necklace she was wearing. "Why on earth would Alessio marry me?"

My mouth dropped open. "He refused? I thought he was your boyfriend, and you were in love. Doesn't he understand he could lose you to another man if he doesn't?"

"My boyfriend? He wishes. Alessio isn't my boyfriend."

I closed my eyes and tried for calm. "Don't tell me... he's just another guy you fool around with."

She smiled. "Exactly."

"Have you at least talked to your boyfriend about it?"

She looked at her nails. "Not yet. He's been—"

"Don't tell me. Busy?"

Antonia wrinkled her nose. "Something like that."

"Toni, you need to talk to him before—"

My father's bellow interrupted us. "Antonia! Get in here."

With a groan, she rose from her chair. "Coming, Father."

I kissed your fiancé!

I wondered if calling it out only in my head counted?

Not that I was worried about telling her, not exactly.

I knew my sister really well.

Toni would honestly not give a damn that I kissed Matteo. Unfortunately, that didn't mean she wouldn't relentlessly tease me about it and, worse, dangle it over my head like a ghoulish cat toy whenever she wanted something from me.

It was bad enough I was always bailing her out of one mess or another against my better judgment. The last thing I needed was to give her more firepower against me.

As I prepared to play again, there was a tap at the window.

I turned to see Fino's head just peeking up over the sill.

My eyes widened as I turned my head to check the doorway so quickly, I got a crick in my neck. Racing over to the door, I closed it before running to the window.

After checking the room again, just in case some phantom person suddenly appeared in the tiny library, I threw up the sash.

"What the hell are you doing here?"

"I needed to speak to you, urgently," he said.

"Here? Now? If we get caught—"

I stopped mid-sentence. If it was urgent, that could mean he was about to arrest my father.

Judge Marzio Delluci must have finally looked over all the evidence I had been secretly collecting and finally approved a prosecution. My heart hammered in my chest.

Although there was no direct evidence my father murdered my mother, at least this could open the door for a new investigation. This time by police officers who weren't in my father's pocket.

I leaned closer to the open window and tried to keep my voice low despite my growing excitement. "You have no idea how relieved I am, Fino! This is amazing. You are cutting it very close but better late than never. Trust me, I'm not complaining! I'm just so happy my father is finally going to see justice. This is the best news you could have given me!" I rambled.

He frowned. "We're not arresting your father."

I returned his frown. "You're not? Then why are you here?"

"The Cavalieris."

My heart sank. "What about them?"

"I got approval from Judge Delluci to open a covert investigation. Strictly off the books. You need to collect any evidence you can of their organized crime ties and any crimes you might uncover while you are at Cavalieri Winery."

I whispered harshly, "I already told you I wouldn't do that."

He shrugged as he lit a cigarette with a wooden match. "Do it or any hope of an investigation into your mother's disappearance and your father's business goes poof." With that, he blew out the match.

"You would seriously ignore all that evidence about the murders he orchestrated and the high-ranking officials he's bribed and the construction contracts he's manipulated?"

He took a drag from his cigarette and blew the smoke in my face. "Poof."

"*Vaffanculo*," I spat out.

He shrugged and pointed at me with his cigarette hand. "Any other murders your father commits will be on your conscience, not mine."

"*Va eccati!*" I flipped the backs of my fingers under my chin. "Go throw yourself in the sea."

"Your choice."

I placed my hands on my hips. "What if the marriage doesn't go through? What then?"

He stamped out his cigarette. "I guess you better make sure it does."

"Fino, you can't—"

"Ella! Ella!"

With my sister screaming for me, I slammed the window shut and turned just as she threw open the library door. "Help me!"

I ran over to her. "What's happened?"

"He's here! He's fucking here now! Maria just let him into Father's office."

"Who?"

"Matteo Cavalieri."

I shook my head. "So? He was here last night."

She paced away from me and turned. "This time he brought a freaking doctor with him."

"A doctor? Why?"

She crossed her arms over her middle. "Father says I need to take a blood test. Do you believe that?"

Yes.

"No!"

"I know! He says Matteo is taking one to prove he's"—she raised her arms to do air quotes—"safe, and now I have to, as well."

A very reasonable and smart request given her known reputation.

"What a jerk! How dare he!"

Warming up to the subject, she leaned forward. "It gets worse! He told Father it was to prove I wasn't pregnant with another man's baby before the wedding."

Again, super smart.

I gasped. "How insulting!"

She rushed over and grabbed my shoulders. "I need you to take the test for me."

I twisted my shoulders to break her grasp and backed up, placing a chair between us. "Me? Why?"

She paced away and turned back to me again, throwing her arms up in the air. "Don't be such a stupid prude, Ella."

My gaze narrowed. "Toni, *why* do you need me to take the test?"

While I often wished her actions would have consequences, I never wanted any serious harm to come to my sister. Oh, God! What if she was sick?

She crossed her arms again. "It's not *that*!"

"I didn't say anything."

She smirked. "But you were thinking it."

Fair enough.

"So if it's not *that*, then what is it?"

She huffed and turned to play with the spine of a book on a nearby shelf.

I tapped my foot. "I will not help you if you don't tell me."

"Fine!" She murmured the next below her breath so I couldn't hear her. "I'm pregnant."

I tilted my head so my ear was facing her, certain I hadn't heard her correctly. "You're what?"

She tossed her arms up in the air again and shouted. "Pregnant! Okay, is your stick up the ass nerdy little soul happy now? I'm pregnant."

I ran over to her and covered her mouth with my palm. "Not so loud! They'll hear."

It was pointless to ask her who was the baby's father. She refused to tell me the name of her boyfriend and there was a decent chance it wasn't even his.

Focu 'ranni. What a freaking mess.

Her eyes widened as she mumbled something unintelligible against my hand.

I pulled my hand away.

"Does that mean you're going to help me?"

Fuck no.

"Yes."

What choice did I have?

She was still my sister.

Our father could literally murder her if he found out she disgraced the family by getting pregnant out of wedlock. Not to mention the embarrassment he would suffer after having to call off his daughter's wedding to the powerful Cavalieri family. There would be gossip as to why.

Plus, that asshole Fino implied he wouldn't continue to pursue my mother's murder if the wedding was called off.

Antonia hugged me. "You're my favorite sister! You are the best! I love you to death for this. I'll totally owe you one!"

"I'm your only sister," I grumbled as she dragged me out of the library and upstairs to her bedroom.

She turned her back on me and gestured over her shoulder. "Hurry up. We have to switch clothes. They're waiting."

I lowered the zipper to her dress. "Do you always have to wear such tight, short dresses?"

As she shimmied out of her dress and left me to get out of my own, she fired back. "God, you're such a fucking prude, Ella. Hurry up so I can put some makeup on you and tease your hair. They'll never believe you are me if you walk in looking like a pale nun."

So much for her showing me love and gratitude.

CHAPTER 17

ELLA

*W*ith a clenched fist between my thighs, I wrenched down on the hem of Antonia's precious Prada dress.

It was a waste of time.

No matter how hard I pulled on the fabric, I would never get it below mid-thigh. At least I could raise the zipper over my breasts, so they weren't spilling out.

A small win.

As I stood just outside his closed office door, my father bellowed, "Antonia! Get your ass back here!"

I closed my eyes and took a deep breath before pushing the door open. "I'm here, Father."

Out of the corner of my eye, I saw Matteo standing near the bookshelves which lined the far wall but refused to make eye contact.

That didn't stop the heat of a humiliating blush from rising up my neck and over my cheeks.

There was also a travel-weary looking man in a slightly wrinkled linen blazer who was fussing with cleaning his glasses with an equally wrinkled handkerchief, and a very stylish, beautiful, older woman.

In her early forties, she was dressed to perfection in couture fashion. Everything about her was fabulously bold. From the large gold bangles that stretched up her forearm to the matching large gold hoop earrings to her glossy black hair with a single stylish streak of gray that was arranged in voluminous waves which seemed to defy gravity and the slightly drizzling weather.

Her style reflected precisely what I wished I could pull off, if I weren't so shy and hated attention. It was like she was the embodiment of my inner heroine. The confident queen all those memes and girl boss quotes on Instagram said was within us all, just waiting to break free.

If only. Perhaps one day.

When I finally broke free of my oppressive father, my selfish, demanding sister, and this horribly demoralizing household with all its memories of my ill-fated mother.

My father stormed toward me and grabbed my upper arm to haul me deeper into the room. "What the fuck took you so long to piss? Did you fall in, you good-for-nothing—"

Matteo stepped forward. "I'm going to have to ask you not to finish that sentence, signore."

My father let go of my arm and turned his enormous belly toward Matteo. "That's Don Fichera to you. And I'll talk to my useless daughter however I please. I haven't sold her to you yet."

I winced.

The woman in gold glided between the two of them, effortlessly defusing the tension as she focused her attention on me. "Are one of you gentlemen going to introduce this stunning creature to me?"

Without thinking I turned my head to look behind me,

alarmed to think Antonia had just entered the room despite our plan, before I realized she meant me.

The woman placed cool, manicured fingers on both of my cheeks. "Silly girl, of course I meant you, darling. You're simply breathtaking."

My eyes widened. She wasn't just graceful and beautiful, she was an enchantress with mystical powers, able to read minds.

"My name is Gabriella Sofia De Luca, but you may call me Aunt Gabriella."

Resisting the urge to curtsey, I swallowed past the dryness in my mouth and said softly, "My name is Antonella—I mean—Antonia Carlotta Fichera."

Crap!

I needed to get it together and focus. Any more slipups like that and Matteo would know something was amiss. I wasn't worried about my father.

He barely noticed my sister and me and absolutely not enough to notice if we switched places. *You're both pain in the ass blondes just like your mother. That's all I need to know,* he once said.

Aunt Gabriella looked over her shoulder at Matteo. "She is simply charming, my dear."

My chest warmed with pleasure at her approval before icy reality crept in as I remembered.

She was talking about Antonia, not me. I doubted she would have said the same thing if I had strolled in wearing my boatneck black sweater and black capris with ballet slippers, with only a pale pink nude gloss over my lips.

Matteo stepped closer. "I agree, quite beautiful."

Civility demanded I look at him, despite every fiber of my being screaming not to.

As I looked up, I was immediately caught by the hidden dark depths of his eyes.

There always seemed to be a strange combination of dark humor and intelligence with a cold, sinister edge reflected in his penetrating gaze. As if he were not looking at my face, but staring past it and into my soul to learn secrets he could later weaponize against me.

It was all folly, of course.

I was making Matteo out to be some kind of master spy using advance interrogation and psychological tricks like some Machiavellian tool to get what he wanted.

Obviously, I had read too many romance novels.

I stopped myself from responding in my usual self-effacing way.

I was playing Antonia and if there was one thing my sister loved, it was a compliment.

After clearing my throat, I pasted a wide smile on my face as I attempted to flip my hair. "Of course I am."

The flirtatious movement was ruined when the ring Antonia gave me to wear got tangled in my overly teased hair. I hissed through my teeth at the sharp sting of pain in my scalp when I attempted to yank my hand free.

Matteo stepped close behind me. "Here, let me."

His warm fingers brushed the sensitive skin on the back of my neck as he gathered my hair into a loose ponytail at the nape.

A frisson of awareness coursed down my spine and my inner thighs clenched at the memory of him pulling my hair as he spanked me with his riding crop.

I jumped when his hand wrapped around my wrist.

"Easy," he whispered near my ear. "I'm not going to hurt you."

Not true. His statement was at the very least emotionally false.

A few gentle tugs, and my hair was no longer tangled around my ring. The very second I was free, I shifted to the side, away from him as I lowered my eyes. "Thank you."

His brow furrowed.

Dammit. He knew that was not how Antonia would have answered.

Searching my brain, I blurted out, "I would have hated to ruin my hair."

With that mostly nonsensical statement hanging in the air like a cloud of sulfur, the room fell into an awkward silence. My father finally threw his weight into the chair behind his desk and said, "Let's get on with this. I have more important things to do with my day. I have a business meeting I need to get to."

I inwardly cringed.

I had known for a very long time that my father's *business meetings* could be anything from drinks with a corrupt politician, to beating a small business owner senseless for not paying protection money, to straight up murder.

Aunt Gabriella looped her arm through mine and led me across the room toward the rumpled man in the corner. "Darling, this is a dear family friend, Dr. Pantona. He's going to take the tiniest little vial of blood and run some tests. Just so you know, we're being fair about this. My nephew, Matteo, has already done the test in your father's presence, and he passed with flying colors."

My stomach twisted when she said the word fair. For the first time, the magnitude of what I was doing hit me. If I didn't stop this wedding, then Matteo was going to sleep with Antonia, assuming she was healthy and not pregnant, when at least one of those things was not true.

I pulled back against her grasp. "I don't think—"

My father stood up and leaned forward with his fists on his desk. "Think? No one asked you to think. Sit your ass down and let the doctor stick it to you."

Frightened of what would happen if I tried to delay or object further, I sat in the chair nearest to Dr. Pantona.

Aunt Gabriella turned to my father with a wintry smile. "You have such a confident manner of speaking for a man of your size and intellect."

My father sucked in his stomach and pushed his chest out, strutting from behind his desk. "It comes naturally to me."

She chuckled as she folded her long, elegant fingers in front of her. "I'm sure it does."

I had to cover my mouth and cough to hide my laughter. It was clear my father had absolutely no idea she was insulting him.

Dr. Pantona spoke for the first time. "Roll up your sleeve, please," he asked gently as he gave me a kind smile that softened his tired eyes a bit.

As I moved to do so, my father stopped me. "Wait just a moment." He leveled a sharp glare at Matteo. "Just so we are agreed, if this test doesn't go the way you want it, you pay me half the bride price anyway. And if it does, you pay in full."

Matteo nodded. "I'll honor the signed bridal agreement. You will receive half a million if I'm unsatisfied with the test results. Or a million if I am, and she leaves for Abruzzo tonight *with me*. Either way, you keep your end of the bargain by supporting Dante Agnello, who arranged this little favor for you."

My father nodded back. "Agreed. Salvatore was an arrogant prick, anyway."

Nearly choking at the sum, my mind reeled. A freaking million euros!

Wait, did he say tonight?

I shot out of my seat. "Tonight? She couldn't possibly—I mean—I couldn't possibly leave tonight! I need at least a few weeks to prepare." I struggled to think of reasons that would sound like my sister. "I need time to shop for a whole new wardrobe... and my wedding dress!"

Matteo's gaze moved over me, pausing at my mouth and then dropping lower.

His gaze caressed me, prompting me to check the zipper over my breasts.

His lips quirked up at the corner.

Apparently, his aunt wasn't the only one who could read minds.

He then bowed his head slightly. "We have personal shoppers on retainer who can get you whatever you need. I will also arrange for the different haute couture fashion houses of Rome to travel to the winery to show you wedding dress designs. Trust me, they are used to it."

"Can't I do that here?"

He crossed his arms as his brow lowered, clearly not happy with my objections. "No. I need you in Abruzzo. We must see Father Luca for the banns and then there is the planning of the wedding. It will take a few weeks, allowing us more time to get to know each other before our vows."

With a wave of my hands in front of me, I shook my head. "This is moving too fast. I won't—"

"Enough!" my father roared before backhanding me.

Unprepared for the assault, I fell back onto my chair with a cry as the side of my face exploded in pain. It wasn't nearly the first time he had hit me. I was just usually braced for it.

Before anyone could respond, Matteo lunged.

His arm struck out to grab my father by the throat.

Despite my father's considerable bulk, Matteo effortlessly shoved him backward until he slammed against the wall.

Then Matteo lifted him by the throat until his feet left the floor.

Terrified, I moved to stop him.

Aunt Gabriella stood in front of me as she threw out her arm across my chest. "Leave the men be, dear," she said calmly despite the display of violence.

Matteo ground out through clenched teeth, "If you ever dare

to lay a hand on her again, I will slice your throat and throw your body into the Caspian Sea. Do you understand me?"

My father's face turned purple as he struggled against Matteo's grasp. A white foam of spittle formed in the corners of his mouth as he choked out, "She's my daughter. I'll treat her as I like."

"Wrong. She's my future wife and I will not have her disrespected."

Butterflies fluttered and spun in my stomach at his declaration.

"Do you know who I am?"

Matteo tilted his head to the side. "Sure. You're my wife's *dead* father if you don't concede."

"Fine, you bastard!" my father choked out.

Matteo released his grip.

My father fell against the wall as he wrapped his hands around his throat and sucked in gulps of air. When he could draw in sufficient oxygen, he jeered, "You'll start a war for this."

Matteo adjusted his shirt cuff. "Doubtful. For starters, the humiliating reason the wedding was called off would get out to your associates. I'd make sure of it. Second, you're too fucking greedy to walk away from that much money."

My father's mouth opened and closed several times like a fish out of water.

Matteo leaned in close, causing my braggart father to flinch. "And finally, we both know I'm not a bastard. *I'm a mother-fucking Cavalieri.* Invoking my name alone would call down the full force of the Italian government, the Vatican, and several shadow organizations to rain fire and brimstone on this pathetic stretch of land you claim as your dominion. Let me assure you. If a war is started, there is no doubt who the victor will be."

It was clear this entire marriage arrangement was to avoid

some kind of civil war in Dante Agnello's syndicate involving the Cavalieris.

And Matteo had just risked it all, *over an insult to me.*

Well, technically my sister, but I was the one my father slapped, so it still sort of counted.

It was getting harder and harder to control the obviously immature, hero-worship crush I was developing on my possibly, but hopefully not, future brother-in-law.

My father's eyes bulged as he sputtered a few sounds I was sure were supposed to be words.

Apparently, it was enough for Matteo. "Good. I'm glad we're in agreement. Now sit your ass down and keep your mouth shut until we're finished."

It would not be possible to give me a blood test, because I was certain all the blood just left my body at hearing Matteo order my father to sit his ass down, a phrase my father was fond of yelling at us.

With an angry scowl, my father actually obeyed.

Blinking, I tried to focus past the shocking events to the more pressing matter at hand.

Matteo thinking my sister would leave with him for Abruzzo this very evening.

With a shift of my shoulders, I turned my body away from my father's simmering anger and glares to face Matteo and his aunt. "About your travel plans—ow!" I pivoted to face Dr. Pantona.

Not showing the least bit of remorse for his underhanded deed, the man drew a vial of blood and pulled the needle free then pressed a cotton swab against my skin. "Did I forget to warn you?"

I stared at him for a moment. I had underestimated the good doctor. "Yes. Yes, you did."

He shrugged as he moved to the side table where he had

several tiny glass bottles filled with different-colored solutions and a few Petri dishes and other medical paraphernalia laid out. Talking past me to Matteo, he said, "This should only take about fifteen minutes for all the results."

After casting a cautious glance in my father's direction, I asked, "Could you please give me at least a week before I'm expected in Abruzzo?"

Matteo's eyes narrowed as he stared down at me. He took a deep breath, studying me.

His scrutiny was so thorough, and he took so long to respond, I was alarmed he had figured out I was Ella and not my sister, Toni.

Finally, he said, "Agreed. You have one week, and not one day more."

I nodded, not wanting to push my luck by asking if by one week did he mean five days or seven. I would just assume he meant by Monday.

The hum and rumble of our villa's ancient heating system was the only sound in the room as we all awkwardly stared at the floor or one another for what felt like an eternity.

Out of the corner of my eye, I watched as Dr. Pantona marked off different boxes on some medical form I couldn't read from where I was sitting. It was silly to be nervous. I knew I wasn't pregnant or anything. Still. It was the longest fifteen minutes of my life.

Finally, the doctor straightened his back and lifted the form in his hand. Instead of handing it to me, he gave it to Matteo.

Not wanting to cause another violent scene, I bit my tongue.

Matteo looked it over and handed it to my father.

After a moment to scan the document, an arrogant smile crossed his lips as he rose and puffed out his chest. "I'll need all the money in advance before you set foot off my property with my daughter."

The air in my lungs whooshed out, leaving me dizzy and breathless.

Matteo held up his phone so my father could see the screen. He then pressed a button with the side of his thumb. "Transferred. Now get the fuck out. I want to speak to my bride."

Uh oh.

CHAPTER 18

MATTEO

There was going to be hell to pay with Dante, but I didn't give a flying fat rat's ass.

He wanted help to prevent a territorial war, fine.

But in the end, I was the one who had to live with this piece of shit as a father-in-law, and I'd be damned if I let him think he could keep treating either of his daughters this way.

My chest tightened.

Ella.

Sweet, shy Ella.

There was no way I was going to leave her at the mercy of her father after marrying Antonia.

As far as I was concerned, both sisters would be under my protection.

I could hear my father's voice in my head now. *You're playing with fire, my son.*

I would just have to find a suitable suitor for Ella as soon as possible to remove the temptation.

Simple.

Bile rose in the back of my throat at the thought of Ella in the arms of another man.

I shook it off.

She was not for me. It was for the best.

Antonia suited my dark personality and unique demands in the bedroom better, anyway.

I couldn't even conceive of trying some of the fucked-up kinky shit I liked on her sister, Ella. She was far too innocent and sweet.

No, now that I knew we were both clean, and she wasn't knocked up, I was going to focus all my attention on Antonia.

Starting now.

After her father, who made a big show of leaving voluntarily for a meeting, stormed out of the office, and giving my aunt a farewell kiss with the promise to see her back at the winery, I gave the doctor a quick handshake before escorting them both out of the room.

I then locked the door.

She moved to stand behind the desk. "We need to discuss your travel plans."

I shrugged out of my suit jacket. "*Our* travel plans and they are not open for discussion."

Draping the jacket over the back of a nearby chair, I rolled up my right cuff. "I'd rather continue our discussion from earlier, before your father interrupted us."

She gripped the edge of the desk and pushed her chin out. "I thought that matter was closed. I'd rather talk about Abruzzo."

I turned my attention to rolling up the other cuff. "Since your impertinent ass hasn't felt the sting of my hand yet, the matter is definitely not closed."

Her cheeks took on a very attractive, almost maidenly blush at my comment. She opened and closed her mouth several times but didn't respond.

I stepped toward the desk. "As I recall, you thought it amusing to let me know, in explicit detail, of your exploits with Alessio last night."

Her eyes widened as her lips thinned.

Strange.

It was almost as if this was news to her.

As if she hadn't wrapped her arms around my neck, crushed her breasts against my chest, and told me less than an hour earlier of how she'd been a bad girl to let Alessio fuck her up the ass last night and should be punished.

I continued to circle around the desk, following after her. "And while you certainly took the news that I kissed your sister in stride, we agreed that your transgression was far worse and deserves a *long, hard spanking.*"

The color on her cheeks deepened. "You told her! I mean—I don't think we are done talking about... my sister. Remind me what you said again."

My arm shot out to snatch her around the waist and pull her closer.

Her tight dress left little to the imagination, revealing every curve. While I enjoyed the view, it would no longer be acceptable attire for my future wife now that we were officially engaged.

"I told you, after privately seeking out your sister to invite her to join us at the winery, I let my better judgment lapse and kissed her. I then assured you it would never happen again."

"A lapse in judgment," she repeated softly, lowering her chin to avoid my gaze.

With my thumb and forefinger, I slowly pulled her dress's zipper tab down, revealing the upper swells of her breasts. "Exactly. And I say that again now. I am a man of my word. As of this morning, we are officially engaged, and I plan to honor that commitment."

She pushed my hand away and yanked the zipper back into

place. "Well, I've changed my mind. I'm angry that you kissed my sister."

After wrapping my hand around her wrist, I secured both her arms behind her back. The move pushed her ample chest against mine. My cock lengthened.

I leaned in close and brushed my lips against hers. "I'd believe you... if you hadn't followed my admission with a rather graphic story of your own... *transgression*... last night. And then *begged me* to spank you like a bad little girl. *Just like on my boat.*"

She inhaled a harsh breath. "I didn't beg you!"

My teeth sank into her lower lip, not enough to draw blood, but just enough to deliver a sharp sting. "You most certainly did. Next time I'll video it."

Her throat muscles contracted as she swallowed. "Video it?"

I moved my lips to the column of her neck and placed an open-mouthed kiss there. "Would you like that, you naughty girl? Would you like it if I recorded us fucking?"

She pulled on her arms, but I tightened my grasp.

Using my free hand, I once more lowered the zipper over her cleavage. "Would you like to watch as my hard cock pushes inside you?"

Her breathing intensified.

My mouth moved over the exposed curves of her breasts. "Did you want to see how your little asshole opens and gapes after I pound into you, over and over again, until you scream for mercy and forget all about that dickhead, Alessio?"

It was fortunate for her that my guilt over kissing her sister prevented me from flying into a jealous rage over Alessio.

That would not be the case now that our arranged marriage was official.

From this point forward, I would rip the eyes out of any man who dared to look twice at her.

This wasn't about love or even lust. It was about honor.

No one would touch what was now mine.

Bought and paid for *mine.*

She fell backward, breaking my grasp.

Stumbling to the side, she knocked one high heel off. When she bent over to pull the remaining one off, she gifted me a glorious view of her tits. "I... um... I... you shouldn't talk to me that... um... I... I want to wait until we're married to have sex!"

I reached for my belt buckle. "So we're back to playing the shocked virgin? Fine by me. I like this sex game even more."

She pulled a chair between us and inched toward the door "It's not a sex game!"

Whipping my leather belt through the loops, I folded it in half and snapped it. "I love your commitment to the role. How about I play the stern schoolmaster to your naughty schoolgirl?"

With a half turn, she raced to the office door and reached for the doorknob.

In less than a second, I was upon her. Grasping her long hair at the nape, I pulled her away and dragged her back to the desk. "It's time you learn a lesson about talking back to your teacher."

I forced her to bend over at the waist onto the desk.

She flattened her palms against the surface and tried to push her torso up. "Please! Wait!"

With one hand centered between her shoulder blades to hold her down, I reached for the hem of her short dress. "Bad girls with dirty mouths get their pretty little asses disciplined by the schoolmaster."

"Please! I don't want to play this game."

After wrenching her dress hem up over her hips to pool at her lower back, I was surprised to see a pair of soft white cotton panties again. I would have expected a barely there lace thong My cock hardened even further, her discreet lingerie only adding to the role-playing.

"Tell your schoolmaster you're sorry and beg me to punish you."

"No!"

I wrenched her panties down over her hips until they fell to her ankles. "I'm warning you. Say, I'm sorry for being such a bad girl."

"I won't!"

I lifted my arm high before whipping the leather belt down across both her exposed cheeks.

She rose up on her toes with a cry. "Stop!"

"You can cry out all you want. Your father is gone, and your staff wouldn't dare enter this office."

I whipped the belt across her cheeks a second time. Her delicate flesh jiggled under the impact before blossoming into a pretty pink shade.

She pushed against my restraining hand. "No more! It hurts."

Leaning over her prone form, I cupped her jaw. Using my thumb to stroke her lower lip, I said, "Promise me these holes will now be for my pleasure alone and I'll stop."

My thumb pushed inside her warm mouth, forcing her to suck it. Once it was wet enough, I pulled free and ran my hand over her hip and ass cheek before pushing my fingers between her crack and letting the pad of my thumb graze her sensitive asshole.

Her back stiffened with her sharp inhale.

I forced my thumb inside of her ass.

She yelped, her hips bucking.

I thrust my thumb in and out several times and teased her clit with the tips of my fingers. "Promise me."

Her body shivered. "I promise. I promise! Please take it out!"

"Not good enough. I want to hear it all!"

I thrust my thumb inside her ass as far as it would go.

Tears ran down her cheeks. "I don't know what you want me to say."

A twisted wave of arrogant male satisfaction hit me over how her tight asshole gripped my thumb and her obvious signs of distress and pain. That dickhead Alessio must not be packing much heat if her dark hole was still this small and almost untried.

"I want you to open that pretty mouth of yours and tell me all your holes are mine, and only mine, to use."

She blinked several times as her lower lip quivered.

Damn, she was an excellent actress.

"My... holes are yours to... use," she breathed.

"*Brava ragazza.*"

I circled her clit with the tip of my middle finger. "Now tell me what a bad girl you are."

"Please don't make me."

I pulled free of her ass and picked up my leather belt again. In swift succession, I gave her several painful swipes.

Her hips shifted in her effort to evade the punishing leather kiss. "I'm a bad girl! I'm a bad girl!"

I swept the leather belt across her upper thighs, just below the curve of her ass. "Do you promise to behave from now on?"

"I promise!"

The moment those words left her salty, tear-wet lips, I swept my arm across the desk and cleared the surface before snatching her around her hips and lifting her onto it.

"What are you—"

I ripped her panties all the way off and spread her knees. "Shhh, don't question your schoolmaster."

Pushing my head between her thighs, I swept my tongue between her pussy lips. She was already slick with cream, proving how much she secretly enjoyed her punishment.

She lurched up onto her elbows. "You can't kiss me *there*!"

God fucking bless the misogynistic Neanderthals who thought a woman's orgasm was secondary to their own.

Those meatheads will forever be denied the pleasure of watching a woman come undone just from using the tip of their tongue.

They would never taste the sweet nectar of her arousal.

Nor would they ever appreciate the power and satisfaction that came from knowing you stimulated not just her body, but her brain. It was why a pathetic number of men thought the female orgasm was a myth.

They would never know the secret was fucking both her pussy and her mind.

Running my palms down the backs of her thighs, I gripped her ass, relishing her hissed response to my fingers sinking into her punished skin. "Get used to it, *colomba mia birichina*. I plan on feasting on this sweet pussy at least once a day."

With the tip of my tongue, I flicked and teased her clit, swirling it around the sensitive nub until her hips rose off the desk.

"That's it, babygirl. Show me how much you like having your ass whipped."

Her fingers threaded through my hair. "Oh! Oh! Oh!"

I squeezed her ass cheeks then pushed my tongue into her cunt before returning to torment her clit. Against her sensitive flesh I rasped, "This is only a taste. When I get you home, I'm going to tie you to my bed and whip your ass with my leather riding crop."

Her hips bucked, and my scalp lit up where she pulled sharply on my hair.

I flicked my tongue rapidly over her clit. "Then I'm going to shove the handle so deep inside your ass you'll feel it in your stomach."

Her thighs tightly clamped around my head. "Oh, no! I'm... I'm..."

"And that's when I'll pound my cock into this cute cunt of yours until I fill it with my come."

She screamed as her head pitched backward while her back arched.

I rose to my full height and savored her flavor, sweeping my finger over my lips then sucking the tip.

Wrapping my hands around her hips, I pulled down her dress hem and raised her to a seated position on the edge of the desk. With a bent finger under her chin, I forced her glassy, unfocused eyes back to my gaze. "I'll expect you in Abruzzo in a week."

I gave her a hard kiss on the mouth. "I'm warning you. Don't make me return to Sicily to claim you."

CHAPTER 19

ELLA

*A*fter swallowing my fear at his threat, I silently nodded I had to leave my father's office quickly, before the staff noticed and figured out what had occurred.

I slipped off the desk and almost fell before grabbing the edge of it. My knees were like jelly and my head spun.

The moment Matteo left, a chill had run over my body, goose bumps rising on my arms. He seemed to have taken all the warmth with him.

Damn that man.

My only saving grace was he was not here to see the aftereffects of the intense orgasm he had just given me. I doubted his male ego needed any additional stroking.

After taking a deep breath to steady myself, I wobbled over to my sister's high heels and forced my feet inside. While smoothing her dress over my hips, I pulled the zipper back up over my breasts and left the office.

As I stepped toward the door, I almost tripped over my panties on the floor. Doing my best to ignore the fiery blush that crossed my cheeks, I picked them up, crushed them tightly in my hand, and returned to my bedroom.

I'd barely crossed the threshold when a deep chuckle filled the air.

Antonia was lounging on an upholstered chair near my bedroom window, my cello across her lap like a guitar.

She strummed the strings, making a terrible screeching sound. "Did you have fun, *dear sister?*"

I ripped her dress over my head, hissing when the zipper caught in my hair, tearing out several strands. I tossed the offensive garment into my laundry basket and reached for a pair of black capris.

As I pulled them over my hips, I confronted her. "You told me you only saw him come into the house. You deliberately kept your scandalous conversation with him from me."

She stroked the strings again. "And you, *dear sister*, kept the fact that you tried to fuck my fiancé from me."

In two strides, I had crossed the room and torn my cello from her grasp.

After placing it gently back on its stand, I went over to my closet to choose a black turtleneck. With my back turned to her, I said, "I didn't try to fuck him. The kiss took us both by surprise. It was barely a peck. He came to his senses and broke it off right away. He was just confused over the whole look-alike twin thing."

She snorted. "You wish you looked like me."

I looked *exactly* like her, but since I'd been taunted as being the uglier and more awkward sister by both her and my father for years, I stopped being hurt by it.

Pushing my head through the top, I shoved my arms into the sleeves and ignored her comment. "Besides, you've repeatedly said you don't want him as a fiancé," I continued. Brushing the hair out of my face, I then pulled it into a tight ponytail at my

nape, cringing at the tangles and hairspray crunch from Antonia's "mini me" makeover. "Not that I do... or that it is an excuse
or anything..."

She launched out of her chair, got in my face, and shoved at
my shoulders. "God, Ella, you're nothing but a closet whore who
likes to *tischi-toschi.*"

"I do not like to *tischi-toschi.* The last thing I do is put on
airs!"

I pushed her hands away and backed up, instinctively
blocking her view of my beloved cello.

I vividly remembered when she threw my previous cello out
the window, demolishing it, after getting mad at me over something trivial. Father refused to pay for another one and wouldn't
allow me to get a job to earn money to pay for one on my own,
either. The old cello my mother had given me was smaller,
intended for younger players, so I had to work in secret at the
music school while playing on a borrowed subpar instrument
for two years before I could afford to replace it with my current
one.

"And what else did you call me?"

She placed her hands on her hips. "A closet whore. In public
you *tischi-toschi,* and are nothing but a judgmental prude, but
secretly you're a fucking slut. At least I'm honest about who
I am."

My mouth fell open at her harsh words even as my cheeks
burned. Although I wouldn't call myself a *judgmental* prude, it
was true my recent clandestine activities with Matteo were not
exactly Christian.

I pointed a finger at her chest. "You're the one who came to
me for help! You're the one who's insisting I pretend to be you!
What did you think was going to happen if I went to Abruzzo
for you?"

She snorted. "You're just jealous of how hot I am, because you could never get a man like Matteo Cavalieri to look twice at you."

I flattened my palm against my chest. "We are *identical* twins!"

"Don't remind me."

Inwardly, I fumed.

She was missing my point.

I moved over to the bed and fished out my ballet flats from under it. Shoving my feet inside them, I said, "You're lucky we are, or you'd be fucked. Father would have killed you for failing that blood test because you're pregnant. Did you know Matteo's paying him a million euros for this marriage?"

She lifted one shoulder. "Why not? I'm worth it."

What must it be like to be that confident?

I wished I had inherited a fraction of her moxie in our mother's womb. "*E cu è, Totò Termini?*" I quipped back. "Don't you have a rather high opinion of yourself. Have you considered the consequences of marrying someone else without Father's permission? What happens if he learns about the baby?"

She frowned. "How would he find out?"

I threw my arms up in frustration. "Because if I can't get out of going to Abruzzo to save your ass, eventually they are going to learn that *I'm me and not you!*"

"So? Matteo will get the poor man's version of me. At least you're still a Fichera daughter, if not the hot one."

My jaw hurt from how hard I clenched my teeth. "I'm not marrying Matteo Cavalieri for you, Toni. Besides, that's not what he or Father wants. There are *reasons* why they want you, not me."

Wow. Why did that hurt so much to say out loud?

"What reasons?"

I sighed. "If I had to guess, I'd start with the fact that everyone knows you're sleeping with Alessio, who is married and a top-ranking officer in Father's ... *business.*"

"So? That's nothing new."

"Obviously, something changed. They mentioned that horrible man who used to come to dinner, Salvatore, and his murder. Somehow Father and the Cavalieris are mixed up in it. I don't know the details. The point is, they want *you* out of Sicily and married off, not me."

She narrowed her eyes and lifted her upper lip in a sneer. "Why not? You two certainly seem to get along." She then raised an eyebrow. "In fact, he seemed extremely comfortable with the idea of bending me over Father's desk and spanking me … almost as if he'd done it before. He mentioned something about his boat?"

To cover my guilt, I marched over to my jewelry box and tore off her heavy Bottega Veneta gold-drop necklace and replaced it with Mother's simple pearl strand. "It was cruel of you, Antonia, to set me up like that, knowing I was only trying to help you."

I took a deep breath and lied my ass off, which by the way was still sore from the belting Matteo had given me earlier. "It was only because he kept insisting that you leave for Abruzzo tonight that I got away from him and his… demands."

She snatched her gold necklace from off my bureau top. "I know."

I froze, feeling all the blood drain from my face. While clasping my shaking hands, I attempted to speak with a light voice. "You know?"

Sciatiri e matri! Was she eavesdropping outside the office? Did she hear my moans and all the dirty things Matteo said?

"Maria came upstairs and started packing my things. Father's orders."

Air rushed back into my lungs. "Well, don't worry. I bought us another week."

She snorted. "You mean you bought you another week.

Remember your promise," she chanted in a twisted singsong as she sauntered out of the bedroom.

* * *

THREE DAYS HAD PASSED in a sickening rush.

In the meantime, I had broken the news to Antonia that I had to stay in Sicily.

I had realized the only way to get the wedding called off was my original plan of getting Father arrested for Mother's disappearance and probable murder.

In order to do that, I couldn't be halfway across the country in Abruzzo.

Fino was ignoring my calls and would only respond with increasingly threatening text messages about me going to spy on the Cavalieris for him.

I resigned myself to finding a way around him to speak directly to Judge Marzio Delluci. Even if I had to camp conspicuously outside the Judge's office.

That there was no way I could even be in the same room as Matteo after what happened between us, let alone pretend to be his bride for a few weeks, had no bearing on my decision. Nope, no bearing *at all*.

I should have learned my lesson on the boat… and then in the gazebo… but now I'd definitely learned it. I was staying far, far away from the man.

So over the short time we had left together, I tried repeatedly to coach Toni on what to say to Matteo to get him to call off the wedding, or at the very least to postpone it for as long as possible. It was like talking to a wall.

She refused to even acknowledge she was leaving for the Cavalieri winery in two days.

I sat on the edge of her bed. "You seem very calm, considering you're about to be carted off as purchased property sold by Father."

She stood in front of me and gently pushed my ponytail back over my shoulder as she gave me a deceptively sweet smile. "Because I trust you will fix everything. *Like you promised.*"

Oh hell.

Once again, I would have to go into the long, tedious explanation of why I couldn't go to Abruzzo. I swore, sometimes dealing with my twin was like dealing with a hyperactive toddler who just did a speedball of sugar.

"Listen, Toni. We've talked about this…"

"Hold on." She left the room and returned moments later with a bottle of red wine and two short glasses. "I don't want us to fight anymore. Let's share a drink first."

Reluctantly, I held both glasses as she poured.

She took one glass and held it up. "To my *dear sister.*"

I raised mine. "*Salute.*"

Alarm bells went off in my head the moment I saw her lower her glass without drinking.

The room spun, causing a wave of vertigo to hit me.

My eyes widened as the glass slipped from my numb fingers onto the floor. "Toni, what have you done?"

CHAPTER 20

ELLA

Stale cigar smoke. Rubber. Leather. Chemical pine scent.

It hurt to breathe in too deeply, so I kept my breathing shallow.

Whirr. Thud. Whirr. Whirr. Thud. Whirr. Whirr. Whirr.

The monotonous but strangely soothing sound of wheels running over a road.

When I tried to open my mouth, my lips briefly stuck together, they were so dry.

My eyelids flickered, but even the small amount of bright light filtering through my lashes sent a spike of pain through my temples. I squeezed them shut.

With a twist of my neck, I moved my head then rolled my shoulders, wincing at the dull pain.

Fear tightened my chest as I next attempted to move my arms.

After shifting, I determined my wrists were not tied together. Shifting again, tormenting pins and needles ran up and down my right arm, which had fallen asleep.

Grasping my right upper arm with my left hand, I pulled myself upright. My teeth clenched as I swung my arm out and back several times, forcing blood back into the limb, ignoring the spike of pain.

Finally, I opened my eyes.

I was in the back of a sedan with the darkened glass privacy divider between the driver and the back seat up. There was no point in letting the driver know I was awake until I assessed the situation. Especially because the person involved was an accomplice in my abduction.

The moment I sat upright, my head exploded in pain, as if the headache had been waiting for just the right moment to strike. I took a deep breath to fill my lungs with air and tried to focus past it.

With a slide across the leather seat, my attention shifted to the window.

By the magenta and orange sky, it looked to be about early dawn, which meant I had been out cold for several hours since the last I remembered it was evening. Long enough to be on the ferry over from Sicily and then to drive deep into the mainland, at least.

From the rolling hills filled with gnarled olive trees and the distant winding roads lined with the distinctively tall, slender cypress trees, I was definitely traveling through Tuscany. At least I thought it was Tuscany.

All I could see for several kilometers were neat rows of dead-branched orchards and one lonely medieval town perched on a mountain far in the distance.

With an eye on the privacy divider, I stretched out my arm and tried to flick up the door lock. It wouldn't budge. The child locks were engaged. Because my brain needed further validation beyond that logical conclusion, I still tried the door handle. Nothing.

My nails dug into my skin as I scratched at my neck.

That was when I realized I wasn't wearing my own clothes.

Instead of my comfortable capris and black turtleneck, I was in a ridiculous rhinestone-embroidered mesh minidress.

From the short A-line cut, it was classic Prada, my sister's favorite designer. My nails scratched at the faceted crystal low scoop-neck collar again.

After the pins and needles had disappeared, I moved my right arm and pulled on the short hem. It was then that I observed a small piece of paper balled up in my palm.

In my sister's chicken-scratch scrawl was written...

I'M SORRY.

I'll try to save you from Matteo in a few weeks.

Wait for a message from me.

Love,

Toni

I CRUMPLED the note and shoved it in the hidden dress pocket.

Of course.

The wine.

The sneer on my sister's lips.

Everything going black.

She drugged me.

My own sister fucking drugged me.

A further inspection of the back seat proved fruitless. No mobile phone. No purse. Nothing but the clothes on my back. Her clothes.

Matteo had said he was sending a car and bodyguard.

Perhaps the man wasn't aware he had a kidnapped passenger. Knowing how clever Antonia could be when she wanted something, there was a chance she somehow got me into the car under false pretenses, like telling him I was drunk or something.

It was time to alert the driver I was awake.

My stomach twisted. This could either go really well, or really, really badly, but what other choice did I have?

Closing my hand into a fist, I pounded on the divider.

I held my breath, waiting for a response.

Several moments later, the air rushed out of my lungs. I took another deep breath before pounding once more.

Then again.

And again.

After several minutes of pounding, the car lurched to the side of the road so violently the tires screeched, and I fell into the footwell. With my gaze fixed on the divider, I climbed back onto the seat, searching for a sign it was about to lower.

So I was unprepared for when the passenger side door swung open.

A pair of beefy hands at the ends of hairy forearms, exposed by rolled-up cuffs, dragged me out of the car. The moment was too sudden for my still recovering brain.

Everything shifted and blurred as my stomach flipped. Acid burned the back of my throat in my struggle not to vomit.

My head bobbled on my shoulders as if my neck could no longer support it when he slammed my back against the side of the car.

A slightly crooked finger with dirt under the nail pointed at my face. "I don't want any trouble from you. Understand?"

I blinked several times to clear my vision.

I recognized the man. His name was Tasso or Terzo or Tomasso. Something like that.

He was an old boyfriend of Toni's.

"Why are you doing this?"

"Toni asked me."

I rubbed my temples. "Seriously? You'll commit a crime because an old girlfriend asked you?"

He licked his lips. "Well, she didn't just ask me, she also—"

"Stop! I get it."

I didn't need to hear what filthy sexual favor my sister had done to convince him.

"Listen, you have to take me back to Sicily."

He crossed his arms. "I'm taking you to Abruzzo."

Of course. The Cavalieri winery.

"I don't want to go to Abruzzo."

"I don't care what you want. I was hired to drive you to Abruzzo, and that's what I'm doing."

"You can't just drug and kidnap someone, there are laws."

He snorted. "Honey, since when has the mafia ever cared about the law? We make the laws. We don't follow them."

That's right. He was also a *soldata* for my father.

I tried that angle. "What is my father going to say when he learns you kidnapped his daughter?"

His bushy eyebrows frowned, causing them to blend into one big hairy caterpillar over his lowered brow. "Toni didn't say anything about your father."

I nodded sagely. "I bet there are a lot of things Toni didn't tell you. Like the fact that she drugged me. Like it was my father's wish that she go to Abruzzo, not me. Like how my father is going to kill you and chop you up into little pieces when he finds out about this, and not necessarily in that order."

Who knew this would be one of the few times my father's heinous reputation would actually come in handy?

Tasso/Terzo/Tomasso backed up a step and reached into his pocket for his mobile. "Don't move."

I raised both palms. "I won't."

It wasn't like I had anywhere to go. He had obviously been told to stay off the major thoroughfares. We were clearly on some borderline dirt road through nothing but farmland.

He pressed a few buttons and then said, "Yeah, it's me. You said your sister was drunk."

Called it.

He continued. "And that you didn't want your father to know before her trip to Abruzzo. She's saying you drugged her, and your father is going to be pissed at me."

Although I couldn't make out the words, I could tell my sister was yelling at him by the way he pulled the phone away from his ear.

He opened the front passenger door. "Where? In the glove box? Yeah. Yeah. Yeah. Fine, but you better put out when I get back and I'm not talking the normal stuff. You know what I like. And make sure you get the cherry-flavored lube, not that strawberry crap."

Ewww.

He ended the call and tossed the phone onto the front seat. When he turned back to me, he held a syringe in his hand.

I backed up several steps, desperately searching for another car or perhaps a laborer in the field. "Please, you don't have to do this."

Tasso/Terzo/Tomasso shrugged. "I kind of do. You know what Toni is like when she doesn't get her way."

We circled around the car. "I can pay you. How much do you want?"

"Nice try. I know your daddy doesn't give you girls any money. Toni complains about it all the time."

Dammit.

I looked over my shoulder, further down the road.

"If you run, you'll only piss me off and when I get pissed, I punch."

My eyes widened as I continued backing around the other side of the car until we were almost back to where we started.

He held up the syringe. "We got at least another six hours of driving. You'd be more comfortable sleeping through it."

"That's not sleeping. It's drugged-out."

"Same difference."

Not really.

I raised my arms again. "Please don't do this."

"We're wasting time. You want it in the arm?" His gaze traveled down my body. "Or the ass?"

The thought of this man lifting my skirt to shove that needle in my ass was just the outrageous image I needed to throw all common sense to the wind... and bolt.

I didn't get far.

His bulk slammed into me from behind, pushing my face into the dirt. His weight pinned me down as he reached for the hem of my dress. The calluses on his dirty hands scraped my thighs as I struggled.

Cool air hit the exposed skin of my hip.

Panic blurred my vision, and all I could hear was the blood rushing in my ears.

It was strange how being in the situation with Matteo Cavalieri was somehow a taboo, erotic rush, and being in it with this man was a terrifying violation.

I looked over my shoulder in time to see him raise his fist.

Oh, God! He's going to punch me.

His other hand painfully squeezed my ass cheek. Then his arm came down to jab the syringe deep into my flesh. "Remember to tell your father you made me do this."

While my mind screamed fight, my body surrendered as the sedative took hold.

I was a limp rag doll when he lifted me over his shoulder and trudged back to the car.

Roughly tossing me across the back seat, he quickly shut the door. Seconds later, I heard as if through a long, deep, dark tunnel, the sound of the door locks tripping.

My eyelids were too heavy to lift.

Darkness descended as the car engine turned over.

Whirr. Thud. Whirr. Whirr. Thud. Whirr. Whirr. Whirr.

CHAPTER 21

ELLA

A slap to the face woke me up.

"Get up. We're here."

My head lolled to the side, coming to rest against the jamb of the car door.

"Here" looked to be a train station. After rubbing my eyes to clear them, I could make out the words Cavalieri Porta Nuova on a rectangular sign with a dark blue background and gold letters.

Cavalieri.

The Cavalieri family was so rich and powerful they had an entire freaking city named after them.

As if I were just an uninterested passenger watching the world go by, I stared as Tasso/Terzo/Tomasso unloaded my suitcase onto the nearby platform before tossing my cello case on top.

I supposed my sister thought letting me have my cello would soften the blow of her betrayal.

Tasso/Terzo/Tomasso pointed to the north. "The Cavalieri

winery is over there a few kilometers from town, in the foothills of the Apennine mountains. Now get out."

"You're just going to leave me here?"

He yanked on my arm, pulling me from the car. "Yeah, you think I'm stupid or something?"

Even through my drugged haze, I knew better than to answer that honestly.

He continued. "I'm not going up to the winery so those arrogant bastards can shoot me. If you wait here long enough, I'm sure someone will come to help a pretty girl like you, especially dressed like that."

I scratched at the faceted crystal neckline again. Leave it to Toni to put me in a completely inappropriate cocktail dress just to be a bitch.

As the car pulled away, the passenger side window rolled down. I ran up to it, thinking he had changed his mind. My purse hit me in the face as he threw it through the window. Then drove off.

Frantically, I searched inside while rubbing my cheek where the zipper hit. I lifted my mobile out of the bag although it was pointless, I could already tell it was dead.

I slumped onto the top of my suitcase. Great.

Just then the *capostazione*, the stationmaster, with his official gold-braided coat and cap came running out to the platform. "*Sei una bella ragazza! Che begli occhi!* It breaks my heart to tell such a beautiful woman as you that you have missed the last train of the night."

"Actually, I—"

He sidled closer and placed a proprietary hand on my suitcase handle. "You should come inside to my office, where I could keep you warm."

I bit back a retort. Already in enemy territory; there was no reason to pile on more.

Giving him my most gracious smile, the one I used for all my father's grabby-hands cronies, I said, "Actually, if you would be so kind as to direct me to Cavalieri Winery."

His gaze narrowed. He lifted his hand from the suitcase as if it suddenly burned him. "What business does a woman"—his gaze traveled over my highly inappropriate attire—"like yourself have to do with the Cavalieris at this time of night?"

I wrapped my arms around my ribs and rubbed my upper arms against the chill. Of course, Antonia didn't think to put a jacket on my comatose form.

Why would she? She rarely wore one herself, saying it covered up what everyone came to see.

Despite his attempt to flirt with me before clearly changing his mind, I didn't begrudge the *capostazione* his judgmental tone.

Without looking in a mirror, I was certain after being drugged, *twice*, and spending the last thirteen hours thrown in the back of a sedan while wearing one of Toni's highly inappropriate, super tight and short dresses, I was not making the most gracious first impression.

Although I hated to do it, until I got ahold of my sister I had no choice but to play the part of Matteo's fiancée. Might as well start now.

Clasping my hands to my chest, I softened my gaze and tilted my head to the right, the way I've seen Toni do when she wants something from my father. "Please accept my apologies for my attire. I've had a nightmare trip."

That is an understatement.

His lips thinned as he continued to eye me speculatively.

I sighed dramatically, looking off into the distance, somewhere over his shoulder.

Antonia once called this her damsel look, as if she were searching for her knight in shining armor.

"If only my fiancé, Matteo Cavalieri, were here to vouch for me, I'm sure you'd be more sympathetic to my plight."

I batted my eyelashes for good measure.

The *capostazione's* eyes became round as he threw his hands in the air before crushing them down on his cap. "Holy Madonna! What kind of man am I to be keeping Signore Cavalieri's beautiful fiancée out in the cold with my silly questions? Please forgive me."

He swept his coat off his shoulders and put it over me. "Please, follow me and I will personally call up to the winery to arrange for someone to escort you."

My shoulders turned as I reached behind me for my suitcase.

The *capostazione* stopped me. "No! Please. Allow me." He gestured toward a small door a few steps away. "Please, go inside and get warm by the stove while I see to your luggage."

"You are very kind."

Clutching my purse to my chest, I entered the office. Despite feeling guilty, I knew I treated the man better than my sister would have.

I perched on the edge of a wooden high-back chair close to the fire.

The *capostazione* entered right behind me with my suitcase and cello, then marched straight to his desk phone and dialed. "Put Alfonso on the phone. Hello? Alfonso? I need you at the station right away. Matteo's fiancée has arrived. No. No. Yes, very. No."

The buckle from my purse dug into the center of my palm from my grip on the strap while I listened. I was completely clueless about his response, but the negatives weren't likely positive.

He hung up and faced me, rubbing his palms together. "Someone from the winery is coming to get you."

I wrinkled my nose. "I'm sorry to be so much trouble. My hired driver was… unwilling to venture deeper into the country-side in the evening."

Translation, my kidnapper didn't want to get caught.

He waved his hands in the air. "No trouble at all, signorina. No trouble."

Cold air blasted through the door's reopening. A man in a police uniform walked in.

The stationmaster greeted him warmly. "Benito, you must meet my honored guest."

The police officer stood silently as he eyed my curious, completely inappropriate attire.

My eyes watered slightly as I forgot to blink. The tip of my finger smoothed under my lashes to brush away the tear as I used the gesture to cover my nervousness, then winced when my fingertips brushed at flecks of dirt left on my cheek from my close encounter with the ground during Tasso/Terzo/Tomasso's tender care.

The stationmaster continued. "She is Matteo Cavalieri's fiancée. Come here from Sicily."

Frenetic questions crashed around my brain.

Did he know I wasn't Antonia?

Did he know I was kidnapped?

Did he know I was the daughter of an infamous mafioso?

Did they both know it was an arranged marriage to avoid a mafia war?

Did he know I was sent here to spy on the Cavalieri family?

I frowned slightly, since I had mentioned nothing about Sicily. For a medieval hilltop town, Cavalieri was very large, with at least eight thousand people from what I understood, but I guessed the gossip about its most famous citizens would run rampant.

Benito pulled a hand-rolled cigarette from behind his ear and placed it in his mouth before reaching into his slightly wrinkled pants pocket and pulling out a pack of old-fashioned wooden matches.

After lighting it, he took a long drag and then finally smiled as he gestured toward me with the hand holding his smoke. "Gabriella is going to love you."

Not wanting to give up an opportunity to seem legitimate, I snatched at the name. "I've met her. She's a… something else."

Through a haze of cigarette smoke, his eyes sparkled. "Yes, she is. An amazing woman."

The stationmaster patted Benito on the shoulder. "Do not talk to this man about Gabriella. She is the great love and loss of his life."

Benito smiled before lifting the cigarette to his lips again without denying it.

Not knowing what to say, I tilted my head and smiled back. "Well, you never know. Life can take some unexpected turns."

Understatement of the year.

I then chastised myself.

Antonia would never say that.

She probably would have asked him how he fucked up, or comment on how Gabriella was too posh to consider dating a policeman or something else equally cruel but hidden behind a thin veneer of what she liked to call honesty.

I'd lost count of how many times she had said something awful to me and then shrugged and commented that she was *only* being honest before asking if I'd rather she lied.

I often wondered how we could be sisters, let alone twins. Sometimes I thought Antonia took after my father and I took after my mother, but then uncertainty would creep in.

My memories of my mother were becoming like an old photo

in a box under my bed. I might not quite remember where or when it was taken. I assumed it was a joyous occasion because I was smiling, but for all I knew it could be one of a hundred thousand times I was told to smile and put on a show for my father and his associates.

The pretty blonde twin girls. Definitely not prized possessions, but still possessions, like two little trophy babydolls sitting on his shelf.

Like that photograph, my mother's memory was becoming less fixed and more of an impression, a lingering emotion. The more the details blurred, the more my mind filled them in. My mother was becoming less real and more idealized. A dangerous prospect.

But wasn't that what always happened with victims?

Whether my father forced her to abandon us or, worse, killed her, I was certain my mother was a victim. It was a horrible thought, but I had to cling to it for justification for what I was about to do in Abruzzo.

Benito stubbed his cigarette out in the overflowing ashtray on the nearby desk. "No, signorina. A man only gets one chance to hold sunshine." He tipped his hat. "Welcome to Cavalieri. I hope you are happy here."

He pulled another hand-rolled cigarette from his shirt pocket and cupped his hands to light it, before opening the train office door to an icy gust of wind just as a large man entered. His shoulders bent down slightly as he crossed the threshold. The moment he entered, he filled the room.

Dressed in a pair of mechanic's overalls with a wool blazer, scarf and tweed cap, his gaze immediately found me in the corner. He swiped the cap off his head and nodded. "Good evening, Signorina Fichera. My name is Alfonso. I'm here to take you to the estate."

Unlike Benito and the stationmaster, his gaze did not travel over my attire with a questioning gaze. I nodded in return. "I'm very sorry for the inconvenience. I traveled here sooner than expected."

"It is no trouble, although please excuse my attire," he answered with a half smile as he reached for my suitcase. "Please stay here while I load the car."

I rose and reached for my cello. "I can help."

His jaw clenched as he gave me a hard look.

I backed away. "Or not."

His smile returned. "I'll only be a moment."

As soon as my bag and cello were safely loaded, I turned to the stationmaster as I slipped his coat off my shoulders. "Thank you for your kindness."

"It was my pleasure."

I took a deep breath to brace for the cold, but it never came.

Before he opened the door, Alfonso slipped his own blazer off his shoulders and swept it over mine. It smelled faintly of wood smoke and fresh hay.

Again, I tried to object.

Again, I was met with a thin-lipped response.

"Thank you," I whispered, following him out into the night.

The interior of the luxury car was warm and toasty as I slid along the leather back passenger seat, too shy to boldly sit up front with him.

The lights of the town gave way to pitch darkness and only flickering starlight as we drove along a narrow winding path deep into the countryside and higher up the mountain.

The car finally slowed at a massive wrought iron gate emblazoned with the Cavalieri family crest surrounded by two rearing horses. Two men holding vicious-looking semi-automatic rifles guarded it. At a nod from Alfonso, one of them pushed open one side and let us through.

Driving into the darkness, I glanced back through the rear window. The massive gate closed with a resounding clang, echoing ominously in the winter night.

I no longer had the advantage of being on my home turf.

I was in Matteo Cavalieri's territory now.

CHAPTER 22

ELLA

A shaft of warm light lit up the cobblestones as the heavy wood and wrought iron front door opened.

Alfonso nodded toward it. "Go ahead. I'll bring your suitcase and instrument along."

I was greeted by a woman around my age. "Good evening, come in."

A shiver went up my spine when she closed the door behind me. "My luggage."

"Alfonso will take it up the back way."

I nodded as I dug my nails into the soft leather of my purse, trying to keep my gaze forward and not gawk at the elegant entranceway like some ingenue who was unaccustomed to such luxury...like me.

My father had money, but he mostly spent it on himself. Only the rooms that he or his guests occupied in our house were properly decorated for his status and wealth. The rest of the house had seen no decor updates since my mother disappeared.

The woman interlaced her fingers and held them before her, rocking back and forth on her heels. It was a minor comfort to realize she was feeling the awkwardness of the moment as much as I was.

Finally, she said, "The others aren't here."

I nodded, too exhausted to come up with any more lies or excuses.

After another painful pause, she said, "Sorry. We didn't know you were coming. Matteo said you would arrive later in the week."

My cheeks burned. It was on the tip of my tongue to say neither did I, but I just gave her a tight-lipped smile.

She clasped her hands behind her. "The housekeeper, Rosa, is visiting her sister, and Don Cavalieri is with Amara at her cottage."

Again, I nodded sagely, not sure if I was expected to know who those people were or not.

I was pretty sure Don Cavalieri was Barone Cavalieri, the head of the family who ran the winery.

Amara must be his new girlfriend, who gossip said he met when she was a server at his son's doomed wedding.

She tilted her head to the side and gave me a questioning look. "Did Matteo tell you when he was expected to dock later tonight? I just want to know so I can be prepared for his arrival. I'm here waiting for him."

Porca miseria. That was probably something a fiancée was expected to know.

I winced. "Sorry, he didn't."

She gestured to the purse I clutched like a life vest in a storm. "Maybe you could call him and ask?"

I nodded slowly as I tried to think of a response. I threw my arm up as if upset. "Yes. That would be a great idea except that my mobile died."

She returned my nod. "Oh."

Another long, painful pause.

Peering around her toward the impressive staircase behind her, I asked, "Maybe you could show me to a room?"

Her face lit up. "Yes, of course. How silly of me. This way, please."

"What's your name?"

She flashed a smile over her shoulder as we ascended the stairs. "Lucia. I'm named after James Joyce's daughter, who died in an insane asylum. My mother is Irish, but my father was Italian."

"Wow. That's definitely unique."

Lucia wrinkled her nose as she smiled. "I sound a little loony myself whenever I say that, but I can't help it. I blame a childhood full of kids assuming I was named after Lucrezia Borgia, with mean boys clutching their throats and pretending to die after asking me for a bite of my school snack."

I laughed. "Kids suck, especially boys."

Her nose wrinkled in that funny way again as she sighed. "They do, don't they? It's such a shame they grow up to be sexy men who torture us with their charming smiles and arrogant bullshit."

An unexpected stab of hot jealousy pierced my chest.

Her seemingly nervous chatter.

Telling me she was *waiting* for Matteo.

Just how well did this woman know my fiancé? Crap, I meant my sister's fiancé.

Was she some kind of girlfriend on the side, despite his new situation?

"Rosa allowed me to choose which guest suite to prepare for your arrival. I chose my favorite one which is above the library and has a view of the private enclosed garden. It's also decorated in the most gorgeous emerald-green and golds," Lucia continued in her same animated fashion.

I followed her down the impressive hallway, which was decorated with clearly priceless artwork and various small half-moon tables topped with statuettes and expensive vases.

Listening to her animated chatter, my momentary unease left me. It was silly to have even thought of it. It wasn't like I was the one marrying Matteo. Right?

As she paused at a set of double doors, she asked, "What's your name? Sorry, but Alfonso only told me to expect Matteo's fiancée. When I called Rosa to ask for instructions, she mentioned it, but I forgot."

I placed my hand over my chest. "How rude of me. My name is Antonella." Following her lead, I said, "Unlike your interesting story, I, unfortunately, was just named after my father."

"Yes, that sounds familiar. Although now that I think of it, I could have sworn Rosa said it was Antonia. I'll have to let her know."

This time, the spike of unease punctured my heart, draining every drop of blood from my body… or at least that was what it felt like. I forced a laugh past my stiff lips, which sounded more like a gruff bark. "Did I say Antonella? Sorry, that's my twin sister's name. I'm Antonia."

After opening the doors, she turned toward me, brow furrowed. "Um… okay."

My fingers pressed into my temples. "I'm just so worn out and tired, I barely know what day it is, let alone my own name."

Her face softened. "Oh! Of course. Sorry for prattling on."

"No, it was nice to meet you."

"The villa is usually this crazy hive of activity and noise, but the family are all away for the night so most of the servants took the evening off. Until you arrived, it was actually a little creepy being here all alone."

I could totally picture that. Despite the darkness, it was hard not to appreciate the massive ancient villa or the surrounding buildings and home that made up the Cavalieri estate.

According to an architecture and decor article I found online, it was updated back in the fifties when large house parties were all the rage. It was converted from twelve bedrooms down to six, plus a massive main bedroom.

Each room was supposed to have its own ensuite bathroom, living area and even a fireplace.

Not that I cared or anything.

It then hit me what she was saying. I bit my lip. If the villa was usually the hub of the winery, then this might be my only opportunity to snoop around.

Lucia crossed to the glass doors leading to a private balcony and pulled on the gold rope tassel which held the emerald taffeta curtains back. The heavily lined fabric swooped forward, covering the doors and enveloping the room in cozy elegance, especially with the cheery fire already lit.

A glance to the right showed my luggage, as if by magic, was already on a luggage rack across from the bed and near the bathroom entrance. And my cello case was leaning against the other far wall.

I was the lowest form of a snake for even thinking of spying around the villa.

What if something looked like it was disturbed, or someone noticed that a file I took was missing?

They would blame poor Lucia, who was going out of her way to be so kind.

"Do you need anything else for now?"

"No, you've been more than kind. Thank you."

She nodded and left, closing the doors behind her.

I raced over to the coffee table and dumped the contents of my purse, as well as Toni's crumpled note, onto the surface. Snatching my phone and the coiled-up charger, I plugged it in and pressed the "power" button. A groan left my lips as the stupid outline of the battery with its red stripe appeared.

"Come on, come on. Charge."

Like the phone would listen and hurry for me.

Finally, there was enough juice to allow a phone call. I pressed the "favorite" button for Antonia so hard my nail turned white.

I had to call three times before she answered.

"Buonasera, Ella."

"Don't you 'buonasera' me. How could you?"

She spoke in that annoying baby voice she used with Father's older associates. "Don't be mad at me Elly-bear," she whined, using a nickname she hadn't called me since we were kids.

"It's not my fault," she continued. "I panicked."

"*Orva di l'occhi!* You're lying through your teeth. It's not panic when you clearly planned this all along."

"I couldn't be sure you'd keep your word and go ... and really, this is all your fault, not mine."

I paced back and forth as much as the phone charger would allow. "My fault!" I yelled, then glanced at the closed door.

I lowered my voice in case Lucia was not telling the truth and there was someone else in the villa listening, while I jammed my finger into the center of my chest. "How the hell do you figure this is *my fault?*"

"You said you would take my place and then you said you wouldn't. What was I supposed to do?"

I stared up at the ceiling, praying to the Madonna for patience. "Well, the first thing that comes to mind to start with is"—I pulled the phone away from my ear, and forgetting my earlier caution, shouted into it—"not drugging your twin sister!"

She let out a long, drawn-out groan. "This is getting tedious. Besides, I have to go. Alessio is taking me to the movies."

"I'm sorry. Is my relating how I was drugged by that goon you used to date boring you?"

She snort-laughed. "Tomasso really is a goon, but a useful one."

I clenched my jaw. "I'm not staying here."

"Oh yes, you are!"

"No, I'm not."

"You don't have a choice. If you leave now, it'll be an enormous embarrassment for Father and he'll never forgive you."

I frowned. "What about Father? Hasn't he asked why I'm in Abruzzo and not you?"

She was silent.

"Antonia?"

There was a dramatic sigh. "I might be wearing your stupid, ugly clothes and I might have dragged out your old stupid cello and pretended to play it."

Wow. So much wrong.

"First off, put my cello back."

It was the one my mother first got me, and I'd be devastated if it was harmed in any way. Not that I could tell Antonia that. She always enjoyed using my favorite toys and stuffed animals as leverage against me when we were kids.

"Second, you can't seriously tell me Father is falling for it?"

"It's not like he pays attention to us when his friends aren't around for him to parade us in front of."

True.

"He didn't think it was weird the cello you were playing was super tiny and meant for a child?"

"God, only you would know something that lame, Ella."

Me and millions of people who were even only vaguely familiar with the instrument, but okay.

"And speaking of your stupid cello, why aren't you thanking me?" she protested.

My jaw dropped. "What exactly for?"

"For including your stupid cello with the luggage."

Called it. I knew she'd expect me to be grateful. It was like a kidnapper expecting a thanks for giving their captive water.

Raising the pitch of my voice until it was high and dripping with bitter sugar, I said, "Oh, yes. Thank you so very much, *dear sister*, for including my cello in your kidnapping kit."

"You're being very dramatic. It's not like you're in Naples. You're staying at a luxury villa. I'm the one slumming it in Sicily."

"You want to trade places?"

"Ha. Ha."

"Seriously, Toni. I can't stay here."

"You won't have to. I'm seeing my boyfriend in two weeks and—"

"Two weeks! You can't leave me here for two weeks."

"There is nothing I can do. He's on vacation with his wife right now."

I closed my eyes. "Your boyfriend is married."

"Duh."

"Is this the same man who got you pregnant?"

"I know what you're thinking, and it's not like that. He loves me. He'll totally want to marry me once he finds out about the baby. His wife doesn't understand him or his needs. No competition."

"What is Father going to say when he finds out about all this?"

"Who cares. Besides, my boyfriend is way better than some stupid horse farmer. I'm sure I'll be able to convince Father of that, later—when it's too late."

I absently wondered what Matteo, a billionaire with generational wealth and prestige, would think about being referred to as a "stupid horse farmer."

I slumped down onto the chair close to the fire. "You really are a selfish bitch, you know that?"

"Flattery won't get you anywhere. Come on, Ella. Just pretend to be me for a few tiny weeks… *like you promised.*"

Before I could respond, there was a soft knock on the door.

I rose to answer it.

Lucia stepped over the threshold, holding a tray of food with a small glass carafe of red wine. "I thought you might be hungry. I'm not as good of a cook as Rosa, but I made you *radicchio con pancetta e parmigiano reggiano.*"

I looked down at the roasted boat-shaped leaves of radicchio which were covered in salty pancetta and partially melted cheese. My stomach growled.

"Hold on, Toni." Speaking to Lucia, I said, "That was very nice of—"

My sister cut in. "Tip the tray."

I held up my finger to Lucia and mouthed, *one moment* as I took a few steps back and whispered into the phone. "What?"

"Knock over the tray."

"No."

"Do it."

"Absolutely not. That's rude."

"Precisely. You're me, not you. Remember the time I dumped that bowl of soup over Maria's head when she brought it up to my bedroom when I was sick?"

"Yes. You were mad at her for tempting you with food when you were hoping to lose ten pounds from the stomach flu like that chick from *The Devil Wears Prada.*"

"So tip the tray."

I looked over at Lucia, who was staring at the floor, probably trying to pretend that how I was acting wasn't super weird.

Antonia ground out, "Tip the fucking tray, Ella! They have to think you're me."

The acid in my stomach roiled as I stepped closer to Lucia.

"Do it," growled Antonia into the phone.

Taking a deep breath, I raised my arm and slammed it down on the edge of the tray. It flipped out of Lucia's grasp and landed face down on the Persian carpet.

For a moment, we both just stared wide-eyed at one another as if neither of us could believe what just happened.

I swallowed past the choking dryness in my throat and channeled my sister. "If I wanted something, I would have asked for it."

Antonia cackled into the phone.

Lucia swiped at a tear on her cheek as she kneeled to clean up the tray. "You're right. I'm so sorry for presuming. I'll clean this up."

This was too much. I couldn't stand there and watch her cry as she picked up the tray.

Forcing an edge to my voice, I said, "Just leave it and get out."

Lucia lowered her head and nodded before rushing out of the room.

I slammed the door after her and leaned against it. "I really hate you," I whispered into the phone as my own tears fell.

"Whatever."

She hung up.

I lowered to my knees and gingerly picked up the shattered glass and pieces of pancetta.

CHAPTER 23

ELLA

I awoke with a start when the covers were ripped off me.

Matteo was standing over my bed. "Who the hell do you think you are?"

Not having the energy to dig into the suitcase earlier, I just ripped off the itchy faceted overlay to my dress, ditched my panties and bra and collapsed into bed wearing the short silk shift.

Shocked, I scrambled to pull the blankets up over me. "How did you get in here? The door was locked."

He drilled me with a look. "There is no such thing as a locked door to me. Now explain yourself."

"I don't know what you're talking about."

"Lucia," he growled. "She's crying because of you."

He was standing over me in just a pair of gray sweatpants riding low on his hips with his hair still wet. His muscled chest and strange passionflower cult tattoo were on full display.

It took a moment for me to comprehend what he was saying, and then a wave of shame washed over me.

Forgetting all about how I was supposed to be Antonia, I clutched the covers to my breasts as I shook my head. "I'm so sorry. I don't know what came over me."

"You're damn right you should be sorry. Our staff is family here. We don't treat them like garbage."

I took a deep breath to slow my rapid heartbeat.

Whether or not I liked it, I needed to do this.

This was a matter of survival.

Channeling my sister and forgetting about my skimpy attire, I rose on my knees with hands on hips. "I didn't ask to be dragged to the middle of nowhere to marry some... stupid horse farmer... and I certainly didn't ask for her to bring me any food. If her feelings were hurt, it's her own damn fault."

I swept my arm wide to gesture to the bedroom entrance where the broken glass and tray were on a side table. "It's not like I ordered her onto her knees to clean it up!"

Fuck, how does my sister live with such darkness inside of her?

Those words were like an evil black tar coating my lungs.

Matteo's arm whipped out so quickly I didn't have time to react or defend myself. He wrapped his hand in my hair at the nape of my neck. "Horse farmer? I'm trying to be patient, but I have had it with this queen bitch attitude of yours."

My mouth fell open as I pressed my palms against his naked chest to push back. "My attitude? What about your arrogant, misogynistic attitude?"

No matter how hard I pushed with straightened arms, his grip did not slacken. His skin was distractingly hot beneath my palms. I had to resist the impulse to thread my fingers through his dark chest hair.

Why did a man's chest have to be so damn sexy? The low-slung gray sweatpants certainly weren't helping.

Warming up to my anger, I lashed out further. "And patient?

Don't make me laugh. All you do is order me about, expecting me to jump to your command the moment you snap your fingers."

He wrenched me so close, my arms collapsed, and I was pressed against his chest.

His mouth lowered until his breath caressed my lips. "It's not the snap of my fingers you're about to hear, but the snap of my riding crop against your flesh."

I screamed as he released his grip on my hair and swept me into his arms. "Put me down!"

He marched across the room to the living room area, where a low fire was still burning. Skirting around the sofa, he gave the tufted coffee-table ottoman a kick to push it closer to the fire.

The swift forward motion sent the black lacquered tray filled with cream pillar candles sliding along the gold velvet fabric to crash onto the floor.

Matteo then dropped me onto the center and reached into his pocket for what looked like a handful of black ribbons.

The moment my bare ass hit the ottoman, I tried to roll off it.

He snatched my right wrist, secured a strip of black fabric around it, then knotted the other end to the mahogany leg post.

Immediately, I twisted my torso and stretched my left arm across my body to untie my wrist.

He grabbed my left wrist and pulled my arm to the other side and, with frightening speed, easily secured it to the other leg post.

"Stop! What are you doing?"

My back and head hit the ottoman's cushioned surface as he yanked my hips toward the end of it then pushed my shoulders down flat, to better secure the ties to the mahogany leg posts.

He then wrapped his large hand around my right ankle.

I kicked out with my left leg. "No! Untie me!"

The heel of my foot contacted his shoulder. My only reward

195

was a dirty look and a small grunt as he easily bent my right knee and secured my ankle to the lower post. He then did the same for my left leg.

I was now tied spread-eagle over the rectangular ottoman like some pagan sacrifice on an altar, my upper arms out wide and my knees bent over the bottom edge.

"If you don't untie me this second, I'm going to scream until the entire household comes running."

Matteo pulled another black strip between his clenched fists as he smirked. "There is no one here to hear you. Besides, it's going to be tough to scream when you're gagged."

My eyes widened. "You wouldn't dare!"

He placed both knees on either side of my hips on the ottoman and leaned over me. "We're going to play a new game."

"I don't like your games."

His head tilted. "I'm really going to have to start videotaping these to prove you wrong, *colomba mia birichina*."

My cheeks burned as he opened his mouth and flicked the tip of his tongue at me. An erotic reminder of how he licked my pussy while I was stretched across my father's desk like a complete wanton.

Sciatiri e matri!

The skin around my wrists chafed as I yanked on my binds. "You cad! Untie me!"

As his hands hovered close to my mouth with the gag, I closed my lips and turned my head to the side. Strong fingers wrapped around my jaw, causing the edges of my teeth to press into the soft skin inside my cheeks.

Against my will, my mouth opened.

He slipped the fabric between my lips and lifted my head to tie it securely. It was tight enough to prevent me from talking, but not so tight that it cut into the corners of my mouth.

My tongue ran along the dry fabric as I still tried to talk, but all that came out were muffled, unintelligible sounds.

He stroked my cheek with the backs of his knuckles before he trailed his fingers down my neck and along my collarbone where they dipped along the scooped neck of my shift dress. With both his hands, he gripped the neckline.

I shook my head and tried to plead with him through the gag.

It was no use.

The harsh sound of silk tearing as he tore the dress in half rent the air over the crackling of the nearby fire. The silk floated to rest on either side of my torso, exposing my breasts and pussy to his gaze.

He winked. "Much better."

Rising off the ottoman, he crossed the room and returned with a black duffel bag. Unzipping the top, he pulled out a riding crop. This one differed from the one on the boat. The leather keeper was large and triangular, with two shiny metal circles in the center.

He locked eyes with me as he pressed the leather keeper against the pulse at the base of my throat. "This game is called stable master, and you're my defiant little

pony who needs to be broken in."

My hips bucked as I pulled on my restraints.

He ran the riding crop down between my breasts and over my stomach. "*Tsk. Tsk. Tsk.* You're being a very bad pony," he warned. "You better calm down and behave."

I cursed at him through my gag. "Uuph modder ffffter."

The tip of the riding crop stopped between my thighs and over my pussy.

"Don't say I didn't warn you."

A green light lit up on the handle of the riding crop at the press of his thumb against a small button.

I cried out as a pulse of electricity buzzed my pussy. It didn't hurt me as much as it shocked me, *literally*. My thighs quivered and strained against my binds in my effort to close my legs.

Matteo moved the riding crop back over my stomach to caress the lower curve of my right breast.

I shook my head violently from side to side, my eyes pleading with him.

"I'm sorry, babygirl. Whether or not you realize it, you need this."

He slapped my nipple with the riding crop, sending a sharp, intense pain radiating over my breast. His arm rose again. My muffled cry mingled with the snap of the leather against my left nipple.

"Just like a wild pony. You are acting out."

Just as the pain ebbed, he slapped my right nipple again.

I twisted my torso in an effort to turn onto my side to shield my left breast, but the binds around my wrists were too tight. He flicked my left nipple with as much force as before.

When I looked down, both nipples were bright pink, fully erect and swollen, as hot pain sparked over the sensitive flesh.

"And just like a wild pony, you need a firm hand."

The riding crop tongue circled my right aerole several times before he laid it over my nipple—and pressed the button.

My hips rose again as the shock hit me, sending pulsating waves through my breast. It was like an intense static shock. Again, it didn't hurt as much as it made my heart race and all the nerves along my skin stand on edge.

His cock lengthened down the inside of his thigh, a thick bulge pressed against the soft fabric of his pants. "You need to understand that I'm now your master, and I will not tolerate your obstinate behavior and willful disobedience."

My stomach clenched as the leather slid over it, then down the top of my thigh.

He circled around the ottoman until his spread legs straddled my head. Peering down at me, he shifted the leather keeper to my inside thigh.

I moaned as I once more tried to close my legs and attempt to talk around my gag.

Using his free hand, he caressed my lower lip. "Next time, I'll gag you with a metal bit between these full lips." His hand moved to cup my breast. "And perhaps a tight leather corset to make it feel like you're wearing a saddle. Would you like that, baby?"

He leaned over me and pressed the keeper along my exposed skin. "And a nice silver plug with a pretty pink horse's tail."

The idea of me wearing a leather corset with a horsetail plug shoved up my ass while he guided a bit between my teeth should have had my mind screaming with fear and shock.

It definitely should not have caused a wave of arousal to course down my spine and settle like warm, liquid metal in the center of my core.

"With e-stim play, anticipating a shock is as sensually torturous as the shock itself. Wouldn't you agree, my naughty little pony?" he asked as he rubbed the rod of the crop between my pussy lips.

My mental focus was fixated on the leather keeper. My breath seized in my lungs every time it moved close to my clit.

Matteo chuckled as he went down on his haunches. The underside of his arm brushed my still overly stimulated right nipple as he continued to work the rod between my pussy lips. "My poor baby, did you think only the tip was electrified?"

My eyes widened as I cried out in protest.

To my horror, he pressed the button on the handle again. The rod of the riding crop sent a zing of electricity straight to my clit, sending an intense vibrating pulse straight through the vulnerable nub.

The moment the pulsing ebbed, he shocked me again.

ZOE BLAKE

A low, keening wail slipped from my throat. I was helpless to stop his erotic punishment.

"Is my naughty pony starting to understand how this works?"

I whimpered.

"Right now, I'm only using the low setting, but if you should disobey me..."

He left the rest of his threat unsaid.

I shook my head again, hopefully conveying to him he would not need the higher setting.

There was a tug behind my head as he loosened the gag. He pulled it from between my lips and over my chin, then rose to tower over me.

"You don't speak without permission. Do you understand?"

My tongue flicked out to lick my dry lips as I nodded.

He ran the riding crop up my other inner thigh. "Who is your master?"

My voice trembled as I answered. "You are."

"*Brava ragazza.*"

Dark and twisted pleasure poured over me at his praise.

He gently tapped my pussy with the keeper. "You've disrespected your stable master with how you've behaved. Show me how sorry you are for being a bad little pony by asking me to whip your pussy."

"Oh my God, please don't!"

He whipped my inner thigh.

I yelped in pain.

"That wasn't what I asked. Do you need me to put the gag back?"

I shook my head.

"Then tell me what I want to hear."

A tear slipped out of the corner of my eye. "Please, I'm sorry I was mean to Lucia. I promise I won't do it again."

"Not good enough. You've made it clear that your pretty

promises are worthless. The only way you are going to change is through the disciplinary kiss of the lash, like a true wild pony."

It was on the tip of my tongue to confess everything to him.

To tell him I was Ella, not Antonia.

That I wasn't his intended bride, in the hope he would spare me the humiliation of his punishment, but in a flash of clarity, I realized it would be in vain.

Whether I was pretending to be Antonia or being myself, I had still shown him the ultimate disrespect by behaving deplorably to his staff after being offered a kindness.

A shiver racked my body. I opened and closed my mouth several times but couldn't force the words out. Finally, after swallowing past the dryness, I whispered, "I was a very bad pony. Please punish me."

He lifted his arm and swatted me between my legs several times, ignoring my cries.

Then, to my embarrassment, just when I thought I couldn't take the painful stinging anymore, he forced the rod between my pussy lips again and shocked me.

But this time he didn't stop at just one pulsing shock.

CHAPTER 24

MATTEO

*H*er slim thighs quivering with each pulse from the e-stim riding crop I held was easily one of the most erotic sights I had ever laid eyes on.

I had lost my temper a precious few times in my adult life.

My father had drilled into me from a very young age that anger was one of the easiest emotions for an opponent to weaponize. Other emotions, such as love or even lust, required time to develop before a target could be manipulated, whereas anger could be instantly triggered, like a bolt of lightning.

Upon docking and racing overland back to the winery, I discovered with fury the poor impression my disobedient bride had made with her unexpected early arrival.

It was after I had taken a shower and gone down into the kitchen in search of something to eat that I heard Lucia crying. She hesitated at first to tell me why. Then, because she was a kind soul, she tried to blame herself.

She sniffed. "Please, it was all my fault. She was tired from her trip. I had to have bored her with my endless chatter. It was presumptuous of me to bring up a tray after she said she was worn out. And she seemed very upset that I rudely interrupted her phone call with Tony."

My brow furrowed.

Tony?

Mother. Fucker.

Not wanting to give away my jealousy and anger that my bride was talking to another man within minutes of being under the roof of my ancestral home, I told Lucia to take the rest of the week off and stormed up the stairs to confront Antonia.

As I stood over her bed, I was at first struck by how innocent and sweet she looked in sleep.

Then I remembered that even a violent, wild animal could look cuddly when it was curled up with its eyes closed.

And that was how I needed to treat her ... like a wild creature in need of taming.

And so I did.

Her pussy lips were swollen and bright pink by the time I switched my attention to flicking the crop against her inner thighs. When I decided she had been suitably punished for her transgression, I turned to her reward.

Although she might feel scared at first, I knew that the electrical stimulation would deliver a powerful, vibrating sensation to her inner muscles, resulting in an orgasm of such intensity that it would border on pain.

Without warning, I pressed the low button after wiggling the rod between her cunt lips.

Her hips shot off the ottoman.

I kept the button depressed despite her cries.

While she maintained her raised hips and arched back, I lowered myself onto my haunches and whispered in her ear. "You like that, little pony? You like feeling the waves of electricity pulse over your clit, then deep into the muscles of your tight hole, causing it to clench and vibrate?"

"Oh... oh... oh..." she moaned, her breathing fast and shallow.

With my free hand, I cupped her breast and rolled her swollen nipple between my fingers.

She screamed her release as her fingers opened and closed into fists, her body shaking.

I released the e-stim button, but still shimmied the rod between her lips several times as her limbs continued to tremble.

Finally, her hips slumped back down onto the ottoman. Her skin glowed in the firelight from a bright sheen of sweat.

Tossing the riding crop onto the edge of the bed, I stroked her hair. "Time for the next phase of your punishment."

Her eyes flew open. "But..."

I raised a single eyebrow. "Were you about to object?"

She blinked. "No, but I..."

"But what?"

"Nothing."

"Nothing... who?"

"Nothing... stable master."

I caressed her silky locks, already looking forward to the next time we played this game, when I would pull her hair back into a tight braid and place the bit between her teeth right before I seated the anal plug horse's tail deep inside her bottom.

"You see, the way to properly train a naughty pony is through both pain and pleasure. First pain, then pleasure, then pain and pleasure again. And again. Until the naughty pony learns her proper place."

Her lower lip trembled as tears filled her eyes.

I ran my hand over her locks again. "Shhh. Soon you will learn to behave and not let this smart mouth of yours get you into trouble. Then it will be all pleasure, although I suspect my kinky *piccola colomba* will still want just a hint of pain."

My thumb brushed her tears. I then ran the tip over my lower lip before my tongue flicked out to taste the salty wetness. Soon, I would savor her sweet cream.

Hooking my thumb into the waistband of my sweatpants, I lowered them until my shaft sprang free. The thick length bobbed up and down several times right over her face as I straddled her head.

Her sharp intake of breath sent a spike of need straight to my balls.

"Now, are you going to be a good pony and do what you're told?"

"Yes," she rasped.

I released both her ankle and wrist binds and carried her to the bed. Placing her in the center of the mattress, parallel with the headboard, I then gripped underneath her arms and pulled until her head was dangling over the edge.

"*Brava ragazza.* Now I want you to open your mouth as wide as you can, so you can swallow my cock deep down your throat."

"Wait."

I slapped my open hand against her pussy. "What was that?"

She bucked. "Sorry!"

"Are you going to open your mouth?"

She sniffed as fresh tears trickled from the corners of her eyes. "Yes, I'll be good."

I pushed the head of my cock between her lips just as I placed my palms on either side of her hips and leaned over her, in the sixty-nine position. With my tongue, I skillfully maneuvered between her pussy lips and flicked her clit.

The vibration of her shocked cry ran up my shaft.

Without warning, I thrust.

She choked as her teeth scraped the sensitive skin on the underside of my shaft. The pain only spurred me on.

I thrust again, feeling the resistance at the back of her throat against my cock head.

Her fingernails clawed at my thighs as her legs kicked out.

My hands clamped around her hips, keeping her in place, as I thrust my own hips again.

This time, the bulbous head of my cock pushed past the tight ring of muscle at the top of her throat.

She gurgled and choked on my shaft as I shoved deeper down her throat.

Using my grip on her hips, I shifted my hands under her body to cup her ass. I then lifted my arms, pushing her pussy harder against my mouth.

Christ, her mouth was tight and wet.

I flicked her clit harder with my tongue, lapping up the sweet cream of her arousal. I needed her to come again before I would allow my own release.

Her thighs wrapped around my head and squeezed as I lifted my torso even higher. This movement pushed my hips forward. My balls rested against her face as I forced her to swallow my shaft to the base.

I thrust backward, pulling out for a moment to allow her to suck in a gasping breath.

As I tilted my head to the side, I playfully nipped at her inner thigh with my teeth. "I won't stop face fucking your pretty mouth until you come, understand me?"

"I can't. It's too much! I can't," she responded breathlessly, her nails digging into my thighs in a feeble attempt to keep me from pushing back inside.

"Then you'll be choking on my cock all night until you do," I said before I pushed deep inside the sweet warmth of her mouth again.

It was extreme, and I'd never dream of engaging in this type of rough sexual play with a virgin, or someone less experienced than my future bride.

However, I knew there were two critical things that needed to happen if our marriage was to have any chance of success.

The first was she needed to recognize my authority.

And the second was I needed to recognize her need for validation through sex. A need that had driven her to seek ever increasingly taboo and kinky sexual experiences. Just one of those being fucking her father's *soldati,* only to move on to the even more dangerous *capos.*

Only through the hot sting of the lash would I be able to achieve both objectives with her.

Knowing her clit was still stimulated from the electrical pulses, I knew, better than she, that she was capable of another intense orgasm.

Increasing the rhythm of my tongue, I laved, licked, and flicked the tiny nub until her thighs clenched around my ears, her body stiffening and her hips bucking.

The moment the ripples of her release ceased, I lowered her legs back to the bed.

Gazing down at her pink lips stretched around my thick shaft, I knew I wouldn't last much longer either. "That's it, baby. Swallow my cock. Choke on it."

She gasped as I pulled back, then thrust in.

By now, her gag reflex had weakened. My cock slipped easily down the column of her throat. Fascinated, I gently wrapped my hand around her neck and felt the press of my cock through her thin skin against my palm as I thrust.

"Fuck, baby. You're being such a good girl by taking my cock down your tight little throat," I rasped as my balls tightened.

The pressure along my shaft increased.

"Here it comes, baby. Don't you dare fucking spit it out this time," I growled.

After several long thrusts, I threw my head back and roared as I shot my come into her mouth.

Her shoulders shook as she choked.

I pulled back slightly, fisting my shaft and watching my come coat her tongue, then pool inside her mouth.

Using the head of my cock, I traced her lips. "Swallow."

With her mouth open and filled with come, she shook her head slightly while breathing through her nose.

Stretching my arm out, I retrieved the riding crop from its precarious perch near the footboard.

Without warning, I whipped both her nipples as I pressed the electric shock button.

Her legs curled up as she cried out... allowing my come to slip down her throat.

She choked again, and then turned onto her side as she swallowed it all.

I perched on the edge of the bed, running my thumb across her lips and collecting the drops of come from the corners before holding her jaw and pushing my finger between her lips. "Suck."

She blinked several times up at me as she closed her lips around the base of my thumb and sucked the come off it.

To help her resist the temptation to impulsively talk back to me despite the painful lesson she just learned, I kept my thumb in her mouth. "I hope you appreciate that I've shown you the kindness you failed to show my staff."

Her brow furrowed as she pulled on my wrist, attempting to dislodge my thumb. "Kumdpness?"

"You'd be wise to remember... a stable master doesn't break in a pony with taps from a riding crop while she is tucked into her stall."

She stilled.

I thrust my thumb in and out of her mouth to emphasize my point. "He forces her to accept the weight of his body on her back and ruthlessly rides her repeatedly while whipping her bare ass. Until all the fight has left her body and she learns to accept her new master."

A jolt of awareness rocked her body with my thinly veiled threat.

After freeing my thumb, I leaned over her and forcefully yanked her hair, tilting her head back. "Tonight, I respected your wish for no true sex until marriage—"

Although I knew she was only requesting consideration to delay the inevitable.

"—but defy or disrespect me again and next time there will be no such kindness."

CHAPTER 25

ELLA

A tremor ran over my body causing my teeth to rattle before I clamped my jaw tight. The musky taste of him still on my tongue.

Matteo pulled me onto his lap. As he swept his hand over the side of my cheek to brush my hair back, he said, "What am I going to do with you, *mia piccola colomba?*"

Too busy fighting the comforting feel of his powerful arms wrapped close around me, I didn't respond.

Matteo leaned to the side and grabbed the gold quilt that was still neatly folded at the end of the bed. He then swept the soft, heavy folds over my shoulders. "Let's go get you something to eat."

Clamping the edges of the blanket over my breasts with my fist, I shook my head. "I'm not hungry," I whispered.

He must not have heard me because he stood, and after adjusting the waistband of his gray sweats, he secured the blanket more firmly around my body before lifting me in his arms.

As he carried me across the bedroom, I said more loudly, "I'm not hungry."

He winked at me. "I heard you the first time."

I huffed out a sigh. "Then where are you taking me?"

"To the kitchen."

"But…"

"No more arguments tonight."

For once, we were in agreement.

I was too tired, too emotionally and physically worn out, to argue anymore.

Easily navigating the narrow back servants' stairs, we emerged into a spacious kitchen.

At first glance, it appeared like a rustic, country kitchen with its exposed brick and the rough wood ceiling beams with hammered copper pots dangling from wrought iron hooks. But on closer inspection, it was easy to spot the high-end appliances and luxurious details.

Matteo set me on the polished stone kitchen island.

I shifted my hips forward, intending to hop off, but a dark look of warning from him stopped me.

He reached over my head and pulled down a heavy cast-iron skillet. After turning up the flame on the gas oven range, he warmed the skillet while he retrieved a loaf of fresh ciabatta from the bread bin. After cutting the entire loaf into thin slices, he drizzled a healthy amount of olive oil into the now heated skillet, and tossed them in.

As I looked on silently, he used his fingers to gingerly flip the slices, exposing the golden-brown toasted side glistening with olive oil.

I inhaled sharply when his arm brushed my hip as he reached past me.

Inwardly, I rolled my eyes when his own gaze focused on

mine. Of course he would have heard my soft gasp. There wasn't the smallest detail this man ever missed. It was super annoying.

The corner of his mouth lifted as he held the dishtowel he had reached for aloft. "There's nothing to be afraid of."

My eyes narrowed. "Said the wolf to the lamb."

With a laugh, he leaned over and kissed the sensitive space just below my jaw. "When you're not being a pain-in-the-ass little brat, you really are adorable."

My lips thinned as I leaned over to my left and rubbed my hip. "I don't know what you're complaining about. I'm the one who has a literal pain in my ass."

He raised an eyebrow. "Well, technically not *in* your ass... *this time.*"

Heat radiated off my cheeks to rival the cast-iron skillet.

Thankfully, I was saved from a response when his attention returned to the skillet. With the towel wrapped around his hand, he grabbed the hot handle and slid the toasted slices onto a nearby pewter platter.

Matteo then opened the refrigerator door and pulled out a mason jar filled with what looked like whipped ricotta cheese and then a similar mason jar of dark honey from a nearby cabinet.

He placed both items on the counter near me then opened a drawer and retrieved two spoons before closing it with his hip.

My mouth watered as I watched him spoon a light and fluffy dollop of rich, creamy ricotta cheese onto the warm crostini. He then lifted the wooden dowel out of the honey and spun it, drizzling the whole thing with a thin stream of sweet honey.

Turning to me, he held the crostini up to my lips. "Open your mouth."

I turned my head. Knowing I was risking another punishment, my hunger and lack of sleep got the better of me. "The last time you said that, I nearly choked to death on your... your thing."

He grasped my jaw and turned my head to face him. "It's called a cock."

I blinked as I clamped my teeth together.

His fingertips pressed into the soft flesh of my cheeks. "Say it. Cock."

I breathed through my nose. "No. It's not ladylike," I replied, keeping my jaw clenched.

"Says the *lady* who's repeatedly *propositioned* me to fuck her ass."

Repeatedly?

God, I really hated my sister sometimes.

Like now. Now was a really good time to hate her for this mess she shoved me in.

He raised his eyebrow again. "I'm waiting."

Shifting my gaze to the ceiling, I bit off, "Cock."

"*Brava ragazza.* Now, take a bite before it gets too cold."

"I told you, I'm not hungry."

He released my jaw and leaned back against the counter across from me. Staring straight at me, he sank his sharp, white teeth into the whipped ricotta crostini. His eyes closed, and he gave a moan while he chewed.

With my hands balled inside of the blanket, I wrapped my arms tightly around my middle to keep my stomach from growling.

He moaned again. "This is so good. Are you sure you don't want a bite?"

The second half of the crostini was held up to my mouth again. Drips of honey threatened to fall off the sides, making me want to flick them with the tip of my tongue.

Distracted by the simple, yet decadent, treat taunting me, I didn't notice at first when Matteo slipped his hips between my knees as he moved closer. "Come on, baby. Take just a small bite. For me."

He brushed the toasted crust of the crostini, with its drips of honey, against my lower lip.

The tip of my tongue swept out to taste the golden sweetness. With my guard down, my stomach rumbled when I forgot to continue to clench my abdominal muscles.

"That's it, little one. Just open your lips and let me slip it inside."

My gaze clashed with his at his erotic double entendre.

Mesmerized by his dark gaze and the allure of the crostini, my mouth opened, allowing him to push the final bite inside.

Like him, I closed my eyes and groaned as my teeth crunched down on the crostini, releasing the earthy flavor of the olive oil just as the whipped ricotta melted onto my tongue. Complimenting the rich creaminess was the burst of sweetness with a touch of floral from the honey.

My eyes still closed, the rough edge of another crostini brushed my lower lip.

"Open," he commanded.

I obeyed.

This time cutting the crunchy yet chewy crostini in half with my front teeth. As I chewed, I opened my eyes in time to see him place the rest of the bite into his mouth.

Outside of sex, I couldn't imagine there was anything more intimate than sharing food.

The corner of my lips tickled as a drizzle of honey escaped my mouth. Before I could flick my tongue out to capture it, Matteo brushed the pad of his thumb over the droplet. He then pushed his thumb inside my mouth.

An instant connection to him doing the same motion earlier, as he made sure I swallowed every drop of his come, made me lightheaded. In my mind, I tried to blame my exhaustion and hunger, but knew it was a lie.

Rattled, I reached for my own slice of crostini and spooned some ricotta on it before shuffling my hips a little further down the kitchen island.

Matteo followed me with the jar of honey.

Reluctantly, I held it out as he spooled a thick drizzle onto my slice.

As he did so, he said, "I know your secret."

My world tilted off its axis.

Afraid my now shaking hand would drop it, and needing time to think before I responded, I shoved the whole crostini into my mouth. Forcing myself not to groan as the sweet creaminess hit my tongue.

He knew my secret?

He knew I was Ella and not his intended fiancée, Antonia?

How much did he know?

When had he figured it out?

Matteo chuckled. "Careful, little one. Dirty talk in the bedroom is fine, but I don't truly want you to choke."

With wide eyes, I nodded as I struggled to chew. My fingers gripped the edge of the island. When I had finally swallowed, I rasped, "I can explain."

No, I couldn't!

I couldn't come remotely close to explaining *any* of this madness.

Where would I even start?

What if I confessed to being the one on the boat with him that time, when he assumed I was Antonia?

What would I say if he asked where Antonia was?

Or why I was taking her place?

Or worse, why I let him practically fuck me, *more than once*, when I knew he was promised to my sister.

216

Sciatiri e matri!

Was he going to kill me now for trying to trick him?

I was all alone in an empty villa with Matteo Cavalieri in the middle of Abruzzo. Helpless.

My head swam as a fevered lightheadedness once again took over.

If I fainted and cracked my skull on the slate floor tile, would he take pity on me?

His knuckles brushed my neck as he pushed my hair back over my shoulder and lifted the blanket higher after it slipped down my shoulder. "There is no need for any explanation."

There isn't?

With embarrassing swiftness, my mind spun out an alternative tale.

Was it possible Matteo had known from the beginning, but went along with the deception because he preferred me to my sister?

My heart leapt at the thought.

Was it possible that the moment we shared in the gazebo was real? *Like really real?*

It was almost inconceivable to imagine someone preferring me over my sexy and outgoing sister. All my life, I had played the shy wallflower to her bold, attention-getting personality.

The lesser twin.

Always overlooked.

Always compared and found wanting.

Always the poor man's Antonia.

Was it possible that for once, someone had decided I wasn't just the *other* sister, but had truly seen me as an individual?

"There isn't?" I squeaked.

Matteo placed his hands on either side of my hips. "Of course not. You're safe here, Antonia."

My heart fell.

217

Antonia.

He didn't know I was Antonella. My so-called secret was safe.

I should have felt a rush of relief, but instead a weariness that was bone-deep caused my shoulders to droop as I lowered my head.

Matteo once more pushed back the cascade of blonde curls I was attempting to hide behind. "I know why you and your sister, Ella, insist on starving yourselves. And why you acted out with all those men."

I swallowed past the lump in my throat as hot tears filled my eyes. I had to clear my throat before answering. "Do you, now?"

He stroked my cheek with the backs of his knuckles. "It was your father. The man should be shot for using his own flesh and blood as trinkets he dangled before his men. He should have been sheltering and protecting you both, and instead he berated and taunted you with cruel memories of your mother."

My lower lip trembled as I raised my chin and stared up at the ceiling to try to keep from crying.

I was hanging on by the thinnest of threads. If Matteo continued to mention my poor mother, I'd lose it.

He continued. "I know the truth. How you behave is all an act. You're really more like your shy, sweet sister. You've just been forced to conform to the bullshit demands of your father as a coping mechanism. But you're safe now. You don't have to pretend anymore."

If he only knew. Everything and nothing about my sister was an act.

She was just as superficial, selfish, and toxic as my father.

That Matteo called me *sweet* only twisted the knife in further.

I sniffed as I pushed my blanket-covered fists against his shoulders. "Thank you for the crostini. I'm exhausted. I'm just going to head back up to bed. *Alone.*"

Matteo sighed. "Very well, but this isn't finished."

I swiped at a traitorous tear. I really needed to get the hell out of this kitchen. After hopping off the island and stepping out of the shelter of his arms, I backed away. Tightening the blanket around me, I said, "Yes. It is. I don't talk about my family with strangers."

His arm shot out to snatch the folds of the blanket between my breasts.

With a sharp tug, he yanked me to his chest.

Releasing the blanket, he fisted my hair and pulled as he towered over me. "We're not fucking strangers."

I had no choice but to open my arms to try to push him away, which only crushed my naked breasts against the warm skin of his chest. "Neither are we family."

"You're my wife."

I pushed, but he didn't budge. "Not yet, she's not. I mean... I'm not."

The pointed edges of his canine teeth were exposed when his upper lip curled in anger. "I'm warning you. Whatever you're planning in that adorable little head of yours? Don't. You won't like the consequences."

My eyes widened. "Is that a threat?"

"You're goddamn right it is."

My gaze narrowed. Throwing his own words back at him, I sneered. "So much for being *safe* here."

He leaned down low and pressed his lips against my cheek-bone as his hot breath caressed my chin. "You are safe. Safe from that piece of shit you call a father's toxic influence. Safe from being pawed at by one of his cronies. Safe to eat as much as you want without judgment. What you're *not* safe from are my rules."

Before I could object, his mouth claimed mine, both of his hands cupping my jaw, holding me prisoner.

We both tasted like sweet honey and sex.

I was breathless when he finally released me. "Let me go."

"This is your only warning, baby. Drop the act and start behaving. I won't tolerate any more of your games. This is my family's ancestral home. You will treat it, and the people here, with respect."

Finally having a use for channeling Antonia, I flipped my hair and laughed without mirth, cocking a hip. "I have news for you, *future husband*. It's not an act."

Just as he opened his mouth to respond, there was a burst of laughter from down the hall.

Someone from his family must have returned.

The moment Matteo turned his head toward the sounds, I broke free and bolted for the stairs.

I froze on the first step as he called out. "Antonia."

Not wanting him to see the tears that had already fallen, I only tilted my head to the side but refused to turn to face him.

He growled, "For your sake… it had better be a fucking act."

Without responding, I bolted the rest of the way up the stairs.

CHAPTER 26

MATTEO

*A*fter watching my bride flee from me, I strolled outside onto the veranda.

Uncle Barone was throwing a log into the iron brassier, causing the fire's flames to rise and spark.

Enzo tucked a heavy fur blanket over Bianca's lap before reaching for a bottle of Rosa's homemade green walnut liquor that was set out on a sideboard. "Joining us?"

I nodded. "But I'll take red wine instead."

Having never acquired a taste for the sweet yet bitter *Nocino*, a classic Abruzzo digestive, I preferred the wine.

Uncle Barone leaned back in his chair as he used a twig from the fire to light a cigar. After blowing a blue ring of smoke, he asked, "I heard Antonia is already here. Is that why you hurried back from your sail to Sicily?"

The rattle of ice against metal covered my momentary silence as Enzo prepared the chilled cocktail before pouring it into three small martini glasses. I thought over how much I wanted to divulge about Antonia's arrival and my motivations.

I shrugged as I passed Bianca and then my uncle each a glass before settling into one of the padded loungers surrounding the fire with my wine. "Not bad. Good winds. I made great time around the point."

Apparently, the answer was not much.

Bianca leaned forward. "Is your lovely bride joining us? I just want to know if I should sip or guzzle this."

Enzo cleared his throat as he joined her on the loveseat lounger.

She shrugged. "What? I said lovely."

He placed his arm over her shoulders and pulled her closer. "Just because Milana or Aunt Gabriella aren't here doesn't mean you need to fill the sarcasm void."

She leaned up and kissed the edge of his jaw before rubbing her thumb over the lipstick stain she caused. "Agree to disagree."

I swirled my glass to aerate the red wine and release the distinct aromas. Not wanting to discuss my bride, I asked my uncle, "Where's Amara?"

"Cesare left for Milan for a few days, so she's staying over at their place to keep Milana company."

Enzo tilted his head toward me. "In other words, she's on guard duty."

I rubbed my eyes. "Did Milana try to sneak into the office while I was gone?"

Uncle Barone rose and poured himself a glass of Scotch from the bar setup Rosa prepared before leaving, instead of a second *Nocino.* "There was no trying about it. The damn girl was there all week, for hours at a time. Cesare nearly tore my head off when he found out."

Bianca threw her head back and laughed. "She hid in your office because you were in Sicily."

As I lifted the wineglass to my lips, I smiled. "Clever girl," I said before taking a sip.

My uncle took his seat again, but not before dropping the

small plate of dried fruit and *sfrappole* Rosa had also prepared on the veranda table in front of us all. "Should I bother asking if there is anything you'd like to tell us?" Powdered sugar wafted off the pastry he snagged from the plate.

My gaze hardened. I was well aware of my family's displeasure with my decision to marry Antonia. And of their hope it would all go sideways during my visit.

And it very nearly did.

I thought of her sister, Ella.

So sweet and shy and vulnerable and yet intelligent, with a curious inner fire. It was admirable how, despite her obvious trepidation about doing so, she still spoke her mind to me. Still stood up for herself. Or at least she tried.

Not that I listened. Especially when she tried to leave me to return to the dinner party, when it was clear she was suffering from lack of food and needed a moment.

Ella probably thought I hadn't noticed how she did her best to protect her sister, my bride, from her countless gaffes and social missteps. But I had.

I stared down into my wineglass.

Although I had no choice, it bothered me I left her behind with her bastard father.

Logically, I knew I'd already pushed against the line when I threatened Antonius over his treatment of Antonia. If I went to the mattresses over Antonella too, it would have possibly blown the entire agreement.

And then I would have no way of saving either sister.

I worried about Ella's safety. Her father had all but announced he'd be arranging a marriage for her next. Inwardly, I cringed at the idea of that sweet girl married off to some obnoxious, possibly violent, crony of her father's.

If I were completely honest, the primary reason I pushed to have Antonia here as soon as possible was to get Ella here as well, under my control. The moment the wedding was over, I would be Antonia's husband, family to Ella. That would give me hopefully just enough leverage.

Especially if I offered to pay her father's *bride price* and found a husband for Ella.

I took another sip of wine.

My father hadn't raised an idiot. I knew I was dancing into a minefield, given my attraction to Ella.

I hoped for the sake of our future marriage that I was right about Antonia only acting out as a reaction to her father and that, separated from his influence, she would become more like Ella.

There were so many times I would have sworn I saw Ella reflected in Antonia's eyes.

More than once, I had even...

No, it was obnoxiously American Hollywood ending to even think it.

It was not possible that the girls had switched.

For starters, I couldn't see Ella mistreating poor Lucia that way.

On the other hand, Antonia was either an extremely accomplished actress or had dramatically inflated the rumors about her level of sexual experience with all her overt propositions and brash talk.

There was no denying my babygirl's response to my touch at times.

As if she were shocked to her core at some of my more inventive bedroom games.

Is it possible?

Once more, my mind wandered to the possibility the sisters had switched positions.

I had witnessed firsthand Ella's willingness to shield and protect Antonia. While also witnessing Antonia's equally selfish and self-centered demeanor. The precise type of personality who would strong-arm and take advantage of, say… a more kind-hearted sister.

It would also explain my supposedly *very much so no longer a virgin* bride's insistence on no traditional sex until the wedding.

I didn't have to ponder the reasons. It was no secret Antonia wanted this wedding even less than I did, but did that mean she would go to the lengths of forcing her sister to replace her?

No.

Not possible.

No matter how much I might secretly wish for it.

I rubbed my eyes again. There was no point in this type of wishful thinking. The die was cast. The agreement set. Antonia would be my wife in less than a month. Hoping for a different outcome, even one as outlandish as the two sisters switching places, was pointless and borderline cowardly. I gave my word I would marry Antonia, and that was what I was going to do.

After draining my glass, I rose to pour another.

While I was standing, I poured a generous amount of *Nocino* over ice, at least enjoying the burst of vanilla, cardamon and citrus peel scent, if not the taste, as I gave the cocktail shaker a vigorous shake. I turned and replenished first Bianca's, then Enzo's glass before holding out the ramekin of deep crimson cocktail cherries for them to select as a garnish.

As I did so, I shook off my strange musings and focused back in on their conversation.

Enzo turned to me. "Are you getting to the destemmer-crusher tomorrow?"

With a toss, I threw the empty wine bottle into a nearby recycle bin as I answered. "Yup. I'm going to need a few of the men to disassemble the fittings, clamps, and seals in order to get to the differential switch."

Uncle Barone asked, "Do you think it blew because of a strain on the crushing component?"

"I do. I'll know more tomorrow."

He nodded. "Well, I can spare Alfonso and two others, but no more. Right now, my priority is pruning back the vines and getting rid of the dry brush. If we wait much longer, we're risking a fire in late spring."

With each passing month, as the temperature warmed, orographic lifting would lead to air being forced up our side of the mountain, leading into thunderstorm season. And thunderstorms meant lightning.

Every winery in the area took the possibility of a brush fire from a lightning strike very seriously, which was why after the harvest, it was common to take a brush mower to the wide, dry brush areas to cut down the fire fuel while also cutting back the vines.

"Understood. I'll only need them for an hour or so in the morning and then again later, after I'm done installing the new part. Just in case, I already ordered a new one. It arrives on the afternoon train."

He nodded. "Sounds like a plan."

Before our conversation could continue, music floated down to us from an upper bedroom. It was the deep, mournful notes of a cello.

It was then I realized we were actually under Antonia's bedroom.

Through my research, I'd learned that only Ella played. According to my report, Antonia wasn't the least bit musically inclined. She didn't have the patience or discipline for it, apparently.

I had noticed yet ignored the instrument in the bedroom's corner earlier.

It was odd, but I was too focused on confronting her over her earlier behavior to ask questions.

The sorrowful melody carried over the chilled night air We all fell silent and listened. It took me a moment, but it finally clicked that she wasn't playing a classical piece as I'd have expected.

She was playing an instrumental version of Guns N' Roses "Don't Cry."

And playing it very well.

Extraordinarily well.

Bianca frowned at me as she leaned forward and whispered, just in case Antonia's window was open. "I didn't know Antonia played the cello."

My gaze remained steady on the soft light of my bride's bedroom window. "She doesn't."

CHAPTER 27

ELLA

"Yes, I do," insisted Antonia.

I could practically hear the childish stamp of her foot over the phone.

With a grunt, I lifted the suitcase onto the sofa. As I leaned over the top to unzip it, I fired back at her. "No, you don't."

The idea that my twin sister took the tiniest bit of responsibility for her actions was laughable under normal circumstances, let alone now.

After lifting the lid, I groaned. Not a single item was neatly folded. "Are you fucking kidding me, Toni?"

"What?"

I flipped the phone to speaker and tossed it onto the cushion next to the sofa as I rifled through the mess. "This suitcase looks like a squirrel on cocaine packed it."

She made a dismissive huff. "Sorry I didn't follow your majesty's packing rules. I was in a rush."

With my own angry huff, I tossed several dresses over the back of the sofa as I rummaged through the pile looking for something halfway decent to wear. "I'm so sorry if you having that thug ex-boyfriend of yours drug and kidnap me made you pressed for time. And don't call me your majesty."

I hated when she called me that. "It's just common adulting decency to know how to pack a suitcase properly."

"Tomasso is not my boyfriend."

My back straightened as I snatched the phone back up. Pressing it to my ear before remembering I had it on speaker, I pressed the "phone" button and raised my voice. "That is what you have an issue with? Not the drugging and kidnapping me part?"

"How much longer are you going to harp on me about that?"

My gaze narrowed as I wrapped my arm around my middle and propped my other elbow on it. "Well, considering it's been less than a week, I'm pretty sure it's going to come up in conversation at least a few more times," I snapped back.

I hated the person Antonia turned me into.

Even when we were little, I never talked or shared things with her. It was as if every interaction with her was just a string of negative reactions.

My father was to blame.

If he hadn't murdered my mother, then it wouldn't have forced me into the role of parent to my own twin. Prematurely ending my childhood, while apparently extending Antonia's.

Life wasn't fair, I knew that, but damn, it would have been nice if my patience and selflessness were rewarded just a little bit, like, say... me not being forced to impersonate my sister in a sham arranged marriage.

Or me not falling for her fiancé.

The unbidden thought shocked me to the core.

Nooooo.

This situation was already way too fucked up for me to suddenly think I was falling for Matteo Cavalieri.

My gaze wandered over to my cello. My only solace. My

companion. My best friend in many slightly pathetic ways. I knew it was dangerous to play it.

Everyone knew Antonia didn't play the cello.

I was lucky Matteo was so angry with me over how I treated Lucia that he didn't comment on it last night. Still, I needed the consolation it provided. Like a hug from a friend.

It wasn't my choice of music that was disturbing me.

It was how I had closed my eyes and imagined Matteo's arms around me as he hugged me close and whispered the lyrics against my cheek.

It was the way my stomach flipped at the idea of him telling me everything was going to be okay, and that he loved me.

The fantasy that, for once, someone was watching over me, protecting me, instead of the other way around.

Afterward, I cried myself to sleep. Alone.

Because that was all it was... a fantasy.

Even if I once again dreamed of the moment we shared in the gazebo. The only time during this entire farce that he knew he was holding me, Ella, not my sister.

That he knew he was kissing me.

At least in my dreams, I left out the part where he immediately regretted it.

"Was there a point to this call?" Antonia's acid-laced voice broke my reverie.

"Have you told him yet?"

"Who?"

"Your boyfriend! Have you told your boyfriend that you're pregnant?"

There was a long pause. "Not yet."

"Toni!"

"I will! He's refusing my calls right now, but I have a plan."

A headache threatened. "I'm not going to like it, am I?"

"It's fine. I'm going to threaten to tell his wife if he doesn't meet with me."

"Antonia, who is he? If he's one of Father's men, that could be very dangerous."

"You worry too much. I have to go. I want to buy a new outfit in case I need to meet with the wife, and I have a two-hour drive to Catania."

"Why are you going to Catania?"

She let out a long, exaggerated groan. "Because that is where his vacation home is. God, Ella, keep up."

I raced over to the small desk on the other side of the bedroom and grabbed the pen that rested on top of a small notepad, which of course had the freaking Cavalieri Winery logo on it. It was as if I were being held prisoner at a resort spa. "Um, sorry. You're right. So silly of me. What was his name again?"

She snorted. "Nice try. I'm not telling you, because you'll get all judge-y."

After tossing the now useless pen aside, I wrapped my arm around my middle as I leaned a hip against the desk. "Too late. I'm kind of already there, so you might as well tell me his name."

"Fine, you sort of already know him. He's a—"

She suddenly cut off.

I pulled the phone away from my face to make sure the screen was still lit and we were connected. "Antonia?"

Nothing.

"Antonia?"

I listened and heard a feverish, hushed conversation.

Straightening, I strained to listen but couldn't make out the words. "Antonia? Is someone there with you?"

Still nothing.

"Antonia!"

Finally, she must have put the phone closer to her mouth

because I could hear her address the other person. "I wasn't going to tell her his real name, God!"

"Antonia? What is going on? Who is there with you? Toni?"

It was too late. She'd hung up.

With a resigned shake of my head, I tossed the phone aside and tackled the suitcase contents again. "Ewww," I groaned as I picked up one dress that was clearly dirty with a suspicious white stain on the lower back.

Not caring how expensive the dress might be, I crossed to the trash can and threw it away. There was literally nothing even remotely suitable to wear in the entire suitcase.

It was filled with Antonia's signature too short, too tight, designer dresses and even tighter, brightly colored tracksuits.

I briefly thought about, then discarded, the idea of wearing a pair of the black track pants under a dress. For starters, I'd look ridiculous. And there was no way anyone would believe Antonia would wear something like that.

Seeing no other option, I selected the least offensive dress, a long-sleeved, black knit one that barely reached to mid-thigh. If I wore her pair of thigh-high boots, at least it would leave only a few inches of bare skin.

I pressed my ear to my door and listened to make sure I didn't hear any voices before I opened it only wide enough to poke my head out.

After surveying the hallway to confirm it was empty, I stepped out of the bedroom and headed to the main staircase, walking on the balls of my feet. Just like at home, I wanted to avoid clacking my high heels against the hardwood floor and announcing my presence.

With another yank on the hem, I descended to the first floor All was silent.

I had deliberately waited until late morning to emerge,

hoping to avoid Matteo and his family as they headed out for their daily routine.

Still walking on the balls of my feet, I headed down the hallway toward the back of the villa, where I figured the kitchen would be. I wasn't entirely sure since Matteo had taken me down the servants' staircase last night.

I didn't dare go that way since it passed several of the upstairs bedrooms. Better to be safe than sorry, in case the Cavalieris liked to sleep in.

Especially since I had absolutely no idea if Matteo was staying at the villa or not. The last thing I wanted was to pass a doorway and have Matteo emerge from his bedroom.

My cheeks warmed at the thought as a vision of him in his gray sweatpants and naked chest with a rumpled bed in the background popped into my head. *Stop it!*

As I made my way down the hallway, to the left was an open room filled with bright winter sunshine. Peeking inside, I saw a large executive desk filled with chaotic piles of files and stray paperwork. Pushed up against it, at an angle to create an "L-shape," was a quaint shabby-chic desk made of reclaimed barnwood. On it were neatly stacked colored files and a small bud vase.

Shifting my head left to right down the hall, I strained to hear any signs of life.

All was still silent.

This was a terrible idea.

Absolutely terrible.

The worst idea ever.

Don't do it, my mind raged.

After another nervous glance, I stepped over the threshold. The space was clearly an office. Maybe if I glanced through the files enough to sound knowledgeable about Cavalieri's business the next time I met with Fino, he would leave me alone about spying on them further.

I headed to the messier of the two desks.

The other desk was clearly that of a neat and organized female. Someone like that would be smart enough to file away anything incriminating. The other desk looked like controlled chaos. It would be much more likely that a piece of paper or file that was supposed to be hidden would get overlooked in the mess.

My fingertips slid over the disjointed edges of the closest pile of files as I forced air into my lungs. Fear made my chest tight. With one eye on the door, I tried to scan through the file tabs.

Invoices. Shipping orders. Website updates. Purity tests. Maintenance records. Payroll.

Maybe the payroll file would prove informative.

As if criminals put other criminals on the formal payroll.

Still, it was a place to start.

My right hand shook as I attempted to steady the unruly pile to slide the file out from the middle.

I was so focused on my task, I didn't hear him enter.

"Can I help you?"

With a small shriek, my hand jerked, destabilizing the whole pile. I cried out as I bent my knees and surged forward to capture as many of the slipping files in my outstretched arms as I could before they tumbled to the floor.

I wasn't successful.

Most of the papers slipped between my arms to crash in a guilty pile at my feet. I fell to my knees to gather them up. "I'm so sorry. I'm so sorry!"

The handsome older man stepped forward. He placed his espresso cup on the edge of the desk and went down on his haunches before me. His large, warm hands pressed down on the tops of mine. "Stop."

His voice was soft but firm.

I slowly tilted my head back to look at him. After moistening my lips, I said again, "I'm very sorry."

He gripped my hands and rose, lifting me off my knees. There was no doubt he was a Cavalieri. He had the same dark eyes, firm jaw, broad shoulders, and imposing height as Matteo.

My eyes widened as I took in his salt and pepper hair.

Oh no.

Oh no.

Oh, please if there is a God, no.

It couldn't be...

Life isn't this cruel.

The corner of the man's mouth lifted as he stared down at me. "I'm Barone Cavalieri. And who might you be?"

Nope.

I was wrong. Life is this cruel.

Of course, it would be Barone Cavalieri.

My lips opened to speak, but no sound came out.

Just then, a soft, female voice interrupted. "Barone, you're scaring her."

I turned to see a pretty woman who looked close to my age enter. Her dark hair hung in thick waves over her shoulders as she entered the office casually dressed in an outfit I would have killed to be wearing at this moment: a heather-gray cashmere sweater over a pair of capri pants, with a simple strand of pearls around her neck.

My arms slipped to my sides, where I pulled on the short hem of my borrowed dress.

The woman held her hand out. "Hi, I'm Amara. You must be Antonia."

Her smile was so genuine and warm, I had to stop myself from cringing away from her touch, worried I would sully her with my craven, guilty lie. "Yes," I forced out through tight teeth, pushing my lips into a false smile.

Barone lifted his espresso cup off the desk. "Well, Antonia. It is nice to finally meet you. I apologize for our rudeness in not greeting you last night. We weren't expecting you so soon."

My cheeks burned. "Please, it was my fault for not announcing my arrival. My departure from Sicily was... unplanned."

He raised a single eyebrow as he raised the cup to his mouth, then paused. "Interesting. Can I ask what you were looking for on my desk?"

Amara swiped the cup from his grasp. "Caffeine pulls fluids from your body and impedes wound healing." She then fixed her dark, sharp gaze on me as she ignored his resigned sigh. "And I'm sure she has a perfectly good reason for being in our office."

Barone wrapped his arm around her lower back and pulled her close. He then kissed the corner of her mouth. "Fine. You're responsible for coming up with another way to get a rise out of me in the morning, then."

Amara blushed prettily. "The doctor said no to that as well."

He nuzzled her hair. "No. He changed his mind and agreed with me it was just the kind of exercise I needed to heal."

She pulled her head back and gave him a playful glare. "Only after you threatened to kill him if he didn't."

Barone shrugged. "All I remember is the doctor saying we should fuc—"

Her eyes widened as she slapped her hand over his mouth. "Barone!" She then tilted her head to the side in my direction.

His dark eyes fixed on me as if he had truly forgotten I was in the room.

What would it feel like to have a man so enamored and in love with me he forgot everything that was going on around him, including a stranger who had clearly been boorishly rifling through his desk?

The silence stretched as they both stared at me expectantly.

I cleared my throat. "A reason? Yes, of course, I have a reason."

As soon as I think of one.

After clearing my throat a second time, I said, "I was just looking for... Matteo! Yes, Matteo. I don't have his mobile phone number and the winery is so large that I thought maybe he had a schedule posted that would tell me where he would be right now."

They exchanged a look.

They didn't even remotely believe me. The question was whether or not they would call me out on it.

Barone took a deep breath and narrowed his gaze.

Uh oh.

Finally, he said, "Matteo is in the main winery building, helping repair the destemmer-crusher machine. I can escort you there."

I held up my palms. "No. I don't want to inconvenience you. I'll just help clean these up and then go find him."

Before I could kneel again to pick up the piles of files, Amara intervened. "Leave it. I'll handle it."

Under normal circumstances, I would have objected and insisted on helping, but it was clear they were suspicious.

I nodded. "Of course. Sorry again."

Barone nodded his head toward the window. "Matteo is in the rectangular brick building just over there."

Not wanting them to see that the dress I was wearing barely covered my ass, I backed up, facing them as far as I could before turning and fleeing.

* * *

As I crossed the courtyard, my right ankle rolled slightly after stepping on a stone.

These stupid high heels. I missed my ballet flats.

Once again, I shifted up onto the balls of my feet and stepped gingerly down the path, careful to avoid any more stones. There was a slight hitch to my step as I favored my right leg, causing my hips to sway.

The moment I entered the building, I was immediately self-conscious.

Despite the whirr and hum of machinery, all human activity seemed to come to a standstill as the predominately male staff stopped to stare.

Again, I tugged on my hem as I lowered my head to conceal my face with the fall of my hair.

Ignoring the looks, I walked down the wide, tiled corridor, searching for Matteo.

And that was when the catcalls started.

"Ciao bella!"

"Dammi un bacio!"

"Bel culetto!"

"Vuoi scopare?"

Offensive as some of the comments were, there was only one voice I heard above all the others.

"Goddammit," growled Matteo.

CHAPTER 28

MATTEO

*A*lfonso kicked my boot from where he stood over me. "Matteo, I think you're needed."

The sound of my men calling out had barely caught my attention as I wrestled with a rusted bolt on the destemmer-crusher machine I was helping disassemble.

My boot heels dug into the tile floor as I bent my knees to slide the rolling creeper I was lying on out from under the machine. "What's up?"

Alfonso gestured with his chin.

I turned my head to see my girl in a tiny dress and fuck-me boots. With each step, her generous hips swayed in an exaggerated saunter as if she were deliberately trying to capture the attention of every red-blooded male in the building.

But I knew better... now.

There was no doubt in my mind that she was Ella, not Antonia.

A part of me had known all along, but I had ruthlessly ignored the red flags.

The signs had been there.

The tiny blunders in her speech whenever I talked about our upcoming marriage or the latest outrageous thing her sister had said to me.

Her innocent response to my touch.

Her blushes at our sex games.

Deep down, I think I knew it wasn't Antonia playing at being a shy virgin.

No one was that good at hiding their true nature.

It wasn't just the sex, or her thin excuse not to fuck me until we were wed.

It was more than that.

There was a warmth and intelligence that shone through Ella's eyes, which was lacking in the vapid snake eyes of her sister. I had seen it firsthand at dinner and afterward in the gazebo.

And last night in the kitchen.

Then I heard her play the cello, and I knew... *I knew.*

What I hadn't known was what I was going to do about it.

There was no turning back at this point.

Not after I'd held Ella in my arms. The idea of tossing her aside to honor my original agreement to marry her sister, Antonia, was repulsive to me.

As was the idea of letting Ella go.

She was mine now.

And right now, she was still playing the part of her horrid whore of a sister, for my benefit.

It was time to put a stop to this bullshit game of hers.

"Goddammit," I cursed, tossing the wrench aside. The heavy metal tool clanged where it bounced against the tiles as I launched myself off the wheeled cart to my feet.

Lowering my head, I charged toward her.

With each step, my anger grew as she pulled nervously on the hem of her skirt and hid behind her hair. Not understanding men, she probably thought she was diffusing the situation.

She was wrong.

She was inflaming it.

All my men saw was a cascade of soft, golden waves and her hand drawing attention to the curve of her hips and the exposed skin of her upper thighs.

"Knock it the fuck off," I shouted.

The men fell silent and turned back to their work.

Her eyes widened as she observed me stalking toward her.

I closed in on her.

With a slight cry, she tried to turn, but stumbled in the ridiculously high heels.

Her shoulders shifted as she turned toward me. Holding up a small hand, she only got out a faint, "Wait—"

Before I lowered my shoulder and swept her up high.

My men cheered as I adjusted her squirming form on my shoulder and kept walking without missing a step.

"Back to work," I yelled, tightening my arm across her upper thighs.

"Put me down," she cried out as we crossed out of the building and into the sunshine.

Her nails dug into the fabric on the back of my T-shirt in her attempt to lift her torso.

With my open palm, I gave her ass a sharp spank. "Keep still."

After that, the only peep I heard from her was a gasp and a plea not to drop her on our way across the courtyard to enter the villa via a side door, taking the servants' stairs two at a time. With determined steps, I stormed down the interior corridor to her assigned bedroom.

The moment we got inside, I tossed her onto the bed and strode over to lock the door.

By the time I turned back, she had already hopped off the

mattress and was backing up to the furthest corner of the extensive suite.

I tried but failed to check my rage. "What the fuck do you think you're doing strutting around dressed like that, Ella?"

Her hands went to her hips, emphasizing her curves even more. "I can dress however I— What did you just call me?"

I stalked toward her. "You know damn well what I just called you."

She blinked several times, backing into the sofa arm and then moving around it. As if something like a piece of furniture would keep me from grabbing her. "I'm Antonia."

I ground out through a clenched jaw, "No more lies. Do you have any idea the danger you both have put yourselves in with this childish prank?"

Her chin rose. "It wasn't a prank! I mean... I mean... I'm Antonia! How dare you call me my sister's name! It's an insult."

My hands curled into fists in my effort to resist the urge to wrap them around her upper arms and shake her.

We circled the room. When she neared the door, she pivoted on her heel, throwing out over her shoulder, "I don't have to take this!"

Her fingers barely grazed the doorknob before I pounced.

Vaulting over the sofa, I spun her around and slammed her against the wall. Anchoring her there with my hips. "The hell you don't."

I reached up to grab her jaw when I realized I still had my thick canvas work gloves on.

Leaning back, I wrenched them off my hands and threw them to the floor, hitting a nearby brass trashcan.

The contents spilled out, drawing my attention.

Strewn on the floor was a dress. A dress with a clear come stain on the fabric, next to a crumpled note with the name Toni.

Ella leapt forward, kicking the dress and note under the table.

Pushing her aside, I snatched the dress and note from the floor. Unfurling the wrinkled paper, I read the message—and saw red.

I'm sorry.
  I'll try to save you from Matteo in a few weeks.
  Wait for a message from me.
  Love,
  Toni

WITH A LOWERED BROW, I lifted my head up and glared at her.

It was all a lie. Every fucking bit of it.

I had assumed my innocent Ella had been dragged into this farce by her manipulative sister.

The thought of her being so heartlessly used as a pawn had angered me more than the initial subterfuge. And that was despite the fucking hot mess their prank had created for my family and Dante.

But now.

Now I knew another man was involved.

A man who had professed his love for Ella.

My Ella.

And make no mistake, she was mine now.

I had branded her smooth skin with my hand and my riding crop. I had tasted her sweet pussy. She had swallowed my seed. I would kill any man who even tried to touch her now.

My lip curled. "You're not leaving this room until you tell me who the fuck Tony is and where I can find him."

Her eyes widened. "It's not what you think."

I stepped closer and threw the come-stained dress at her feet and pointed to it. "The fuck it's not. Another man jizzed on my property."

The only reason I wasn't bellowing with rage was I was certain she was still a virgin. Whoever this man was, he had not taken the ultimate intimate step with her. If she had been any other woman, I would not have cared, as I hadn't with her sister. I would never judge a woman for enjoying the same pleasures as a man.

And yet...

Something primal and dark had reared up inside of me at the thought of being the *only* man in Ella's life. I wasn't ashamed to admit it. I wanted her for my own. I wanted her to be mine and mine alone. As if I were selfishly snatching a unique and precious treasure and raging *mine, mine, mine,* like that troll from that movie.

Her arm flew up as she slapped me across the face with her open palm. "I'm not an object you can just buy."

My hand moved to my jaw as I shifted it to the right and left. My girl packed a nice wallop. It was a strange moment to feel proud, but I did. "Wrong. And I have the bank receipt to prove it."

Dammit.

I needed to get back in control.

My anger was getting the better of me.

She didn't deserve me saying that. Just the idea that I could lose her to another man, all for being too stupid to realize it was her in my arms each time, not her sister, was untenable to me.

The way I was feeling in this moment, nothing—absolutely nothing — was too extreme for me to hold on to her. Even if I had to chain her to my bed, I would do it if it prevented her from leaving me to go running to that other man.

I needed a second chance with her, like I needed my next breath.

After witnessing firsthand Cesare and Enzo's struggles to hold on to the women they loved after monumental fuck ups, I was determined not to share the same fate.

Yes, I fucked up.

Yes, I should have realized sooner that the sisters had switched.

Yes, this was going to cause a shitstorm of issues with Dante.

But fuck no. I would not let that stop me from claiming her.

She didn't belong with them, or that other man.

She belonged with me.

Her gasp cut through my tense thoughts. "Fuck you."

She threw the door open and tried to run down the hall to the main staircase.

She didn't get far, especially not wearing her sister's fuck-me heels.

Chasing after her, I didn't even break my stride as I wrapped an arm around her waist and lifted her off the floor then marched toward the bedroom I often used when I stayed at the villa.

What happened next would not happen in her bed... but mine.

"Let me go!" she cried out as she clawed at my forearm.

A shout from below reached us.

Uncle Barone called up. "Matteo, is everything okay up there?"

Shifting her weight to my hip, I leaned over the wrought iron banister. "Perfectly fine. Just setting down some rules for my new bride."

Ella cried out. "No, it's not! Help! He's holding me against my will!"

Uncle Barone nodded as he lifted an espresso cup off the saucer he was holding in a mock salute. "Carry on," he said before moving on to his office.

Ella shook her head and yelled at the ceiling. "I hate you Cavalieris!"

After adjusting my grip, I continued down the hallway as I tossed out, "That's a shame, since you're about to become one."

The moment we crossed the threshold to my suite of rooms, I dropped her onto a tufted ottoman before pivoting to lock the door. After turning the brass key, I removed it from the lock and placed it high on top of the doorframe, out of her reach.

I turned to face her.

Ella was pacing back and forth on the other side of the room, stumbling every few steps.

"Take those fucking boots off before you break your ankle."

Once more, she yanked on the hem of her sweater dress. "Stop telling me what to do. You're not my..."

I raised an eyebrow. "Not your what? Boyfriend? Fiancé? Future husband?"

She matched my expression. "As a matter of fact, no, you're not."

I inhaled deeply through my nose as I ran my left thumb over the scarred knuckles of my right hand. Despite my work gloves, my dominant hand was stained with machine grease. The black grime making the small spidery scars from years of bare-knuckle fights stand out like small white veins.

Only a monster would touch an innocent woman with dirty hands.

Only a monster would consider what I was planning.

Knowing for certain Ella had switched places with Antonia, I should've contacted Dante immediately. I should have arranged to have her returned to Sicily.

I should have honored my word.

But for the first time in my life, I was going to break it.

There wasn't a chance in hell I was sending her back.

SCORN OF THE BETROTHED

In my mind, Ella was not a Fichera, subject to her father's rules or even Dante Agnello's mafia syndicate.

She was a Cavalieri now.

My wife in all but name and deed.

No, it wasn't the obstacle of the fallout I was concerned about in this moment...

I stormed toward her.

After her futile attempt to evade my grasp, I maneuvered her into a corner. Placing my hands above her on either wall, I leaned in close. "You're right, *colomba mia*. I am none of those things to you."

The tension in her shoulders visibly relaxed as she kept her face averted. "I'm glad you agree. Now let me out of here."

With my right hand, I clasped my fingers around her throat, forcing her to meet my gaze. My thumb caressed the sharp edge of her jaw, leaving a black smudge. "Not so fast, little one. Who I am is the man who's tasted your sweet mouth. Who's felt you tremble in his arms with each release. Who knows you secretly like it when I push my thumb inside your tight little ass while we role-play."

She covered her ears with her hands. "Stop it! Stop! You're my sister's fiancé."

I yanked her hands down. Clasping both her wrists in one hand and holding them against her chest, I growled, "No. I'm the only man who'll ever have the right to touch you again. Now, I'm going to ask one more time. Who is Tony?"

Her eyes flashed with defiance as she raised her chin. "He is—"

"I'm warning you. I am barely holding on to my rage right now. I wouldn't recommend lying to me again."

Her lips clamped shut as her gaze shifted to the side. "He's my sister. She's my sister, I mean. Toni is short for Antonia."

My brow furrowed. Of course. If I hadn't been so consumed with jealousy, I would have realized that sooner. "What does that note mean?"

The delicate muscles in her throat contracted as she swallowed. "I didn't come here... willingly."

Shocked, I released her and stepped back. Rubbing a hand over my eyes, I muttered, "Goddammit."

In that moment, she slid out from behind me, turning to face me after she was more than an arm's length away. "Before you get mad at Antonia, you're just as much to blame for this mess."

Her eyes glistened with tears as she raised her arm and pointed an accusing finger at me. "I told you Antonia didn't want to marry you, but you insisted on going through with this farce."

I spread my arms wide. "There wasn't a choice."

This was not the time to explain to Ella how Antonia had put her life in danger with her manipulative escapades.

While I may have offered to marry Antonia to save my family from being pulled into a territory war within the Agnello syndicate, it was also to rescue her from the almost certain unmarked grave in her near future.

Ella fired back. "There's always a choice. You just made the self-serving one."

I stepped closer. "Not then I wasn't—but I am now."

She backed up. "What do you mean?"

My gaze narrowed. "What do you think is happening here, Ella?"

Her arms folded over her middle. "I think you're angry my sister and I tried to fool you. But I'm not here to force you into marrying me instead, if that's what you think."

God, she was beautiful.

Standing before me, clearly afraid, and yet defiant and proud.

Sweet, intelligent, talented, fiercely loyal, everything a man could want or need in a wife.

My arm swung out to snatch her to me. Tightening my grasp as she wriggled to try to break it, I rasped against her lips, "No, baby. That's what *I'm* here to do."

CHAPTER 29

ELLA

I grasped his upper arms. "I don't understand."

His lips moved over mine. "Yes, you do."

The breath I inhaled was his own. "This whole thing was wrong from the beginning. You need to send me back to Sicily. I'll explain to my father—"

He shifted his hand to grasp my hair at the base of my skull, holding my head steady as he kissed the corner of my mouth. "You're not going anywhere, Ella."

My fingers twisted into the fabric of his T-shirt. "You have to let me go. I don't belong here."

"No."

I opened my lips to object further, but before I could utter a single word, his mouth claimed mine. His tongue swept inside with such fierce determination, it stole my breath.

With his arm still around my waist, he lifted me off the floor, pressing his hips into mine.

The hard ridge of his cock pushed against my stomach as he swung our bodies around and walked toward the bed.

I tore my mouth free and craned my neck to the side. "Let go."

"Never."

"You can't do this."

"Watch me."

The backs of my thighs hit the edge of the mattress, and I panicked. Twisting my hips, I wrenched free of his arms and skirted around the bed.

I held out a restraining hand. "Matteo, you're angry. You're not thinking straight."

He whipped his T-shirt over his head, exposing the chiseled ridges of hard muscle across his chest and abdomen. There were far too many scars, some faint, some more recent, for anyone to call it perfection. Anyone but me. Damn the man.

Even with his hands dirty and scarred, they were still sexy in that masculine, big and strong way. When he ran them over my skin, I loved how slightly rough and strangely heavy they felt. As if he were restraining their power so he didn't bruise my flesh.

The very idea sent a warm spark of awareness straight between my thighs.

This was madness.

I had to stop this before we both did something we regretted. "I won't tell anyone about the… the… things we did…in bed… not even my sister."

He probably assumed he would now be forced to marry me instead of her if my father found out about all the kinky sex games he had been playing with me.

His hands reached for the tarnished brass buckle of his belt as he kicked off his boots. "You had better not," he growled.

I shook my head. "I won't. I promise!"

The leather belt slid through the loops of his jeans as the corner of his mouth lifted in a knowing smile. "I'm a jealous man. I barely tolerate another man looking at you, let alone picturing your sexy body writhing with pleasure."

My eyes widened. "That's not what I meant."

He tossed the folded belt aside. "I know what you mean, baby. And what we're about to do has nothing to do with your sister or your father or Dante or any of that bullshit. I'll deal with all of that later. This is between us."

My fingers curled into fists at my sides. I knew I'd angered him with this stupid stunt of Antonia's, but there was no cause to taunt me like this. He could just say his piece and send me back to Sicily. He didn't have to act as if there was something between us.

After all, I was no one. *Just the shy, sweet sister.*

"Us? There is no us. Until today, you thought I was my sister." I fired back.

As scary as it was, I needed the terrifying, slightly unhinged side of him back.

I couldn't handle this determined, obstinate side.

He tilted his head to the side as he studied me. "That's fair."

The breath I had been holding escaped past my lips. Nothing like having your worst fears confirmed.

I'd played a secondary character to my sister's starring one in my own story for my whole life. There was no reason having it confirmed once again should hurt this much. Still, some tiny part of me had hoped he had noticed I wasn't *her.*

To avoid looking into his eyes and seeing pity or, worse, disgust in them, I shifted my gaze down and locked it on his hands again.

His masculine, scarred, dirty hands. Hands that would leave marks on my skin.

With his fingers splayed wide, he ran his right hand over the tight ridges of his abdomen. My cheeks burned as I glanced up to catch him watching me. The corner of his lips lifted as he moved his hand in a slow circle before dipping just the tips of three fingers into the waistband of his jeans.

My mouth went dry.

Matteo took a step toward me.

This time, I was too mesmerized to shift away.

His voice was low and calm, as if he were soothing a wild animal. "Let's play a game."

My gaze snapped back up to his. "I've had enough of your games."

He was so close by now, he reached out and captured my chin to tilt my head back. "I think you'll like this one."

I clenched my stomach muscles to keep from trembling. I wanted to blame my overwrought emotions, exhaustion, stress—anything but his nearness—but I knew the truth.

My tongue flicked out to wet my dry lips. "What happens if I win?"

His gaze focused on my mouth as he ran his thumb over my lower lip. "Oh, babygirl. You're not going to win."

My throat muscles contracted as I tried to swallow. There was an unmistakably sinister threat to his words.

"Then I don't want to play."

He stepped closer, pushing me back against the wall. "Too late. We've already begun."

His hand wrapped around my neck as he leaned down to nuzzle the sensitive skin just below my ear. "The rules are simple. I'll tell you a moment I remember. And you tell me if it was you... or your sister."

My eyes filled with tears. My heart already expecting the pain his game would cause me. Hating how pathetic I sounded, I sniffed. "I don't... I don't want to play this game. Please."

His lips skimmed my jaw, then moved softly over mine. "Shhh, *colomba mia*, trust me."

It wasn't as if I had a choice. He had me pinned against the wall with his hips.

His fingers gently cupped the base of my skull as he moved his mouth over my skin to kiss my forehead. "I remember the fresh clean scent of your perfume as I held your body close when we swayed to the pounding drumbeat of a *pizzica tarantelle*."

When I didn't answer at first, he curled his fingers into my hair and tugged. "Me," I rasped.

"Good girl. Round two. I remember the soft vibrations of your moan the first time I kissed you. Even then I was struck by your innocent response."

This time when I didn't answer right away, he pressed his hips into mine, further emphasizing the threat of his hard cock.

"Me," I squeaked.

He ran the tip of his tongue between the seam of my lips. "How about the moment I pushed my fingers into your tight pussy as we watched those two men fucking that woman in front of the bonfire? Do you remember that, babygirl? Do you remember how you trembled in my arms as you stared in wide-eyed fascination?"

My fingers splayed wide as I pushed against his warm, naked chest and tried to turn my head to the side. "Please, I don't want to play this game."

His voice took on a dark, sharp edge as all gentleness fled. He yanked on my hair, forcing my head back and my chest forward against his. "What's the matter? Can't handle the truth, that no matter what I called you, I knew the woman in my arms. I knew the taste of your skin. The weight of your breast against my palm. Even the cluster of freckles between your shoulder blades in the shape of a crescent moon."

I tried to pull away as salty tears stung my cheeks. "Please, don't say any more."

This wasn't fair.

Ruthlessly, he continued. "You think it matters that I called you Antonia when I stared into your eyes and saw the hope and longing last night after I said you were safe with me? You think that moment was any less real? I know the hell your father has put you through."

Using his grip, he swung me away from the wall and pushed me back several steps as he shoved both hands into my hair, holding me by the neck. "I know about the empty ache inside your chest from growing up without a mother's love. Always feeling as if you've been deprived of some essential human experience. Always knowing you'll never truly be whole."

Oh God, did he know about my mother?

About my fears?

Had he truly seen through this entire facade the whole time and guessed my motives for going along with it?

He leaned his forehead against mine. "I can make you whole, Ella."

Tears blurred my vision. "It's too late. It's too complicated. This whole thing is a mess. There's nothing you can do to fix it. I'll go home to my father. I'll convince him to give you your money back."

With a curse, he released me and paced away before turning back. "I don't give a damn about the money. I care about you. You think your father's just going to welcome you back with open arms?"

He was right. I couldn't go home. My father saw my sister and me as commodities. Once the scandal broke of why Antonia's engagement to the powerful Cavalieri family ended, both of us would be ruined. My father would think of us as useless trash, just like my mother.

I ran my hands over my arms as a shiver ran down my spine. For years, my mother's ghost had called out to me as I imagined her in a lonely, unmarked grave. The irony that my efforts to

SCORN OF THE BETROTHED

find her would see me share the same fate was too cruel to contemplate.

"What happens to me is none of your concern."

His jaw clenched as he narrowed his gaze on me. "What did you just say to me?" he growled.

My resolve faltered, but that didn't change the truth. Backing up a step, I whispered, "It's out of your control."

Matteo cupped his right fist in his left hand and cracked his knuckles. "No, little one. It's not."

Beg. Plead. Tell him you're sorry. Tell him it wasn't your idea. Scream. Run.

The competing impulses crashed into my brain.

"What are you going to do?"

"What I should have done when I first suspected it was you who had come beautifully undone in my arms that night on my boat, and not Antonia."

259

CHAPTER 30

MATTEO

There was no goddamn way I was sending her back to her father.

And there was only one way to make certain no one—not her father, not Dante, no one—took her from me.

Stalking forward, I pushed her back until her legs brushed against the bed. "Get on the bed."

"Why? What are you going to do?"

"I told you. What I should have done that night in the gazebo. I'm going to fuck you."

There would be no disputing my claim to become her husband once her father learned she was no longer a virgin. While it would not have mattered in my eyes, I knew her father would consider her ruined.

With a cry, she turned to run.

I caught up with her in two strides. With my arm around her waist, I lifted her off the floor.

She kicked out with those ridiculous boots she was wearing. "No! No!"

With a twist of my torso, I flung her onto the bed. "I guess we're doing this the hard way."

With her natural submissive nature and dangerous impulse to please the people in her life, it was not surprising she would feel an overwhelming sense of guilt over what we were about to do.

And I had just the way to break her out of that mentality.

Like an adorable Catholic penitent, I'd already learned my sweet little dove needed pain before her mind would let her enjoy the pleasure. Punishment burned away the guilt.

Before reaching for my belt, I pulled my knife out of my back pocket and flicked it open.

Her eyes widened as she tried to shimmy back on her hips. "Oh, my God!"

The corner of my mouth lifted. "Save the praise for when I'm licking your pussy."

Her cheeks blossomed with bright pink color.

Fuck, I loved her innocent blushes.

My fingers twisted into the woven fabric of her sweater dress. I lifted the hem as I prepared to shove the tip of the knife into it.

Her hand grasped the edge as she tried to wrench it from my fingers. "No! My sister will be furious if I ruin this dress."

Blinking in disbelief, I shook my head. After all her sister had forced on her this past week, she was still worried about making her angry? It was my girl who should be in a rage, not the other way around, and definitely not over a stupid fucking dress.

"Good," I growled as the sharp metal point slid into the wool fibers, tearing them. "I look forward to telling your *dear sister* where she can shove the torn remains of it."

Tossing the knife aside, I twisted the torn edges of her hem in my hands and yanked upward, severing the dress in two.

Although I didn't think it was possible, my anger only rose as

I stared down at her sweet body on display. Instead of a cute pair of modest silk panties, like before, today she was wearing a trashy scrap of lace that ended in a thin string over her hips, no doubt a thong.

Under her breasts and across her ribcage were harsh red marks where the too tight bra had dug into her sensitive skin. Leave it to her sister to be the type to torture herself with a lower size bra just to push her breasts up high.

"Dammit, woman."

Retrieving the knife, I placed a restraining hand on her abdomen as I slid the sharp edge through the string over her hip. Then, ignoring her cry of protest, I gripped the strip of fabric between her breasts. "Hold still."

She held her breath as the cold, dull edge of the knife slid along her skin to slip under the bra. I had to saw it back and forth a few times to cut through the wire and thick elastic but finally the fabric snapped. The black lace extra-padded cups fell away, exposing her sweet flesh... and more marks.

I dropped the knife and placed a knee on the bed as I leaned over her. With utmost care, I ran the tips of my fingers over the thin scratches. I swallowed past the tightness in my throat. "Never do this to yourself again. Do you hear me?"

"It doesn't hurt, and Toni says..."

With my hand cupping her jaw, I placed my thumb over her lips. "And definitely never quote your sister's advice to me."

She sniffed. "She's not a bad person. Not really. You have to understand that she just chose to... *cope*... with our father's difficult ways differently than me."

My lips pressed to her forehead. "I know, baby. And I love that your sweet soul still gives her the benefit of the doubt. You have my word. I will do everything in my power to still try to save her. But right now, saving you is my only concern."

It was the wrong thing to say.

Her dark eyes hardened as she rolled away from me and leaned up on her knees, grasping the edges of the torn dress over her naked breasts. "Saving my sister is *my* job, not yours. And I've told you before, I'm not your concern, and I don't need saving! I'm perfectly capable of figuring out this mess for myself once I'm back in Sicily."

She was just being stubborn. There was no way she hadn't noticed telling me that her safety and well-being were not my concern was like waving a red flag in front of a bull.

I couldn't help it.

I was a Cavalieri man.

It was bred into our DNA to be attracted to damsels in distress who needed our help and protection. Hell, I was surprised our family shield wasn't a dragon instead of two horses with the Latin motto *Interfector Draconum*, Slayer of Dragons.

With my gaze trained on her, I rose off the bed and reached for my belt. "We seem to be at cross-purposes. Care to guess which one of us is going to win?"

Her gaze trained on the thick strip of leather I was slowly wrapping around my fist. "This is insane. My sister never wanted to marry you. Whatever plan you and my father and Dante concocted for her is clearly over. There is no point in threatening to keep me here."

My head tilted to the side. "First of all, it's not a threat. Second, where else would my wife be, but at my side?"

Her cute lips dropped open. "You're serious about that?"

I raised one eyebrow. "If you got the impression I was joking, then I need to work on my *persuasion* skills."

She shifted backward, dangling her feet off the edge of the mattress. "I won't marry you. I *can't* marry you. My father and sister would—"

"Enough," I ground out. My arm snapped out to grasp the forearm holding her dress in place.

Her knees slid along the silky bedcovers as I yanked her toward me until she collided with my chest. My torso twisted so I could swing her around and over my lap while I sat on the bed.

I restrained her with my right hand holding the back of her neck, leaving a faint dark smudge on her skin. Then I flipped up the torn shreds of her dress to expose her naked ass. "If you are going to insist on acting like a petulant child, then I will treat you like one."

Her head twisted to stare at my raised arm with my belt firmly grasped in my hand. "Matteo Cavalieri, don't you dare spank me with that belt!"

"If you didn't want a spanking, then you should have been a good girl and done as you were told."

"You can't force me to marry you with a spanking!"

I winked. "Watch me. And it won't just be a spanking."

My arm came down with swift determination. The leather end of my belt slapped across her cheeks with a satisfying smack.

Ella's back arched as she let out a howl of indignation.

The belt smacked across her ass a second and third time, raising a pretty pink blush.

She swept her arm back and tried to cover her ass with her hand. "Stop! It hurts."

My fingers wrapped around her wrist and anchored her arm at her lower back. "Stubborn little girls get sore bottoms."

Her flesh jiggled with the next strike as she kicked her feet. The ridiculously high heels of the boots struck the bed's footboard, making a matching *thwack* sound in rhythm with the belt.

If the only way to move her past her guilt and sense of family loyalty was to punish her ass, then so be it. For good measure, I slapped the leather tongue of the belt across the tops of her thighs and just under the curve of her ass several times.

Only when her skin was a warm, bright red and hot to the touch did I set the belt aside. She was so small and delicate, I needed to be careful not to raise welts on her sensitive skin.

With the palm of my left hand, I rubbed slow, sweeping circles over her punishment-warmed skin and loosened my grip on her neck.

She whimpered and squirmed on my lap. The movement only making my already aching cock harder. "Shhh, little one. Your punishment is over."

Ella knuckled her tear-filled eyes as she sniffed. "I hate you."

God, she was adorable. "No, you don't. And I'll prove it. Raise this pretty ass of yours up."

"No," she grumbled.

"Did you want me to get my belt again?"

"Fine," she huffed as she shifted her knees closer to my left thigh, raising her hips.

"Good girl."

I continued to caress her ass in soothing circles as my left hand moved closer and closer to the juncture of her thighs. "Spread open your knees, baby."

"What are you—"

"Do as you're told."

Her knees spread open slightly.

I slipped my hand between her legs. Her pussy was wet and ready for me.

She whimpered again. "Don't say anything, *please*."

Another time I would enjoy the embarrassed blush on her cheeks as I regaled her with all sorts of filthy, dirty talk about her sweet, wet cunt. But for now, I remained silent.

I slipped my two middle fingers along the seam of her lips, teasing her clit.

Ella gasped and arched her back, trying to shift her hips forward.

Reaching under her, I cupped her breast and gave her nipple a hard pinch. "Back into position."

"Ow!" Her hips moved back.

I increased the pressure of my fingers as I rubbed between her legs harder and faster. After every few strokes, I would move my hand over her ass and tease her puckered hole with my thumb. Her body would jerk and stiffen in response before I swept my hand once more between her legs. This time pushing first one, then two fingers inside her tight pussy.

Unlike before, I pushed in deeper with each pulsing thrust, until her body's resistance pressed against my fingertips.

So she was still a virgin.

No, not just a virgin.

Mine and *only* mine.

My soon-to-be wife and the mother of my future children would belong only to me.

I was a twisted, misogynistic bastard for even thinking it, but I didn't give a damn. My cock lengthened to the point of almost pain at the idea of being the only man to possess her.

Especially after reconciling myself to the idea of her sister, a woman who had spread her legs for more men than I could count. Reconciling myself to the knowledge that I would never be fully certain any children she bore in the marriage would be of my blood. It had been a tough pill to swallow.

But now a change in fate had brought this sweet creature into my life instead and although I sure as fuck didn't deserve her, I was going to hold on to her with both hands.

My fingers thrust in and out of her pussy. "Now you're going to be a good girl and come for me."

She moaned as she fisted the bedcovers. Her thighs clamped around my wrist. "This isn't right."

"This is exactly right. I need you to come so your pretty cunt is nice and slick for when I push my cock inside."

She leaned up on her forearms. "No! You can't. Can't you just... do what you did before?"

I wrapped my right hand around the back of her neck to push her head down and arch her back, which pushed her hips against my hand as her knees spread open.

The perfect submission position.

If I had my way, she'd start and end each day sprawled over my lap just like this.

"No, babygirl. There is no turning back now."

CHAPTER 31

ELLA

I was trapped.

Although could I really call it a trap if, as the prey, I willingly stepped into the cage?

The hard truth was, I could have stopped this madness at any moment by simply telling Matteo the truth.

I knew his kinky games and harsh punishments were only because he had assumed I was my much more experienced sister. And yet, I did nothing to stop them.

Because the obscene truth was, I liked it. I liked being dominated and subjugated by him. There was something about having your sense of control torn from your hands that was both terrifying and thrilling.

Even now, as I lay shamelessly half-naked across his lap, I knew if I truly screamed or cried out, he'd stop.

I moaned as his fingers pressed harder inside my pussy.

Biting my lip to prevent myself from screaming "harder... deeper."

I wanted this.

I wanted him.

Fuck the consequences.

My scalp stung as he pulled my hair, bowing my back even further. "Come now, babygirl," he commanded in that dark, authoritative voice of his.

And I obeyed.

A ripple of pleasure ran up and down my spine as my hips ground against his leg, my inner muscles contracting around his fingers. "Oh, God! Oh God! Oh! Oh!"

Lost in the rush of pleasure sweeping over me like warm water, I barely registered it when Matteo shifted me off his lap and onto the cool silk of the bedcover.

His powerful hands gripped my waist as he guided me flat on my stomach. His knees forced my legs open wider. "I can't wait any longer," he breathed against my shoulder.

Although some, I was sure, would think it cruel, I was grateful he didn't turn me onto my back to face him. I didn't think I could do this if I was forced to look him in the eye.

The sound of him lowering the zipper of his jeans was like a buzz saw in the tense silence.

His hips then pressed against the underside of my ass.

I hissed. The skin was still deliciously swollen and sore from his belt.

The head of his cock pushed against my pussy. "This is going to hurt, baby. I can't be gentle. Not now."

"Make it hurt, Matteo." I needed the pain to assuage my guilt.

It burned as he pushed the wide head of his shaft past the tight ring of muscle guarding my entrance. I gritted my teeth, feeling my body stretch to accommodate his thick girth.

My fingers once more dug into the covers and I breathed out in short, erratic gasps.

"That's it, baby. Take my cock."

I moaned as I shifted my hips under him, trying to ease the building pressure.

He pushed in slowly, opening me. Sensations bombarded me. His calloused fingers gripping my hips. The coarse denim on his legs brushing against the soft skin of my inner thighs, exposed above the leather top of my borrowed boots.

My senses were hyper aware. Every touch. Every sound. Every brush of his skin against mine sent a bolt of electricity between my legs.

The head of his cock pushed against my maidenhead.

My body stiffened as guilt, doubt, and fear crashed over me. "Wait! I think…"

He pulled back… was he actually going to stop?

Before I could react, he thrust violently forward, breaking through my inner barrier, tearing my body in two.

I screamed as I curled up on my knees, trying to move into the fetal position.

Matteo covered my body with his as he wrapped his arms around my middle and cupped my breast with his right hand. Holding me tightly to him from behind, he paused for a moment then thrust again and again as I struggled in his embrace. "Hold on, baby. Use the pain."

Tears blurred my vision as my pussy contracted painfully around his cock to force him out of me.

He pulled my body up and back until I was practically sitting on his cock.

The movement forced him deeper inside of me.

My head fell back onto his shoulder as he shifted his head to kiss my forehead. Breathing heavily against my cheek, he rasped, "You're being such a good girl for me."

I whimpered again, trying to get past the pain of having him penetrating me.

His left hand moved over my stomach to tease my pussy as he continued to thrust inside of me.

"Please come," I begged. "Please come. I can't take much more."

"Yes, you can, baby. God, you're so tight."

I collapsed forward onto the bed.

He followed me down with the weight of his body. This time, he moved his hand to grip my hair. Yanking on it, he quickened his thrusts. Pounding into my vulnerable body repeatedly.

The fast rhythm and relentless pace stirred something deep inside of me. A low hum. A vibrating awareness as the hard ridge of the head of his cock seemed to taunt the sensitive nerves deep inside of me.

"Oh! Oh!" I breathed.

"Fuck, babygirl. I need you to come on my cock. Now," he growled with such ferocity, I didn't dare disobey.

My knees bent backward, and I hit him on the back with my heels as my thighs gripped his hips.

My own hips rocked against the mattress as I came a second time.

This orgasm was so fierce and overpowering, I saw stars behind my eyelids.

"God, yes! Yes! Fuck!" roared Matteo as he thrust several more times before releasing his liquid heat inside of me.

His body trembled as he thrust several more times before pulling out and collapsing to the side of me.

I was shocked how quickly I felt empty and cold without the press of his body on top of me.

But that was short-lived.

Matteo rolled onto his side and pulled me into the curve of his body from behind. "Don't start thinking."

My shoulders tensed. "I don't know what you mean," I lied.

He pushed my tangled hair to the side over my shoulder and kissed my cheek. "Yes, you do. I'm going to handle everything. There is nothing to worry about."

Nothing to worry about?

Sure.

Only what my sister was going to say, and her safety.

What my father was going to do.

How Dante was going to react when he found out what I'd done.

Matteo's arm tightened around my waist. "You're thinking."

My brow furrowed as I squirmed in his embrace. "Am not."

His amused chuckle tickled my ear. "Liar."

I let out a long sigh. "Well, there's a lot for me to think about."

He rolled me onto my back and braced his forearm near my head as he leaned over me. "No, there's a lot for *me* to think about and do. You are going to take a nice warm bath and then I'm going to drive you into town to get some new clothes."

"Antonia's clothes are fine for travel. I'll just borrow a coat or something."

He nodded. "A good plan. *If* you were traveling. But you're not going anywhere."

"Matteo, I—"

Before I could finish, he cut me off. Leaning down to kiss the corner of my mouth, he whispered against my lips, "Answer one question and I'll consider letting you leave."

My breath hitched. Later, I would wonder why a sudden sickening weight settled in my stomach at him agreeing to let me leave him. As much as I was fighting it, there was something nice about having him insist on keeping me by his side. I'd be foolish not to admit it was nice to be wanted.

"What's your question?"

He raised an eyebrow. "I want a truthful answer. Remember, I'll know if you're lying."

With thinned lips, I nodded, then huffed. "Fine."

His dark eyes bore into mine. "In all those frenetic thoughts

273

that just raced through your adorable brain, did you, for even a moment, think of yourself?"

I blinked as I opened my lips to answer, then closed them. His question caught me completely off guard. My gaze shifted away from his probing one. "Why are you asking?"

"Just answer the question. Did you think of your own situation, or were you more worried about how your sister and father would react?"

I swallowed as I shifted my hips. "You're crushing me."

"No, I'm not. And you're stalling."

I let out another frustrated breath. "Well, so what if I thought of them first? Most people would consider family loyalty a good thing."

He tapped the end of my nose. "And I'm one of them. Your fierce loyalty and protective nature are some of the things I adore about you, but what I see as a strength, your family is exploiting as a weakness."

My hands pushed at his shoulders, but he wouldn't budge. "I don't need you judging me or my family situation. You don't know me. Until a few hours ago, you thought I was my sister!"

His hand cupped the left side of my face. "Let's get a few things straight right now. If you think this ridiculous plan of yours and your sister's would have lasted beyond today, you are sorely mistaken. The only reason you fooled me this long was because of my guilt."

I shifted my head away from the distracting warmth of his hand. "I don't understand."

Matteo rose off the bed and zipped his jeans.

I took that moment to snatch the bedcovers over my naked shoulders.

He rubbed his eyes as he paced away and then turned back to me. "I wanted her to be you."

His words were so unexpected I was certain I didn't hear him correctly.

His hand moved to rub the back of his neck as he clearly chose his words carefully. "You talk about family loyalty. As much as I detest how much you have sacrificed for your family, I am guilty of the same thing. Your sister didn't want to marry me? The feeling was mutual."

I scooted back deeper onto the center of the bed, drawing my knees up and wrapping the blanket more securely around me. "So why did you agree?"

His rough hands moved to his hips. I stared at the dark smudges on his right hand. Had he tattooed my skin with his touch?

He continued. "I've told you. Your sister was in danger, and my family owed Dante a favor in return for his protection. It was as simple as that. That night on my boat..."

Once again, he paced away, then returned to stand before me. "I shouldn't have treated you so brutally. The harsh truth is, I thought a silver lining in this whole clusterfuck of a mess was I'd be getting an experienced bride who liked it rough and kinky in bed."

And just like that, the cold emptiness returned.

I swallowed past the thick, swollen sensation in my throat as tears threatened. Bowing my head to cover my face with my hair, I leapt off the bed, not caring about my nakedness, and ran to the bathroom as I tossed over my shoulder, "You don't have to say anything else."

Slamming the door behind me, I choked back a sob as I reached behind me and turned the lock on the doorknob.

Second to my sister... again.

Matteo pounded on the door. "Ella? What the fuck?"

"Just go away."

The doorknob rattled.

"Open this door."

I glimpsed my reflection in the mirror. At first, I was confused, genuinely not realizing I was staring at myself. I looked like a discarded rag doll. My makeup was smeared. My hair a tangled mess. The red scratches from that terrible bra were still visible along my ribcage.

And then there were his marks.

Black smudges around my neck and a distinct handprint over my left breast.

Then there was the faint smudge of blood and come across my inner thigh.

Oh God!

I jumped when the door rattled as Matteo pounded on it. "I'm giving you one second to open this damn door."

Instead of answering, I moved to snatch a large cobalt-blue towel from a neatly folded stack in a wicker basket below the white marble sink.

"*Sciatiri e matri!*" I shrieked, jumping and almost dropping the towel as the locked door splintered and flew open.

CHAPTER 32

MATTEO

I was fucking this up.

The problem was, I couldn't afford to fuck this up.

After kicking the door open, I stormed inside the bathroom. "You're going to listen to what I have to say."

She wrapped the towel around her middle and clutched it between her breasts. "I get it. You were hoping to get the sexy sister, and you got the nerdy one instead."

My bark of laughter echoed around the bathroom.

She straightened her shoulders and lifted her chin, preparing to do battle with me.

God, I was going to love having her as a wife. Life would never be boring with my adorable little dove around. Although right now, my little dove was like an indignant bird with ruffled feathers.

I shook my head. "You can't help it, can you, babygirl?"

Although I wasn't a patient man, it was clear I would have to learn to be one if I was going to break through years of her being told she was the lesser of the two sisters.

Shoving her hair out of her face, she gave me a half smile. "Sorry."

I gathered her into my arms and kissed the top of her head. "It's okay. I get it."

My arm swept under her knees, and I lifted her into my arms, walking over to the edge of the oval whirlpool tub and sitting down with her on my lap. "This time you're going to let me finish without interrupting."

She opened her mouth and started to speak.

I placed a finger over her lips. "Without interruptions," I repeated firmly.

Her lower lip protruded in a pout as her brow furrowed. "Fine."

"I was trying to make the best of a shitty situation. And then I met you. And fuck... you were so goddamn sweet and intelligent and thoughtful. I just wanted to pick you up and put you in my pocket."

Her cheeks bloomed with a pretty pink blush. "That's not true," she whispered.

I tapped the end of her cute nose again. "I promise I'm not lying. From that moment on, whenever I interacted with you while you were pretending to be Antonia, I would see the tiniest glimpse of the real you."

Her soft skin caressed my palm as I cupped her cheek. "And you do not know how fucking badly I wanted it to really be you. So badly, I convinced myself that your sister was just acting as this crass, selfish bitch out of necessity. That she was just going through the motions for your father."

She laughed as she put her head on my shoulder. "No, trust me. It's not an act."

The moment she said it, her head popped back up and she covered her mouth with her hand. With wide eyes, she gasped, "I shouldn't have said that."

"Why not? It's true."

Ella shook her head. "No. She's in trouble right now and depending on me and here I am making fun of her. I'm a horrible—"

"Unless you want another spanking, I suggest you don't finish that sentence."

Her head fell back onto my shoulder. "What are we going to do now?" she whispered.

Tightening my arm around her waist, I leaned back and turned the tub's brass faucet on. With the tips of my fingers, I checked the water temperature before plugging the drain. "Right now, you're going to get a bath."

"But I don't want—"

"That's an order. You're going to be sore from earlier and a bath will help."

The tub filled quickly. I rose and placed her on her feet. Gently pulling the towel away, I saw the dirty smudges I had left on her pristine skin. Although I should've felt like a real asshole, I didn't. There was something crazy sexy about having my hand-print on her breast. It was almost a shame to let her wash it off.

I held her hand as she stepped over the tub ledge and sank into the warm water.

After selecting a glass vessel with a pearlescent liquid, I pulled off the stopper and tipped it under the faucet stream. Then I hit the button for the whirlpool jets.

Shimmering white bubbles rose in large fluffy clouds, rising to the top of her shoulders.

"Ahhh! You put too much soap! The bubbles will flow over the edge," she cried out with laughter, flattening her palms over the soapy mounds to tamp them down.

I washed my hands in the sink, concentrating on scrubbing the grime off my right hand, then tossed some water over my face and chest before grabbing a hand towel. "That is what towels and mops are for. Enjoy your bath. Don't let me see you out of it until I return."

As I turned to leave, she grumbled under her breath. "Fine, Mr. Bossy."

"I heard that," I called out over my shoulder before leaving the bathroom. Snatching a fresh shirt from a drawer, I tossed it on before picking up my mobile and padding barefoot down the hallway to my Aunt Gabriella's suite of rooms.

It took several moments to get my bearings in her vast walk-in closet. Eventually, I found a fuzzy pink sweater and a pair of what looked like short black pants that looked like they would come close to fitting my girl. I then selected several more items. I knew Aunt Gabbie wouldn't mind.

It had become a running joke in our family about her wardrobe becoming public property for our girls.

Next week, I'd take Ella shopping in Rome. She'd probably like that.

I smiled at the uncharacteristic domestic thought. I was definitely beginning to see the charm of having a woman in my life. My cousins weren't wrong.

Neither was my father. Speaking of whom...

I reached into my back pocket for my mobile and dialed my father's number.

"Hello, son. Change your mind yet?"

Ever since I had agreed to Dante's plan, my father, Benedict Cavalieri, the rather infamous black sheep of the family, had started every conversation with the same question.

This time, I finally had a different answer. "As a matter of fact, I have."

"So you finally came to your senses. Good. I'll start placing calls to some of our contacts to take the temperature in Sicily," offered my father.

I winced as I flung several dresses over my shoulder and

headed out of the room. "About that. I have a feeling it's about to boil over."

After filling him in, there was a long stretch of silence.

Finally, he chuckled. "Damn, son, when you step in the shit, you really jump in with both feet."

"Says the man who fell in love with his brother's almost-assassin."

"You know damn well Liliana didn't pull the trigger,' he gruffly, but good-naturedly, replied.

"Yes, but you didn't when you first fell for her,' I taunted.

"Be nice to your stepmother or I'll dock your allowance."

My head fell back as I laughed. It was a running joke in our family that my new so-called stepmother was actually a year younger than me. Their new nicknames inside the family were the Old Billy Goat and his Little Nun, because of Lili having been raised in a convent and their age gap.

Although none of that mattered.

Not only did I genuinely enjoy Liliana's friendship, I was especially grateful for how happy she made my father. For the first time in his life, he seemed content in that way only a truly fulfilled life could make a person.

I wanted that for myself.

Sobering, I crossed the threshold back into my bedroom. "Listen, we have to locate her sister and get her the fuck out of Sicily before Antonius finds out his daughters switched places."

"Agreed. I'll head down to the winery tomorrow and then to Sicily. It would be best if Dante heard all this in person. Do we know the sister's location?"

My attention was divided as Ella came into view, standing next to the broken bathroom door wrapped in my blue robe. It was so large on her, the hem scraped along the floor and the sleeves draped well past her fingertips.

Although I was annoyed she had disobeyed me and gotten

out of the tub, she looked so damn cute I couldn't be that angry with her. "Hold on."

I approached Ella and cupped her cheek. God, she was so beautiful. I still couldn't wrap my mind around the fortunate turn of events. "Baby, is your sister at your father's house?"

She broke eye contact with me as she tightened the belt on the robe. "Yes, she should be."

CHAPTER 33

ELLA

I held my breath as Matteo continued to tower over me.

Would he believe me? Could he tell I was lying?

After what felt like an eternity, he turned away and continued his conversation on the phone.

Only then did I let the air out of my lungs in a dizzying rush.

Despite what had just happened between us, I couldn't tell him the truth about Antonia's whereabouts. Not yet. Not until I had a chance to think through everything.

Matteo turned and gestured to a small pile of clothes on the bed. *For you,* he mouthed before gesturing that he would be another minute.

When he left, I grabbed the clothes and snuck down the hallway when the coast was clear, back to my own room.

Rifling through the pile, I was secretly pleased to see the pink Balenciaga cashmere sweater and a pair of capris. There was even a pair of Prada Napa leather ballet flats. They looked like they'd be a size too big, but I could stuff tissues into the toes to make them fit.

I leaned over and checked the entrance to the bedroom to see Matteo pacing just out in the hallway. Holding the clothes to my chest, I scrambled back into the far corner of the bathroom, away from the broken door, to change.

By the time I emerged, Matteo was waiting for me. "Ready to go?"

The towel wrapped around my wet hair slipped onto my shoulders. "Go? Go where?"

Was it possible he was taking me to the train station so I could return to Sicily like I asked?

"Into town. I have to pick up a part. Come with me."

"I think I'll just stay here."

He approached.

Once more, I had to tilt my head back to meet his gaze. He was just so tall. His shoulders alone were half my height. My cheeks burned at the thought of all that heavily muscled weight pinning me down only a half hour earlier.

"It wasn't a request, little one. While we are there, we can stop in to see Father Luca."

"Father Luca?"

Fuck, I sounded like a demented parrot just repeating his phrases back to him.

Matteo tugged on one wet curl. "Yes. I need to inform him about the wedding. We'll need the next possible available date."

"The wedding?"

For the love of God, stop repeating everything the man says.

"Yes. *Our* wedding."

Why was it so hard to breathe? It was like I had to consciously focus on expanding my lungs. "About that. We need to talk."

"We'll talk about the details while we are in town. Have you eaten anything yet?" His brow furrowed as he asked.

"I'm not hungry."

"That's not what I asked. We'll get some food first." He then turned and tossed over his shoulder, "Dry your hair and meet me downstairs in thirty minutes."

I followed him into the hallway. "But I'm not hungry. And I don't want to go into town," I called after him, addressing his back as he was already descending the staircase.

He paused with his hand on the wrought iron railing and looked up at me. "Thirty minutes."

Then he was gone.

Returning to the bedroom, I just stood there in shock.

What have I done?

The full ramification crashed down on me so hard my knees buckled. Like a child, I sat on the carpeted floor with my legs curled up and hugging my knees, wishing I could just hide in the closet like I used to when my father would rage at my mother.

I never asked for any of this.

I had just wanted a quiet life in Sicily, giving cello lessons to the local children and perhaps playing in a local quartet for the tourists. Knowing who and what my father was, I had never even dreamed about getting married or having a family.

Dreams like that were for women with options. I had known from a very young age my future husband would be chosen for me by my father.

The mafia was infamous for securing loyalty through marriage like some leftover of the medieval feudal system.

The best I had ever hoped for was a husband who, if not kind and loving, would at least allow me the space and freedom to play my cello.

Now I was in Abruzzo, the fiancée of a Cavalieri. A family name that had a legacy of power, wealth, and dangerous influence stretching back to before Italy was even a country.

Even though I was present almost every step of the way, I still couldn't seem to follow the twisted path which had led to this moment.

It was as if I were staring at a sheet of music. I could recognize the notes, but the melody was out of tune.

Staying on my hands and knees, I crawled the short distance to where I had my cello propped against the bureau. With my hand wrapped around the fingerboard, I moved to sit on the ottoman. Even as I did so, memories of the night before and Matteo's buzzing riding crop bounced around my mind like discordant notes.

My fingers gingerly turned the screw on my bow to tighten the strings. Then, placing the instrument between my legs, I played my favorite portion of Stravinsky's *The Rite of Spring*. The savage and strange dissonance and chaotic notes matching my own internal emotions.

Playing centered me.

This entire mess, pretending to be my sister and dealing with Fino's constant threats as well as the increasing danger my father posed, had me questioning who I was.

When I played, my world came back into order. I could think clearly.

As much as I was developing feelings for Matteo, I had to accept the fact that it would never work. For starters, there was my father. Then there was the inevitable scandal, since it had already been announced Matteo would marry Antonia not me.

With Antonia pregnant and it sounding less and less likely that the father would divorce his wife and marry her, there wasn't a question that my father would force Matteo to honor his original agreement and marry her for the sake of the family name.

Even though I may want to, I could never go against my family's wishes. Although I hoped my father would be arrested for what he may have done to my mother, I wasn't foolish enough to think that would be the end of his influence over us.

And, as horrible as she was to me, Toni was still my sister. I could never sacrifice her well-being for my own. She was safer with Matteo.

My bow screeched along the strings, then rattled against the wooden lower bout as I dropped it.

I swiped at my tears before picking my bow up and setting my cello aside.

Resolved, I picked up my phone and pressed the button to autodial my sister. After several rings, it went straight to voicemail. "It's me. It's urgent. Matteo knows I'm me and not you. Call me back as soon as you get this."

There wasn't a chance in hell I would tell her what had just happened between Matteo and me. That was a secret I would take to the grave, but I needed to warn her I had been found out.

Realizing I had already wasted too much time, I quickly dried my hair and dug around in her suitcase until I found the makeup bag again. Adding some blush to bring some color to my ashen cheeks, I also put a little concealer under my eyes to hopefully mask that I had been crying. I finished with a swipe of mascara and some tinted ChapStick from my purse before racing out of the room and down the stairs.

* * *

I crossed the exterior courtyard in time to see Matteo approach.

My heart lurched at the thought of what could have been.

He was just so strong and capable and intelligent. True he was also domineering, arrogant, and far too confident, which I was sure came from being a freaking walking god among men with a godlike fortune to match, but still ... it was equally obvious that he was also funny and sweet and caring.

287

Although I couldn't trust my current rising feelings for him since they were easily influenced by the unusual stressful circumstances, I suspected if things had been different, given time I could have easily fallen in love with him.

I laughed mournfully at myself.

Could have? How about *already did* fall in love with him?

As he got closer, his smile turned into a frown.

Before I could stop him, his arm wrapped around my waist, and he pulled me against the hard strength of his chest. His hand pushed into my still slightly damp curls at the nape of my neck. "Are you okay? Was I too rough with you earlier?"

My gaze shot to the left and right. "Not so loud! People will hear!"

He chuckled. "I promise you. Fucking my beautiful fiancée in the middle of the afternoon is the least scandalous thing my family could possibly hear." He pushed a lock of my hair behind my ear. "In fact, we may have to try harder to raise some eyebrows or my cousins are going to consider us boring."

I bit my lip. "Matteo, about the whole fiancée thing."

CHAPTER 34

ELLA

*H*e turned, pulling me with him. "Later. Let's go get some food."

He led me into the massive stables next to the villa, which apparently housed both horses and cars. No one could consider themselves an Italian and know nothing about cars. Which was why I was shocked to see him casually lead me over to a shiny, black, vintage Alfa Romeo 6C 2500.

He opened the passenger-side door and let me in.

As I slid down onto the buttery soft leather seats, I noticed the key was already in the ignition.

When Matteo got in behind the steering wheel, I asked, "You just keep the keys in a six-hundred-thousand-euro Alfa Romeo?"

Was this what it was like having insane amounts of family money?

I meant, my father definitely had some wealth, not that he shared much of it with his daughters, but I had grown up around what most would consider comfortable luxury.

That being said, I didn't grow up around anyone treating a mint condition, vintage Alfa Romeo as if it were a crappy Fiat

Argenta with the keys just casually dangling from the ignition for anyone to steal.

He glanced over at me. "You like cars?"

I shrugged one shoulder. "More like I know cars."

"Did you want to drive?"

My eyes widened at even the thought of getting behind the wheel of such an expensive antique car. I shook my head. "No way!"

He laughed as he started the ignition. "Maybe on the way home after a few *Amarena Spritzes* for courage."

My head twisted sharply. How did he know that was my favorite drink? Father didn't really approve of women drinking, so it wasn't often that I could indulge.

I asked Matteo as much.

His mouth lifted at one corner. "You'd be surprised how much I know about you, Antonella."

For the rest of the ride into Cavalieri, I remained silent. Staring out at the valley below as we descended from the winery to the base of the mountain. The whole time trying to decide if what he had just said was meant to comfort or threaten me.

After slowing down to navigate the narrow cobblestone streets of the ancient medieval city, another testament to the wealth and power of the Cavalieri legacy, he pulled into a reserved space just off the piazza.

When he opened my car door, he held his hand out palm up to help me alight. The warmth of his fingers wrapping around my own sent a spark of uneasy awareness straight to the pit of my stomach.

Matteo gestured with his head. "That is the headquarters for our other family business, Cavalieri Enterprises. And over there is Enzo's place, where I've been staying while I help at the office."

"I thought you worked the horse farm with your father?"

"Raising champion horses in the Dolomites is more my

father's thing. Although I love it up there. It's absolutely beauti-ful, especially in winter."

He placed a hand on my lower back and led me through the bustling piazza. As we navigated past various stalls and vendors, he continued. "I prefer the property development side of our family interests. I work closely with Milana, Cesare's fiancée, who you'll meet soon."

It was impossible to miss all the turning heads as we made our way to a small cafe with heated outdoor seating on the other side of the piazza.

Although I rarely liked being the center of attention, that was my sister's job, it was hard not to feel a feminine thrill at being on the arm of Matteo Cavalieri.

It was like I was walking the halls of school as the girlfriend of the best midfielder at the local football club.

He pulled out one of the wicker chairs for me before taking a seat across the small, round table. A server in a long white apron came rushing over.

Without even asking me or looking at a menu, Matteo ordered an *Amarena Spritz* for me and an *Americano Perfecto* for himself. He then ordered some roasted olives, a small plate of pesto and tomato crostinis, a platter of *spiedini di mare* with shrimp and calamari, a *frico,* and some eggplant *polpettine.*

As the waiter scurried away to fill our order, Matteo propped his elbow on the back of his chair and leaned back. "Just a little *apertivo,* since we'll be having dinner with the family later."

As we waited for our drinks, I rubbed my upper arms. Despite the warm glow from the heaters, I had a chill. Abruzzo was much colder than Sicily.

Matteo leapt from his chair as he pulled off the wool blazer he had tossed over his T-shirt. "I'm an ass. I can't believe I didn't snag you a proper coat from Aunt Gabbie's closet."

My eyes closed briefly as the warm, cologne-scented fabric

settled onto my shoulders. "It's fine. I'm used to it, really. Antonia doesn't"—I held my hands up to do air quotes—"believe in coats. That's why there wasn't one in her suitcase. She thinks they ruin her outfits. So whenever we go out, she won't let me wear one either."

He frowned down at me, then lifted his head. "Wait right here."

Before I could object, he had left the small, enclosed area of the cafe.

When the waiter returned with our drinks, he raised an eyebrow at Matteo's empty seat.

"He'll be right back."

The waiter didn't look like he believed me. "Uh huh."

Feeling peevish, I reached for the garnish pick in my drink and scraped my teeth along the wood to eat the three brandied cherries.

Usually I saved them for last, but I figured I'd earned a small treat. I then used the garnish pick to stir the ice cubes, mixing the teaspoon of dark ruby cherry syrup and balsamic vinegar that had sunk to the bottom with the *Punt e Mes* and *Carpano Bianco* vermouths with the bubbly prosecco.

I took a sip, needing the fizzy sweet drink with its pungent bite of bitters. As I watched the bubbles from the pilsner beer coat the slice of orange garnish in Matteo's drink, I resisted the urge to look for him over my shoulder.

It was bad enough I could feel all the curious gazes of the other patrons on me. I didn't want to give the impression I was nervous or I had just been ditched.

The waiter returned and with what was definitely a smug look asked, "Perhaps you'd like to be moved to a less *public* table since it does not seem Signore Cavalieri is returning."

I raised my chin. "This table suits me just fine."

After a pause, the waiter nodded.

He then raised his hands and clapped. Several more waiters streamed out of the restaurant. They weaved through the other cafe tables carrying trays like a demented parade of ants. One by one they dropped various plates, bowls, and platters, covering the table's already small surface.

Clearing his throat, my new enemy, the waiter, announced each dish with a flourish of his hand. Pointing to the slightly greasy paper cone which had small fried breadcrumb balls spilling out of it onto a rectangular platter, he said, "Here we have your *polpettine de melanzane*."

He then pointed to a small, still sizzling cast-iron pan. "And this, of course, is the *frico* made with Montasio cows' milk cheese. Please stop me if you don't understand anything I'm saying, I know in Sicily you people choose to use different words from us Italians."

I swallowed as I focused on the edge of the table, knowing my accent had given me away. It was no secret that mainland Italians viewed Sicilians with a certain amount of disdain. As popular as it was, that stupid American movie *The Godfather* painted all Italians as corrupt mobsters, and the mainland blamed the Sicilians.

Since my father was a corrupt mobster, there wasn't much I could say to defend myself.

"Thank you, no. I understand everything. You don't need to point each item out," I whispered as my cheeks burned.

The waiter smiled. "Perhaps that is not how they do it in Sicily, but here in Abruzzo, there is a proper way of doing things." He then pointed to the grilled skewer of shrimp and calamari. "Here, of course, is your *spiedini di mare* using *Amalfi* lemons."

Another tiny dig at one of Sicilians' proudest exports, our lemons.

"Then, of course, we have the roasted olives and the pesto

crostini. The pesto is made the proper Italian way with pine nuts, not with almonds, as I believe you Sicilians prefer."

Once again "Sicilian" was said as if he were spitting out something bitter.

"Then take it back," came Matteo's dark, commanding voice from behind both of us.

I turned in my seat to see him only a few steps away carrying an emerald-green paper bag.

The waiter shook his head. "I'm sorry. What did you say, Signore Cavalieri?"

Matteo stood behind me as he pulled an Elide Vivianna coat with wool camel sleeves and a brown-and-gray houndstooth pattern from the bag. "Stand up, babygirl."

With my head lowered so I wouldn't meet the gaze of the waiter, I pushed my chair back and stood.

Matteo took his blazer from my shoulders and held up the coat for me to slip my arms into . The moment it was on, he pulled me back against his chest and wrapped his arm across my shoulders from behind.

His breath moved wisps of my hair as he addressed the waiter again. "I said to take it back and make it with almonds."

"But, signore, we simply do not…"

"Do I need to call Chef Giuseppe and tell him that a waiter is refusing my simple request?"

Through the covering cascade of my hair, I observed the arrogant waiter's reaction.

His mouth puckered, then thinned, before he bowed his head. "Of course not." He reached for the platter of crostini. "I will let Chef know you would prefer your pesto with almonds. The Sicilian way."

With his arm still tight around my front, Matteo kissed the top of my head, which barely reached above his shoulder, before nodding toward the table. "And make me a fresh drink while you're at it."

"Of course."

After the waiter left, Matteo turned me around to face him. He pulled on the lapels of the coat to button them. "Not bad. A little big, but since you'll probably fill out these cute curves after a few months of Rosa's cooking, I'm sure it will be fine. We'll get you something more appropriate when we're in Rome."

He then pulled the white price tag attached to the collar off and pushed it into the front pocket.

All while my anxious gaze looked past his upper arm to the surrounding patrons, who were now openly staring at us.

Stepping back, I crossed my arm over my middle. "It's fine. You didn't need to get me a coat."

Matteo ran his knuckle over my cheek. "Yes, I did. It's my responsibility to take care of you."

A warmth that had nothing to do with my new coat spread from my belly. Not since my mother had anyone given a damn about taking care of me. It was always me sacrificing to take care of others.

He kissed me on the forehead. "Let's eat."

Oblivious to the collective gasp that just radiated over the patrons like a wave, Matteo took his seat and reached over for my plate.

"I'll just take a few roasted olives and a crostini, please."

Completely ignoring me, he piled two shrimp skewers, a wedge of the potato cheese pancake, several fried eggplant balls, and two of the re-made crostini. Topping the whole pile off with a few roasted olives.

The moment he placed it before me, I gingerly picked up the skewers and started to return them to the platter.

"Don't you dare," he warned.

"I'm not hungry."

My stomach took that moment to growl.

Matteo raised a single eyebrow at me.

With thinned lips, I matched his expression, arching my brow. "Fine. I *might* be a little hungry, but it isn't ladylike to scarf down a full trough of food in front of people."

Too many years of my father's taunting had made me practically incapable of eating in front of people. Not that I didn't eat or like food.

As we were sitting on the edge of the cafe's patio facing the piazza, Matteo dragged his chair around from across the table to beside me, directly to my left. His broad shoulders and back now effectively blocked the view of all the patrons. "There. No one's looking. Eat."

I picked up a skewer and pulled a grilled shrimp off the end with my finger and thumb as he picked up his own skewer and sank his teeth into a tender piece of calamari, ripping it off the wood stick.

Catching my gaze, he smiled and winked at me as he chewed.

The sweet yet salty bite of shrimp with its hint of citrus cutting the earthy taste of the olive oil it was grilled in practically melted in my mouth. A groan escaped my lips before I had a chance to stop it.

Matteo leaned in close. "Fuck, you're sexy as hell when you eat."

My eyes widened as I swallowed my bite and then exclaimed, "You, sir, are a bald-faced liar."

His gaze focused on my mouth.

He then reached up and brushed his thumb over my lower lip. "If I hadn't promised not to fuck that beautifully tight pussy of yours the other night, I would have drizzled your breasts with honey, spread your knees, and pounded my cock into you while I suckled your honey-coated nipples."

"*Sciatiri e matri,*" I breathed, my shaking hand reaching for my drink. I took a large swallow, choking as a few droplets went down the wrong pipe. "You shouldn't say such things to me. Especially not in public."

His large hand wrapped around the arm of my chair. The legs screeched against the ancient stone floor as he pulled the chair away from the table.

Then he reached for me.

I recoiled as all the heads in the cafe turned to watch us. "What are you doing?"

He grasped my hips and lifted me out of my chair and onto his lap. With the folds of my wool coat shielding his hand from view, he wedged his fingers between my thighs.

Nuzzling my ear, he rasped, "If I didn't know your pussy was too sore from earlier, I'd take you up to my office right now, bend you over my desk, and fuck you all over again."

My head spun from a dizzying blend of humiliation and titillation. The edges of my palms pushed against his chest. "You have to stop. People are staring."

"Let them stare."

"They'll think we're together."

His brow lowered. "We *are* together. You're my fiancée."

"No, we are not. Just because you broke your word and we had… we had…" I lowered my voice to barely a whisper. "*Real* sex changes nothing. I am not your fiancée. My sister is your fiancée."

His finger and thumb clasped my chin as he forced my gaze to his. With narrowed eyes, he ground out, "The fuck it doesn't. *You're mine now, Ella.* I don't give a shit what happens with Dante and your father and the whole rotten lot of them. You *will be* my wife."

CHAPTER 35

MATTEO

*C*learly the only way to silence Ella's objections was to marry her or knock her up.

Preferably both.

The idea of this sweet and talented woman carrying my child made me want to drag her back to my bed and not let her out of it until she was pregnant.

Looking at her now, thinking about a future together, I finally, truly understood the drive to preserve and protect the Cavalieri name.

Finally understood the importance of fostering the next generation and the weight of that responsibility.

Like our grapevines, we grew stronger with each generation.

And each new generation carried the honor of caring for those vines for the next one to come.

I had almost poisoned the vine by marrying her sister.

Someone who would not have respected our family's legacy.

While it may or may not have been the right decision for the present, it could've had terrible ramifications for future generations. Greater families than ours had been destroyed by the actions of one errant father, or one weak-willed son.

Legacies were fragile. It would only take the wrongful actions of one generation to ruin the hard work and dedication of the ten generations before.

In marrying Ella, I was at least still stepping up and saving someone who was vulnerable and needed my protection, while also responsibly securing my family's future.

That was assuming we survived the ticking time bombs that were Dante, Antonius, and her sister, Antonia.

My father would be here tomorrow.

And I already received a text from Sebastian Diamanti that he was coming in as well.

Although not directly involved in our conflict with the Agnellos, the Diamantis had an enormous amount of power and influence which could tip the scales in our favor if things turned ugly and the Agnello syndicate fractured. It was a distinct possibility and one we worried about when I first stupidly agreed to the arranged marriage.

Dante was still a new Don and did not have his entire power base solidified. There was a chance Ella's father could make a play for the throne.

So tomorrow our plan was to basically come up with a new plan on how to deal with Dante, Ella's father, and the fallout from Liliana's godfather's death without starting a full-out mafia war in Sicily.

And that plan definitely would no longer include me marrying Antonia.

Because of their little "parent trap" prank, Ella was now in just as much danger as her sister, this time from her own father, especially if the rumors about her mother were true.

She now needed my protection more than ever.

And I planned to provide it by giving her the protection of the Cavalieri name and fortune.

Even now, I considered Ella my wife in all but name… something I would rectify as soon as I talked with Father Luca.

That even after I compromised her reputation by taking her virginity Ella would still sacrifice her own well-being to help her wretched sister galled me to no end. Those people didn't deserve her unwavering loyalty.

Her hand pushed against my chest. "It's not that simple. There are… *things*… you don't know about."

I moved my hand to clasp the side of her neck. "What things?"

She turned her head away. "Nothing. *Just things.*"

My jaw clenched as I used my grasp to force her head back to face me. "Ella. What. Things?"

"My father's a *capo* in the Sicilian mafia."

The tightness in my chest eased. "You really are adorable"

Did she honestly think I didn't know about her father?

I reached over and selected one of the warm *polpettine*. Holding it close to her lips, I said, "Open your mouth and swallow my ball."

Her slender fingers wrapping around my wrist, she tried to push it away, her head pivoting to look around us. "You did not just say that so loudly!"

It was so much fun making her blush, in and out of the bedroom.

I sank my teeth into the savory ball. After chewing, I winked at her and teased, "You really should try a bite. They are very salty and there is a surprising burst of *creaminess* at the end."

She covered her face and moaned from behind her hands. "*Oh. My. God!*"

Fuck, I loved the sound of her little moans.

Lifting my hand, I held it close to her mouth again. "My ball was probably too big to fit into your mouth. Did you want—"

Her mouth opened like a cute little baby bird as she wrapped her lips around my fingertips, then used her tongue to flick the bite into her mouth. Sucking my fingers as she pulled back, she covered her mouth with her hand as she said, "There. I tried it. Now, for the love of God, please stop talking about your balls!"

I shifted in my seat as the hand around her lower back squeezed her close. That was going to be difficult since my cock was now hard. Fuck. Just the sight of her sucking my fingers, despite the innocent intent, sent a kinky shock wave straight to my shaft.

Taboo sex was fun.

Taboo sex with an innocent, shy beauty I was forcing to accept my dominating desires was next level, mind-blowing, ecstasy.

As my hips moved, her eyes widened. She looked down at her lap where I had placed my hand between her legs, already regretting selecting pants for her to wear.

"Are you?" She leaned in further and whispered, "Are you... *hard?*"

"Woman, are you serious? Of course my cock is—"

She waved her flattened hand in front of my face. "Shhh, keep your voice down."

I wrapped my hand around her neck and pulled her close until the tips of our noses almost touched. "Of course, I'm fucking hard. You just sucked my fingers."

"I took the bite you offered!"

"Same difference."

"You're impossible. Let me up!"

"Not until I watch you eat another ball."

"You can't be serious."

I waited her out.

With a huff, she reached for a *polpettine* and shoved the whole ball into her mouth. Her cheeks hollowed and her full lips puckered as she chewed it. Finally, she swallowed and said, "There. Happy?"

My gaze focused on her mouth as I thought of all the absolutely filthy things I wanted to do to it. "Not right now, but I will be later."

She slid off my lap back onto her chair next to me, then reached for her drink. "This isn't strong enough," she muttered.

I chuckled. "Well, that's all you're getting for now. We have dinner with my family tonight. You'll want to be sober, with your wits about you."

"Why?"

I shrugged as I reached for a cheesy wedge of *frico*, lifting a long, gooey strand of cheese up to my mouth first. "My cousins and uncle will be fine. It's the girls you need to worry about. Don't get me wrong. They're amazing, but they will make you work for it. I don't think Milana and Amara will be there, but Bianca and Aunt Gabbie, who you've already met, will be."

"No, I meant, why are we having dinner with them?"

I rested my forearms on the table as I studied her. "Because they want to meet you formally and because having dinner together is something that families do."

She played with a button on the coat, twirling it around and around. "Do I have to meet them?"

"No, but it will probably get awkward in the hallways and at the breakfast table tomorrow if you don't."

"I just don't see the point in doing a big formal introduction if I'm leaving for Sicily as soon as possible."

I inhaled a deep breath. *Patience*, I reminded myself. "That would be true *if* you were leaving, but you're not."

"Matteo, it's just not possible—"

"What if you're already pregnant?"

She blinked. "What?"

After cupping the back of her head, I pulled her close to whisper into her ear. "I came deep inside your sweet, tight pussy —filling you. It's possible..."

She opened her mouth to respond.

I cut her off. "Before you say something I'll make you regret, know that I will not tolerate even a slim possibility of my child being born a bastard. Until my mother finally told my father about me, I was labeled a bastard and it's not something I would wish on my own son or daughter."

"We simply cannot marry! You're my sister's—"

"Go ahead. Piss me off by saying it again and I'll pull you over my knee and spank your ass right here in the middle of the cafe."

"You wouldn't dare!"

I leveled a stern look at her. "Watch me."

Before she could respond, a distant train whistle sounded.

I stood and reached for my wallet. Pulling out several euro bills, I tossed them into the center of the table. "I need to go meet the train. The part I need to finish repairing the destemmer-crusher is on it."

Leaning over, I kissed the top of her head, then gestured toward the center of the piazza. "There is a string quartet setting up for the evening crowd. Stay here and enjoy the music until I return."

"We haven't finished talking about this, Matteo."

I curved my hand under her chin and lifted her face. "Of course not, babygirl. There are the wedding arrangements to discuss."

She called after my retreating back. "That's not what I meant!"

Ignoring her, I gestured for the manager as I crossed the patio.

"Yes, Signore Cavalieri."

I placed a hand on his shoulder. "Elio, keep that arrogant prick waiter away from my girl. And while you're at it, send over an espresso and something sweet for her to eat."

"Yes, sir. I'm very sorry about the pesto."

I patted his shoulder. "And tell the Chef it wasn't personal. I was just making a point."

"Yes, sir. Right away, sir. And might I say, sir. She's exquisite. You are a lucky man."

Glancing over my shoulder at Ella, I nodded. "That she is, Elio. Inside and out."

* * *

AFTER RETURNING from the train depot and stashing the part Alfonso was waiting for in the car, I returned to the cafe for Ella.

But she wasn't there.

CHAPTER 36

ELLA

*T*here was no freaking way I was staying at the café to be stared at like some zoo animal.

The moment Matteo was out of sight, I left.

Naturally, I gravitated to the musicians setting up. There were four men. By the looks of it, they were not a standard quartet. Instead of two violinists, a violist, and a cellist, they instead had one violinist and a bassist.

They started with a favorite of mine, "Con te partirò." I always teared up from the bittersweet lyrics. I even adored the British version, "Time to Say Goodbye."

With my eyes closed, I swayed to the melody.

It wasn't until the song was finished that I realized I had been air playing along with my bow hand.

The cellist noticed. *"Bella signora,* you play?"

At my nod, he beckoned me closer. Stepping to the side, he gestured to his instrument. "Play for us."

"Oh no, I couldn't."

He then addressed the small crowd which had formed.

"Everyone clap to encourage this beautiful woman to play a song for us."

The crowd enthusiastically clapped.

Since I usually spent several hours a day playing my cello and had barely played a few songs over the last few days, I couldn't resist the opportunity. The one time I wasn't shy around others was when I was holding my cello and playing for them.

Tucking a lock of hair behind my ear, I smiled. "Okay. I'll play."

The man held up both his hands. "Ah, it will be an honor to have my instrument held by such a beautiful woman."

Brushing off his typical Italian male praise, I shrugged out of my coat and sat on the small stool he offered. Spreading my knees, I rested the cello against my left inner thigh as I positioned the fingerboard close to my left ear. "What shall we play, gentlemen?"

"Whatever the lady wishes."

I thought for a moment, knowing they'd want me to choose something that would be popular among the residents and the tourists. So that, of course, meant something Bocelli sang. "How about "Vivo per lei?"

The man clapped again. "Perfetto!"

Since Bocelli's version was a tribute to his love of music, I knew the musicians would like my choice as well.

The cellist took a position in front of the group to act as a conductor. After counting us in, we all played.

When we reached the bridge and shifted the string arrangement to modulate to a different key, building tension to the first of the dramatic emotive moments, the man circled the crowd with a red plastic bucket. The audience tossed bills and spare coins inside.

At the end of the song, I rose and prepared to hand the cello back to its owner.

He folded his hands in front of him as if in prayer. "No. No. No, signora. One more song. I beg you."

Seeing the large crowd forming and knowing he enjoyed the attention a female cellist was drawing, I conceded. "You choose this time."

He raised his arms with a flourish and announced to the crowd. "'Io che non vivo!'"

It was a superb choice. The tourists would soon realize it was the Italian version of Elvis's "You Don't Have to Say You Love Me."

Usually, the lyrics were just the lyrics, and I was more concerned with the music, but it hit hard as the man sang along. The plaintive loneliness of the words as the person in the song begged their lover not to leave them caused a lump in the back of my throat.

At the final strains of the music, I opened my eyes to see Matteo watching me intently. His dark gaze seemed to miss nothing.

With a watery smile, I rose and bowed my head to the cellist as I handed him back his cello. "Thank you."

The man gestured to me. "A round of applause for our pretty cellist."

The crowd erupted into applause just as Matteo approached with a singular purpose.

Without saying a word, he wrapped his arm around my waist and swung me in an arc, just as the quartet began to play "Dance Me to the End of Love."

Held close to his warm body, I clung to his upper arm as my other hand was enveloped in his firm grasp. "No one else is dancing."

His voice had a fierce edge to it. "I don't care. The music could stop, and I'd still dance with you."

As he effortlessly moved me around the small piazza, other

couples joined in. "You looked magnificent up there. I could watch and listen to you play for hours and never tire of it."

He was so strong it was as if I were dancing on my tiptoes, nothing more than a leaf flitting on the breeze. "You say that now. But say that again after I've been practicing scales for three hours straight."

"As long as you do that thing with your tongue while you're playing, I couldn't care less if all you did was play 'Chopsticks' over and over again."

My brow furrowed. "What thing with my tongue?"

He winked. "When you play, you close your eyes as you sway with the movement of your bow. While you're doing that, your lips open ever so slightly, and the cute tip of your tongue runs along the upper edge of your teeth."

"I don't do—" Wait, I did do that. Usually I was aware of it and could stop it. I must have been too caught up in the music, but how did Matteo notice something so inconsequential?

As if reading my thoughts, he said, "I notice everything about you, baby. Your face is my favorite work of art."

What nonsense. Right? I meant, it was silly. And meaningless to say such things.

Yet, it *was* awfully nice to hear them. And to think... maybe...

Matteo leaned down and softly sang the wedding lyric in my ear as he tightened his arm around my waist.

At that moment, I let myself believe in the fairy tale.

Maybe, just maybe... was it possible?

Could the tiny spark between us be sheltered through the coming storm?

Could it survive the raging winds which were sure to come from Sicily the moment my father learned of my sister's and my subterfuge?

If any man was strong enough to hold me through the rain, it would be Matteo Cavalieri.

Tilting my head back, I stared up at him, losing myself in the comforting darkness of his gaze.

And that was when I saw him...

His long sallow face and his small beady eyes fixed on me.

Fino Buratti had followed me to Abruzzo.

At the sight of him, I stumbled.

Matteo lifted me off my feet to press my body harder against his body. "Are you all right?"

"I'm... I'm fine," I stammered as I tried not to stare at Fino, worried Matteo would follow my gaze and ask if I knew him. Or worse, recognize him from Carnevale in Palermo.

"You're tired. Let me get you home."

As Matteo turned to retrieve my coat, Fino came toward me as the crowd surged forward to request more songs. As his shoulder connected with mine, he pressed a folded piece of white paper into my hand.

Matteo stormed back, calling after Fino's retreating form as he placed the coat over my shoulders. "Who was that man? Did he hurt you?"

I slipped my arms into the coat sleeves before sliding my hand into the pocket to conceal the note. "No. I don't know him. I'm sure he meant nothing by it."

Matteo's eyes narrowed as he squared off in front of me. "Then why did he pass something along to you?"

The blood in my veins froze. Not knowing what the note said, I at least knew it would be disastrous for Matteo to read it. "He passed nothing on to me."

"I saw a piece of white paper in your hand, Ella. Don't lie to me."

The crowd cheered and danced as the musicians played a rousing rendition of "Tu vou fa l'Americano."

Matteo grabbed my upper arm and dragged me across the

piazza back to the car. "I want an answer, Ella. Show me the note."

My fingers closed around a piece of white cardstock inside my pocket. I pulled it free and handed it to him. "Here. This is what you saw."

He stared down at the coat's price tag.

I shrugged. "It was in my pants pocket. I pulled it out intending to toss it."

His jaw shifted to the side as he focused his gaze on me.

I crossed an arm over my middle. "You can apologize any time now for being an overbearing boor."

Giving me no warning, he pinned me against the side of the car. With his forearm on one side of my head and his hand at my throat, he leaned in. "It will be a cold day in hell when I apologize for being *overprotective* of you. You're marrying a jealous man, *colomba mia*. Get used to it."

His mouth claimed mine.

There was no stopping his tongue as it swept past my lips to taste and plunder. The insistent press of his hips pushed his hard cock against my stomach as I rose on my toes to try to escape the onslaught, to no avail.

He only deepened the kiss. Crushing my lips against my teeth as he tightened his fingers around my throat, holding me still and under his command.

When he finally lifted his head, I was breathless and dizzy, but it did not stop me from shooting daggers at him with my gaze.

Matteo chuckled as he cupped my cheek. "Save your poison looks for someone else, babygirl. And before you try to object one more time to us marrying, I'll remind you I'd have no qualms about bending you over the hood of this car, flipping up your coat, and fucking you right here in the street."

The air I was sucking in became a gasp. "You wouldn't—"

"Dare? Trust me, I would." With both palms rested against the top of the car, he once more leaned over me. "And there isn't a damn person in this entire village who would stop me. You know why?"

I slowly shook my head as I stared back at him, mesmerized by the fierce threat of his words.

"Because I'm a goddamn Cavalieri. And that's why my name is going to protect you from your father's retribution and why"— he kissed my forehead—"you're marrying me whether or not you like it."

Keeping his gaze trained on me, he reached over and swung open the passenger-side car door. "Get in."

I hesitated for just the barest of seconds.

Matteo reached for his belt buckle.

With a cry, I dipped my head and dove inside the car.

Heat radiated off my cheeks at his amused chuckle which carried into the car's interior as he circled around and got in behind the wheel.

I crossed my arms over my middle. "I hate you."

"Keeping telling yourself that, babygirl, and I'll keep enjoying proving you wrong."

As we drove back to the winery, I watched him out of the corner of my eye as I slipped my hand back into my coat pocket and touched the traitorous note from Fino.

CHAPTER 37

ELLA

*M*y back pressed against the closed bedroom door. After waiting a moment to reassure myself that Matteo had not followed me, I unfolded the note.

MEET ME AT 8PM.
 By the gate off the library veranda.
 Do <u>not</u> disobey me.
 -Fino

I CRUMPLED the note and tossed it on the floor. Then, stumbling over the side table that I forgot was there, I raced across the room to find my phone. I had left it behind because I didn't want to risk Antonia calling while I was with Matteo. I did not know we'd be gone for so long, though.

My poor sister had probably been trying to reach me this whole time in a panic.

It wasn't there.

For half a second, I feared Matteo had taken it.

Then I realized none of my stuff was here. Or technically none of my sister's stuff, but especially not my cello.

I spun in a circle, taking in the entire bedroom.

All my belongings were gone.

Forcing myself to think, I tried to reason where my belongings would be. I dove for the closet doors and swung them open. Empty.

Just for good measure, I fell to my knees and checked under the bed for the suitcase. Nothing.

Peeking into the bathroom, I could see even my few toiletries were packed up.

Where on earth?

Then it came to me.

Matteo's suite.

My hand covered my mouth as I stopped myself from screaming in panic and humiliation.

Someone had seen the crumpled, sex-stained sheets.

Someone knew what Matteo and I had been doing in his room earlier.

Sciatiri e matri!

What must they think of the broken bathroom door?

And then anger took over, my lips thinning as my fingers curled into fists. *That arrogant, domineering man!*

Throwing open my bedroom door, I marched down the hall to the rooms assigned to Matteo.

Sure enough, neatly stacked on a small bench next to the fire was the suitcase, my cello, my borrowed clothes, and purse.

Slinging my purse over my shoulder, I hefted the suitcase to the floor and tossed the clothes over my other arm, before grabbing my suitcase handle and picking up my cello case. I then stumbled and struggled with my off-balance load all the way back to my own assigned bedroom. After dropping everything in the center of the room, I locked the door.

I then turned over my purse, dumping the contents on the bed, and reached for my mobile.

There were no missed calls.

It had been over four hours since my last call. She had to have received my voicemail.

Dialing Antonia, I got her voicemail again. "Toni, this is serious. You need to call me back."

I leaned against the door again with a huff.

And started when the frame rattled from a pounding knock. "Ella? Open the door."

One broken door was bad enough, but two would have the entire villa talking about us.

I twisted the lock and opened the door just a sliver. "What do you want?"

Matteo placed his palm on the center panel and pushed the door all the way open. "What are you doing in here?"

I raised an eyebrow. "You're going to have to be more specific. Do you mean in Abruzzo? Because my sister's thug ex-boyfriend helped her to drug me and send me here in her place. Or do you mean here at the winery? Because my sister's thug fiancé is refusing to let me leave. Or do you mean in this room?"

The corner of his mouth lifted as he leaned a shoulder against the doorjamb and crossed his arms over his chest. "You're like a wet dove with ruffled feathers when you're angry. All big dark eyes and cute little coos."

"Don't try to distract me with more of your sweet talk. You had no business moving my stuff."

He tilted his head to the side. "And what stuff would that be? You're going to have to be more specific. Is it the suitcase filled with your sister's trashy wardrobe? Or the borrowed clothes from my aunt? Or the—"

I pursed my lips to keep from smiling. "You've made your point."

"You're not staying in here. You're staying with me for tonight, then I'm moving us to the house off the piazza."

I backed up a step as I caught sight of the crumpled white note on the floor only a few paces away. "I can't move into a house with you alone. That would be completely inappropriate. We're not married." I shifted to block Matteo's view of the bedroom floor and the note.

But the second I said it I regretted it.

Matteo threw his head back and laughed. "Finally. We are in agreement. The answer is yes, my darling babygirl. I *will* marry you."

I stamped my foot. "That was neither an agreement nor a proposal."

He placed his hand over his heart. "A man can hope."

"I thought you were going to leave me alone to rest before dinner."

"I am. I need to go help Alfonso with this part. I just wanted to make sure you knew which bedroom to go to."

"I did. *This* one."

He smiled. "Have it your way, little one. I'll be back to escort you into dinner at six."

I closed the door and leaned against it.

My gaze lighted on the crumpled note, as if it were Poe's tell-tale heart furiously beating underneath the floorboards to rat me out.

What the hell am I going to do?

CHAPTER 38

MATTEO

*I*n a completely uncharacteristic manner, I was nervous about this evening.

I gave my dark gray wool blazer a final sweep down both arms with the lint brush and then spritzed some cologne on. After checking one more time that I had removed all the machine grease from my hands, I left my suite of rooms.

There was no reason to be nervous of course. This was my family.

Yet, I wanted them to not just like Ella but to fall in love with her.

I wanted my girl to feel as though she was welcome and belonged. Although I would have hoped for the same had I been forced to go through with the arranged marriage to her sister, this was on a different level.

At no point had I imagined the possibility of a truly happy marriage with Antonia.

I had envisioned eventually purchasing her a flat in Rome where we would live polite, but separate lives. After she had given me an heir of course. In fact, the only enjoyable prospect of the whole arrangement was the twisted, kinky sex I assumed we would have in my pursuit of a child.

Tucking my finger in the tight collar of my shirt, I loosened my tie as the uncomfortable knowledge of how I treated Ella those first few encounters sat like a lead ball in my stomach.

I will forever carry the stain of my rough behavior toward her.

I *knew* there was something off but didn't look into it further, as I should have.

While it was true the gods smiled on me by giving Ella a deliciously dark appetite in the bedroom equal to mine, it didn't excuse me from guilt.

She should have been introduced to my more demanding desires slowly, in a safe space.

Not all at once, bent over my fucking bed as I whipped her with a riding crop while I shoved my cock down her throat. *Jesus Christ.* I was lucky she didn't run screaming to her father and Dante that very night when she had ample opportunity to do so.

That she could have told me she was Ella and not Antonia and stopped the whole thing was not her fault.

Clearly, my poor girl was placed in an impossible situation by her manipulative sister.

With two knuckles, I knocked on Ella's *temporary* bedroom door.

Fortunately, that was all behind us.

I would introduce her to my family tonight as my true bride. They would fall in love with her sweet, engaging personality and the rest of the obstacles to our marriage be damned.

Now that she was mine, I wasn't letting her go.

After a long pause, the door opened a sliver.

Ella's cute face was barely visible in the dark room.

She held her fisted hand to her lips and coughed. "I'm sorry, Matteo. I'm not feeling so well. I'm going to have to miss dinner."

God, she was cute.

And a terrible liar.

Again I internally chastised myself for not seeing all the flapping red flags around her subterfuge earlier.

I frowned. "That is a shame. You do look very pale."

She lowered her eyes and entertained me with another delicate cough. "Yes, I'm very pale and tired. I should just rest quietly, completely undisturbed for the rest of the evening. I guess I'll see you tomorrow morning."

As the door closed, I placed my palm against it, pushed it open, and stepped inside the dim interior. "What kind of fiancé would I be if I just left you alone in this vulnerable state?"

She clutched the collar of the white robe we kept in the bathroom for guests tightly around her throat as she backed up several steps. "I'm sure I will be fine after a night of undisturbed sleep."

I nodded sagely as I stalked after her. Matching her step for step.

My head tilted to the side. "You know, as I look closer you seem less and less pale. In fact, there seems to be an almost feverish blush to your cheeks."

Her hands went to her hot cheeks. "Yes! I must have a fever. You should go. I wouldn't want you to catch what I have."

The backs of her thighs hit the edge of the bed.

My hand rested over my heart. "Don't be silly, darling. You are to be my wife. My life partner. What's mine is yours and vice versa. That is true in all things. I would never abandon you in your hour of need because I was afraid of catching your illness. I can think of no greater honor than to share the same germs as—"

She waved her hand in front of her face as she let out a harsh sigh. "Oh, stuff it. You know perfectly well I'm not sick."

I swept her into my arms and settled her on my lap as I sat on

ZOE BLAKE

the edge of the bed. "So what's going on in that adorably chaotic brain of yours."

She averted her face. "I don't want to meet your family."

"I can understand that."

Her gaze swung back to meet mine. "You can?"

"Of course, they're terrifying."

She huffed again. "You're not helping."

"You have nothing to worry about. I'll be by your side the entire time."

"That's part of the problem! You're going to tell them my real name and then claim we're getting married."

"We are getting married."

"No. We're not."

"Agree to disagree."

She threw her arms up as she tried to slide off my lap. "You can't agree to disagree over something like marriage."

I tightened my grasp on her waist. "Watch me."

"You're impossible."

"And yet you still love me."

Her spine stiffened as she sucked in a gasp of air and held it. After a long, tense pause, she licked her lips and said, "Who said anything about love?"

After caressing her cheek and pulling a lock of hair behind her ear so I could better study her face, I replied, "I just did."

Her fingers twisted into the robe's belt. "You barely know me. We barely know each other. It's ridiculous to even joke about being in love."

With my hand on her chin, I turned her face toward me. "Who said I was joking?"

Her brow furrowed. "You're lying. You're only saying these things to get me down to dinner."

She'd soon find out just how mistaken she was if she didn't

322

start moving. "We both know I don't need to lie to get you down to dinner. I'm way bigger and stronger than you. All I'd have to do is toss you over my shoulder and carry you into the dining room."

She gasped as she clutched at the collar of her robe. "In my robe? You wouldn't dare."

The corner of my mouth lifted. "Are you sure about that?"

"Have I mentioned how impossible you are?"

"Once or twice."

"You don't love me."

My gaze roamed over her beautiful face. "Don't tell me what I can and cannot be. Whether or not you like it, I am in love with you." I leaned forward as I wrapped my hand around the side of her neck and pulled her closer. "And... whether you like it or not... you're in love with me."

Her breath teased my lips as she whispered, "Don't tell me what I am."

She really was magnificent.

My mouth captured hers as my tongue swept inside, unable to resist tasting her another moment longer.

She let out the smallest of moans as her palms pressed against my chest.

When I finally relented, we were both breathless. Her lips were the color of dark, crushed berries which only complimented the bright blush high on her cheeks.

Running my mouth along her jaw, I nipped at her earlobe. "You have five minutes to get ready or I'm ripping this robe off you, fucking you senseless, and then carrying you buck naked down to dinner to meet my family with my come still drying on your thighs."

"Oh. My. God!"

She stumbled off my lap and raced toward the pile of Aunt Gabbie's clothes draped over the back of the nearby sofa. After grabbing a dress, she stormed over to the bathroom and called out before slamming the door, "You're impossible."

* * *

TEN MINUTES later we crossed the threshold into the parlor where most of my family were already gathered.

Ella hesitated and swayed backward.

I wrapped my arm tightly around her lower back. "I'm right here, baby."

Then addressing my family, I said, "Everyone, I'd liked you to meet *Antonella*, my bride."

Since I had already apprised Aunt Gabbie, who had arrived earlier from her villa on the Amalfi Coast, of the situation, I knew the rest of the family would be aware as well.

Amara and a heavily pregnant Milana rushed forward to hug Ella. "Welcome to the family!"

Bianca soon followed. "We heard you playing your cello the other night. You are amazing. I hope you'll play for us later."

As they did so, Cesare shook my hand. "Congrats, cousin."

Enzo patted me on the shoulder and said with a wink, "Glad you came to your senses."

Uncle Barone pulled me in for a bear hug. "Marriage is going to suit you just fine."

Cesare smirked. "Yeah, it's a shame you won't be joining us in blissful matrimony any time soon, Papa."

Amara gave him a playful punch on the shoulder. "Don't you start, or I'll never hear the end of it."

Uncle Barone lifted her off her feet and swung her around as she laughed. "Good. You should be ashamed of yourself, forcing me to live in sin like this."

After he set her down, he pointed a finger at Cesare. "Although, low blow."

Cesare wrapped his arm around Milana's shoulders from behind. "You deserve it for not watching over this one more closely while I was gone."

Milana leaned her head back onto his shoulder. "I had project proposals to complete, and Bianca was waiting on my approval of the marketing campaign graphics for the San Benedetto del Tronto development."

Bianca chimed in. "Oh no, you don't. Don't drag me into this. I saw what Cesare did to Matteo's office."

I frowned as I turned to Cesare. "What the hell did you do to my office?"

Cesare shrugged. "I *Milana-proofed* it."

Amara threw her head back as she laughed wholeheartedly. "He took the door off."

"What the fuck, Cesare!"

Cesare pointed to Uncle Barone. "Don't blame me! Talk to your unobservant uncle over there. Two weeks. Two full weeks she was sneaking into your office right under his nose."

Before Uncle Barone could defend himself, Aunt Gabbie swept into the parlor holding a pitcher of *prampolini* with Alfonso following closely behind carrying a large silver tray with empty glasses, sliced oranges, and a crystal ice bucket.

She pointed to Enzo. "Darling, clear off that table so Alfonso can put the tray down." Then she pointed to Cesare. "Go back into the kitchen and tell Rosa I forgot the *Cedrata* soda." Then she nodded to Uncle Barone. "Come take this pitcher from me and pour. If I do it, I'll just make a mess of things."

As the men all hopped to obey her commands and the women approached to help fix the red wine and vermouth *apertivi*, I took advantage of the moment of distraction to look down at Ella.

During the familial onslaught, she had pressed closer to my side with her arm wrapped around my middle and her head tucked against my shoulder. Her eyes were wide as she silently took in the chaos.

I leaned over and kissed her temple. "Don't worry, *colomba mia*. You'll get used to them in time."

She gazed up at me with trusting eyes.

As she did so I stroked her hair, then cupped the back of her head. "Until then, just stay close to me."

Ella nuzzled her head against my chest, as Aunt Gabbie approached us both, a drink in each hand. "Of course she looks beautiful, Alfonso. She's wearing one of my dresses. *Auguri ai novelli fidanzati!*"

"*Grazie,*" I responded to her congratulations as I accepted the drink.

Surrounded by my amazing family, with the woman I loved tucked under my arm.

There was nothing I wanted more than to savor this incredible evening with us all together.

At least for now… everything was perfect in the world.

CHAPTER 39

ELLA

here was nothing I wanted more than for this evening to be over.

Everyone was just so warm and friendly. Even with all the teasing, it was obvious they all loved one another and were comfortable in each other's company.

It was *really* weird. Almost unnatural.

While the others chatted animatedly, Alfonso approached us. Remembering the embarrassing circumstances of my arrival in Cavalieri, I sidled closer to Matteo as I shifted slightly behind his protective body.

Alfonso smiled as his gaze moved over my attire. Not in that creepy way my father's friends would look at me, always stopping at my chest for longer than was polite, but more in a polite, appreciative way.

As I slipped my hand into his outstretched one, he bowed and kissed the back. "May I offer my congratulations, signorina. And may I say, you look beautiful tonight."

Matteo's arm tightened across my back. "Don't go trying to compete for my girl, old man," he teased.

Alfonso winked at me before placing a hand on Matteo's shoulder and shaking his head. "As if there would be a competition."

Matteo nodded. "Exactly. Wait..."

I covered my mouth as I laughed.

Matteo moved his hand to pinch my ass. "Don't you encourage him."

"Afraid I'll choose a better option?"

He leaned in close. "Yes. That's why I'm not giving you a choice." He then gave me a hard kiss on the mouth.

The whole room burst into a round of cheers, applause, and shouts.

Completely embarrassed, I buried my face against Matteo's chest.

I was saved by a matronly woman announcing dinner. I later learned her name was Rosa, their beloved housekeeper, but everyone treated her like the de facto *nonna* of the family. Just like they treated Alfonso, their general operations manager and head mechanic, like family.

As Matteo led me into the sprawling dining room, I shook my head.

Everything about this was weird.

My offer to help was ignored as each family member filed into the kitchen and returned holding a platter.

For the antipasti course alone, there was asparagus with a Parmesan butter sauce and *caponata di melanzane*. The roasted eggplant was garnished with farm-fresh boiled eggs. Then came a brightly decorated porcelain bowl piled high with *acciughe fritte*. The lightly tempura-battered anchovies were served with a garlic aioli on the side. There was even a wooden board with *pesche grigliate con Burrata e prosciutto*.

And this was just the appetizers.

I glanced at the antique grandfather clock tucked into the far corner of the dining room.

It was already past six thirty p.m.

Fino would be waiting for me on the veranda off the library in an hour and a half.

As his cousins circled the table pouring glasses of *Cavalieri Montepulciano*, Matteo lifted my plate and asked what I wanted to eat.

Knowing he wouldn't take no for an answer, I pointed to the *Burrata*. "I'll take a half of a peach and some *Burrata* but no *prosciutto*, please."

After selecting the prettiest peach half on the platter, he spooned some creamy *Burrata* next to it. He then forked several spears of asparagus on my plate. With a wink, he said, "Rosa would have my head if you didn't have at least a little of the asparagus. She's very proud of her butter sauce."

I gave him a slight smile.

After his Uncle Barone led everyone in grace, they all started talking at once over each other.

Alfonso, Enzo, and Matteo talked about the status of clearing the brush and overgrowth from the vineyard fields. Apparently they were concerned about the pace of the project and resolved to start a controlled burn of the dried brush as soon as possible.

Bianca and Amara chatted about new artwork for a set of special edition wine labels.

While Gabriella and Milana talked about the latest fashions and what she'd be able to wear once the baby was born.

Rosa and Cesare debated the old Italian wives' tale that a baby would be born with birthmarks if the mother didn't indulge in her pregnancy cravings.

Since everyone was distracted, I decided to take the opportunity to sneak my full plate into the kitchen, as I had been trained to do at dinner parties since I was a teenager.

As I grasped the plate edge and prepared to rise, Matteo's

hand reached out and covered my wrist, halting me. His head was still turned away from me in conversation, so the movement startled me. He then twisted his head and whispered in my ear. "This is not your father's house, babygirl. Eat and enjoy." He winked and returned to his conversation about the danger of brush fires, while keeping his hand wrapped around my wrist.

When I hesitated, he said, "Seriously. Rosa will notice and have my head if you don't try her roasted peaches."

My gaze rose to the formidable-looking Rosa.

Not wanting to anger her, I picked up my fork and sliced the edge through the soft, delicate peach flesh. Sweeping the bite through the creamy *Burrata,* I had to stifle a groan of appreciation as the smoky-sweet peach juice combined with the rich, salty creaminess of the cheese and melted on my tongue.

The plates were soon cleared.

More wine was poured.

And a cheer went up around the table as Cesare proudly held aloft a platter displaying a perfectly formed *pasticcio di maccheroni* for the *primi* course. Rosa followed with a large carving knife, beaming with pride.

As thick slices of the baked pasta pie were cut and dished out to the passing plates, I once more glanced at the clock.

Seven fifteen p.m.

Less than an hour until I was supposed to meet with Fino.

My gaze caught Rosa staring intently at me as I rolled a piece of macaroni back and forth across my plate with the tines of my fork without eating. Feeling the weight of her stare, I pierced the soft pasta and swept it through the chicken giblet ragu before forcing it into my mouth.

All eyes at the table turned to me.

"What do you think?" asked Amara. "It's one of Rosa's specialties. I helped her this time." Her eyes shone with pride.

The food stuck in the back of my throat as I tried to swallow it while being the subject of the entire table's regard. Snatching my glass of wine, I took a large sip before nodding. "It's delicious."

The massive platter was cleared, and all the men rose to go into the kitchen. Just like before, they returned in an impressive line holding platters aloft like we were in the middle of a medieval feast. All that was missing was the roasted peacock and the brass horns playing.

Once again, the table was weighed down with dish after delicious dish. For the *secondi*, there was an impressive *branzino al sale* nestled on a bed of sea salt and sliced lemons taking pride of place in the center. Then several roasted chickens with garlic and cannellini beans and a large, still steaming pot of *polpette al forgo con mozzerella*.

Cesare, who was sitting to my right, offered me a spoonful of the *polpette* with a generous helping of gooey, baked mozzarella on top. "Do you like meatballs, Antonella?"

Choking, I lifted my napkin to cover my mouth.

Matteo patted my back as I coughed. "Why thank you, cousin. She loves meat*balls*."

My gaze narrowed at him in warning.

Completely unfazed, he pierced a meatball with his fork and raised it to his mouth. Keeping his gaze locked on mine, he sank his sharp, white teeth into the savory flesh before slowly chewing the bite as he winked at me.

Once again, the table burst with spirited chatter. Food, work, wine, babies, the village, the weather. It didn't matter. They listened, laughed, and spoke with enthusiasm to each other.

And all I wanted to do was scream.

My heart sank as I looked over at the clock.

Seven forty-five p.m.

I watched as the second hand clicked around the dial, like a ticking time bomb.

So intently was I staring at the clock that Barone's question took me by surprise. "So, Antonella, tell us about yourself."

The table fell silent as everyone turned to stare at me. For once, the whole room was silent.

My chest hurt as my lungs squeezed tight, the few bites of food I had in my stomach turning to pure acid. The red wine made my cheeks and nose feel hot.

I rubbed my sweaty palms along the thighs of my borrowed dress as I struggled to think of something interesting or witty to say about myself.

Nothing.

My mind was blank.

All these interesting, boisterous, fun people were looking at me and realizing that I was nothing like them. That I was small, and useless, and boring. A music nerd who spent most of her days cloistered away from the rest of humanity in a moldy gazebo playing her cello.

A nobody who...

Matteo's firm, warm hand rested over the top of mine on my thigh. He then gave it a squeeze. "She's an amazingly talented musician. The boys who usually set up in the piazza let her play earlier and you should have seen the crowd that formed."

Bianca clapped. "Oh, how exciting! I'm sorry I missed that."

Matteo continued. "She's the children's favorite teacher at the Academy of Music in Palermo."

How did he know that?

"Although I haven't heard her play it yet," Matteo said, "I have it on very good authority from Dante that she is also the only cellist in Sicily who was invited by the Church to play Mozart's *Sinfonia Concertante* for the Pope's visit last spring."

Gabriella raised her glass in a toast. "That is very impressive, my girl. I'm familiar with that piece and I cannot imagine the courage it took to play it in front of His Holiness, no less."

"Is there a video or recording of the performance?" asked Amara. "I'd love to hear it."

Milana's eyes lit up. "We should host a party and invite everyone we know to listen. What a brilliant way to introduce Antonella to the village."

Barone pointed to Alfonso. "We could work it into the winery festival program for the *Festa di San Giuseppe*."

Alfonso nodded. "I could have the men set up a screen with some speakers. We could project it onto the side of the main winery building."

Rosa then chimed in. "While everyone listens it would be the perfect time to serve the *zeppole di san Giuseppe*."

"Great idea, Rosa," responded Bianca.

My eyes teared over.

It was the proudest moment of my life.

The *Sinfonia Concertante* was considered one of the most difficult pieces of music for any cellist to perform because of its complicated arpeggios, quick scales, and the necessity for precise bowing.

I'd been a nervous wreck about performing it in front of so many people, let alone in front of the Pope. I'd practiced for three months straight, until the tips of the fingers on my left hand cracked and bled and my right hand cramped from holding my bow for hours straight day after day.

When the day finally arrived, neither my father nor Antonia could be bothered to attend.

And here was a table of complete strangers talking about making a scratchy, second-rate recording of it the centerpiece of their Feast of St. Joseph celebration.

I broke.

Throwing my napkin over my plate, I pushed back my chair and ran out of the room.

As I crossed over the threshold, I heard Barone's deep baritone say to Matteo, "Let her go."

Yes, Matteo, for your own sake… *let me go.*

CHAPTER 40

ELLA

"What are you doing here?" I whispered harshly as I looked over my shoulder at the darkened library windows.

Fino emerged from the shadows. "Don't use that tone with me. You've been ignoring my phone calls."

I shifted closer to the shadows along the high veranda wall. "There is nothing to tell you. I searched the Cavalieri offices and found nothing suspicious."

It was mostly the truth.

Fino reached into his suit jacket and pulled out a crumpled soft pack of cigarettes. Placing the unfiltered end between his lips he lit it and took a long drag.

Then blew the smoke in my face.

I waved it away, coughing and choking.

He pointed with his cigarette hand. "Well then, you're just going to have to keep searching until you find something."

"I've been watched just about every moment of the day. Even if I wasn't, the whole villa is crawling with family members and employees."

He flicked a piece of ash off his shirt. "If you don't find me something incriminating on the Cavalieris, I will be forced to take other, unpleasant measures."

I glanced down at the dark screen of my phone. "Have you done something to my sister? Is that why she isn't returning my calls?"

He took another long drag as he shrugged one shoulder. "One of the beautiful things about betrayal. It is so easy to turn the tables. For instance, if your father were to hear all my recordings of you ratting him out. What do you think he would do to you?"

I staggered backward with faltering steps.

Antonia had been pretending to be me back in Sicily.

If Fino told my father...

Not only would my sister be in danger, but there would be no hope of finding out what happened to my mother.

My lower lip trembled. "You won't get away with this. I'll go straight to Judge Delluci. I'll tell him what you've done."

His arm struck out so fast, I had no time to defend myself. The jagged, unkept fingernails of his right hand dug into the skin around my throat as his fingers squeezed.

Gasping for air, I clawed at his wrist and forearm and tried to scream.

With two steps forward, he covered my nose and mouth with his free hand and pinned me against the stone wall of the enclosure, striking my head against the bricks. My vision blurred as he bared his yellow-stained teeth.

His breath was rancid with garlic and stale tobacco as he hissed, "Don't you dare threaten me, bitch."

The edges to my vision darkened as I tried to twist my head away from his hand while at the same time straining to stay on the tips of my toes to ease the pressure on my throat. My lungs strained and burned as the last vestiges of oxygen left my body.

Matteo.

I wanted Matteo.

Tears streaked along the sides of my face as the pain of regret seemed to weigh my body down further. A deep, crippling exhaustion enveloped me as I slowly lost consciousness.

My mother's face flashed before my eyes. *I'm so sorry, Mama. I failed.*

Then all I saw was Matteo. His crooked smile. His winks. His powerful hands.

I should have told him. I should have told him everything. I should have trusted him.

As my arms fell slack at my sides, my head lolled to the side.

A strange euphoria took over.

I was just so tired.

Fino released his grip on me.

I fell to the dirt. At first, too stunned and out of it to even think to breathe.

Then primal instinct took over.

My mouth opened and I sucked in a choking gasp of dust and air which only made me choke harder as I clutched at my sore neck.

Fino kicked me in the stomach. "Shut the fuck up. Do you want the whole household to hear you?"

My body curled into the fetal position as I clutched my middle. He hadn't kicked me hard, but it was enough of a blow to hurt as I was trying to expand my lungs with precious air.

He squatted down on his haunches. "Get me the information I want, or your father will find out you're nothing but a snitch and a rat. Then your sister will wind up fish food, just like your mother."

Fino took a final drag of his cigarette and blew the smoke in my face again, causing another choking fit.

With a flick of his index finger, he tossed the still lit cigarette onto the dirt where it rolled near some brush. "If I even suspect that you went running to the Cavalieris for help, I'll burn this place to the ground with all of them inside. Understood?"

He disappeared back into the shadows without waiting for my response.

Tightening my arm around my waist, I forced myself onto my knees, gathered the skirt of my dress, and crawled through the dirt to the lit cigarette butt, putting it out before the dry branches could catch fire.

I then rolled onto my back and took my first real breath as I stared up at the cold, unfeeling winter skies. The bright flashes of white starlight seeming to mock me.

* * *

"ELLA? ELLA ARE YOU OUT HERE?"

Oh no.

I tried to roll back onto my knees as Matteo's voice came closer.

"Ella are you—Jesus Christ."

His powerful arms lifted me off the ground.

My cheek rubbed against the softness of his shirt, the scent of his cologne comforting.

"Baby? Baby, what happened? Who did this to you?" His voice was a low growl. "I'll fucking kill them."

I reached up and clutched at his shirt. "No. No one," I rasped. "I came out here for some air and… slipped."

Nausea rolled through my stomach as the lie soured in my mouth.

He carried me into the warmth of the villa. Bending his knees to lower me onto the nearby sofa, he said, "I'm going to get some help."

My fingers dug into his shirt in a tight grasp. "No! Please don't! It's too embarrassing. Please, Matteo. Please!"

After adjusting his grip, he straightened. "Shhh, it's okay, babygirl. I won't tell anyone."

He pressed his lips to my forehead then carried me out of the library and up the stairs to his bedroom.

His jaw tightened when in the light from the bedroom, he saw the dirt on me and my borrowed dress, and my scraped knees. "What the hell happened, Ella? The truth."

I eased back onto the edge of the mattress where he set me down. "It was stupid. I was crying and I went through the library out onto the veranda and must have slipped on a branch or rock or something on the ground. It knocked the wind out of me."

Kneeling before me, he reached up and cupped my cheek as he searched my face. "Did you hit your head?"

Yes.

"No. I don't think so." I reached up and felt the back of my skull. "There's no bump."

Not trusting my response, he moved his hand to massage the back of my neck and the base of my skull as he searched for any sign of injury. "Why do you smell like cigarette smoke? I know you don't smoke."

I swallowed painfully. My brain was so fuzzy it was difficult to think of so many lies in quick succession. "I think there was a security guard who was smoking nearby."

Puzzled, he asked, "Why didn't you call out for help?"

"I was too embarrassed. I'd already disgraced myself in front of your family. I didn't want to make the whole thing worse."

He sighed as he reached down to pull off my now ruined ballet flats. "You silly little girl. Do you have any idea how fucking worried I was? I've been tearing this place apart looking for you."

Seeing the genuine concern in his eyes, I had to swallow the bile that rose in the back of my throat.

I was a horrible person. I didn't deserve his concern. "Matteo, I need to tell you—"

He looked up as he ran his hand over my legs. "Yes?"

Tell him.

Tell him!

Tell him everything.

Then Fino's final threat came back to mind.

I licked my lips. "I—I'm sorry I caused a scene at dinner."

His strong arms reached around me to unzip my dress. "You should be more sorry for running off into the darkness like that. You could have been seriously hurt."

I lowered my gaze. "I know. I'm sorry."

He pulled the dress off my shoulders. As I slipped my arms through the sleeves, he ran his calloused hands over my skin, still searching for injuries. "I'm fine. Really. I was just jarred from the fall, that's all. I'm more embarrassed than anything else."

He stood, towering over me as he lifted my chin with his right hand. "You probably got dizzy from not eating enough at dinner, like before at your father's. I've warned you to knock that shit off."

I blinked at his stern expression. "I know. I'm sorry. Old habits die hard."

He stroked my hair and sighed. "Stop saying you're sorry," he said gruffly.

"Sorry. I mean, okay, I'll stop."

The corner of his mouth lifted in that slightly crooked smile I had already come to love. "It's hard to stay angry at you when you look like a little dove who fell out of her nest."

He pulled the dress off my hips.

I crossed my arms over my breasts.

After going into the ensuite bathroom, he returned with a heavy black robe. "Take off your bra and panties."

I reached for the garment. "I can just put the robe on over them."

He held it out of my reach. "Do as you're told. I'm in no mood right now, Ella."

When my arms reached behind me to unclasp the bra, I winced.

He cursed low under his breath before brushing my hands away and unhooking it himself. "Are you sure you didn't fall on something and crack a rib?"

Did getting kicked count?

"Yes, I'm sure."

The robe was soft and warm, and he gingerly placed it over my shoulders and then gently picked up my wrists to thread my arms through the sleeves. Before allowing me to close it, his firm hands wrapped around my ribcage, just below my breasts.

I sucked in a breath and held it, not expecting the spark of awareness between my legs at his intimate touch.

His dark gaze clashed with mine. Then his fingertips reached out to touch my throat. "Christ, are these bruises from me? From earlier? Fuck, babygirl. I'm so sorry. I promise I'll be more gentle next time."

My hand flew to my neck. Only a monster would let a man who was being so kind think he had caused the bruises Fino gave to me. "It's fine. They don't hurt."

It was official. My sister had turned me into a monster.

With all of my lies and manipulations and bullshit, I was now no better than her.

The tense silence stretched between us.

Finally, he pulled back as he cleared his throat. "Stay here. I'm going to get the first aid kit for your knees."

341

"They're fine. I just need to wipe off the dirt."

"Ella. Stay."

"Yes, sir."

The moment he left, I buried my face in my hands. I should have told him. I would tell him. As soon as I talked to Antonia and warned her. Then I would tell him everything.

I lifted my head and looked around the room. I couldn't help but smile when I noticed my borrowed clothes, suitcase, purse, and cello neatly stacked in the corner.

Matteo returned carrying a tray with two silver cloches, a small bowl of water, and a first aid kit. Resting the tray on the bed near me, he wet a washcloth and cleaned my knees before carefully rubbing a salve on the slight scrapes. When I hissed from the sting, he pursed his lips and blew cool air on the wounds.

The spark in my belly ignited, as if he had been blowing on an ember to get it to flame.

After changing out of his clothes into just a pair of gray sweatpants, his naked chest showing off his unique tattoo, he leaned against the headboard and pulled me onto his lap.

For once, I didn't object and simply buried my head against his shoulder.

I needed this.

I needed the comforting strength of his arms.

I needed the reassuring beat of his heart.

At least for a moment, it made me think everything was going to be all right.

He leaned forward and pulled the tray closer before lifting the two cloches. Under one were two bright orange persimmons cut into quarters and drizzled with what smelled like a traditional vanilla and rum sauce. Under the other was a bowl of *zabaione*.

Matteo dipped a spoon into the warm and frothy *zabaione* and lifted it to my lips. "Open your mouth, my clumsy little bird."

Not able to resist the velvety dessert, I obeyed. The wine, sugar, and frothed egg yolks soothed my sore throat.

When he dipped the spoon in a second time and held it to my mouth, I said, "I can feed myself."

"Shut up and let me feed you."

I obeyed, letting him slip the spoon inside my mouth. I licked my lips, savoring the creamy sweetness.

His gaze focused on my mouth, a deep rumble vibrating inside his chest. Against the backs of my thighs, his cock hardened. I shifted. "Maybe I should—"

His arm tightened around my waist. "Don't move," he growled.

The air in the room thickened.

Keeping his gaze locked on mine, he reached over and picked up a piece of persimmon and held it close to my mouth. "Bite."

When my teeth sank into the soft flesh, the boozy glaze dripped down through the opening of my robe, onto the inner curve of my breast.

As I moved to wipe it off, he wrapped his fingers around my wrist and pulled my arm away.

Still keeping his intense gaze on me, he lowered his head. The tip of his tongue swept over my skin to lap at the vanilla-sweetened drops.

"Oh, God," I breathed out in a rush as my heart raced.

He slipped his hand inside the robe and opened it wider, loosening the belt. He then lifted my thigh and bent my knee to swing me around on his lap so that I was straddling him.

Picking up another piece of persimmon, he held it to my lips. "Open your mouth, baby."

Mesmerized by his dark eyes, I bit into the bright, sweet flesh.

343

This time he squeezed the piece of fruit as I did so, deliberately sending a cascade of sticky rum droplets over my breasts and stomach.

As he leaned his head down to lick the curve of my left breast, I fell back onto my forearms, pressing his hard thighs against my back.

He groaned as he shifted so his mouth could reach my breasts and stomach, peppering them with open-mouthed kisses. "So fucking sweet."

His large hands slipped under my hips and lifted me.

"What? Oh! Oh!"

My lower body was tilted up toward his face as he anchored my bent knees over his shoulders. His thumbs went to either side of my pussy lips, opening me. The tip of his tongue flicked against my clit.

My fingers dug into the blankets as my back arched, pushing my hips against his jaw. A high-pitched moan escaped my lips; my body felt like it was floating in his grasp.

His hot breath brushed my inner thigh. "That's it, babygirl. Sing for me."

The tip of his tongue moved faster, swirling around and around, increasing the pressure with each full circle.

My own finger or a vibrator could never compare to the feel of his mouth on me.

Easily keeping my body aloft with his left hand, he shifted his right to between my thighs. His thumb pushed inside my wet entrance. After several thrusts, he pulled out to press the tip of it against my puckered hole.

Instinctively, I tightened it. He increased the pressure while varying the rhythm of his tongue.

There was this odd suspense as my body braced for the moment he'd force his thumb inside my ass. A shock of sensation raced up my spine when he scraped the sharp edges of his teeth against my clit. My brain splintered and I forgot to keep my asshole clenched.

He thrust his thumb inside.

The dark, elicit pleasure of it sent me over.

I came undone.

My hips bucked as my bare feet kicked at the headboard. This time the stars I saw were shimmering with white glitter and warmth.

His left hand flattened over my abdomen as he slowly lowered my hips back to his lap. My knees hugged his sides as he growled, "Fuck, I love how responsive you are."

He moved his hand to cup my hip as he lifted his cock and positioned it at my entrance.

I whimpered, knowing I was still sore from earlier.

"Shhh, little one. I promise I won't thrust. I just need to be inside you right now."

There was a momentary sensation of pressure, and then the thick head slipped inside me. He wrapped both hands around my hips and slid my body closer to him, forcing me to impale myself on his cock.

"Fuck, babygirl. You're so goddamn tight."

My inner muscles burned as they stretched to accommodate his girth. When my ass was against his hips, he was fully seated inside of me.

There was an odd sense of pride and accomplishment about being able to take his full, long length inside of my tight pussy.

True to his word, he remained still. Moving his hands over my stomach, hips, and breasts in slow, soothing circles.

My hips shifted as my body luxuriated in the feeling of fullness and completion.

My eyelids drooped.

His dark voice came to me as if through a long, dark tunnel.

"That's it, *colomba mia*. You're safe now. Fall asleep with my cock inside of you. I'm here."

My cheek rested against the top of his leg as the sound of his voice and the feel of him lulled me.

The last thing I heard before falling into a deep sleep was him whispering, "I'll always be here for you, baby."

Please don't let me go.

CHAPTER 41

MATTEO

"*S*he's lying to me."

Enzo passed a cappuccino to me before making the foam for a second one.

I joined Cesare at the kitchen table as he reached for a *cornetto*. "What makes you so certain?"

At his nod, I slid the small jar of homemade apricot preserves down the table toward him. "She's a terrible liar."

Enzo took his seat across from me. As he raised his cup to his mouth, he chuckled. "Well, that's going to make marriage easier. Assuming you're still marrying the girl?"

It wasn't even a question. "Fuck yeah, I'm still marrying her. The sooner the better."

Cesare broke off a piece of the buttery pastry and popped it into his mouth before leaning back in his chair. "If you want to keep your edge, keep her away from Milana. I swear to God, that woman could sell someone two left feet and convince them they are a better dancer for it."

Uncle Barone poked his head in. "Amara?"

Enzo waved him in. "It's safe. She's with Bianca and Milana getting ready for Liliana's visit."

He stepped into the kitchen as he rubbed his hands together. "Finally, I can enjoy an espresso in peace."

He pressed the fresh coffee grounds into the filter basket, before locking it in. The machine hissed as he pulled a shot. The room once again filled with the acrid, earthy scent of coffee.

After placing the cup on a saucer, he leaned his hip against the kitchen island, closed his eyes, and took a moment to inhale the rich scent.

Before he could even lift the cup to his lips, Aunt Gabriella drifted in and snatched it from his hands without even stopping on her way to the table. "Thank you, darling. I needed this."

Taking a sip, she grimaced and held it aloft over her shoulder. "Ugh, Barone, you know I take steamed milk."

His brow lowered as he said through clenched teeth, "That wasn't meant for you."

She pivoted on him as she adjusted one of her heavy gold and diamond loop earrings which completed her deep purple and cobalt blue turban and caftan morning outfit. "Don't be silly. Of course you made it for me."

She then raised one elegantly arched eyebrow. "Otherwise, that would mean *you* were about to drink it, and I'd hate to start the day having to impart *nasty* gossip to sweet Amara."

Uncle Barone pointed a finger at her. "You're an evil woman, you know that."

She laughed as she took a seat at the other end of the table. "So I've been told many, many times, darling."

He placed the espresso with added steamed milk in front of her, then poured himself some orange juice. "Matteo, how's your girl?"

Leaning an elbow on the table, I rubbed my eyes. "To be honest, Uncle, I'm worried about her. I need to get this mess settled, and quickly. I'm afraid if I don't, she might do something stupid."

Enzo shook his head. "Not going to happen, cousin." He gestured around the table. "We'll all be watching out for her. We'll keep her safe, even from herself."

Cesare pushed the platter of *cornettos* toward Gabriella.

She waved him off. "No thank you, dear. I haven't eaten carbs in the morning since carrying a Fendi logo bag was fashionable. Are we talking about Ella?"

"I think she's lying to me."

She shrugged. "Of course, she's lying."

"You haven't even heard why I think it."

Gabriella put her espresso cup down and waved her hand in my direction, her signature gold bangles jangling, as if they were the theme music of her life. "You've met her father, and we all know about the dreaded sister. No one survives a toxic family environment like that without developing survival skills."

Her words gave me pause.

She continued. "I imagine the poor girl is forced to lie through her teeth to those two selfish egomaniacs on a daily basis just to get a moment's peace."

I switched seats to be closer to her. "But she's no longer in that environment. She's safe here. Why is she still protecting them?"

Her soft hand covered mine as her red lips lifted in an understanding smile. "Because family's family, dear. If human beings didn't have a high tolerance for their loved ones' bullshit, we would have died out as a species long ago." She patted my hand. "Like I said, survival instincts."

Suspicion that Ella was lying about how she was injured last night itched at the back of my brain. I stayed up half the night watching her sleep, going over it in my mind.

My connection with her last night was something I had never

experienced with another woman. It was amazing. While never being called a selfish lover, I'd never put a woman's needs completely and absolutely above my own.

When I sank my cock deep inside her sweet pussy, it had taken all my willpower not to thrust hard and fast until I filled her with come. Especially after my realization that I wanted her to bear my child. But I didn't.

I kept still and watched her body relax and accept having me inside of her.

Just when she was about to fall asleep, I lifted her into my arms and slid down in the bed until she was lying on top of me, her cheek resting against my heart as I held her close.

Not wanting to break our connection or shatter the moment, I must have stayed like that for over an hour just stroking her hair and listening to the gentle sound of her breathing.

This situation needed to be fixed, and fast. I never again wanted to see the fear and stress in my baby's eyes.

Although I hadn't ordered her not to tell her sister, because I hadn't wanted to place that kind of pressure on her, it would be foolish not to assume she had.

We would now have to proceed with the assumption that Antonia knew her scheme hadn't worked. The difficulty was in guessing what she would do next.

The idea of locking Ella safely in a room until this was all over was becoming more and more attractive. A vision of her wide, frightened eyes flashed through my mind again. She'd looked so haunted and afraid last night. It was all I could do not to just grab her by the shoulders and shake her, begging her to confide in me.

If I had learned one thing working side by side with my father for the brotherhood, it was that trust couldn't be rushed. It needed to be earned, even under false pretenses.

I leaned back in my seat. "Yeah, well, fuck her family. We're her family now."

"Spoken like a true, arrogant Cavalieri," boomed my father as he entered the room, the cool morning air still clinging to his clothes.

I rose. "Father."

We hugged, him slapping me on the back before cupping my face. "You look good, son."

My father crossed to Gabriella and gave her a kiss on the cheek. "Gabbie."

Her lips twisted in a smile. "Old Goat."

He laughed then said hello to Enzo and Cesare, who rose to greet him.

Uncle Barone handed him an espresso. "How was the trip down?"

The brothers stood shoulder to shoulder, looking almost like identical twins despite the few years' age difference. "Uneventful."

Uncle Barone checked his watch. "Sebastian should be here soon, but I say we don't wait. Let's head down to the old office where we won't be overheard."

Just then Alfonso entered carrying three green metal ammo boxes.

The room fell silent.

Ever the pragmatist, we knew Alfonso was stocking up. We usually kept plenty of bullets for our hunting rifles, but no more than a nominal amount beyond basic security needs for the handguns in the armory. That needed to change.

There was a fight coming.

One that would likely be violent, bloody, and dirty.

As most clashes with any mafia syndicate often were.

The mafia rarely cared about body counts when their interests were threatened.

If the shit hit the fan over Antonia and Antonella's scheme and if Dante couldn't hold on to power, the possibility of this fight coming to the winery's doorstep was very high.

Alfonso cleared his throat. "I'll just put these in the armory and meet you all down there."

I rose and leaned down to kiss Aunt Gabriella on the cheek. "Watch out for Ella. I left a note next to the bed that she should come and find you if I wasn't finished by the time she rose."

I was pivoting to follow the other men when she snatched my wrist. I turned back to her inquiringly.

"Don't send her back."

I frowned. "What?"

Her grip tightened. "Don't send her back. Don't even let them discuss that as an option."

I closed my hand over hers. "That's not going to happen, Aunt Gabbie."

Her eyes filled with tears.

Alarmed, I retook my seat. "Aunt Gabbie?"

Tilting her head back, she patted her manicured fingers under her eyes. "I'll ruin my makeup."

"What's going on?"

She stared at me for a long moment. Then sighed. "Women can be silly, complicated creatures. Sometimes we fight tooth and nail against what we want most in the world. Don't let her get away with it. Hold on to her."

"Are you speaking from experience?"

Aunt Gabbie took a deep breath, leaned back, and fluffed her hair. All signs of vulnerability gone behind a mask of steely elegance. "It's in the past and as you know, a lady never admits to having a past."

I chuckled as I leaned over and kissed her cheek again. "I love you, Aunt. And don't worry. I have no intention of letting Ella go. No matter how hard she tries to leave."

CHAPTER 42

ELLA

*W*as that a freaking helicopter that just landed on the lawn?

Didn't movie villains always arrive in ominous black helicopters?

Zipping up the back of my borrowed, off-the-shoulder, Sarra Porcelain Flower Ralph Loren dress, I dug through my purse looking for my phone. I had placed it on silent/vibrate last night so no one would know if I had received a text or phone call from Antonia during dinner but me.

It wasn't in my purse.

My heart raced. Had Matteo taken it? I dumped my purse out to double-check. There wasn't anything incriminating on the phone per se, but there were the multiple calls from Fino and all my calls to Antonia.

That was when I remembered, I left it in the library. I had stashed it there right before meeting with Fino because I wanted it close.

After listening at the top of the main staircase for signs of life,

I crept down the stairs and tiptoed down the hallway to the library. So far, the villa was quiet.

With all the animated talk about clearing away brush, fixing machinery, and approving wine label graphics at dinner last night, it was more than likely they were all at work.

Although I considered myself a disciplined person when it came to practicing my cello, being forbidden to work by my father had led to the rather lazy habit of sleeping in late. I consoled myself with the fact that I usually rose by ten a.m. compared to my sister who never showed her face before noon.

Despite that, I was exhausted and... rattled.

Last night with Matteo was... different.

Between his domineering and kinky ways and my pretending I was my sister, in a way, I had been able to disassociate myself during our escapades. I was free to respond and take pleasure in things that should have shocked me to the core, because it was me, but it wasn't me. Like putting on a costume and pretending just for a little while that I was this desirable, sexually promiscuous wanton.

And even when we had sex for the first time, there was still an atmosphere of high emotion and anger and pent-up passion that made it frenzied and almost chaotic.

But last night...

Last night was quiet and... intimate.

There was no hiding behind a mask. Funny how we first met at a masquerade and how, up until last night, I had kept that facade like body armor.

But last night...

There was no hiding. I'd been scared and vulnerable. Naked in every sense of the word.

The comforting strength of his powerful arms as they held me tight until I fell asleep with him still inside of me was borderline a religious experience. It was as if I transcended all the chaos around me. As if he had lifted me out of my body and mind to place me safely in the clouds.

It was fanciful nonsense of course, but I couldn't help wondering if that was what love was supposed to feel like. As if he had me safely curled up in the shelter of his palm and nothing or no one could hurt me.

Then with the glaring light of the morning sun, reality crashed me back to earth.

My head swiveled from left to right, then left again, triple-checking that the coast was clear before I ducked into the library.

I went straight to a far shelf where I had wedged my phone between an English copy of *Bonfire of the Vanities* and *La Divine Commedia*.

How prophetic of me.

The screen glowed in the dim room as I checked my text and voice messages.

Nothing.

Damn her.

I pressed Antonia's contact and was startled when she answered after only two rings, having once more been expecting to get her voicemail again.

"Hello?"

Nothing. Just the sound of rustling.

"Hello? Antonia? Are you there?"

More rustling.

My alarm rose. "Toni?"

"Ella, is that you?"

Her voice was strained and high-pitched. "It's me. What's going on?"

At first, she didn't respond, there was just the sound of more rustling and her erratic breathing. "I'm in trouble, Ella."

"Oh my God! Where are you? Toni, talk to me."

This time there was a bang and a clatter as if she had dropped the phone. "What's happening?"

In my agitation, I pulled my phone away and checked the screen as if it would suddenly switch to video or a map.

"Ella, you have to help me."

"What's going on? Is it Father? Does he know?"

"Ella, you have to— No! No! Please, we didn't mean it! Please!"

"Toni? Who's there with you? What's happening?"

A piercing, bloodcurdling scream was my only answer.

Then the line went dead.

For several seconds I just stood there staring at my black phone screen, not able to fully take in what just happened. Then my body shook, my mouth opening on a scream.

Falling to my knees, I tried calling her over and over again, shouting into the dead phone line, "Toni? Toni! Oh my God! Oh my God!"

Tears clouded my vision, and my hand shook so badly I dropped the phone several times.

No matter how many times I called, there was no answer.

It didn't even ring.

As if her phone were dead... as if she were... oh my God!

My phone fell from my hand as I clutched at my middle and rocked back and forth.

What had we done?

What had we done?

Strong hands lifted me from the floor and turned me into a solid chest. A powerful arm circled over my shoulders while another pressed my head against a masculine shoulder.

As I continued to shake and tremble, the hold on me tightened. "Shhh. Shhh."

At first, I thought it was Matteo. It took several moments for my shell-shocked mind to catch up to what was happening.

It was the man's cologne, an icy scent of juniper, pepper, and sage.

It lacked the spicy warmth of Matteo's, which smelled more like pinewood and burnt sugar.

And this chest was solid and firm but different from Matteo's bulkier muscles.

I pulled my head back sharply and stared up into the towering form of... *diavolo*.

The sinfully handsome man with piercing black eyes and jet-black hair smiled.

That was when I realized I had whispered the word, devil, out loud.

It wasn't my fault.

The man had appeared like Mephistopheles, straight out of *Doctor Faustus*. Dressed in unrelenting black, his lowered brow, high cheekbones and sharp jawline turned his appearance into the living embodiment of the devil or some classic villain from literature.

"That isn't the first time I've been mistaken for the devil by a beautiful woman."

His voice was like ice sliding on glass, cold and smooth.

With my palms, I tried to break his embrace. "I'm so sorry. You startled me."

He held tight as he cupped my cheek and wiped away my tears with the side of his thumb. "What has made you cry, *bellissima*?"

I was too overwrought to lie. "My sister, Antonia. Something has happened to her."

His large hand moved to stroke my hair. "Ah, you must be Matteo Cavalieri's *piccolo piantagrane*."

I bristled at being called Matteo's *little troublemaker*. "You presume too much, signore. Please unhand me."

His gaze narrowed as his lips thinned.

I was sure the rolling thunder I just heard was only in my imagination.

Or at least was pretty sure.

"Careful, *piccolo piantagrane*. This stunt of yours has made you many enemies. I wouldn't recommend adding me to the list."

A fist twisted inside my chest as my lungs seized. I had to force my words out. "Were you sent by my father to kill me?"

His eyebrow lifted. "I give those type of orders, I don't take them. Especially not from an insignificant *zip* from some back-water town. But tell me, why would you assume your father wants you dead?"

My father would go absolutely apoplectic if he heard this man referring to him as a *zip*, essentially an unsophisticated and undisciplined Sicilian mafioso with no skill or tact.

"Who are you?"

His hand moved to my chin. Tilting my head back, he glared down at me. "Do I strike you as a patient or kind man?"

My eyes widened as I jerked back, once more trying to break free.

His grip on me was too powerful.

I licked my lips, regretting the action the moment his gaze fixated on my mouth. I shook my head, then whispered, "No, signore."

Common sense would have dictated that I lie to placate him, but the dangerous energy that literally radiated off him like cold fusion warned me against it.

He nodded as the corner of his mouth lifted. "Exactly. So why would you risk annoying me by asking me a question instead of answering mine?"

The lump of fear in my throat nearly choked me. "I'm sorry."

There was a subtle tic over his right cheek as he waited for me to continue. Clearly, he was losing patience with me, something he had all but warned me would be detrimental to my well-being.

Again, my mind screamed for me to *lie, lie, lie* my ass off, but I couldn't.

Like the devil, this man's soulless black eyes seemed to see right through me.

"Because I think he murdered my mother years ago and may have just harmed my sister."

There was a bitter taste in my mouth after uttering the accusation out loud. I wasn't sure if it was because he was a stranger, my fear, or the strange sense of betrayal from telling this man before I confided in Matteo.

Without a word, he released me.

I fell backward against the bookshelves. Reaching behind me, I clutched at the nearby fireplace mantle to remain upright since I didn't trust my knees not to buckle again.

Keeping his unnerving gaze on me, he reached into his designer black suit jacket.

I gasped, then held my breath, expecting him to pull out a gun.

Would he shoot me right here, in the middle of the Cavalieris' library?

Would he at least show me the kindness of hitting me between the eyes so there would be no pain?

As badly as I wanted to, I didn't close my eyes. They burned and stung as I forced my eyelids to remain open. If he was going to shoot me in cold blood, I would at least make him look me in the eye while he did it.

My breath slipped past my lips in a rush when he pulled out a slim, gold business card holder. As he flipped it open, I saw the unmistakable family crest engraved on the top.

It was a rearing medieval dragon and unicorn protecting a large diamond and a scroll with a Latin phrase.

Crede nullis. Vince omnes.

Trust none. Conquer all.

The Diamantis.

Porca miseria. The freaking Diamantis!

Which meant this must be… *uh oh.*

The man pulled out a card and handed it to me. "My card."

It was heavy, black card stock with the same family crest embossed in gold and ice blue. On the other side it had only his name and a six-digit code under it, no email or phone number. As if you needed to be a member of some ultra-secret society to be able to contact him.

Sebastian Diamanti

13 7 23 3

I should have recognized him. Most people outside of Italy knew him as the CEO and heir to the House of Diamanti, a diamond and jewelry empire dating back over a hundred years.

But Italians knew better.

Sebastian Diamanti was one of the most dangerous men—and the eldest son of one of the most powerful families—in all of Italy.

Certain people might fear the influence of the Sicilian mob, but they were terrified of the Diamantis.

Legitimacy gave them way more power. It was the same reason Fino was showing so much interest in the Cavalieris.

They were equally wealthy and influential, although their reputation wasn't quite as ruthless. Only because they were tucked away in Abruzzo as opposed to Rome, where the Diamantis lived.

"Thank you." I didn't know what else to say.

In the tense silence, I glanced down at my phone as my eyes filled with tears.

His hand covered the screen. "No more of that. You're a Cavalieri now."

I wiped my cheek with the back of my hand. "No I'm not." I sounded like a petulant child but didn't care.

Sebastian chuckled. "Fair enough. You soon will be a Cavalieri. They protect their own. And they have the full support of my family in doing so. *No matter what is required.*"

The weight of his words hung heavy between us.

I sniffed. "But my sister."

He buttoned his suit jacket. "Matteo was right. You are adorably sweet and very loyal. Almost too loyal. Don't worry, *piccolo piantagrane.* Your man is aware there is no happiness with you, without first securing the well-being of that sister of yours."

That sister of mine. So it seemed he was aware of Antonia's reputation for trouble. If anything *she* was the little troublemaker not me. Although I guessed I now shared in that after the last few days.

But wait. Matteo had talked about me to him?

It was silly but it definitely gave me a warm, fluttery feeling to know he had spoken about me.

Me.

Not my sister or me pretending to be my sister, but me.

He touched my cheek. "No more tears. Now, I must go meet with your man to discuss how we are going to deal with the both of you without causing a nasty little war."

I stepped forward. "I should go with you."

His back was already turned to me. He barely bothered to turn around, only casting a quick glance over his shoulder. "Absolutely not. Matteo will handle this for you. It's his duty as your future husband."

And with that he was gone.

I looked around the room, half expecting to see a puff of smoke. I knew I wasn't imagining that the room seemed warmer without him in it.

I shivered.

Just then my mobile rang.

It was Antonia.

"Toni? Are you okay?"

"Ella?"

"Yes, it's me. Are you okay?"

"Help me, Ella. Help me," she rasped before the line once more went dead.

No matter how many times I tried to call her back, she didn't answer.

I stared at the empty doorway where Sebastian had just been. He had said the men were planning something, but he had also called Antonia *that sister of yours.*

Could I trust them to prioritize saving her? They didn't even know she was pregnant. Would that make her chances better or worse?

My hand tightened around my phone.

I couldn't risk that chance.

Family was family.

Sicily was at least ten hours' drive from Abruzzo not counting the ferry.

If I left now, I would be there before midnight.

My decision made, I ran upstairs and grabbed my purse before sneaking out of the villa to the stables, where I knew Matteo's Alfa Romeo would be... with the keys in the ignition.

CHAPTER 43

SEBASTIAN

"We should just send in an extraction team for the sister and be done with it. Let Dante sort out the rest of the bloody mess," argued Benedict as I opened the heavy oak door to the carved-out cave that passed for the formal office of the Cavalieri headquarters.

Barone responded. "I would agree, except we know damn well that Dante has no loyalty to us. He could lay that same bloody mess at our doorstep to deflect and distract."

Enzo raised his arm and gestured with his drink hand. "Hate to admit it, but it would be an elegant solution to his problem."

"*Buon pomeriggio*," I said as I stepped into the room.

The men rose.

Barone crossed first, hand out. "Sebastian, good of you to come."

"Always."

I nodded to the others.

Then I turned to Matteo. "You should head to the villa. *Now*."

He frowned. "Why? What's wrong?"

I accepted a hand-rolled cigarette from Cesare then cupped

my hand over the match he struck to light it. Pulling back, I blew out a cloud of blue smoke, before saying, "I have a feeling your girl's about to do something *very* stupid."

With a curse, Matteo bolted out of the room.

After shaking Benedict's hand, I took the glass of *Cynar* he offered before unbuttoning my suit jacket and settling in one of the oxblood leather seats arranged around the ancient fireplace. "So, gentlemen. How many guns and men do you need?"

CHAPTER 44

MATTEO

A quick glance in the stable proved she had taken the Alfa Romeo.

Clever girl.

Fortunately for me, that vintage car had a tricky clutch.

Sliding behind the steering wheel of the nearest black Range Rover, I sped out of the villa grounds.

It didn't take long to find her stalled along a secluded side lane to the main road to the village. She must have pulled over onto the narrow unpaved road when the car gave her trouble.

She was dressed in a pretty blue-and-white dress completely unsuited for the chill in the air, circling the car with her mobile raised high, looking for service.

She wouldn't find any.

The open country between the winery and the village was a dead zone.

I pulled up behind her and shrugged out of my heavy canvas coat, placing it over her shoulders. "You silly little thing. What are you doing out here?"

Ella leaned the top of her head against my chest. Her voice was barely above a whisper. "I broke your super-expensive car."

My arms wrapped tightly around her as I stroked her hair. "You didn't break the car, babygirl. Not that I would give a damn if you had."

"It just sputtered and then stopped."

"It has a trick clutch. Tell me what's going through that adorable head of yours. Why did you steal a car and try to leave?"

"I screwed up. I should have told you everything when I had a chance. Then maybe—"

She pulled back. As she did so, my oversized jacket slipped off her shoulders.

I yanked on the lapels, then gently pushed her arms through the sleeves. "Tell me now."

After swiping at the tears on her cheeks, she shook her head. "I can't. It's too late. Please, just let me go back to Sicily. My sister needs me."

My jaw tightened at the mention of her sister.

The idea that my girl had put herself in danger—again—for that woman made me want to howl with rage, but I kept it in check. She was too vulnerable. Too scared and conflicted. The last thing she needed was me going all caveman on her now.

That would happen later.

When this was all resolved.

Then I'd lay down the law when it came to always telling me the truth and never hiding her problems from me. And the consequences for doing so.

I brushed her thick blonde curls away from her face. "You've just deprived me of a big, dramatic car chase like in the movies. The least you can do is talk to me."

Her lips twisted.

I tilted her chin back. "Is that a smile?"

She grasped my wrist as she tried to lower her head. "Don't

make me smile. It's bad. Really, really bad. I think something's happened to my sister. I need to get back to Sicily."

"You're not going anywhere, Antonella. I forbid it."

She broke free. "You can't forbid me from helping my sister."

"The fuck I can't. Your sister is nothing but trouble. She's no longer your problem. She's mine."

Ella paced back and forth in front of me with her arm wrapped around her middle. "You don't understand. You don't know what's going on."

"Babygirl, I am holding on to my anger by a very thin strand. You are two seconds away from being bent over the hood of that car and having your skirts flipped over your head while I spank your pretty little ass raw as punishment for this *latest* stunt."

Her arms reached behind her to cover her ass. "You wouldn't dare. Not here. Not out in the open."

My hand rested on the silver belt buckle of my leather work belt. "Watch me."

Her cheeks bloomed with bright color as her lower lip pushed out in a pout. "You're not being fair."

"Trust me, baby. I'm being *very* fair right now. If this were my father or uncle, you'd already have a red bottom. Now talk."

She crossed her arms and leaned against the car. "It all started when Antonia told me she was pregnant..."

* * *

"So you told your sister I was at Carnevale, and she still refused to leave with you?"

The only tiny kernel of redemption in how I'd treated my girl that first night was she at least got pleasure out of it. That still didn't forgive my barbaric behavior toward an untried virgin. That I thought she was her sister was not enough of an excuse for my guilty mind.

* * *

I WRAPPED my left hand over my right fist. "He did what?"

She had barely gotten to the part where her sister drugged her and then pawned her unconscious body off on some thug ex-boyfriend and already there were several people I wanted to straight up murder.

"I'm going to need his full name when you're done."

Hell, Dante might not have enough soldiers in his mafia syndicate to continue once I was done cleaning house. Problem solved.

* * *

MY FINGERS DUG into my brow bone as I rubbed my eyes. "So that's why you tipped the tray over?"

Ella spread her arms wide. "Antonia told me I had to make it believable!"

Just another link in the chains I would be wearing in hell for how I'd treated this sweet, innocent creature in the beginning. Christ, that was the night I treated her like a pony and used an e-stim riding crop on her.

Fuck, I was totally going to hell.

I kept my eyes shielded as I groaned, "Continue."

* * *

I PACED in front of her, running my hand through my hair. "You're telling me that you've been handing over all sorts of incriminating shit to this asshole, Fino, for months now?"

She twisted her hands in front of her. "He said if I gave him information on my father, he'd look into my mother's disappearance."

My lungs filled with crisp winter air as I took a deep breath and prayed for patience. Desperately trying to keep my voice even and calm, I asked, "Would I be correct in assuming all this evidence can be traced back to show you're the one who took it?"

She bit her lip and grimaced. "Yes, but that's not the worst part…"

My girl had a "fun" definition of bad if she thought making a mortal enemy of not just her own father, but Dante as well, wasn't the worst part. She obviously didn't consider that in her zeal to reveal her father's criminal actions, she would be implicating the entire Agnello syndicate.

It was a fucking miracle she wasn't already dead and rotting in some unmarked grave.

Placing my hands on my hips I stared down into the dirt, afraid I'd shake her if I met her gaze. I sighed before asking, "What is the worst part, baby?"

She gestured to me. "See, you're angry. I don't want to tell you now."

I wrapped my arm around her waist and pulled her close. After kissing her forehead, I said, "Yes. I'm very angry. Possibly the angriest I've ever been in my life, but not at you. Now tell me."

"You'll yell."

"I promise I won't."

* * *

"ARE YOU MOTHERFUCKING KIDDING ME?" I yelled once she finally related the true circumstances of how I found her last night.

She stamped her foot. "You promised you wouldn't yell."

Through clenched teeth, I growled, "That was before you told

369

me some asshole snuck onto my family's land and tried to choke you to death."

"He wouldn't have really killed me. He needed me alive to…" Her voice drifted off. "Spy on your family," she finished in a small voice.

I threw my arms in the air. "Well, that makes all the difference."

A tentative smile crossed her lips. "It does?"

Storming toward her, I wrapped my hand around the base of her skull and pulled her close before slamming my mouth down on hers. Thrusting my tongue inside her sweet mouth, I devoured her in a hard, possessive kiss before breaking free.

I leaned my forehead against hers as I rasped, "No, my sweet girl. The only difference it makes is instead of putting a bullet between his eyes, now I'm going to use a knife to puncture every major vein in his body and force him to watch as the blood slowly drains from it."

She blinked. "You're not serious, are you?"

"Deadly serious."

She gripped my shirt. "You can't kill him."

"I assure you, I can."

"You don't understand. I need to get to Judge Delluci to convince him to arrest my father. And Fino is the one with access and all my evidence. I think my father has attacked my sister. I already might be too late. Toni called me earlier screaming for help. I haven't been able to reach her since."

There was very little chance the phone call Ella received was genuine.

Because my father informed me not an hour earlier that Antonia had made her way to the mainland yesterday, having fled the moment she learned I knew of their switch.

And there being no evidence her blowhard father even knew anything was amiss, it was doubtful it was real.

Probably just another manipulation attempt by her sister.

But I couldn't say that and risk the possibility Antonia really was injured.

I placed my hands on her upper shoulders. "You have my word, I am going to handle all of this, but first I need you—'

She frowned and pointed. "What is that?"

I followed her gaze over my shoulder.

There was a thick, black plume of smoke rising over the horizon.

Cavalieri Winery was on fire.

CHAPTER 45

BARONE

"$\mathcal{W}$e need to set up a defensible perimeter!" I shouted to the boys as we all ran hell for leather toward the blaze.

A dense copse of trees between the villa and the winery facilities were engulfed in flames.

Thick smoke and ash carried on the wind, burning my eyes and increasing the danger of the fire spreading through flying embers.

With my arm shielding my face from the blast of heat as we approached, I yelled out, "Assessment."

Enzo coughed then called out, "We've already moved half the barrels into the wine caves where they'll be safe, but we still have about five hundred barrels racked."

The rack room was the first building in the blaze's path. Five hundred barrels was over twelve thousand cases of wine at risk. That was about a hundred and fifty thousand bottles, half this year's inventory. We couldn't let that happen.

While the barrels themselves would be able to withstand a degree of heat, the physical wooden racks they were stored on would not. If they were compromised, the barrels could crash to the stone floor and break open.

I covered my mouth with the crook of my arm. "Vines?"

Cesare spoke through his shirt which he had lifted to cover his face. "They'll withstand the worst of the heat blast because of the water content, but it's the drip hoses I'm worried about. Thank God we replaced the north and west quadrants with steel pipes, but if the wind shifts and the lower southeast acres get hit, we're done for."

Fuck. Centuries' worth of vine growth.

The Cavalieri legacy.

It all could be wiped out in an instant if the older irrigation pipes ignited. The plastic would melt onto the vines, killing them.

Then there were the stables, bottling facility, and other buildings to worry about, not to mention the main villa and Cesare's home.

With my forearm, I wiped the soot from my eyes. "All right. We all know what to do."

Sebastian Diamanti threw off his suit jacket. "Where do you need me?"

"I need to dig a ditch between the fire and the winery buildings."

He nodded. "Done."

As he raced toward my men, he held out his arm, snatching the handle of a shovel from one of them as he shouted orders and gathered a team.

Benedict gestured to Alfonso. "We need to move the horses out of the stable and clear the sheep to a lower pasture."

Instead of using a masticator to mulch and to control erosion, we used sheep to clear all the brush and grass from between the vines. There were about three hundred head that had just been let out into the northern acreage.

Enzo gestured to the winery buildings. "There isn't enough heat to trigger the sprinkler systems. I'm going to go do it manually. If we soak the barrels and racks that will give us extra time."

I patted him on the shoulder to show my agreement before sprinting toward Amara and Liliana who were struggling to drag a coil of canvas hose across the yard. Leaning down, I hefted the coil onto my shoulder and ran to the water pipes.

Dropping the cumbersome hose in the dirt, I yanked on the open end, unfurling it. "Hook it up nice and tight, *dolcezza*, then get back to safety."

As I ordered her, I realized Milana and Bianca were struggling with the second hose coil. My head pivoted in a semicircle, but all my men were occupied with digging a defense perimeter or hooking any exposed vegetation piles to pull them away from the inferno.

Just then, one of our Range Rovers roared into the courtyard.

Before the vehicle had even come to a full stop, Matteo had thrown open the driver's side door and jumped out. Seeing Bianca and a heavily pregnant Milana wrestling with the hose, he ran over to them.

He lowered his knees and hefted the coil onto his shoulder before racing for the other water pipe. "Girls, get back! Get back!" he ordered as he ran.

By now Gabriella had appeared. Wrapping her hand around Bianca's forearm, she yelled, "We'll turn on Matteo's water." She then pointed to Milana. "Take the Range Rover and drive to the gate to direct the villagers."

Smart woman.

The villagers would have seen the smoke by now and would be coming in droves to help. We needed someone at the gate to control the situation. Plus it got Milana and her unborn baby as far away as possible from the toxic fumes and heat blast. With Cesare occupied securing the lower fields with another defensive perimeter, he would expect us to watch out for his girl.

I tightened my grip on the water hose and raised my fist in the air to signal to Amara.

The hose jerked and vibrated in my grasp as over thirty bars of pressurized water rushed through the oiled canvas.

Through the corner of my eye, I saw Benedict burst through the stable doors riding one of our horses bareback while holding the reins of three others.

Alfonso shielded his face in the crook of his arm as he ran toward me right when the water burst forward onto the flames.

He gestured wildly toward the villa then made a shoveling motion.

I nodded as I directed the water into the belly of the beast.

Matteo circled to my left with his own stream of water as we tried to quell the flames from two different angles.

Gabriella shouted out orders from behind me to the women. "Girls! Liliana and Bianca, go help Rosa with setting up an infirmary for any injured. Amara, get on the phone and find out what's taking the fire brigade so long."

As we were in the mountains and had an extensive amount of land, we didn't entirely rely on the village fire brigade for our first response. It was expected for us to have several lines of defense in place like water pipes, hoses, and sprinklers. But we would definitely need them in case the wind shifted, or worse, one of the main buildings caught fire.

Gabriella called out to Ella, Matteo's girl. "Ella! Antonella!"

The girl seemed to be transfixed by the flames. She stood unnaturally still, the glow from the fire flickering across her dangerously pale face.

Finally, she shook her head and blinked as if coming out of a daze. "Yes! Yes, what can I do?"

"Milana is sending the villagers up. The ones with buckets."

She threw her outstretched arm to the left. "Direct them to the sand pits. The ones with shovels, divide them between Sebastian and Alfonso's ditch crews."

Ella nodded and took off in a run toward the gate to meet the villagers who had already begun to arrive.

A gust of wind sent the flames higher. "Get back! Get back!" I roared over the deafening thunder of the fire.

It wasn't the flames that killed, it was often the heat blast from the six-hundred-degree air which could travel farther and faster than the fire itself. It would scorch a person's lungs and melt their clothing to their skin before they even saw the flames.

Matteo yelled out to me as he gestured violently. "The supply barn!"

Fuck.

In that instant, Matteo, Alfonso, and I all came to the same conclusion.

With the wind shift, the old barn we had converted into an inventory building was now at risk.

Housed inside were over fifty sintered titanium filters. Titanium was a highly combustible metal which would not only react violently to the heat, but the water we used to put the flames out.

An explosion would be deadly.

Shoving the water hose into the chest of one of my nearby men, I took off toward the barn. My lungs burned from the hot air I was forced to breathe as I pushed every muscle in my body to the limit.

Matteo was on my heels as Alfonso approached from the right flank.

We were too late.

A spark had already ignited the roof. It went up like a tinderbox.

The explosion mimicked the sound of a sonic boom.

A rush of fast-moving air, wood shards, and flames rolled over us in a wave, knocking Matteo and me off our feet. My body was suspended in the air before slamming into the ground several lengths away from where I'd been standing.

Knocking me out for a moment.

Dazed, at first I thought the high-pitched bell was my ears ringing from the impact.

Then I realized it was screaming.

Amara's slight body fell over mine as she threw herself over my chest. "Barone!"

Wrapping my arms tightly around her, I rolled my body, shielding her as I pressed her into the ground.

Out of the corner of my eye, I saw Matteo doing the same for Ella. Curling his body over her shaking and crying one.

The second blast sent out another wave of hot air and more wood shards. I clenched my jaw and growled as several lodged in my back and shoulders.

The ground vibrated with the pounding of an approaching horse's hooves.

Benedict appeared through a plume of thick, pitch-black smoke. He had covered the horse's eyes with his torn shirt.

Another piercing shriek lost somewhere within the thick clouds rent the air.

Gabriella.

My God.

With his fists clutching at the horse's mane, Benedict propelled the beast forward, galloping toward her screams.

Cesare and Enzo fell on their knees before us, smothering Ella and Amara with drenched wool blankets before lifting them in their arms and running to safety as Matteo and I followed in Benedict's wake.

Benedict jumped off his horse and smacked its ass, sending it running in the opposite direction, away from the fire, just as we arrived on the other side of the barn.

Gabriella was on her knees in the dirt, desperately clutching at a still burning wood beam.

Alfonso was pinned face down underneath it.

"Help me! Help me!" she cried out.

Benedict and I pushed her aside so we could each wrap our hands around the massive support beam.

The sickening smell of burnt hair and scorched flesh made me gag and choke as I fought my body's primal instinct to release my grip.

I opened my mouth in a silent yell, straining with my brother to lift the heavy beam off our friend.

Matteo yanked on Alfonso's feet as soon as he was clear, pulling him from under it.

Gabriella turned him over. "Alfonso? Alfonso!"

Her hands frantically moved over his chest and face.

Ignoring the searing pain in my burnt hands, I bent down and shouldered Alfonso's right arm as Benedict did the same on his left side. We dragged his unconscious body to a clearing upwind of the blaze.

The moment we laid him on the grass, Gabriella fell over him. "Alfonso! Open your eyes! Please, open your eyes!"

Her tears made dirty tracks down her cheeks through the soot.

Benedict and I exchanged a look as we stared down at Alfonso's slack features.

Enzo returned with Dr. Pantona in his wake.

Benedict wrapped his arms around Gabriella's middle and forced her away from him.

"Let me go! Let me go!" she shrieked, her arms straining to reach out to Alfonso.

Benedict held on firmly. "Give the doctor room, love."

He turned her in his arms and clutched her to his chest.

I fell to my knees beside Alfonso and grabbed his hand in my injured one as Dr. Pantona pressed his fingers against his neck, searching for signs of life.

Tears blocked my vision and burned my previously heat-dried eyes as I tightened my grip on Alfonso's hand. The scorching pain in my palm and fingers anchoring me. "Come on, old friend. Stop lazing around. There's work still to be done."

Shrill sirens and a truck's horn blast signaled the arrival of reinforcements. With the added manpower of the fire brigade, I knew the already waning fire would soon be under control.

Dr. Pantona leaned over Alfonso and pressed his ear to his chest.

Everything stopped.

All the chaos around us stilled.

It seemed as if even the flames froze in jagged spikes as they reached for the now darkened skies.

We all waited, holding our breaths, willing him to hear a heartbeat.

Leaning back, the doctor met my gaze and slowly shook his head.

Gabriella broke free of Benedict's grasp as she threw herself over Alfonso's lifeless body. "Nooooooo!"

Her heartbreaking sobs ripped my soul to shreds.

"Do something! Save him!"

Dr. Pantona tried to place a comforting hand on her shoulder. "Gabriella, he's—"

She bared her teeth at him. "Don't you say it. Don't you dare fucking say it!"

Her palms gripped Alfonso's face, before she raised her arm and slapped him. "Alfonso! Wake up! Don't leave me! Wake up, damn you!"

Then her small hands curled into fists as she pounded on his

SCORN OF THE BETROTHED

chest, in a desperate attempt to get the heart she loved, the heart that was so strong and brave, so loving and loyal, to beat at least one more time. Her signature gold bangles rattling with each strike to his unresponsive chest.

"He's not dead! He's not dead! He's not dead!" she raged through her sobs.

Her black hair was in a tangled disarray, whipping across her face as she turned her head, looking at us with wild eyes. "Help him! Please!"

My throat tightened, making words almost impossible as I reached over and placed my larger hands over her fists, stilling them. "He's gone, Gabriella. Let him rest."

She pulled her hands free and gripped her hair, throwing her head back and wailing before falling forward over his body, burying her face against his neck as she clutched at his shirt.

Benedict went down on his haunches and tried to pull her back. "Come away, love. We need to move him."

She rounded on him. "Don't you touch him!" She then cradled Alfonso's head in her lap and bent over his body, holding him close as she rocked back and forth, sobbing.

Another cry pierced the air. Despite her advanced pregnancy, Milana came running toward us.

Before she reached Alfonso's body, Cesare intercepted her, sweeping her up into his arms. Milana stretched out her arm over his shoulder as her face contorted with grief. "Alfonso! Nooo!"

Despite their relatively short acquaintance, I knew she'd shared a special bond with Alfonso.

This shock could endanger her already risky pregnancy.

I shared a look with Dr. Pantona, who nodded. "I'll go to her. Then I'll see to the other injuries."

Dammit. My men. The winery. My responsibilities.

My head rose in time to see Sebastian taking control in that ruthlessly efficient, cold manner of his. He caught my gaze and nodded before raising his arm and shouting out more orders.

With that, my gaze returned to my old friend. Disbelief fighting reality.

He couldn't be gone. He just couldn't be. Shock wouldn't allow me to accept it.

For as long as I could remember, Alfonso had been my closest friend. Always supporting me, no matter what, with solid, quiet determination and his own brand of dry wit.

There wasn't a single stretch of grass over all the Cavalieri lands that we hadn't trodden together a thousand times, side by side.

And now he was gone.

And nothing would be the same again.

I swiped at my eyes with the sleeve of my shirt. Through a haze of tears, I saw Amara sprinting toward us. Catching her against my body, I pressed her close and stroked her wet hair.

"I know, *dolcezza*. I know," I murmured against her temple as I moved my hand in circles over her back, letting her sob against my shoulder.

Matteo followed closely behind her. He stared down at Alfonso's body in silence but the pain in his eyes spoke volumes. He curled his hand into a fist and turned first to Benedict, then me. "This wasn't an accident. The fire was deliberate."

My arms tightened around Amara's quaking shoulders. "This means war," I growled.

CHAPTER 46

MATTEO

*C*lawing past my grief, I searched for Ella.

A primal need to protect and shield her drove me.

She wasn't there.

The villa grounds were filled with fire vehicles, villagers' trucks, and countless people still sloshing through the mud created by the narrow rivers of water streaming over the cobble-stones away from the drenched, charred trees.

It was chaos… but silent chaos.

The whole scene was muted.

As if I had cotton wool in my ears.

There were no distinct sounds, just warbles and thumps.

Everyone moved as if suspended in molasses. Which made the sympathetic glances I was getting, as word of Alfonso's death spread, seemed to last forever, making them that much more painful.

Where was Ella?

I needed to find Ella.

I needed Ella.

Shouldering my way through the crowd, I searched every face.

I finally spotted her standing under a far-off tree. There was an unnatural stillness about her form.

Terrified she was injured, I bolted down the small hill and across the enclosure until I reached her side.

Her unseeing eyes didn't even blink at my approach. My hands wrapped around her upper arms. "Ella? Baby? Are you hurt?"

It wasn't until I gave her a little shake that she finally blinked and stared at me.

The moment she did, her face crumpled as she used her forearms to break my grasp. Her head shook from side to side and tears fell down her cheeks. "It's all my fault."

I reached for her. "Baby, no."

Holding her palms up in defense, she backed away. "Yes, it is. Fino said he would burn it to the ground. I didn't take him seriously. He warned me if I told you anything, he would burn it to the ground."

She clutched her head and fell to her knees. Rocking back and forth, she sobbed, "That nice man is dead and it's all my fault."

Goddammit.

The harder I tried to shield her from all the evil surrounding us, the more it dragged her down.

It seemed as if a storm of cold air swirled around her, sucking the heat from her body. No matter how hard I held on to her, no matter how much I shared my body's warmth, she seemed to slip further and further into the grips of icy darkness.

She was too vulnerable, too sweet, too naive to survive in this treacherous world alone.

If I let them, her family would slowly strangle my little dove until there was no light or love left in her.

Fuck that.

I wouldn't let that happen.

They couldn't have her.

They had already taken too much from us.

They weren't going to get her too.

I bent down to scoop her into my arms. Her wild and unfocused eyes turned on me. "No!"

With bent fingers she clawed and fought my embrace. She slapped my face, then pounded on my chest. "Why didn't you let me leave? Why? Why?"

I fought past her flailing arms and snatched her to me. Then I grabbed her thighs and lifted until her legs wrapped around my waist. My arms enclosed her.

If it were possible, I would have ripped open my ribcage and tucked her inside my body close to my heart just to keep her safe and warm.

Her tears wet my neck as she clung to me.

Ignoring the trauma around us, I carried her into the villa.

In my own shellshocked mind, I had only one single purpose —to get her warm and clean.

She was covered in the filth of another's treacherous deed.

In my helpless desperation, I vaulted up the stairs two at a time, as if she weighed nothing in my arms.

Storming down the deserted hallway to my suite of rooms, I marched straight into the bathroom. After stepping into the glass stall still fully clothed, I used my fist to turn the shower lever on full blast.

Ella pulled back at the initial shock of cold water. Her beautiful pale face with streaks of makeup and soot stared at me as if seeing me for the first time. "Tell me it's all a bad dream. Tell me none of this is happening. Lie to me."

As the warming water drenched her hair, turning it from a

golden blonde to a deeper brown, I cupped her face. "I can't, babygirl. You have no idea how badly I wish I could."

Her face became pinched, her mouth opening on a cry.

Unable to take her pain another moment, I slammed my mouth down on hers. As if I could somehow swallow all the anguish and guilt tormenting her.

Swinging her to my left, I lifted her up and slammed her back against the tiles, pressing my hips into hers as I deepened the kiss. My lips moved over hers as my tongue swept inside.

But it wasn't enough.

I needed something... I needed more.

My fingers twisted in her wet curls as I sank my teeth into her full lower lip.

She cried out and jerked her head back.

With my breath coming fast and heavy, I stared at the pink tip of her tongue sweeping along her lip to taste the droplet of blood that had formed there.

Her hands grabbed my jaw as her gaze fixated on my bared teeth. "Hurt me again, Matteo."

My brow furrowed even as a primal urge rose in my chest. "Ella—"

"I'm so cold and numb. The guilt is too much."

My fingers dug into the flesh of her hip where I held her anchored between me and the shower wall. "Baby, you don't know what you're asking. I'll be too rough."

She buried her face in the crook of my neck and... bit me. Hard.

An animalistic growl rumbled from my chest.

All the pain. All the grief. All the anger vibrated through every limb.

My hand fisted in her hair, and I captured her mouth again. Giving no quarter.

The beast was unleashed.

Hot water stung the scrapes on my back from the explosion, spurring me on.

Lowering her feet to the slick tile floor, I gripped the front of her dress and tore it open, snapping the fragile plastic clasp of her bra at the same time. My mouth descended. I sucked her nipple into my mouth, using my teeth to scrape the sensitive flesh.

Ella groaned as her fingers threaded through my hair, then pulled hard.

Moving my mouth over the soft curves of her breast, I sank my teeth into her flesh.

She cried out but didn't move away, only yanking on my hair harder.

A sick, possessive satisfaction gripped me as I stared down at the red, crescent-shaped bite mark on her flesh.

Mine.

Marked as mine.

Forever mine.

And no one was taking her from me.

I spun her around. After ripping the dress off her arms, it fell in a sodden heap at our feet. "Hands on the wall."

Her fingers splayed out as she braced herself against the wall.

She wasn't wearing any panties.

I ran my hand over her ass cheek before raising my arm and spanking her. Her wet, warmed skin bloomed with a bright hand mark.

Good.

I wanted to mark every inch of her skin. If I could, I'd tattoo my mark in permanent ink, so she'd never forget who owned her now.

Hating having to take my hands off her even for a second, I made short work of my shirt, tearing it over my head and throwing it aside before spanning my hands over her generous hips.

I wrenched her hips backward until her ass slammed against my hips.

Twisting my hand in her hair, I reached for the almond shower oil. I squeezed the bottle until a thick stream of golden liquid streamed down her lower back to pool between her ass cheeks.

The bottle clattered against the glass shower wall as I threw it away from me and ran my fingers along her crack, pushing inside until the tips skimmed her tight, puckered hole.

Pushing one finger inside, I worked the oil in deep before lowering my jeans zipper.

Released from the confines of my jeans, my hard cock sprang forward, bobbing against the top of her ass. My oil-covered hand clasped my shaft in a rigid grip as I coated it before stroking it against her skin several times then pushing it between her cheeks.

Pressing my hips forward, I pushed the head against her hole.

Ella fought my grasp on her hair as she tried to look over her shoulder.

"Eyes forward," I commanded.

She whimpered as I pushed against the constricted muscle ring again.

I leaned over her back to rasp in her ear, "You want the pain, babygirl?"

She moaned.

I yanked on her hair. "I asked you a question," I growled.

"Yes, sir."

I nipped at her earlobe like a stallion preparing his mare. "Beg me for it."

The wet surface of the tile squeaked under her moving hands. "Please. I need this."

The head of my cock pushed inside her ass.

Ella yelped and rose onto her toes.

"Remember, this is what you wanted, baby."

The voice inside my head warning me to go gentle was drowned out by a primal need to claim.

I thrust forward, impaling my cock deep inside of her.

Her body bucked as she screamed.

The sight of my thick girth forced deep inside her tight hole was one of the most erotic things I'd ever witnessed.

It was the ultimate act of submission.

For her to accept the pain, to accept my dominance over every part of her.

"Oh, God! It hurts," she whimpered.

I pulled out slightly and thrust in again as her body clenched around my flesh. Releasing my grip on her hair, I pressed my chest against her back and reached around us to cup her breasts.

All restraint gone, I pounded into her like a rutting beast, squeezing her breasts, pinching her nipples.

My thrusts were so ferocious her knees buckled.

My legs absorbed the impact as I followed her to the shower floor.

With her on her hands and knees before me, I grasped her hair again. Her back bowed as I reared upward. Raising my arm, I smacked her ass before I increased the feverish pace of my thrusts.

Scorching hot water pounded down on us, filling the chamber with steam and making it hard to breathe.

After several more punishing thrusts, I moved my hands to her ass. Splaying her cheeks open wide, I watched my cock open her now sore hole, taking sadistic pleasure in forcing it to accept me.

My balls tightened at the sight. Pressure rippled down my shaft. With a final thrust I roared my release, pulling back so I could watch my come coat her gaping hole before the water washed it away.

Lightheaded from the intensity of my release, I wasn't finished.

I turned her onto her back. Sliding her forward so the shower stream would strike her breasts not her face, I lifted her hips and hooked her legs over my shoulders. I then pushed my face between her thighs and feasted.

Licking and sucking at her clit until her body bucked and she cried out her own release.

Only then did I lower her legs to straddle me so I could pull her up against my chest.

My arms wrapped securely around her, she burst into sobs.

I cupped the back of her head and buried my face in her wet hair, my own tears now falling.

CHAPTER 47

MATTEO

*H*er tears spent, I held her close until her body went limp in my embrace.

Only then did I maneuver onto my knees and then rise, still holding her close.

Turning off the shower with my elbow, I carried her wet and clinging to my neck back into the bedroom. With one hand, I tossed back the blankets and crawled into bed, using its warmth to dry our bodies.

Neither of us spoke.

I clung to her until her body stopped trembling with emotion and finally stilled.

Brushing the hair away from her face, I stared down at her closed eyes. She had fallen into an exhausted sleep.

Breathing in the clean scent of her skin, I kissed the top of her head and whispered, "You're safe, baby. I'm here and I m going to fix this. God help me, I'm going to fix this."

Her lips rested near my tattoo.

I stared at the bright purple and gold colors of the passion-flower with the Triad crown over a crimson pomegranate.

One of the proudest moments of my life was standing next to my father during the brotherhood marking ceremony.

At the time, I'd felt an almost divine purpose to my life. Knowing that, unlike so many who squandered their wealth and privilege on selfish pursuits, I would have a higher calling.

This moment superseded that.

My life's purpose was now solely focused on keeping this beautiful, delicate creature in the light. I would not let the cold darkness of her treacherous family consume her.

With slow and gentle movements, I shifted her away from my chest so I could slide from the bed. Standing over it, I watched her curl up under the blankets like a little rabbit.

Padding barefoot and naked over to the window, I drew back the curtains and stared down at the courtyard below.

Unlike the usually serene view of the winery and the vine-yards beyond, there was disorder and an ominous energy that hung over the place like a dark cloud.

The aftermath of any disaster, whether it be natural or manmade, was always the same.

Shock. Disbelief. Rage.

As if the tangled mess of sodden rubble and charred remains offended our human need for control and order in the universe.

Father Luca's car appeared, slowly navigating around the hoses, discarded shovels, and lingering groups of exhausted villagers.

And I knew what needed to be done.

Marching over to my closet, I drew on a fresh pair of jeans, socks, and a soft cotton T-shirt to cover the scrapes on my back before tossing on a charcoal cable-knit sweater.

I then selected a pair of dark blue sweatpants and another cream-colored knit sweater. Having no other option, I grabbed a second pair of thick wool socks.

I knelt down by the side of the bed and caressed Ella's cheek. "Baby, I need you to wake up."

Her eyelids fluttered as she moaned and turned to bury her cheek in the pillow.

God, she was so beautiful. Even with her tearstained eyes, tangled hair, and no makeup, she was easily the most stunning woman I'd ever laid eyes on.

"Baby, I need you to sit up."

She groaned. "Why?"

I sat on the edge of the bed and scooped her onto my lap. Knowing she'd immediately feel the loss of the warm blankets, I swept my sweatpants over her legs. "Lift your hips."

She leaned against my chest and did as she was told.

"Good girl."

Capturing her left foot, I slipped one of the socks on as she rested her head against my shoulder. "Please, I don't want to face it. Not yet."

"I know, baby. I know. But there is something that can't wait."

After slipping on the second sock, I leaned back and grabbed the sweater. "Arms up."

She crossed her arms over her breasts. "Where are we going? Are you sending me away?"

"Never. Now arms up."

The sweater fell over her slim arms and form like an over-sized poncho.

I flipped her still damp hair out from the collar and smoothed it down her back. "It won't take long and then you can go back to bed, okay?"

Cradling her in my arms, I carried her out of the room and down the stairs into the parlor, where I settled her in one of the plush chairs. Snatching a crocheted blanket from the back of the sofa, I wrapped it around her hips. I then leaned over her and kissed her forehead. "Wait right here. I'll be right back."

She reached out and grabbed my wrist. "No, please don't leave me."

I stroked her cheek. "You're safer in here. Plus I don't want you to get a chill from wet socks. I promise I'll be right back."

My chest warmed at her need for me. While the circumstances were the most horrific I could imagine, it pleased me that she was finally turning to me for support.

Heading outside, the first person I encountered was Sebastian.

We hugged, then he patted me on the back. "Alfonso was the best of us."

A lump formed in the back of my throat. "That he was. Thank you for all your help."

He gave me a rare smile. "Your uncle is more of a father to me than my own. There is nothing I wouldn't do for your family. Nothing. I hope you know that."

His intense look matched mine.

The true meaning of his statement was left unsaid. No words were needed.

We both knew today's actions would fracture the Agnello syndicate and lead to a mafia war.

One we were now heavily involved in.

Sebastian promising the support of the Diamanti dynasty wasn't just symbolic, it carried a significant weight. By getting involved, he risked shattering the myth that the Diamantis were nothing more than a powerful diamond empire.

Once he lifted that veil, there would be no going back.

It was an enormous sacrifice. One I knew he didn't offer lightly.

Despite his closeness with my Uncle Barone, Sebastian had a secret.

One only my father and I were aware of.

One that demanded his sacrifice, even though it was freely given.

My grip on his shoulder tightened. "Always."

Gesturing behind me, I asked, "Can you watch over Ella? She's in the parlor. I need to find Father Luca."

He nodded and headed into the villa.

After several minutes, I located Father Luca. He was wiping something from his face with a handkerchief as he leaned against a stone wall. "Dr. Pantona said he gave your Aunt Gabriella a sedative, but let me assure you, it has *not* taken effect yet."

I grimaced. "Sorry, Father. She's upset. As we all are."

He nodded as he straightened and pushed the handkerchief which now smelled like Scotch into his back pocket. "Your Aunt is an amazingly passionate woman. It only makes sense that she would grieve just as passionately."

I couldn't resist. "You too, Father?"

A ruddy blush stained his cheeks. "Not in that way of course, I'm an honest man of the cloth. But I doubt there's a man alive who hasn't fallen prey to your aunt's charms. She's a very engaging woman. Eve had nothing on her."

A scratch formed in the back of my throat as my eyes misted. Rubbing my jaw, I cleared my throat as I forced myself to focus on the issue at hand, Ella's safety.

Alfonso would be pissed as fuck looking down on me from heaven if I put my grief ahead of protecting my girl. He loved all our girls like daughters and now that he was gone, it was our duty to honor him by keeping them safe.

"Father, I need a favor."

CHAPTER 48

ELLA

"*A*re you crazy?"

Matteo's lips thinned, his hands anchored on his hips. "This is happening, Ella."

I shook my head and scanned the stern male faces staring back at me.

Soon after Sebastian had entered the room, Matteo followed with a priest and Lucia.

At first, I didn't register the priest, too intent on speaking with Lucia. "I'm so very sorry for the unforgivable way I behaved. You have every right to hate me."

She laughed and brushed me off. "It's fine. Really. Amara explained it all to me. I think it was exciting to be part of your..." She lowered her voice and glanced around conspiratorially. "*Secret cover.*"

"That is very sweet of you."

Even as I said it, a lead ball formed in my stomach. All the Cavalieris and even their staff were being so freaking nice to me and all I had done was bring grief and misfortune to their doorstep.

My face crumpled as a deep, aching sadness dropped over me, suffocating me.

Matteo rushed forward. "I know that face. Stop it. None of this was your fault."

I sniffed. "Fino said if I told anyone he'd—"

"Exactly. Fino said. These are his and his bosses' actions, not yours."

Swiping at my tears, I tried to reason with him. "But I lied to you, to your family. I—"

"You had your reasons… and now so do I."

He stepped aside and gestured for the priest to step forward. "This is Father Luca."

I nodded. "Hello, Father."

Matteo stared down at me so intently, an unease settled in my chest.

Looking between them, I asked, "What's going on?"

Matteo clasped his hands around mine and took a deep breath. "Father Luca is going to marry us."

My eyes widened. "Are you crazy?"

"This is happening, Ella. It's for your own safety."

I broke his hold and gestured wildly toward the windows and the somber aftermath of the fire. "We can't get married. Alfonso just—" My throat closed, and I couldn't finish my sentence as my vision blurred.

"That is precisely why. And trust me, Alfonso would be the first person to agree with me. It's the only way to fully protect you from what is about to happen."

Turning to Father Luca, I pleaded, "You can't possibly agree with this."

He gripped his Bible more firmly to his chest. "That depends. Have you and Matteo engaged in any…" he raised his eyebrow, "*extramarital* relations?"

My cheeks burned as I lowered my gaze. Lying was one thing. Lying to a priest was another.

I tried another tack. "This can't possibly be legal. There are forms, a license."

Matteo tossed a question over his shoulder. "Father, in the eyes of God, would we be married?"

"Yes, son. God's law is above man's."

He nodded. "That's good enough for me. We'll worry about the government paperwork later. All your family needs to know is that the marriage is binding and since we've already consummated—"

I covered his mouth with my hand as my cheeks burned brighter. "Don't you dare," I whispered.

He spoke against my palm, tickling my skin. "Then you better say yes."

I pulled my hand away, shaking my head. "You know I can't."

He turned to Father Luca. "Father Luca, what is the Church's opinion on shower anal—"

"Oh my God! Yes! Yes! I'll marry you. Just stop talking!"

Father Luca's face burned almost as brightly as mine as he cleared his throat. "Very good. Will the witnesses stand behind the couple, please."

Lucia called out. "Wait!" With that she ran from the room and soon returned holding a large bunch of pale blue hydrangeas.

She wiped the stems off on her dress before handing them to me. "I pulled them from a vase in the hall. Every bride needs a bouquet."

Holding my makeshift bouquet in one hand and the rolled-down waist of Matteo's sweatpants in the other, I stood with Matteo before Father Luca.

We were married.

I was now Matteo's wife.

His wife.

And all hell was going to break loose when my family found out.

* * *

MATTEO SWOOPED me into his arms before kissing me hard on the mouth. Everything and everyone faded into the background as I lost myself in his kiss.

Lucia broke the spell. "Throw the bouquet."

I tossed her the bouquet as Matteo thanked Father Luca and Sebastian before he carried me out of the room.

It was surreal.

Less than thirty minutes after leaving it, I was back in Matteo's bed under the slightly damp covers. "You can't expect me to take a nap now! After everything that just happened."

He tapped the tip of my nose. "I can and I do."

"But I should be down there helping at least."

"Everything is being handled. You are a target, and I won't have you wandering around out in the open with so many strangers on the grounds."

"But—"

"No buts. I'm going down to help now. You rest. That's an order."

He gave me another quick kiss before closing the drapes, enveloping the room in darkness. "Sleep."

He closed the door softly behind him.

My last thought was there was absolutely no way I was going to be able to sleep under the circumstances—right before exhaustion overtook me.

* * *

WHEN I AWOKE LATER, the thin streaks of sunlight were no longer visible through the cracks in the drapes.

A dark form leaned over me.

I leaned up on my forearms as my eyes adjusted to the dark interior. "Matteo?"

A cloth with a cloyingly sweet scent was thrust against my nose and mouth.

I struggled, but with each passing second my limbs became more weighed down until there was nothing but heavy... suffocating... darkness.

CHAPTER 49

ANTONIA

"*E*w. What the fuck is she wearing? Are those sweatpants?"

"Princess, we don't have much time," pleaded Fino.

I gritted my teeth and bit back a snarky retort.

I detested pet names.

Reminding myself that I needed Fino's stupid cooperation, I pasted on a smile. "I know, *darling*, and I'd help you with her body, but my makeup needs to be perfect."

My attention returned to my reflection.

With a makeup sponge, I dabbed more concealer over the purple bruise under my eye.

My boyfriend didn't take the news of my pregnancy very well.

If I had *actually* been pregnant, I might have been offended.

As it was, I was just pissed.

If Judge Marzio Delluci thought he could fill me with come and empty promises and then dump me—he had another think coming.

Nobody fucked over Antonia Fichera. I was, after all, my father's daughter.

Fortunately, I was always several moves ahead of the ignorant men around me.

When Fino stupidly came to me to corroborate my idiot sister's accusations, I at least was smart enough to demand an audience with Marzio. It didn't take long to have him wrapped around my finger. Or, strictly speaking, around my body while I bent over his desk and he fucked me, completely unaware of the small video camera in my purse nearby.

I wasn't trying to save Father. Quite the opposite.

I was going to replace him. All of them.

It was past time the Sicilian mafia had a female *capo dei capi*. With all the changes he was making, it was only a matter of time before someone tried to dethrone Dante.

Why shouldn't that someone be me?

First, I had to eliminate the competition.

Salvatore was the first person the syndicate would turn to if Dante was gone. He had to go first. With his sick appetites and blind ambition, he was the easiest to manipulate.

Salvatore's downfall was the first crack in Dante's rule. It showed his weakness.

Next in line was my father.

My goody-two-shoes twin sister gave me the perfect in and handed me the protection I would need once I took control of the Agnello syndicate. All I needed to do was wait until the judge made a move against my father, which would throw the whole syndicate into chaos.

I would then swoop in and have the power to make it all go away... *for a price.*

It really was amusing how much a girl could learn by simply being in the room or spreading her legs. For years now, I played the dutiful, dumb daughter at my father's table, learning about their criminal enterprises and all their dirty secrets.

Then I gathered blackmail information against several high-ranking soldiers throughout the syndicate. Men were so careless about their business when they thought with their cocks.

The only thing I hadn't planned on was the Cavalieris agreeing to an arranged marriage.

Dante outmaneuvered me there, but not for long.

At first, I thought I'd force Marzio's hand.

What better hiding place for the head of a mafia syndicate than as the wife of a powerful judge?

With my fingertips, I touched the bruise along my cheekbone and grimaced.

I hadn't planned on Marzio being more corrupt than my father and Dante combined... or having even better connections. He now had half the Sicilian police force and half the underworld criminal element looking for me.

Time for Plan B.

I patted my finger along my lower lip, applying the perfect amount of siren-red matte lipstick. "Remember, Fino. Marzio must believe that Ella is me, so make sure you tape her mouth nice and secure so she can't talk."

"Of course, my angel pie."

Vomit.

Putting up with his slobbering, cloddish attempts in bed had been the worst part of all my plans, but Fino had made the perfect pawn to manipulate my sister while also keeping tabs on Marzio's movements.

Thank God, when this was all over, I already had plans for him to die in some terribly embarrassing way. Maybe I'd slip him a drug that mimicked a heart attack right before he went to the bathroom, so he died on the toilet with his pants around his ankles and his pathetic little crooked penis on display. That would be hilarious.

Fino flipped Ella's legs into the trunk and turned to me as he slammed the lid shut. "But explain to me again why you are staying behind."

My hand curled into a fist, digging my long nails into my palm. Taking a deep breath, I forced my voice to sound even and cheerful. "We talked about this, *darling*. You need time to get to Sicily without detection. Besides, by marrying Matteo Cavalieri, I will have access to his millions."

Fino's weasel face twisted. "But I don't like the idea of you being with him. You said you loved me."

I patted his cheek. "And I do, darling." I placed my hand over my heart. "Trust me, I'll be thinking of you the whole time I'm in bed with him."

Sure. That tracked. I'd be thinking of this pasty little ferret with his sweaty palms while the tall, masculine, deliciously muscled Matteo Cavalieri was rutting over me with his big cock.

So I leaned over and kissed Fino's cheek, leaving a large red lipstick smear. It wasn't that big of an ick, I did after all need to blot my lipstick. "And don't worry, *pooky*. As soon as we're married, Matteo Cavalieri will meet with an unfortunate accident, and I'll return to Sicily. The grieving, incredibly rich, widow."

He nodded decisively. "And then we'll marry."

Knowing I would never be able to say it with a straight face, I turned away to zip my makeup bag closed. "Of course. I can't wait to be your wife." *Ew, gag.*

After smoothing my hands over the silk nightgown I had on, I shrugged into a trench coat and slung my purse over my shoulder. "I have to go before Matteo realizes my sister... I mean *I'm*... gone. Make sure Marzio completely believes it is me before you kill her. We can't have any loose ends."

I couldn't wait to see the bastard's face when he learned I was alive and married to Matteo Cavalieri.

Fino leaned in for another kiss, before settling for a peck on my cheek as I turned my head away. "I won't let you down, *schnookems.*"

Ew.

Dying on the toilet was definitely not humiliating enough.

As Fino drove off using a back road to the north of the winery, I took advantage of the chaos after the fire we started to slip into the villa. I had already paid off one of the staff to tell me Ella's whereabouts; my slutty twin sister was staying in Matteo's suite.

Apparently, she wasn't that innocent after all. It was a shame. Had I known sooner, I might have included her in my plans.

Too late now.

Bye, sis.

CHAPTER 50

MATTEO

Something was wrong.

Over twelve straight hours of dealing with the aftermath of the fire had me pushed beyond the point of exhaustion. By two a.m., all I wanted to do was climb into bed and hold my wife close.

My wife.

It felt good to say it. Although I had resigned myself to the concept of marriage, I had not even considered the possibility of finding happiness in marriage. Fate had other plans. Thank God.

Especially in moments like this. It would have been torture to watch my cousins, father, and uncle turn to their girls for comfort in their grief while I had nothing but the cold bed of an unwilling bride. Enzo had been right. Forsaking love and support was no way to live.

After hosing off downstairs and agreeing to allow Dr. Pantona to examine the scrapes on my back, I was finally able to check on my baby.

Lucia was kind enough to bring her a tray of food earlier but told me the room was dark and Ella didn't respond so she just left it on a side table. Although I was concerned that she may have not eaten, perhaps sleep was the best thing for her right now.

Sleep was an escape.

And I'd desperately wanted that same escape.

But the moment I entered our suite, I knew something was off.

It was the smell.

A cloying, sickeningly dense rose perfume.

I knew that scent...

Flipping on the light, I stormed over to the bed and ripped the covers off.

Antonia.

With her hair artfully splayed out on the pillow and her heavy makeup perfectly applied, she pretended to blink and slowly come awake like some demented fairy tale princess rising from a bed of fucking flower petals.

Gracefully drawing her hands under her chin, she arched her back, pushing her breasts which were barely contained in some scrap of silk and lace forward. "Darling, is that you?"

My fist twisted in her hair. I grimaced at the crunchy feel of the thick hairspray covering the tacky curls sticking to my palm. With a fierce yank, I pulled her from the bed. "Don't you fucking darling me. Where the hell is Ella?"

From her position on her knees at my feet, she ran her hands over the tops of my thighs. Her eyes filled with false tears. "Please don't be angry with me. She made me do it."

Throwing off her hands, I prowled around the room. "Bull-shit. I know it was you, Antonia."

I slammed open the door to my closet. "Ella?" It was empty. "What did you do with her?"

Antonia crawled across the room to me. This time reaching up and pressing her hands against my crotch. "Be kind to me.

You have no idea the... the... *unspeakable things...* I've endured to reach you."

My hands wrapped around her wrists as I pulled her to her feet. "You have one second to tell me where your sister is, you miserable excuse for a human being, or I won't be responsible for my actions."

She covered her face and cried. "I told you. This was all her idea. She wanted your money for herself. That is why she pretended to be me at Carnevale and why she kissed you in the gazebo. It was all part of her plan to steal my identity and trick you into marrying her instead."

The false gesture was ruined when I watched her peek over her fingertips to see if I was affected.

My hands curled into fists at my sides in an effort to keep from striking her. Judging by the slight smear of makeup over her cheek, someone already had. "I will ask you one more time. Where is she?"

Her well-manicured hand, long nails painted a glossy black, pressed over her heart. "After escaping my father, I finally made my way here. The moment she saw me, she became enraged. She knew her plan had failed and that I was your true bride."

Jesus Christ.

I stared at her hands. How could I not have noticed Ella's hands sooner than I did? Unlike her sister's claws, Ella's nails were short and unvarnished. More than likely because of her cello playing. I twisted my head to stare at the cello in the corner. Her beloved cello.

Antonia sidled closer to me, her perfume an unpleasant, rank cloud. "I tried to stop her. You must believe me. I begged her not to set the fire."

My gaze snapped back to her. My family's pain and grief were too raw, too fresh for me to restrain myself any further. My arm snapped out and I grabbed her by the throat. "You manipulative bitch. I'll see you rot in hell for Alfonso's death. And so help me God, if you've harmed Ella in any way..."

Her scarlet lips turned up in a smile. Then she bared her teeth as she laughed. "Well, this is interesting. A man only behaves like this when he's had a taste of pussy. Did my sweet, innocent sister give up the goods?"

I matched her smile, taking great pleasure in saying, "Well, it's only fitting that a wife would sleep with her husband."

Her eyes widened before she ran her claws over my wrists, drawing blood. "You're lying."

I released her and backed away, afraid of what I would do if I continued to hold her life in my hands. "Am I?"

Her gaze narrowed as her chest rose and fell with her heavy, angry breaths. "I'd have heard about a wedding."

Trying to turn the tables on her, I said, "Fino didn't tell you?"

"No, he didn't tell—"

So she was working with Fino, which meant Judge Marzio Delluci may or may not be involved as well.

She tilted her head as she sneered. "Very clever. Much more clever than I gave you credit for. Fine. Whatever. Good luck tricking me into telling you where your precious soon to be dead wife is."

I crossed my arms over my chest. "Oh, you'll talk. Trust me."

Antonia fluffed her hair. "Doubtful. And besides, you better be nice to me. Once my sister is dead, Dante and my father are going to make you honor your original agreement and marry me anyway to avoid a scandal."

I'd had enough of this.

Snatching her by the forearm, I pulled her out of the room and down the hall.

She dragged her feet. "Where are you taking me? I'll scream!"

Clenching my fist, I pounded on the bedroom door at the farthest corner of the villa.

After a moment, it swung open.

It was clear from my father's expression and Liliana's naked shoulders peeking out above the covers that I had interrupted something.

My father frowned. "What the fuck is going on? Why is Antonia here?"

I ground my teeth. Of course he would recognize Antonia immediately. Fuck, I was a goddamn fool those first few days with Ella.

Shaking off my disgust with myself, I said, "Ella is missing. She's involved. I need your *special* interrogation skills."

He nodded. "Let me get my tools."

Antonia yanked on my grip, but I held steady. "God, this is so pathetic. You honestly think this scare tactic is going to work on me?"

Fear made her voice quiver at a higher pitch.

I leaned closer over her, as I raised one eyebrow. "You don't think so? I give you less than a minute."

My father reappeared. This time in jeans and a shirt, holding a weathered, leather knife roll. As he shifted it in his hands, the metal tools inside clanked.

Antonia's face paled as her knees buckled.

CHAPTER 51

ELLA

*T*he click of a latch.

A scrape of metal as a slim tray slid along the floor.

Then the bang of the door.

Four meals.

Two days.

For two days, I'd been kept prisoner in multiple windowless holding cells, one no different than the other.

It seemed like every few hours I'd be moved to a different location. I'd tried to listen for any clues as to where I was being taken, but the thick, wool hood over my head muffled any sound.

At first, I thought it might be less because of the number of meals, but then I realized Fino was only bothering to feed me just enough to keep me alive. A *cornetto* and some lukewarm cafe in the morning and some soft polenta with stewed tomatoes in what I assumed was the evening.

Hearing Matteo's voice in my head to eat and keep up my strength until he could rescue me, I choked down the meager meals.

There was a time when I would have thought I wasn't worth rescuing.

Not anymore.

Matteo had shown me how all the loyalty and perseverance I'd wasted on my family over the years could be turned into inner strength.

How ironic.

In fighting him, I'd learned to fight for myself.

And it was through witnessing how his family interacted that I finally accepted a hard truth.

The fact that Antonia and my father were my blood didn't give them the right to walk all over me. It didn't give them the right to take advantage of my better nature. To use me for their own ends. To treat me like I was nothing.

That wasn't family. That was abuse.

Family was love and laughter and support and being there for one another.

Family was choosing to surround yourself with people who not only mattered to you, but to whom you also mattered.

Family was respect.

Fuck that old adage that blood was thicker than water.

It was a stupid saying. You couldn't survive on blood, but clean, fresh water was life-giving. Things grew and thrived with water, like the ancient grapevines at Cavalieri.

Water was the family you chose.

I'd had a lot of time to think while trapped in this cell. My single-minded determination to find out what happened to my mother was part of the reason why I had been so easily led into this mess. But why?

For some childish dream that things would be different in my life had my mother been around? I realized now that was unlikely. My father and sister were who they were. Nothing would have changed with my mother in the home.

And if she wasn't dead, then my selfish insistence on pursuing her disappearance could have led to her discovery. I could have jeopardized the life my mother sacrificed her daughters to achieve.

Although deep down, as much as I wanted to, I didn't truly believe she was living a new life somewhere under an assumed name. I knew she was dead. I also knew the mafia were very skilled at hiding bodies and never facing justice.

And now there was a good chance, if Matteo didn't find me in time, that I would share the same fate.

How ironic.

* * *

ANOTHER CLICK OF THE LATCH.

My chest tightened as my stomach cramped.

Instinctively, I knew it was too early for my next paltry tray.

Something was happening.

The door swung open, and Fino appeared. "It's time."

I started to speak and choked. My throat sore from screaming for help the first day. I cleared my throat and tried again, whispering, "Why are you doing this, Fino? I don't understand."

"Get up."

"Please. If it's my mother's investigation, you don't have to pursue it anymore."

"I said, get up."

"Is it my father? Did he pay you to stop looking into his affairs? Did he pay you to kill me?"

"Shut up."

Rising from the stained prison mattress that served as my only furniture in the cell, I asked, "Are you going to kill me now?"

"No more questions."

He ripped a strip of duct tape from the roll and held it between his hands as he approached me.

"No!"

* * *

THE SKIN around my wrists stung as I pulled and twisted them, desperate to get free.

Despite the duct tape wrapped several times around my head and over my mouth, I still tried to scream for help. In vain.

Terrified, I shook my arms as I tried to break the steering wheel. My wrists were bound too tightly with duct tape to ever hope to free myself that way. My only hope would be to break the wheel and then use it to smash open the window.

Even if I could break free, I knew that Fino and his three thug companions were nearby. I'd never outrun all four of them.

Again I screamed as a clear liquid ran down the windshield, then over the hood. The noxious fumes burned my nose. Fino then appeared as he circled around the car while dousing it in petrol.

After tossing the plastic container aside, he took out his phone and pointed it at me. "Smile for the Judge, Antonia."

Why was he calling me Antonia? He knew damn well I was Antonella.

What the hell was going on?

My eyes widened as I shook my head and tried to object despite the tape. The only sounds I made were muffled whimpers.

Fino laughed. "Wave goodbye, *Antonia*! Oh wait, you can't."

He turned the phone toward himself and handed it to one of the thugs. "Film me."

He then crouched near the open driver-side door and

grabbed the top of my head, forcing me to face the camera phone. "This is your proof, Judge, that I have taken care of the problem for you."

Why would Judge Delluci want Antonia dead? Or me?

Fino released me and reached into his pocket for a Zippo lighter. "And goodbye, Ella."

Flicking the lid open, he tossed the open flame onto the hood of the car.

CHAPTER 52

MATTEO

*F*ire.

For the second time in close to three days, I saw an ominous orange glow in the distance.

This time the destructive flames were potentially killing the woman I loved.

"Fuck!" I screamed. "That has to be Ella. Faster."

Enzo slammed on the gas as we raced toward the remote beach on a deserted stretch of coastland just south of Palermo.

For over two days, we had been tracking Fino's movements after learning he had taken Ella to Sicily from Antonia, who cracked like an egg at just the sight of my father's "tools."

She didn't need to know they were actually pastry tools for Liliana's new baking hobby.

After dumping her in Dante's hands we went on the hunt

But we were always a step behind.

Always getting there too late.

My frustration and anguish grew with each missed opportunity.

It didn't help that she was being shuttled between secret mafia detention centers around northern Sicily. There were no official records of the facilities, and no one would talk openly about them.

We had forked over countless millions in untraceable diamonds provided by Sebastian for bribes just to learn about them. It had taken millions more in diamonds to bribe our way into the clandestine locations to search for Ella.

None of this was done with the local police's knowledge.

Or Dante's.

We couldn't risk it.

As much as I wanted to barge straight into Judge Marzio Delluci's office and demand to know his involvement with Antonia and where he was holding Ella, I had been convinced to hold off.

Sicily was not our territory.

We had no true friends or connections.

There was deception and betrayal at every turn.

Each person we spoke to could be the one to give the order to have Ella killed.

There was no way to know who to trust— so we trusted no one.

Which meant an excruciatingly slow process of bribes and searches.

One prisoner after another.

Each one more disturbingly cruel than the last.

I was absolutely feral in my desperation to find her.

When I did finally locate Fino, I was going to tear him apart limb from limb with my fucking teeth just so I could taste his blood and crunch on his fucking bones.

Finally, we had caught a break.

Unlike before when we missed them by hours, we had only missed them by minutes.

Fortunately, we had a helicopter in the air that was able to track and access any vehicles traveling on the remote roads leading to the secret prison.

It only took a matter of minutes to zero in on the correct ones, one large black SUV and one beat-up white hatchback.

Just as we were racing down the single lane toward the flames, the SUV approached from the opposite direction.

As it tried to veer off the road to avoid us, Enzo wrenched the wheel as he gunned it.

Our Range Rover swung violently to the left, perpendicular to the other car.

I stretched my arm out the window and fired one bullet straight into the grill.

A thick plume of smoke burst around the edges of the hood, before the flat piece of metal flew upward, blocking the windshield.

The black SUV fishtailed then stopped.

The three men inside burst out of the doors and made a break for it.

As Enzo, Cesare and Sebastian pursued them, my father and I searched the abandoned vehicle.

My father cursed. "She's not in here."

The blood in my veins froze.

Two cars. An SUV *and* a white hatchback.

I turned to search the horizon for the origin of the flames.

It was the hatchback.

"My God! She's in the burning car."

Time stopped.

Everything ceased to exist.

There was no breath, no warmth, no life.

All was nothingness except for the thundering in my ears as I ran with every ounce of my strength to reach the car which was already engulfed in flames.

Through the driver's window I could see Ella's horrified gaze as she shook her head violently and gestured with her chin that I should stay back. Even in death, she wasn't thinking of herself.

From past experience, I knew it was useless to try the door. The only way to get her out was through the window and there wasn't much time.

From the looks of it, Fino and his goons had only doused the exterior of the car.

A rookie mistake.

If they had known to soak the interior seat cushions and to douse the engine block, Ella would already be dead.

As it was, having only the exterior hood and roof on fire bought us time.

Not much.

But every second counted.

I stretched out my arm. "I need—"

Before I could finish my sentence, my father was at my side. "Right here, son."

He handed me his Franchi SPAS-12 combat shotgun. "Ella, lean forward," I yelled.

She ducked her head until her forehead touched the steering wheel.

I fired one shot at the upper right corner of the window, shattering it.

"Christ, she's duct taped to the fucking steering wheel."

Ella shook her head as tears streamed down her flushed face. It was clear she was trying to speak to me over her duct taped gag. Although I couldn't make out the words, it was obvious she was begging me to leave and save myself.

Knowing it was important to keep her calm despite the danger and rising flames around us, I gave her a quick wink and teased, "I love you too, baby."

SCORN OF THE BETROTHED

My hand reached into my boot for my switchblade. After flicking it open, I made quick work of her binds.

My father and I both yanked Ella through the window.

I then tossed her over my shoulder and ran.

We needed to get as far away from the vehicle as possible before it—

The car exploded into a searing ball of flame.

* * *

WHEN WE REACHED OUR SUV, my cousins and Sebastian had already dragged Fino and his cohorts back.

I set Ella down, carefully brushing pieces of pebble-like glass from her hair and clothes before placing her in the passenger seat. Crouching down in front of her, I held up my blade. "I need to cut the tape. Stay very still."

Her brow furrowed as she whimpered.

Very carefully, I slipped the tip of the knife under the tape's edge and sliced through it. I hissed as I was forced to gingerly pull the tape off her swollen lips. Rather than pull her hair, I cut the strands still attached to the tape. Her hair was so wavy and full, no one would ever notice the thin, uneven layer.

The moment she was free she threw her arms around my neck. Her voice was hoarse as she whispered against my neck, "I knew you'd come."

I pushed her hair back away from her tearstained face. "I told you, *colomba mia*. I'm never letting you leave me. And that includes even in death."

She cupped my face. "I love you, Matteo. Husband."

With my hand over hers, I turned my face to kiss her palm. "I love you too, Ella. My amazingly brave wife."

Cesare cleared his throat. "Not to interrupt this super

touching scene"—he checked his watch—"but I need to get back to my own pregnant wife. Can we kill these three already?"

I turned back to Ella and winked. "I'll just be a minute."

I rose to my full height and approached the cowering men as I rolled up my sleeves. "Fino is mine."

CHAPTER 53

MATTEO

"Fuck, we're late," I ground out as I navigated through the narrow streets of Cavalieri village.

In the rearview mirror, I saw my father adjust his deep-purple-and-black tie. The colors matching his right eye. "We're not late."

In the back seat, Enzo winced as he shrugged into his suit jacket, which only caused his split lip to open and bleed again. "We're definitely late."

Cesare pulled the pieces of rolled-up, bloody tissue out of his nostrils. "It's not like we don't have a pretty good excuse."

Sebastian turned around from the passenger seat to look at him. "Do you honestly think she'll care?"

He was right. Aunt Gabriella would straight up murder us if we didn't get there soon.

Cesare leaned forward and patted me on the shoulder. "Drive faster."

There were very few things that would pull me away from Ella's side right now, but this was one of them. We had stopped off at the winery only long enough to change and secure Ella in Rosa and Lucia's very capable arms.

Well, Rosa, Lucia and fifteen armed guards surrounding the villa with two posted outside my bedroom door.

While I appreciated the bravery it took for her to offer to come with me, I knew she had already been through too much.

The car fell silent as we neared the center of the village and saw the posters.

They lined the streets like wallpaper. Not a single wall, shop window, or post was left bare.

The town square was plastered with them as well.

The posters announced Alfonso's death and the details of his funeral, as was the custom in Italy.

While usually one or two prominent posters was acceptable, it was a testament to how beloved Alfonso was that everyone wanted to honor his passing by displaying one.

We had to pull over before reaching Santa Maria Church because the streets were clogged with flowers and candles. As we walked together toward the hearse, I swiped at my eyes.

Uncle Barone greeted us. "Cutting it a little close, aren't you, boys?"

My father hugged him. "There was traffic," he quipped. "The girls inside?"

Uncle Barone nodded as his eyes misted. "Yeah." He cleared his throat. "Let's do this."

My uncle moved toward the hearse, preparing to carry his oldest friend's coffin. It was not wise given his recent injury, but not one of us dared to stop him. Not even Amara.

We knew he'd bear the pain to have his friend at his shoulder, side by side, one last time.

Father Luca appeared as the coroner opened the back of the hearse. While the coffin was driven here, this hearse would be exchanged for a horse-drawn carriage after the service for the procession to Alfonso's final resting place.

Father Luca gave our bruised and battered faces a second look but didn't remark on them. "You're late."

"Sorry, Father," we all said in unison.

"Make sure you turn the coffin around, so he enters the church feet first. As is proper."

"Yes, Father."

At the count of three, we lifted the coffin onto our shoulders and walked solemnly into the church.

It was standing room only. Every pew, the aisle, and the altar were covered in white lilies, roses, and chrysanthemums. It was as if spring, pure and fresh, had come early to the village.

As the church's choir sang Allegri's "Miserere," we slowly made our way down the aisle. The girls were sitting in the front pew, comforting a heavily veiled Aunt Gabriella.

After placing the coffin on the catafalque, we took our seats.

Then watched as Uncle Barone opened the lid and gazed upon his friend one last time.

His shoulders shook.

Amara rose and went to him. He wrapped his arm around her shoulders and held her tight as they both moved to their seats.

Father Luca began. "*L'eterno riposo dona loro, Signore, e splenda ad essi la luce perpetua. Nel nome del Padre e del Figlio e dello Spirito Santo.*"

The entire congregation solemnly said, "Amen."

* * *

THERE WASN'T a dry eye in the church after several people, including my father and uncle, rose to give speeches in Alfonso's honor. It then took close to another two hours for everyone to file past the coffin to give their final respects. Funerals, even in a large, more cosmopolitan village like this, were public affairs. Everyone was always welcome to say their final goodbyes.

Father Luca then concluded the service. "May the angels lead you into paradise, may the martyrs come to welcome you and take you into the holy city, the new and eternal Jerusalem. Eternal rest grant unto him, Lord, and let perpetual light shine upon him."

A silence descended over the congregation when Aunt Gabriella suddenly rose. Pushing her shoulders back and her chin up, she approached the coffin.

Lifting her thick, black-lace veil she slipped something out of her purse and placed it in his hand. Then she leaned over and kissed him goodbye.

Lowering her veil, she turned. She seemed to start, as if she saw something in the distance which alarmed her. I turned to look down the church aisle but only saw a sea of mourners.

The assembly held its collective breath as she continued to stand there, a portrait of graceful grief. Then her head lowered, and her body swayed slightly.

Fuck.

Without warning, I vaulted over the pew and dove for her. Catching her in my arms seconds before she would have collapsed to the unforgiving marble floor.

All the girls and Dr. Pantona rushed forward to take her from my arms.

"I'm fine," she whispered. "Just a momentary lapse."

Bianca wrapped an arm around her waist. "Of course, darling. These things happen," she responded in that crisp, authoritative voice which was so comforting during the uncertainty and upheaval of grief.

Liliana moved to Aunt Gabriella's other side. "No one saw a thing. You handled yourself beautifully."

The group moved to a small antechamber off the altar to give her time to recover while we prepared the coffin.

As we moved to lower the lid, we had to rearrange all the mementos and trinkets left inside to shepherd Alfonso's journey to heaven; flowers, rosaries, small flasks of wine, even a tiny teddy bear given to him by a little girl from the village so he wouldn't be alone.

Tucked in his hand was a photo of him and Aunt Gabriella. Her head was tilted to the side as she laughed while he towered over her from just behind, looking on with amusement. It was hard to imagine no longer seeing him quietly standing by my aunt. Like an ever-vigilant sentinel, he had watched over her for as long as I could remember.

After securing the lid, we slowly shouldered the coffin once more and turned so Alfonso would once more leave feet first.

As we made our way down the aisle, countless people openly sobbed. It was as if a ballon had popped, releasing the suspended tension in the room.

There was something about this moment.

This very moment. That made it all finally real.

As if up until now our minds were in denial, not fully accepting the reality of his death.

But then the coffin lid closed.

And it was over.

That strange, unrealistic flicker of hope... extinguished like a forlorn candle stub.

Outside, we placed his coffin into the glass enclosure of the horse-drawn hearse which would take him to his final resting place in the private family cemetery on Cavalieri land. Alfonso had more than earned that honor.

He may not have been a Cavalieri in name, but he was a Cavalieri in our hearts.

As the horses pulled the hearse carriage forward, we filed into a line behind it to begin the procession through the village.

Mourners lined the path, tossing white roses onto the roof of the glass enclosure as it passed.

We slowly walked the several miles behind the hearse, knowing this would be our last walk together with the friend who had always walked by our sides.

As we neared the gates of the winery, a somber strain of music could be heard on the wind.

And then I saw her… Ella seated below a nearby tree, playing Barber's "Adagio for Strings" on her cello as we passed.

And in that moment, I thanked God for having the grace to twist the strings of fate that brought this remarkable woman into my life.

* * *

HOURS LATER.

After all the mourners had left.

My father, Uncle Barone, Enzo, Cesare, and I stood around Alfonso's fresh grave.

Uncle Barone opened a bottle of *Vino Nobile di Montepulciano d'Abruzzo dei Cavalieri,* raised it high, and said, "To Alfonso. Never will a man be missed more." He then took a swig directly from the bottle and passed it around.

After drinking, I swiped the back of my hand across my mouth and spoke to him as if he were still alive. "You missed a hell of a fight, my friend. You would have loved it."

Enzo handed the bottle to Cesare after taking a drink. "Especially the part where that asshole Fino pissed himself."

My father placed his hand on Uncle Barone's shoulder. "Remember the time Alfonso accidentally shot your old vineyard manager in the ass while he was fucking that village woman in the trees over there."

Uncle Barone threw his head back and laughed. "Alfonso didn't miss a beat. As the man ran around howling, clutching his bare, buckshot ass, Alfonso reloaded his gun and said, 'If you fuck like an animal in the woods expect to get shot like one too.'"

For the rest of the day and long into the night, we sat by Alfonso's gravesite, drinking and telling stories... keeping our old friend company through the darkness so he wouldn't be alone.

CHAPTER 54

MATTEO

 *ne month later.*

I PROWLED through the crowd at the piazza.

Shouldering past the many tourists and locals as they danced around the center bonfire.

I nodded to the bodyguard my girl knew about—then to the two she didn't. One of them gestured to the left with his head.

And that was when I spotted her.

Her blonde hair loose and falling in golden waves down her back, drawing every male eye to the generous swell of her hips as she moved and swayed to the music. Her left arm gracefully stretched out then swept over her head in time to the beat, while her right extended toward the crowd, holding a red plastic bucket.

I came up behind her and wrapped my arm tightly around her waist. Drawing her back against my hips and already growing cock, I growled, "Bad girl, swaying your hips like this in front of other men—when you're supposed to be mine."

Ella giggled and turned in my arms. As she draped her left hand around my neck, she tilted her head back and smiled. "I'm all yours, husband."

I gave her a hard kiss on her sweet, full lips. "And don't you ever forget it, wife."

My hand caressed down her right arm to remove the bucket from her grasp. Lifting it out of her reach, I shook it until the coins rattled. "I thought I made myself clear about this?"

She stretched on her toes to reach it but was adorably too short. "Technically yes, but…"

"No buts. We agreed."

Giuseppe approached us with his hand over his heart. "So sorry, Signore Cavalieri. You have my word it won't happen again."

Handing him the bucket, I raised an eyebrow. "See that it doesn't."

Ella had joined the small string quartet that played in the piazza under the strict rule that she was not to move about the crowd busking for coins. For starters, it wasn't a good look for the wife of a multi-millionaire, but more importantly, it was dangerous.

Nothing had been resolved with the Agnellos. Her father was still screaming for war, while her sister had fled to Milan. Which left Dante scrambling to shore up loyalty.

And then there was Judge Marzio Delluci. We had something special planned for him, but it would take a great deal of secrecy and a delicate touch.

In the meantime, we had to keep our girls safe. None of them were crazy about having a bodyguard, which was why we decided to keep the additional two bodyguards under the radar.

Ella pretended to pout. "But I'm bored. Playing cello and then moving about the crowd is fun."

I spun her in a circle as we danced. "I have plenty of ways to keep you *occupied* until we leave for the ranch next week."

She rolled her eyes and gave a dramatic sigh. "Aunt Gabriella says it would be gauche if I allowed you to knock me up in the first six months of our marriage."

"Remind me to thank her," I quipped, pressing Ella closer.

"Besides, I need to focus on the Cavalieri School of Art and Music."

We had decided to turn Enzo's historical house overlooking the piazza into a school, art museum and gallery, and community center for the village.

Milana was overseeing the construction project. Bianca was handling the decorating, and we were headed to the Dolomites to spend a few months on the horse ranch so that Liliana and Ella could work together on the school curriculum. Meanwhile Amara was working the winery's more exalted clients for art donations for the museum while lining up local artists for the gallery.

Ella rested her head against my heart. "I can't wait to see the ballroom turned into a concert hall. The acoustics are perfect. And I already have half the program worked out for the memorial concert in Alfonso's honor to celebrate *Festa di Tutti i Santi* in November."

Just then, she leaned her head back to look up at me. "Thank you."

I frowned. "For what?"

"A few months ago, my life was empty. Now I have so many projects and ideas I don't know what to do with myself. All I ever wanted to do was share my love of music and help people. So thank you."

I cupped her cheek and placed a kiss on her forehead. "You're welcome, *colomba mia*."

She lowered her head and snuggled closer against my chest.

My hand stroked her long, soft hair. "Of course, you could say that I gave you purpose. That before me, your life was cold and meaningless. That I was the one who brought light and warmth. Like the sun, or a god. Maybe you should be worshipping me on your knees—"

Her cheeks turned bright pink with embarrassment as several nearby dancing couples cast interested glances in our direction and smiled at our overheard conversation.

Ella groaned while reaching up to cover my mouth. "Oh my God. Please stop talking!"

CHAPTER 55

BARONE

*A*mara cast a suspicious glance at me as I opened her passenger door. With a narrowed gaze, she looked me over. "What are you up to?"

I offered her my hand to help her from the vehicle, my smile completely innocent. "What makes you think I'm up to something?"

"You've been suspiciously nice all day today."

I placed my hand over my heart. "I'm always nice."

Her mouth dropped open. "Did you seriously just say that with a straight face?"

I wrapped my arm around her waist and pulled her close as my hand tilted her chin back. "You're right. It's been a while since Daddy's punished you with his belt."

Amara tilted her head to suck two of my fingers into her cute mouth. "I know. Maybe I should start misbehaving more."

My answer was a low rumbling growl as I shifted my hand into her hair and claimed her mouth. My tongue swept inside, tasting the vanilla and rum persimmon from our dessert. God, she tasted sweet.

It took all my willpower not to toss her over my shoulder and carry her back to the car then up to our bedroom.

But there were people waiting for us.

As she ran a finger under her lips to check her lipstick, she asked, "Why are we at my mother's cottage?"

Enclosing her hand in mine I guided her along and said, "You'll see."

The moment we passed under the canopy the florist erected of winter jasmine and white hellebores, she knew.

She pressed a hand to her mouth as her eyes misted. "Is it time? Is this finally happening?"

With my hand on the doorknob, I grumbled, "Hell yes it's happening because it is long past time, babygirl."

I swung the door open, and our entire assembled family yelled, "Surprise!"

With my arm wrapped securely around her waist, I pulled Amara closer to my side and kissed the top of her head. "Welcome to your *La Promessa*."

Milana shifted the baby to her other arm as she moved forward to hug Amara. "I'm so excited for you!" The baby stared with wide eyes, fist waving.

Cesare laughed as he lifted the baby into his arms. "Baby Alfonso is happy for you, too."

Bianca clapped her hands. "We can't start celebrating until he actually makes his promise and proposes!"

My palm slapped over my suit jacket, feeling for the ring. "But first."

Since my girl valued tradition, I wanted to do this right.

I turned to Milana and took her hand. "You have always been Amara's best friend, biggest supporter, and surrogate family. I would be honored if, in her mother's honor, you would grant me permission to ask her to marry me."

Milana threw her arms around my neck. "Oh my God! Yes!"

Benedict leaned forward and whispered to Amara, "Are you taking notes? The word to remember is yes." He then winked as she laughed.

Milana hugged Amara again before Liliana gave Ella the cue.

From her perch near the fireplace, Ella played Etta James's "At Last."

The whole room erupted in laughter at the inside joke.

Facing Amara, I lowered to one knee to take her left hand in my own while holding up the diamond ring I had made for her from the Cavalieri family jewels.

"My *dolcezza*, from the moment you literally fell into my life, you have brought a love I truly didn't think I deserved into my world. And I will spend every moment, of every single day, striving to be a man worthy of it, if you would do me the greatest honor of becoming my wife."

She shook her head and leapt into my arms, sitting on my bent knee as she wrapped her arms around my neck and kissed my cheek. "That was so beautiful."

Matteo cleared his throat. "I hate to be a stickler, but we're all going to need to hear a verbal confirmation."

As I slid the ring onto her finger, Amara smiled through her tears. "Yes!"

Gabriella raised her arms and clapped, gold bracelets jangling. "Pour the Champagne! She *finally* said yes!"

EPILOGUE

GABRIELLA

he breeze from over the Tyrrhenian Sea brushed my face.

The salty, citrus-scented air filling my lungs where I stood leaning against the wooden railing of my villa's veranda.

Staring out over the jagged cliff's edge, I watched the foamy white caps form then dissipate as they hit the rocky shore. The relentless beating of the water against the hard stones was a raw reminder of the unsettling, yet inevitable, creep of death.

I sighed and rubbed the space between my eyebrows. Such morbid thoughts didn't suit me.

They were a cold, heavy pit in my stomach And yet...

The ice in my drink rattled as it settled in my *Negroni Sbagliato*.

As the sky filled with the blazing orange and purple colors of the sunset, my thoughts turned to Alfonso, as they usually did at this time of day. The sunset reminded me of him. Quiet and unassuming and yet still a beautiful burst of brilliant color and light.

I tilted my face toward the setting sun.

Despite its fiery colors... there was no warmth. A chill ran over my skin, raising goosebumps on my arms, as if rising from the bitter coldness deep within.

A creak of the deck boards alerted me to someone's presence.

I pivoted and nearly dropped my drink.

"Hello, Gabriella."

His voice was the same dark, melted chocolate that I remembered.

My gaze narrowed. "You have a lot of fucking nerve coming here."

Unable to look at him, I paced away and tried to still my racing heart.

"I saw you at Alfonso's funeral... and I know you saw me."

I rounded on him, my fingers tightening on my glass. "Don't you dare say his name."

He stepped forward.

With my arm stretched out, I ordered, "Get out. Leave. Now."

He shook his head as he stalked toward me. "No, not this time."

With an outraged cry, I threw my drink at him.

To be continued...

The Cavalieris will be returning with five new books in the future.

The past is full of secrets and nothing is as it seems. The only certainty is the truth will always find a way to the surface, revealing the tangled vines of love, lust, and scandal that bind the Cavalieri family together.

Echoes of Obsession, Book Six
Echoes of Deception, Book Seven
Echoes of Temptation, Book Eight
Echoes of Corruption, Book Nine
Echoes of Redemption, Book Ten

ABOUT THE AUTHOR

Zoe Blake is the USA Today Bestselling Author of the romantic suspense sagas *The Diamanti Billionaire Dynasty* & *The Cavalieri Billionaire Legacy* inspired by her own heritage as well as her obsession with jewelry, travel, and the salacious gossip of history's most infamous families.

She delights in writing Dark Romance books filled with overly possessive billionaires, taboo scenes, and unexpected twists. She usually spends her ill-gotten gains on martinis, travels, and red lipstick. Since she can barely boil water, she's lucky enough to be married to a sexy Chef.

ALSO BY ZOE BLAKE

IVANOV CRIME FAMILY TRILOGY

A Dark Mafia Romance

Savage Vow

Gregor & Samara's story

I took her innocence as payment.

She was far too young and naïve to be betrothed to a monster like me.

I would bring only pain and darkness into her sheltered world.

That's why she ran.

I should've just let her go…

She never asked to marry into a powerful Russian mafia family

None of this was her choice.

Unfortunately for her, I don't care.

I own her… and after three years of searching… I've found her.

My runaway bride was about to learn disobedience has consequences… punishing ones.

Having her in my arms and under my control had become an obsession.

Nothing was going to keep me from claiming her before the eyes of God and man.

She's finally mine… and I'm never letting her go.

Vicious Oath

Damien & Yelena's story

When I give an order, I expect it to be obeyed.

She's too smart for her own good, and it's going to get her killed.

Against my better judgement, I put her under the protection of my powerful Russian mafia family.

So imagine my anger when the little minx ran.

For three long years I've been on her trail, always one step behind.

Finding and claiming her had become an obsession.

It was getting harder to rein in my driving need to possess her… to own her.

But now the chase is over.

I've found her.

Soon she will be mine.

And I plan to make it official, even if I have to drag her kicking and screaming to the altar.

This time… there will be no escape from me.

Betrayed Honor

Mikhail & Nadia's story

Her innocence was going to get her killed.

That was if I didn't get to her first.

She's the protected little sister of the powerful Ivanov Russian mafia family - the very definition of forbidden.

It's always been my job, as their Head of Security, to watch over her but never to touch.

That ends today.

She disobeyed me and put herself in danger.

It was time to take her in hand.

I'm the only one who can save her and I will fight anyone who tries to stop me, including her brothers.

Honor and loyalty be damned.

She's mine now.

Fierce Pursuit

Konstantine & Marina's story

I'm the only one standing between her and those who want her dead.

I was married to her sister—a woman who died in the crossfire of my Russian mafia world.

To her, I'm nothing but a monster with blood-stained hands.

She doesn't see they're the same hands keeping her alive.

She's fled from me repeatedly, each escape bringing her closer to the enemies hunting us both.

The hatred burning in her eyes only matches the forbidden heat igniting between us.

The rival bratva won't stop until she's eliminated.

My solution? Make her mine—a marriage placing her untouchably under my protection.

She fights me at every turn, fierce and beautiful in her rage, blaming me for her sister's death and her shattered life—she can never learn the truth.

As danger closes in, I'm torn between my vow to protect her and the desperate hunger that consumes me whenever she's near.

When an ambush leaves her bleeding in my arms, everything changes.

This marriage isn't negotiable anymore.

She'll wear my ring and bear my name.

She'll be mine, even if I have to break her to keep her.

Twisted Proposal

Artem & Viktoria's story

I'm not the hero in this story—I'm the monster who claimed what wasn't his to take.

I was supposed to sell her to the highest bidder, a marriage that would seal alliances and strengthen her family's power.

But seeing her bloodied and defiant changed everything.

Her father and brothers thought they could use her as a pawn.

They didn't realize I was playing a different game entirely.

I destroyed them all, leaving her seemingly free—only to chain her to me instead.

She thinks she can escape, build a normal life away from the violence she was born into.

She doesn't understand that what I protect, I possess completely.

And now, she's mine.

The problem?

She fights me with every breath, refusing to be anyone's property... especially mine.

Her fierce defiance only makes me want her more.

What she doesn't know is that her freedom required blood payment, and that debt is coming due.

As enemies close in, threatening what's mine, my decision is final.

She will be my wife.

She will wear my mark.

She will surrender to me completely.

Even if I have to break her first.

Sinister Promise

Pavel & Alina's story

The only thing more dangerous than what she witnessed…is me.

She was supposed to be a problem—one I would deal with, forget, erase.

Instead, she became my obsession.

A hotel maid drowning in her father's debts, working among killers and Bratva bosses, believing silence would keep her safe.

Then she saw something she shouldn't.

She should have run. Should have screamed. Should have begged.

Instead, she held my gaze, defiant and unbroken.

Now, I can't let her go.

The only way to keep her alive is to make her mine—a marriage that will satisfy Bratva law and place her firmly under my control.

What I offer isn't protection…it's possession.

She fights me with every breath, her body betraying her with each trembling response to my touch.

Her eyes promise escape while her pulse races beneath my fingers.

She swears she'll never belong to me, not understanding that her resistance only fuels my determination.

Every whispered threat. Every stolen kiss. Every brutal promise draws her deeper into my world.

Because I don't just want to own her.

I want to break her. Then claim her completely.

And I always get what I want.

Captive Prize

Roman & Zoya's story

She stole what belongs to me. Now I'll take everything from her.

A problem I need to fix. A war I need to win. A woman I can't afford to desire.

Her fatal mistake? Taking an Ivanov.

My cousin is missing, his pregnant wife left for dead.

The guilt is a noose around my neck, tightening with every second he's gone.

I was never fully Ivanov—half Russian, half Cuban, never enough.

But this time, I'll prove myself.

I'll infiltrate Los Infidels. Find Pavel. And kidnap the fierce mafia princess responsible.

She fights me with every breath—clawing, cursing, daring me to shatter her completely.

The real problem?

I don't just want to break her. I want to possess her.

Hate bleeds into hunger. Revenge twists into obsession.

Suddenly, our war isn't about family loyalty, it's about dominance.

She won't bow.

I refuse to yield.

One of us must fall.

And I never lose.

RUTHLESS OBSESSION SERIES

A Dark Mafia Romance

Sweet Cruelty

Dimitri & Emma's story

It was an innocent mistake.

She knocked on the wrong door.

Mine.

If I were a better man, I would've just let her go.

But I'm not.

I'm a cruel bastard.

I ruthlessly claimed her virtue for my own.

It should have been enough.

But it wasn't.

I needed more.

Craved it.

She became my obsession.

Her sweetness and purity taunted my dark soul.

The need to possess her nearly drove me mad.

A Russian arms dealer had no business pursuing a naive librarian student.

She didn't belong in my world.

I would bring her only pain.

But it was too late…

She was mine and I was keeping her.

Sweet Depravity

Vaska & Mary's story

The moment she opened those gorgeous red lips to tell me no, she was mine.

I was a powerful Russian arms dealer and she was an innocent schoolteacher.

If she had a choice, she'd run as far away from me as possible.

Unfortunately for her, I wasn't giving her one.

I wasn't just going to take her; I was going to take over her entire world.

Where she lived.

What she ate.

Where she worked.

All would be under my control.

Call it obsession.

Call it depravity.

I don't give a damn… as long as you call her mine.

Sweet Savagery

Ivan & Dylan's Story

I was a savage bent on claiming her as punishment for her family's mistakes.

As a powerful Russian Arms dealer, no one steals from me and gets away with it.

She was an innocent pawn in a dangerous game.

She had no idea the package her uncle sent her from Russia contained my stolen money.

If I were a good man, I would let her return the money and leave.

If I were a gentleman, I might even let her keep some of it just for frightening her.

As I stared down at the beautiful living doll stretched out before me like a virgin sacrifice,

I thanked God for every sin and misdeed that had blackened my cold heart.

I was not a good man.

I sure as hell wasn't a gentleman… and I had no intention of letting her go.

She was mine now.

And no one takes what's mine.

Sweet Brutality

Maxim & Carinna's story

The more she fights me, the more I want her.

It's that beautiful, sassy mouth of hers.

It makes me want to push her to her knees and dominate her, like the brutal savage I am.

As a Russian Arms dealer, I should not be ruthlessly pursuing an innocent college student like her, but that would not stop me.

A twist of fate may have brought us together, but it is my twisted obsession that will hold her captive as my own treasured possession.

She is mine now.

I dare you to try and take her from me.

Sweet Ferocity

Luka & Katie's Story

I was a mafia mercenary only hired to find her, but now I'm going to keep her.

She is a Russian mafia princess, kidnapped to be used as a pawn in a dangerous territory war.

Saving her was my job. Keeping her safe had become my obsession.

Every move she makes, I am in the shadows, watching.

I was like a feral animal: cruel, violent, and selfishly out for my own needs. Until her.

Now, I will make her mine by any means necessary.

I am her protector, but no one is going to protect her from me.

Sweet Intensity

Anton & Brynn's story

She couldn't have known the danger she faced when she dared to steal from me.

She was too young for a man my age, barely in her twenties.

Far too pure and untouched.

Unfortunately for her, that wasn't going to stop me.

The moment I laid eyes on her, I claimed her.

Determined to make her mine … by any means necessary.

I owned Chicago's most elite gambling club, a front for my role as a Russian Mafia crime boss.

And she was a fragile little bird, who had just flown straight into my open jaws.

Naïve and sweet, she was a temptation I couldn't resist biting.

My intense drive to dominate and control her had become an obsession.

I would ruthlessly use my superior strength and wealth to take over her life.

The harder she resisted, the more feral and savage I would become.

She needed to understand … she was mine now.

Mine.

Sweet Severity

Macarius & Phoebe's story

Had she crashed into any other man's car, she could have walked away —but she hit mine.

Upon seeing the bruises on her wrist, I struggled to contain my rage.

Despite her objections, I refused to allow her to leave.

Whoever hurt this innocent beauty would pay dearly.

As a Russian Mafia crime boss who owns Chicago's most elite gambling club, I have very creative and painful methods of exacting revenge.

She seems too young and naive to be out on her own in such a dangerous world.

Needing a nanny, I decided to claim her for the role.

She might resist my severe, domineering discipline, but I won't give her a choice in the matter.

She needs a protector, and I'd be damned if it were anyone but me

Resisting the urge to claim her will test all my restraint.

It's a battle I'm bound to lose.

With each day, my obsession and jealousy intensify.

It's only a matter of time before my control snaps ... and I make her mine.

Mine.

Sweet Animosity

Varlaam & Vivian's Story

I never asked for an assistant, and if I had, I sure as hell wouldn't have chosen her.

With her sharp tongue and lack of discipline, what she needs is a firm hand, not a job.

The more she tests my limits, the more tempted I am to bend her over my knee.

As a Russian Mafia boss and owner of Chicago's most elite gambling club, I can't afford distractions from her antics.

Or her secrets.

For I suspect, my innocent new assistant is hiding something.

And I know just how to get to the truth.

It's high time she understands who holds the power in our relationship.

To ensure I get what I desire, I'll keep her close, controlling her every move.

Except I am no longer after information—I want her mind, body and soul.

She underestimated the stakes of our dangerous game and now owes a heavy price.

As payment I will take her freedom.

She's mine now.

Mine.

www.ingramcontent.com/pod-product-compliance
Lightning Source LLC
Chambersburg PA
CBHW072017020726
47501CB00006B/1838